Mary of Lorraine

An historical romance

by

James Grant

Mary of Lorraine
An historical romance
by James Grant

ISBN: 978-93-62768-04-9

Published by

DOUBLE 9 BOOKS

2/13-B, Ansari Road
Daryaganj, New Delhi – 110002
info@double9books.com
www.double9books.com
Tel. 011-40042856

This book is under public domain

ABOUT THE AUTHOR

James Grant, born on August 1, 1822, changed into a Scottish creator famend for his prolific contributions to literature, specially within the genres of historic fiction, journey, and military narratives. His early years had been steeped in a navy environment due to his father's profession in the British navy, which significantly stimulated Grant's writing. Grant's literary profession flourished at some stage in the 19th century, marked via a high-quality output of extra than 90 novels, regularly published under various pseudonyms inclusive of Harry Gringo and Lawrence L. Lynch. His works were recognized for his or her bright portrayal of navy life, regularly drawing from his firsthand reviews and historic activities. "Adventures of an Aide-de-Camp" is certainly one of his remarkable works, depicting memories of navy adventures and reflecting Grant's intimate information of military existence. His writing style changed into characterized via particular descriptions, intricate plots, and a penchant for ancient accuracy, making his narratives compelling and engaging. Grant's literary achievements solidified his reputation as a prominent figure in nineteenth-century literature, and his have an impact on at the style of military fiction stays huge to this day. He continued to jot down and publish till his passing on May 5, 1887, leaving in the back of a wealthy legacy of gripping storytelling and historic insight.

CONTENTS

PREFACE

In the following pages I have endeavoured to describe something of the manners and inner life of the Lowland Scots at the period referred to, modernizing the language, which, to my English readers, might otherwise prove unintelligible.

For the political corruption of the Scottish noblesse at that—as at every other—period of their annals, ample proofs to support me are furnished by "Rymer's Foedera," and "Tytler's History;" while the fact that Henry VIII. and his successors too often employed in Scotland other and very different emissaries than the two I shall introduce to the reader, has been amply proved by the Calendar of State Papers on Scotland, lately published by Mr. Thorpe, who shows us that, in addition to the devastations and burning of his lawless invading armies of English, Spaniards, and Germans, he was base enough to hire secret assassins, to remove all who were inimical to his matrimonial speculations in Scotland.

Incidentally, I have introduced the terrible episode of a Highland feud which occurred in the time of James V. The story of "The Neish's Head" is still remembered in Strathearn; and I believe a different version of it appeared some years ago in a work entitled "The Scottish Wars."

The mode of torture mentioned in the adventure at Millheugh Tower, was not uncommon in those barbarous days. My attention was called, by a friend, to a paper which is preserved at Cullen House, Bauffshire, and which furnished the idea.

It formed part of a collection of MSS. which belonged to the late Rev. John Grant, of Elgin, and which, with his library, he bequeathed to his chief, the Earl of Seafield. It refers to the feud between the Earls of Huntley and Murray (which ended in the murder of the latter, at the Castle of Donibristle, in Fifeshire), and is a copy of a petition from the latter noble, the chief of the Grants, and Dunbar, sheriff of Moray, praying the government of James VI. to grant them protection against Huntley and his followers, and craving redress for injuries which they had sustained at his hands. After narrating many instances of fire-raising and bloodshed perpetrated by the Gordons, it demands justice "for the cruel slaughter of John Mhor, son of Alaster Mhor

Grant, a kinsman and follower of John Grant, of Freuchie, who was hanged and *smeikit in the cruick, till he died,* by Patrick Gordon, brother to William Gordon, of Monaltrie, and five or six others, at the instance and command of the said George, Earl of Huntley."

In this document, which was dated 1591, there is another barbarity which I care not committing to print; but such were the cruelties and recklessness of life, about the times immediately before and after the Reformation, and the regency of Mary of Lorraine.

In the notes I have given a list—the gradual collection of years—of some of those Scottish gentlemen who fell in defence of their country on the 10th of September, 1547; and I have little doubt that many of my readers may discover their ancestors amongst them. I have seen no similar list so ample, save one that I possess of the brave who died at Flodden with King James.

26, DANUBE STREET, EDINBURGH,
May, 1860.

CHAPTER I
THE TOWER OF FAWSIDE

The castle looketh dark without;
  Within the rooms are cold and dreary;
The chill light from the window fades;
  The fire it burneth all uncheery.
With meek hands cross'd beside the hearth,
  The pale and anxious mother sitteth;
And now she listens to the bat
  That, screaming, round the window flitteth.

Mary Howitt.

Ten miles eastward from the Cross of Edinburgh, and two southward from the sandy shore of the Firth of Forth, stands an old and ruined fortalice, named the Castle of Fawside, on a green ridge which rises by gradual and gentle undulations, to the height of three hundred feet above the sea.

In summer the foliage of a group of venerable trees generally conceals much of this ancient mansion, which occupies a lonely and sequestered spot; but its square crumbling chimneys and round turrets, cutting the sky line above the leafy coppice, are visible to all who traverse the roads which lie at the base of the aforesaid ridge. Covered with wood, and a little to the westward, is the hill of Carberry, the scene of Queen Mary's memorable surrender (some twenty years after the period of our present story) to those titled ruffians who styled themselves the Lords of the Congregation.

The more ancient part of this mansion is of unknown antiquity, and consists of a narrow and massive tower, entered by a low-browed archway, built of deep-red sandstone, facing the north. The arch gives access to a suite of those strong dark vaults which form the substructure of all old Scottish houses, and from thence, by a steep wheel stair (which contains a curious and secret hiding-place) we may ascend to a hall, the groined stone roof of which is still remaining, though covered on the top, where once the stone bartizan lay, by a coating of rich grass.

Here, in this grim and narrow tower, in the twelfth century, dwelt William de Fawsyde, a baron in the first parliament of King David I.; and his son Edmund, who stood by that brave monarch's side, when, in the monastery of the Holy Rood, he gifted the lands of Tranent to Thor, the son of Swan. The more modern parts of this ruin are on the south, and consist of a huge gable, having two massive turrets, a steep and narrow circular stair, and several large windows, in which the enormous harrow-shaped iron gratings are still remaining. Stone water-spouts, finely carved, project from these turrets; but no date gives an index to the time of these additions, which are in the Scoto-French style of the sixteenth century.

Like all such edifices in Scotland, this castle is haunted. It is the abode of a spectral lady, who wears a dule-weed, or antique suit of mourning, and appears once yearly, flitting among the ruins, on the anniversary of that Black Saturday in September when the fatal field of Pinkey was fought on the green slope and beautiful plain between the ruins and the sea. Benighted shepherds, gipsies, and other wanderers, who have ventured to seek shelter under the crumbling roof of the old hall, have more than once encountered her, to their terror and dismay; but this restless spirit molests no one. Pale, sad, and silent, she generally sits in a corner of the great northern window, with her wheel or spindle, and like she of whom we read in the "Battle of Regillus," it has been said of her that, —

> "As she plied the distaff,
>   In sweet voice and low,
> She sang of great old houses,
>   And fights fought long ago;
> So spun she, so sang she, until the east was grey,
> Then pointed to her bleeding heart, and shrieked and fled away."

This quaint ruin, which is still engirt by the remains of a high barbican wall, entered by one of those strong yetlan iron gates peculiar to all baronial houses in Scotland, after the portcullis fell into disuse, was the residence and stronghold of the Fawsides of that ilk—one of the oldest families in the Lowlands of Scotland. And now, with the reader's pardon for this somewhat archæological and architectural preamble, we will proceed at once to open our story.

In the year 1547, when the little Mary Queen of Scots was a chubby child of five years old, and her turbulent and rebellious kingdom, then wavering between Catholicism and a new faith, for which there was no other name but Heresy, was governed by the somewhat feeble authority of a regent, in the person of James Hamilton, second Earl of Arran, and next heir to the throne, the tower of Fawside was inhabited by Dame Alison Kennedy, widow of Sir John Fawside, who had been slain in a feud by the Hamiltons of Preston; and this stern woman—for singularly stern she was by nature—was a Kennedy of the house of Colzean, and cousin of that ferocious Earl of Cassilis, who, thirty-three years *after* the epoch of this our history, deliberately roasted Allan Stewart, commendator of Crossraguel, before a blazing fire, having first denuded him of his clothes, and basted him well with grease; and there, sputtering like a huge turkey, the hapless priest was turned upon a spit, until, with his scorched and shrivelled hand, he signed a charter, gifting all the lands of his abbey unto the earl and his heirs.

On the evening of the 1st of August, the Feast of St. Peter ad Vincula (or the Festival of the Chains), 1547, this lady was seated at the northern window of her hall, gazing with fixed and anxious eyes over the tract of country that lay between her castle and the sea. Untouched and neglected, her ivory-mounted spinning-wheel stood near her; close by were six other wheels of plainer construction, evincing that she and the women of her little household had been spinning since the time of dinner, which, in those stirring days, was taken at the hour of twelve.

The sun was setting beyond the purple hills of Dunblane, and its golden gleam lit all the far-extending shores of Lothian and of Fife, with their gray bluffs, green bays, and sandy beaches, the straggling burghs of Grail and Kinghorn, and many a fisher-village, all dark and weather-beaten by the stormy gales that blow from the German Sea. At anchor in Musselburgh Bay were a few of those small craft which were then termed topmen, from their peculiar rigging, and which traded with the low countries in wool, skins, salmon, cloth, silks, and wine. They had huge square poops, and low prows beaked with iron, and were always well equipped with falcons, crossbows, and arquebusses, as a defence against English pirates and Moorish rovers.

Save where a few cottages and a clump of trees dotted the slope here and there, the country was all open between the tower in which the lady sat, and the green knoll crowned by St. Michael's Kirk of Inveresk, and the high antique bridge and the thatched or stone-slated houses of the "honest town" of Musselburgh. This venerable municipality was then terminated on the westward by a beautiful chapel, dedicated to our Lady of Loretto, to whose shrine the late King James V., with taper in hand and feet and head bare, had made more than one pilgrimage for the health of his first queen, Magdalene of Valois, and of his second, Mary of Lorraine; for this old shrine shared all the fame and sanctity of its elder prototype in Italy. A great part of the adjacent town was in ruins, just as it had been left by the English after their invasion under Lord Hertford, three years before the date of our story.

Below the hill of Inveresk lay a deep and dangerous morass, named the Howe Mire, then the haunt of the heron, the wild goose, and coot, the water kelpie, and the will-o'-the-wisp.

Three miles distant from the window at which Dame Alison was seated rose the high and narrow tower of Preston; and when her wandering eyes fell on its grim dark mass, they flashed with a hateful glare, while the gloom of her pale anxious brow grew darker, and its stern lines more deep; for she hated the race of Hamilton, to whom it belonged, with all the hate an old Scottish feud inspired.

On the green slope of Fawside Hill the shepherds, grey-plaided and bonneted, were driving home to fold and penn the flocks which had browsed there the livelong harvest day; and these were all of that old Scottish breed which is now completely extinct, but was small, active, and keen-eyed, with tawny faces, hairy wool, and well-curved yellow horns.

The quiet evening aspect of the pastoral landscape on which the lady gazed was not made more lively by the grisly forms of two dead men hanging upon the arm of an oak tree about a bow-shot from the tower gate, where the black rooks and ravenous gleds were perching or wheeling in circles round them. These unfortunates had been "hangit in their buits," as they phrased it in those days, by order of the baroness; for there was then a law "that ilk baron might cleanse his lands of trespassers thrice in the year;" so, on finding two on her estate of Fawside, she ordered them to be hanged, and, in five minutes thereafter, old Roger of the Westmains, her bailie, had them dangling from an arm of the dule tree. Her neighbours averred that this severity was exercised because the culprits bore the name of Hamilton; and a greater horror was added to the episode by the discovery that certain portions of their limbs had been abstracted in the night,—"Doubtless," said the bailie, "by the witches of Salt Preston, for the furtherance of their damnable cantrips."

"Half-past eight," muttered Lady Alison, as the last segment of the ruddy sun sank behind the dark peak of Dumeyat, "and no sign's yet of horse or man upon the upland road. Woe to you, Westmains, for a loitering fool! Thou art too old to scourge, and too faithful to hang, or, by my husband's grave, my mood to-night would give thee to one or other—the rod or the rope!"

As she spoke her thoughts aloud, in that manner peculiar to those who think deeply and are much alone, she beat the paved floor passionately with the high heel of her shoe. There she sat alone in that quaint old hall, with the shadows of night closing around her—alone, because she was a woman whom, from her stern nature and wayward humour, many feared and few loved.

For the hundredth time that day, she anxiously consulted the horologue. This clock was a curious piece of mechanism, which occupied a niche in the hall, and was supported on four little brass pillars, surmounted by a metal dome, on which the hours were struck by a clumsy iron hammer. It bore the date 1507, and the name *Leadenhall*, having been found in an English ship, taken by Sir Robert Barton, who had presented it as an almost priceless gift to her late husband.

Nine o'clock struck from this sonorous horologue; and then the pale mother, who, in those perilous and stormy days, waited for an only and long-absent son, struck her hands despairingly together, and again seated herself at the grated window of the hall, to watch the darkening shadows without.

Suddenly a sound struck her ear, and a horseman was seen galloping up the narrow bridle-path which traversed Fawside Brae and led direct to the castle wall.

"Nurse—nurse Maud!" said Lady Alison impetuously to an old woman wearing a curchie and camlet gown, who joined her; "my eyes are full of tears, and I cannot see—is that horseman our bairn, or only old Westmains?"

"'Tis Westmains—I would ken his grey mare amang a thousand."

"He rideth fast, nurse, for a man so old in years."

"Yea; but a drunken man and a famished horse come fast home to bower and stall," responded the Abigail crustily; "the hour is late, and Preston's men were at Edinburgh market to-day; so, perhaps our bailie had a shrewd guess the way might be beset between the night and morning."

"Beset!—and my son——" muttered the pale mother through her clenched teeth.

"Fear na for him; he has friends——"

"Friends?"

"Yes, madam—his sword and dagger, and stout hands to wield them! But here comes that drunken carle, the bailie."

As the nurse spoke, the horseman trotted his nag into the paved barbican of the tower, and dismounted.

CHAPTER II
WESTMAINS

Oh, when will ye come hame again?
   Dear Willie, tell to me;
"When sun and moon loup o'er yon hill—
   And that will never be!"
She turned hersel right round about,
   Her heart burst into three;
"My ae best son is dead and gane,
   The other I ne'er shall see."

Old Ballad.

"A light," exclaimed Lady Alison; "a light, that I may see by this loiterer's face whether he be tipsy or sober!"

Candles were soon flaming in the numerous sconces of polished tin and brass that hung on knobs around the hall, and shed a cheerful light through every part of it; yet it was not without what we in these days would deem a quaint and weird aspect. Many centuries had darkened this old mansion, and twelve generations had hung their swords in that baronial hall. It is lofty, arched with stone, and its walls are still massive, deep, and strong. Father Seton, the vicar of the adjacent village, who was locally known as Mass John of Tranent, and to whose writings we are indebted for much that concerns this old family, has left a minute description of all the "gear and inside plenishing of the castle."

Large oak chests, girnels and almries, the receptacles of linen, vessels for the table, food, corn, and beer, occupied the recesses. Trophies of arms and racks of spears stood between the windows. In this apartment there were but two chairs of carved oak. These, as usual then in Scottish halls stood on each side of the fireplace: one, being for the father of the family, had never been used since the slaughter of Sir John Fawside by the Laird of Preston; the other was for Dame Alison. Round the hall were ranged various forms, creepies, and buffet stools; these, like the long table, were all of black old oak from the Burghmuir, and allotted to the use of the family or visitors. The stone seats in the windows were laid over with cushions of Flemish damask, and had footmats of plaited rushes from the Howemire. The stone walls, which, as the season was warm, were divested of tapestry, had been recently decorated by Andro Watson, the late king's favourite painter, and bore numerous gaudy and quaint designs, representing family traditions, such as passages of arms and daring feats performed in war or in the chase.

Over the arched fireplace stood the portrait of umquhile Sir John of that ilk, the work of the same hand. Quaint, stark and stiff, he was on foot, in an old suit of mail of the fifteenth century, jagged with iron beaks; a snowy beard flowed below his girdle, and his right hand grasped the bridle of a white horse, on the back of which this grim figure had frequently been found *mounted* at midnight, as nurse Maud, and other old servants, had more than once affirmed!—for Fawside Tower was haunted even then, as a matter of course. Too much blood had been shed in and about it, and too many of its mailed proprietors had perished by bloody and violent deaths, for the mansion to be without its due proportion of spectral appearances and mysterious sounds.

Thus, an antique copper bell which swung at the gable of the tower tolled of its own accord, and all untouched by mortal hand, when a Fawside died; and on the Eve of St. John, a bearded visage, averred by some to be that of the late laird, peeped in the twilight through the hall windows, though these were more than twenty feet from the ground. The gleaming eyes would gaze sadly for a moment on the shrinking beholder, and then the visage melted slowly away into air.

Above the mantelpiece, as above the barbican gate, were the arms of this old family—gules, a fess between three besants, the heraldic badge assigned to a predecessor who had been in Palestine—Sir Robert of that ilk, having served St. Louis IX. in the last crusade, and taken the motto *Forth and feir nocht*: but enough of this dull archæology, and now to resume our narrative.

Followed by several of the household, male and female, all anxious to learn what the town news was, and chiefly whether there were any tidings of their young master's return from France, where he had been resident nearly seven years, the ground bailie, Roger Fawside, of the Westmains, a vassal and remote kinsman, entered the hall. He was a stout and thickset man, about fifty years of age; his beard was grizzled and grey, like his Lombard coat, which had long hanging sleeves, with rows of horn buttons from the shoulder to the wrist. He wore grey breeches and white ribbed stockings gartered at the knee, a blue bonnet, a sword and dagger, slung at a calf-skin girdle. Doffing his bonnet, he made a reverence to Lady Alison, and walking straight to where, upon a binn, near the hall door, there stood a barrel of ale furnished with a wooden cup, for all who chose to drink thereat; he drew forth the spiggot, and proceeded to fill the aforesaid vessel with a foaming draught. With her brows knit, and her dark eyes flashing, the tall old dame came hastily forward, and by one blow of her jewelled hand, dashed from his the wooden tankard, while she exclaimed—

"Satisfy my impatience, carle, ere you satisfy your thirst! Well, what tidings of my son, Westmains, or of his ship? speak , and quickly too, for you have tarried long enough!"

"A ship supposed to be his, my Lady Alison, was seen on the water of Forth this morning, but she hath not come to land."

"This morning——"

"Yes."

"Art sure of this!"

"Sure as I live, madam."

"And he not here yet!" pondered the lady.

"The skippers at Musselburgh kent her well—a French galley, high pooped and low waisted, with King Henry's banner displayed; men called her the *Salamandre*, or some such name."

"Likely enough; 'tis the crest of the late king's mistress, Diana, the Duchess of Valentinois; and this——"

"Was about the dawning of the day, madam."

"And since then," continued the lady impatiently, "she has not passed the Inch."

"There have been no storms to delay the ship?"

"None, save that made by Girzy Gowdie, of Salt Preston, by baptising a cat in the devil's name last week, as we a' ken."

"But that storm came and went to drown a skipper of Dunbar, who had slighted her daughter."

"And yesterday," added Nurse Maude, "she did her penance under a pile o' tarred barrels on Gulane Links."

"Rightly was she served, the accursed witch!" responded Roger of Westmains, recovering the wooden cup and applying it hastily to the spiggot of the barrel, from whence he achieved a draught of ale; "for 'tis now kenned that when she rode forth on a broom stick, in the auld fashion, thrice a year, to keep the devil's sabbath at Clootie's Croft, on the Lammermuir, she left in bed beside her gudeman, a three-legged stool in the likeness of herself; and the said stool (which was burned wi' her) only assumed its own form when Father John of Tranent, chanced to pass that way, telling his beads, about the matin time."

"Cease this gossip, bailie," said the lady, starting again to the north window; "a horseman!—see, see!—a horseman at last is ascending the brae side."

"But he wheels off to Carberry," added the nurse, in a voice like a moan.

"Alas!" exclaimed this stern woman, as her eyes began to fill with tears—"my son; why comes he not?"

"The dogs howled the lee lang night," said the wrinkled nurse, applying her apron to her eyes; "and 'twas not for nocht that yonder howlet screamed on the cape-house head yestreen."

"What mean ye, Maud?" asked the lady sharply.

"They are kenned omens of evil."

"Of evil say ye!"

"Yes—weel awat it is!"

"Havers, Kimmer!" said the ground bailie, taking another jug of ale; "just an auld wife's havers!"

"Thou art right, Westmains," added Lady Alison; "for I have believed but little in omens since Flodden Field was stricken."

"Why since then, lady?"

"On the morn my husband marched from here to join the king's host on the Burghmuir of Edinburgh, as he combed his beard—and a braw lang beard it was, Westmains"——

"I mind it weel, for it spread from ilk shoulder to the other, covering corslet and pauldrons."

"Well, as he combed it out with a steel comb twelve inches long, and buckled on his armour, lo! there appeared before him, in the mirror—what think ye all?"

"I know not," replied the bailie, in his abstraction contriving to fill a third jug of ale; "but many strange sights were seen in those days. We a' ken o' the spectres that King James saw at Lithgow Kirk and Jeddart Ha', and of the weird spirit-herald who summoned the souls of the slain—the doomed men of the battle at Edinburgh Cross."

"But what think you my poor husband saw!"

"As I live, I know not," replied the bailie; while the hushed crowd of dependents drew near to listen.

"A mort head where his own comely face should have been!"

"Preserve us a'!"

"Our lady o' Whitehorn!"

"Say ye so, my lady?" were the varied exclamations of the servants.

"Yes!—there stood the shining reflection of his cuirass, pauldrons, and sleeves of Milan plate, just as we see them limned in yonder portrait; but the gorget was surmounted by a grinning skull. And yet he fell not with the king on that fatal ninth of September."

"God rest him now, in his grave in Tranent Kirk! He was a leal brave man, our laird!"

"True, Westmains," replied the lady, while her large black eyes kindled. "But none of his race have died a natural death—it would seem to be their doom. All, all have perished in feud or in the cause of Scotland; and though my heart would break were a hair of my Florence's head to be touched, never shall son of this house die in his bed like a fat monk of St. Mary or a lurdane burgess of Haddington."

"Thou art true to thy race, Lady Alison."

"Tell me what other news you heard, Westmains, in yonder borough town?"

"A band of abominable witches have been dancing about the market cross, as they did last Hallowe'en, with the deil, in the likeness of a hairy Hielandman, playing the pipes to them."

"Pshaw! And yet, 'tis strange—this witchcraft, like the spirit of Lollardy, seems to grow apace in the land."

"They have been caught, and are to thole an assize. One is accused of giving devilish drugs and philtres to the Earl of Bothwell, wherewith to win the love of the queen mother"— —

"Mary of Lorraine?"

"Another, of cutting off a dead man's thumbs to make hell-broth, wherein she dipped nine elf-arrows, and shot nine o' auld Preston's kye."

"A murrain on him! Would to Heaven the hag had shot himself! But he is reserved for a better end."

"How?"

"Can *you* ask?" said the lady fiercely. "To die by a Fawside's sword—by the sword of my only son!"

"And there was taken," resumed the garrulous bailie, "a grisly warlock, to whose house in Lugton, last Lammastide, there came the deil"— —

"Save us and sain us!" muttered the servants, crossing themselves—for Scotland was Catholic still, in outward form, at least, and the credulity of the people seems almost incredible now.

"The devil! say you, Roger?" asked the lady, becoming suddenly interested.

"The grim black deil himsel, but in the likeness of a fair woman—the Queen of Elfen,—and was there delivered of a female bairn, who in the space of three weeks grew large enough to become his wife, and through whom he knew as much as ever True Thomas did of old; for he confessed that by taking a dog under his left arm, and whispering in his ear the queer word *macpeblis*, he could raise the King of Evil, his master, at will; and by sprinkling a blanket with Esk water, as a spell, he drew all the clew and verdure of Wolmet-mains to his ain farm land, leaving the other bare and withered. Then, worse than a', when Wolmet's wife was lying in her childbed-lair, by devilish cantrips, he cast the whole of her pain, dolor, and sickness upon John Guidlat, the baron bailie of Dalkeith, who, during the entire time of her travail, was marvellously troubled, with such agonies, fury, and madness, that it took the town drummer, the bellman and piper to boot, to hold him; but the moment the gentlewoman was delivered, John felt himself a whole man, and well; and so, for all these, things, the grey warlock o' Lugton is to be brankit wi iron, and worried by fire at the Gallows-haugh."

"Enough of such tidings as these; heard ye nought else at Edinburgh-Cross, Westmains?"

"Else?"

"Yes, 'tis of my son and the state I would speak,—not the wretched gossip of an ale-brewster's spence. What is the queen-mother,—what are the Regent Arran and his pestilent Hamiltons about?"

"The regent bydes him at Holyrood, the queen-mother at her house on the Castle-hill; and there seems but little love and muckle jealousy between them yet, as I learned from a proclamation anent false coining, for which I saw three Frenchmen hanged and beheaded this morning."

"Anything more?"

"Odslife! I think that was enough to see before breaking one's fast; and then their heads were spiked, where six others girn, on the Bristo Porte."

"Goose! I would thine was with them; for the news I seek oozes out of thee like blood-drops."

"And there was an Irish leper woman branded by a hot iron on both cheeks, for returning uncleansed to her own house in St. Ninian's Row."

"Oh, Westmains, my heart is heavy!" said the lady, seating herself after a pause, during which the ground bailie had filled and drained a fourth cup, to which a fifth would have succeeded had not Nurse Maud, as a hint that he had imbibed enough already, angrily driven home the spiggot: "This day is the first of August; and at noon we heard Father John of Tranerit say mass for St. Peter's benediction, that the shorn lambs might escape the danger of cold."

"Mass according to the ancient wont."

"Mass according to the Church and faith of our fathers," continued the lady, with some asperity; and then she added plaintively, "I was in hopes that my son—*my* absent lamb—would be with us ere sunset, and yet he comes not."

"A braw lamb," said Westmains merrily; "a tall and proper youth, six feet high, in full steel harness, with sword, dagger, and spurs."

"A lamb he is to me, Roger; though I trust he may yet prove worse than a wolf to that old fox, Hamilton of Preston. Oh, why doth he tarry?" continued the mother, beginning to soften; "can danger have beset him?"

"Consult Mass John anent this," whispered the nurse; "his prayers are as spells of power——"

"For those that pay him weel," added the bailie under his beard, while he scratched his chin.

"Will his prayers bring home my bairn, if a fair wind fails him, think ye?"

"I dinna ken. Like Our Lady's image in the Nunraw of Haddington, they bring rain when the Tranent folk need it to gar their kail grow; or make the weather fair and clear, as the case may be; then why may they not bring hame the young laird?"

"Ay, why, indeed!" muttered the nurse.

"Oh, peace, you silly carlin!"

"As you please, madam," retorted Maud. "But there is a wise woman in Preston-grange——"

"And what of her?"

"She can forsee things to come, and the return o' folk that are far awa, by turning a riddle wi' shears."

"Nay, nay; I would rather see my son no more than see him by necromancy and acts against God's holy word, Nurse. But Preston's men have been abroad to-day, and they seldom ride on a good errand," said Lady Alison, starting from her seat with a new glow of anger and terror in her breast; "but woe to them if aught happens to my son, for bearded men shall weep for it, and I will kill Preston on his own hearthstone, as I would a serpent in its lair! If that foul riever, who slew my husband under tryst, and my brave and winsome Willie— — but he dare not!" she added, checking the bitter surmise by a husky and intense whisper; "no, he dare not!"

And, sinking into her chair, with nervous fingers she grasped the arms of it, and fixed her wild dark eyes upon the wall, as if she saw there in imagination the hereditary foeman of her husband's house.

"Yes, yes, he will be here in the morning," she said suddenly, "for the ship has been seen. Nurse Maud, look out the best dornick napery, and have a fire of turf and coal lighted in his room; hang the crimson curtains on the carved stand-bed, and the green arras on its tenter-hooks. See that the kitchen wenches set a posset of spiced alicant to simmer by the ingle—for the mornings are chill now; let them look well to what is in the spence and almerie against his hame-coming. We must make a feast, Nurse; for after seven years in France our auld Scottish fare will be alike welcome and new to him."

"Seven years," said Maud, thoughtfully.

"Yes, Nurse; seven years come yule-tide hath our beloved bairn been absent from our hearth and hame."

Westmains went away to his grange, or farm, which lay westward of the tower. The strong gates of yetlan iron were now closed for the night, and the lady of Fawside retired, to pray for her absent son, who at that moment was only ten miles distant, but lying on his back, bleeding and gashed by three wounds: but I anticipate my story.

CHAPTER III
THE DEATH FEUD

Then pale, pale grew her tearfu' cheek,
  "Let ane o' my sons three
Alane guide this emprise, your eild
  May ill sic travel dree!
O where were I, were my dear lord,
  And a' my sons to bleed;
Better to brook the wrong, than sae
  To wreck the high misdeed."

Hardyknute.

Several days passed; and though the ship had certainly come from France, and lay near the Beacon Rock, with all her sails furled, there came no tidings of the widow's son. Horsemen rode east, and horsemen rode west; the burly Roger of Westmains wore himself almost to a shadow, and every steed in the stables was completely knocked up; but no trace of Florence Fawside had been discovered, from the time he left the barge of M. de Villegaignon, at the old wooden pier of Leith. And now, with the reader's permission, we will go back a little in our story.

The Fawsides of that ilk were neither powerful nor wealthy, and their purses bore no proportion to their pride or their pedigree; but they were landed barons of good repute, who took (or gave, which matters not) their name from their own property, bringing thence in time of war or tumult forty armed men to the king's host. Faithful and true in times of treason and invasion, this fine old race had never failed the Scottish crown; but a deadly, bitter, and inextinguishable feud, one of those hereditary and transmitted hatreds peculiar to some Scottish families, existed between them and the Hamiltons of Preston, whose lofty baronial tower stands about three miles distant from Fawside Hill.

William of Fawside served under David I., in his war against Stephen of England, and saved his life at the Battle of Northallerton. For this service he received, that night, a charter written on the head of a kettle-drum, the only piece of parchment which the Chancellor, Bishop Engelram, had at hand, and it is remarkable for a laconic simplicity peculiar alike to the age and country:—

"*David Dei Gratiæ Rex Scottorum*, to all his people greeting. Know ye that I have granted unto William, son of Adam, son of John of Fawside, the right of pasturage on Gladsmuir, in perpetual gift, until the Day of Doom."

Now, in future years, long after the saintly David and the mailed knight who fought by his stirrup at Northallerton had been gathered to their fathers, there sprang up the Hamiltons, whose tower of Preston was adjacent to this muir or waste land; and the charter of the Fawsides was deemed sufficiently vague to make them claim the right of having the pasturage in common. Scotsmen required little excuse for unsheathing the sword in those sturdy old times; and hence, about this miserable tract of ground, which was covered with broom, whin, heather, and huge black boulder-stones, the rival barons quarrelled and fought from generation to generation, carrying their cause of feud even to the foot of the throne. More than once, in the time of James IV., Fawside and Preston, with their armed followers, had fought a desperate combat at the Market-cross of Edinburgh, and been forcibly expelled by the citizens, led by their provost, Sir Richard Lawson, of Boghall and Highrigs, who perished at Flodden. Again and again, they had been forfeited by the Parliament, outlawed by the King, and excommunicated by the Abbot of Holyrood; but each maintained himself in his strong old tower, and seemed never a whit the worse.

When the Court of Session was established by James V., their dispute "anent meithes and marches" was brought forward, and their case was the first on the roll; but during its discussion (which sorely puzzled lawyers who were unable to sign their names) they so beset the lords with fire and sword on the highway and in their own residences, each threatening to cut off all who were friendly to the other, that the plea was indignantly thrust aside, and they were left to settle it by the old Scottish arbiter of justice, the broadsword.

They were the terror of East Lothian; they fought whenever they met, and each houghed, killed, or captured the sheep and cattle of the other, whenever they were found straying upon the disputed territory.

About twenty years before the period of our story, Sir John Fawside and Claude Hamilton of Preston (both of whom had fought valiantly at Flodden, and rendered each other good service in that disastrous field), accompanied by several gentlemen, their friends, at the particular request of the good King James V.—the King of the Commons and Father of the Poor, as he loved to style himself,—met on Gladsmuir, with the solemn intention of peacefully adjusting the long-vexed question of their boundaries, and setting march-stones upon the common. They were attended by certain learned notaries, who had been duly examined and certified by the bishop of their diocese, "as being men of faith, gude fame, science, and law;" but the tedium and technicalities of these legal pundits proved too dreary for such "stoute and prettie men," as an old diarist terms our two feudatories; and, in short, Sir John and Hamilton soon came to high words. In the dispute, Roger of Westmains closed up beside his leader, and on drawing his sword, received a stroke from the truncheon of an adversary. Roger ran him through the body, and on the instant all came to blows in wild *melée*. Every sword was out of its scabbard, every hand uplifted, and every tongue shouting taunts and the adverse cries of—

"A Hamilton! a Hamilton!"

"Fawside—'Forth and fear nocht!'"

The notaries tucked up the skirts of their long black gowns, and fled, while the clash of swords continued on the grassy common, where many a horse and man went down; but the Hamiltons proved the most powerful, being assisted by the vassals of their kinsman, the Earl of Yarrow. Fawside was slain, and all his followers were routed, and pursued by the exulting victors up the grassy brae to the gates of the tower, on the iron bars of which the Hamiltons struck with their sword-blades, in token of triumph and contempt.

When the brave Sir John fell, his neighbours were uncharitable enough to regret that he had not (before his departure) given Preston a mortal wound; as all deemed it a pity that two such fiery and restless spirits should be separated for a time, even by the barriers of the other world. Denuded of his knightly belt and sword, Sir John's body was found among the green whins upon the moor, and was buried in the church of Tranent, where a tablet in the north wall *still* bears his arms, surmounted by a helmet, and inscribed simply,—

"John Fawside of that Ilk"

Three bullets fired from calivers were found in his body. His widow had these carefully extracted, with the intention of returning them to Claude Hamilton with terrible interest; and thrice she dipped the dead man's dagger in the blood that oozed from his wounds, with the hope that, in a future time, her oldest boy might cleanse the blade in the blood of the slayer.

Dame Alison was a fierce and stern woman, "animated by such terrible passions as the heroines of the middle ages alone possessed." The partner and partaker of all her husband's ideas, his rights and wrongs—real or imaginary,—she now became inspired by one prevailing thought, and one only—*revenge*;—and so absorbed was she by this devouring passion, that nothing in this world seemed to possess the least interest or value, unless it might feed this demon, or further the terrible object she had in view. Secluded in her gloomy tower, with her two sons, William and Florence at her knee, she told them a thousand times the dark, bloody story of the old hereditary feud and hate—of their father's fall, and how, when tall men and strong soldiers, they must avenge it, by slaying him who proved his destroyer in time of truce and tryst—slaying him as they would a wolf in his den, or a serpent in his lair. And as she poured these wild incentives to future bloodshed into their boyish ears, she would point to where the tower of Preston reared its tall grim outline between them and the sea, and say such things as such a mother, living in that wild age and warlike land, alone could say, till the little impulsive hearts of the boys panted like her own, in anticipation of the hour that would lay Hamilton at their feet, and avenge that day's slaughter on Gladsmuir and Fawside brae.

She gave each one of the bullets found in her husband's corpse; the third she reserved and wore at her neck, with the intention that if her sons' hands failed her when they grew to manhood, she had still one left for vengeance in her own.

She would have appealed to the king; but the house of Hamilton was then in the zenith of its power, and complaints against one of a sept so numerous could find no echo at Falkland or at Holyrood; and so the years passed on.

Because Sir John had died unconfessed, and had been suspected of Lollardy, the Vicar of Tranent had at first refused him Church rites. For this affront, the stern dame denied him the corse-presents exacted then by the priests, and until the Reformation, in 1559—to wit, the best cow of the deceased; the *umest-claith,* or uppermost covering on the bed whereon he lay, together with the silver commonly called *Kirk-richts*; and farther, she threatened to send Westmains with a troop of horse, to burn both kirk and vicarage about the ears of his reverence.

Yearly, on the anniversary of her husband's fall, she went, with hair dishevelled, feet bare, and a taper in her hand, to hear mass said for his soul, in the church of Tranent; and after the service, with an irreverence which even the old vicar failed to restrain, she invoked the curses of Heaven on the Hamiltons of Preston. Her sons heard these things; they sank deep into their little hearts, and absorbed all their thoughts.

Often when she prayed at her husband's tomb (it had now become her altar) she imagined that strange sounds came from it; that she heard him chiding her delay in avenging him in this world and joining him in the next; and these morbid fancies fostered yet more her spirit of revenge.

By her injunctions, the gudeman of Westmains left nothing undone to render the boys hardy, stout, and athletic, and expert in the use of weapons of every kind; thus, ere William, the eldest, who possessed great comeliness of face and beauty of person, had reached his twelfth year, he was master of the sword and dagger, the bow and arquebuse; and he could toss a pike, pitch a bar, or handle a quarterstaff with the best man in the barony. His brother Florence had gone to France, as page in the suite of Anne de la Tour de Vendome (the widowed duchess of the regent, John of Albany), who had promised Lady Alison he would return the most accomplished cavalier in Scotland; and, as related, he had now been seven years absent.

Fired by the story which his mother never ceased repeating and enforcing, by touching references to the empty chair which stood unused by the hall fire, to the unused plate that was placed daily on the hall table, to keep alive the memory of the slain man whose rusty arms and mouldering garments were hung in conspicuous places, and to all of which Dame Alison hourly drew the attention of her boys,—fired by the reiteration of all this, one evening, in the autumn of 1541, when Hamilton of Preston had just returned from the battle of Haldenrig, where the army of Henry VIII. had been defeated with considerable slaughter, William Fawside, then in his fourteenth year, without consulting his mother, Father John of Tranent, or his warlike preceptor, old Roger of the Westmains, presented himself at the iron gate of Preston tower, and, while his swelling heart beat high and his smooth cheek flushed crimson with the consciousness of his own audacity, he demanded of the surly and bearded warder admittance to the laird. The servants of the latter narrowly and insolently scrutinized the boy, who bore the arms of his house, *gules,* a fess between three besants, worked in crimson and gold on the breast of his velvet doublet.

"See that he has nae weapon—nae sting aboot him, the young wasp!" said Symon Brodie, the butler, whose name and convivial habits have come down to us in a famous old drinking song.

"They are kittle cattle, the Fawsides," whispered Mungo Tennant, the warder, as they ushered the boy into the high-arched hall, where the grim old laird was reclining asleep in a huge black leather chair, covered by a wolf's-skin, and seated near a fire that blazed on the tiled hearth.

"Bairn!" he exclaimed, with more astonishment than anger, on being wakened, "what want ye of me?"

"My father's sword!" replied young William boldly.

"Your father!—And who was he, my callant?"

"Sir John of Fawside and that ilk— —"

"Aha!"

"He whom ye foully slew under tryst, as all in the Lothians know."

The high, stern brow of old Preston grew black as night. He grasped the carved arms of his high-backed chair, and for a moment surveyed the boy with a terrible frown; then, perceiving that he neither quailed nor shrank under this glance, but stoutly paid it back, though his little heart trembled at his temerity, Preston relaxed his ferocity a little, and grimly replied, under his shaggy moustache,

"Ye lie, ye d—d little limmer!—and they who told ye so, foully lie! I slew him, true; but it was in fair fight, and at open feud, as God and all braid Scotland be my judge!"

"Be that as you will, I want his sword; and, betide me weal, betide me woe, I shall have it!"

"His sword?"

"Yes!"

"For what purpose?"

"That ye shall ken anon," replied the boy with flashing eyes and clenched hands.

"Ye have the dour devilish look o' that termagant Kennedy, your mother, in ye, lad. You are the widow's son Willie, I suppose?"

"I am. Your insolent grooms here ken me weel; and better shall they ken me ere this death feud be stanched! But the sword, Claude Hamilton of Preston!—I say, my father's sword!"

"But what want ye with it, loon?"

"To stab you to the heart, when the time comes," responded the fearless boy.

"By my faith! this little devil takes fire like the match of an arquebuse!" growled the tall, grim laird.

"My father's sword, foul riever!" continued Willie, stamping his foot.

Old Preston now laughed outright, for the boy's daring charmed his warlike spirit.

"Though lawful spulzie, taken in combat and under harness, receive the sword, and welcome, bairn," replied Preston, unhooking from the wall one of those long cross-guarded and taper-bladed swords used in the early part of the fifteenth century, and handing it the boy, who trembled with stern exultation as he there kissed the hilt of polished steel. "It was good King James's gift to your father on that bloody morning when first we forgot our quarrel and fought side by side, like brither Scots, on the green slope of Flodden Hill, where our best and bravest were lying on the brae-side thick as the leaves in Carberry Wood. Take the weapon, bairn. Your father was a leal and gallant man—rest him, God! for Scotland had no better,—and I, the man he hated most on earth, avow it; and ill would it become Claude Hamilton to keep the sword of such a father from such a son. Take it, bairn, and welcome; and I pray Heaven that we may meet no more!"

"False carle, we *shall* meet, and that thou shalt see!" responded the boy, pressing the sword to his breast, while his eyes filled with tears.

Symon Brodie, the butler, here raised his huge hand to smite the boy down, but the laird interposed.

"Beware, fellow!" said he, "and let the bairn alone; yea, and let him speak, too. What have I to fear from a fushionless auld carline and twa halfling laddies?"

"I have been told that you fear not God, although you are a Hamilton; but I will teach you, carle, to fear me!"

"A brave lad!" exclaimed the old laird, with an admiration which he could not repress. "I love to see a lad stand up thus for his father's feud and his family honour. But let this matter end; in twa hunder years and mair we have surely had enough of it! Give me thy hand, Willie o' Fawside, and I will ask pardon for slaying thy father. 'Twas done in hot blood and under harness; and I will even pay unto Mass John of Tranent a hundred French crowns to say funeral services for his soul's repose."

"My hand!"

"Yes, bairn; an auld man asks it of thee."

"Never!" replied William Fawside, shrinking back. "If I gave a hand to thee, my mother would slay me like a cur; and I would well deserve the death. So fare ye well! with a thousand thanks for this fair gift, until—we meet again."

And they did meet, most fatally, five years afterwards.

William Fawside, then in his nineteenth year, was a tall and handsome cavalier, than whom there was none more gay or gallant in costume, manner, or bearing at the court of the Regent Arran, to whom he officiated as Master of the Horse. He was the most graceful dancer on Falkland Green, and there, also, the victor of the ring and butts, with spear and bow; but when he and Claude of Preston, then a man well up in years, confronted each other in the lists under the southern brow of the Castle Rock of Edinburgh, to fight a solemn duel, to which the taunts and open accusations of murder (for so the widow styled her husband's fall on Fawside Brae) had brought him, the young Sir William saw, without pity, that his grey-haired adversary was animated by a reluctance which he was at no pains to conceal, for on many a day of battle his courage had been put to the sternest proof.

Cartels of defiance had been duly exchanged; mass had been said in the chapel of Our Lady in the Portsburgh; and there, in presence of the assembled citizens of Edinburgh, whose provost, William Craik, appeared on horseback in complete armour, and before a chair, in which sat George Earl of Errol, hereditary lord high constable of Scotland, as vicar-general to the infant queen, wearing on his surcoat the three shields of his house, in a field *argent*, and within a listed space, sixty paces long and forty broad, stood the young and resolute challenger, on foot, at the eastern end, and Preston at the western, all according to the custom of judicial combats. Each was in full armour of unpolished but highly-tempered steel, with open helmets; each bore a Scottish target, a sword, and dagger.

They were sworn solemnly by the constable, "That they had not brought into the lists other armour or weapons than such as were allowed by Scottish law, or any firework engine, witch's spell or enchantment, and that they trusted alone to their own valour, as God and His holy Evangelists should help them!"

It was then proclaimed that no man should speak or utter a cry, under penalty of a fine equal in value to twenty cattle; or put forth hand or weapon, under pain of forfeiting limb and life to the queen—the poor little unconscious queen, who was then in her cradle, in time-hallowed Holyrood.

The constable rose from his seat, and waved his white truncheon thrice, exclaiming,

"Let them go! Let them go! Let them go, and do their worst!"

This was the usual formula; and then they rushed on each other.

Preston fought warily; but the fury of his adversary and the wounds he inflicted soon raised the old man's blood, and, by one tremendous stroke of his two-handed sword, he clove the widow's son—her boasted, her fair and comely Willie—through helmet and bone, to the chin, slaying him in a moment; as the quaint records of the lord high constable's court have it, "cleaving him through harnpan and harns to ye bearde with ane straik of his quhinger."

His body was sent home for burial, but denuded of his armour, —every buckle of which had been that morn adjusted by his mother's hands, —of his jewels and rings, which, according to the form of judicial combats in Scotland, became, together with the posts and rails of the lists, the fees of the constable's servants.

Lady Alison was on her knees at her husband's altar-tomb in Tranent Church, imploring God to aid and to protect her son, when old Roger of Westmains arrived, with his eyes swollen by weeping, and his heart swollen by rage and sorrow, to detail the death of her eldest boy by the same relentless sword that slew his father! The fierce, stern woman heard him to an end, and then fell prostrate on the tomb, in a paroxysm of grief, and perhaps of remorse.

If the latter found way in her breast, it did not linger long. Three days she remained in a darkened chamber, without speaking to any one; on the morning of the fourth she came out, graver, more gloomy, and, if possible, paler than before, and said briefly to Westmains—

"Write to France—to the chateau of Anne of Vendome, and desire Florence to come home without delay. I have yet the bullets that were found in the body of his father; and if the widow of John of Albany hath kept her royal word, I may yet have sure vengeance on yonder murderer and his brood!"

"The tenants have brought their herezelds," said Westmains in a low voice.

"Remit them; but say, to put their swords to the grindstone, for the day cometh when I, Alison Kennedy, shall need them all."

The bailie referred to the gift given in case of death to the heir of an over-lord, generally the best cow, yielded by those who held of the said lord an oxgang of land.

There were now TWO places vacant at the hearth, two platters unused on the table, and two scutcheons hung in the kirk of Tranent; but the mangled images of those who were gone remained enthroned more darkly than ever in the heart of the widow and mother!

CHAPTER IV
AN OLD SCOTTISH MATRON

Can Christian love, can patriot zeal,
   Can love of blessed charity—
Can piety the discord heal,
   Or stanch the death feud's enmity?

                         Scott.

Lady Alison of Fawside had been a beauty in her youth, when the stout and buirdly knight Sir John had wooed and won her, in the Castle of Calzean; and in memory of this alliance, the cognisance of the Kennedys, a chevron *gules*, between three cross-crosslets, fitched sable, may still be traced on the roof of the hall; but in the year when our story opens few traces remained of those charms which Huchown Clerk of Tranent, the old macker (*i.e.* troubadour) extolled in his poems, and for which he was rewarded yearly by a silver chain an ell long, three French crowns, and a camlet gown lined with Flemish silk, until his death, which happened about the close of the reign of King James V.

The widow was of great stature, yet her figure was graceful, noble, and commanding; her features were fine; her nose was straight; and her black eyebrows, which met above it, together with the peculiar lines of her mouth and chin, expressed firmness and unflinching resolution. Her complexion was deadly pale. Her once-black hair was grey and escaped in grizzled locks from under her escallop or shell-shaped cap, which was made of thick point-lace, like her close-quilled ruff and ruffles. Her attire was always a black damask dress, buttoned by small silver knobs, from the lower peak of her long stomacher, up to her ruff. She wore a rosary and cross of ebony, and a black locket containing the hair of her late husband and his slaughtered son; but no other ornament. Her pocket sun-dial, or perpetual almanac, a brass plate inscribed, "This table beginneth in 1540, and so on for ever," with her keys (and huge antique keys they were), her scissors and huswife hung at her girdle; and she used a long ivory-mounted cane to assist her in walking, and as gossips averred, wherewith to chastise her lacqueys and serving-men. Her busk was of hard wood, and contained a bodkin. This was literally a dagger seven inches long, and worn for defence in those stirring and perilous times.

Four-and-thirty years ago this stern woman, without shedding a tear, had seen her husband and all his kinsmen ride forth on that invasion of England which terminated at Flodden; but she welcomed him with transports of joy when he returned. Alas! old Westmains, covered with wounds, was the sole representative of forty stout men of Lothian, well horsed, with jack and spear, who had followed Fawside's pennon to the field. After this catastrophe, they had a few years peace with the Hamiltons of Preston, whose men had all escaped, being a portion of those many thousand Scots who melted away a week before the battle, and left King James with his knights and nobles to confront the foe alone.

Lady Alison was a Scottish matron of a very "old school" indeed, and possessed a stern and Spartan spirit incident to the times of war and tumult, raid and feud, amid which she had been born and bred. The annals of her country record the names of many such, who, in extremity of danger, possessed that resolute spirit with which Scott has gifted his imaginary Helen MacGregor, and the coolness of the Lady of Harden, who, when the larder was bare, placed a pair of Ripon spurs in her husband's plate at dinner, as a hint to mount and ride for England, where the fat beeves browsed on the green hills of Cumberland. There was black Agnes Randolph, the Countess of March, who, for five months defended her castle of Dunbar against the troops of Edward III., and foiled them in the end; there was the Lady of Edinglassie, who, after her husband had been slain by the Laird of Invermarkie, had the head of the latter cut off, in September, 1584, and conveying it "by its hoar locks" to Edinburgh, cast it at the feet of the startled James VI., as a token that she could avenge her own wrongs without appeal to Lowland judge or jury; there was the Lady Johnstone, of Annandale, who, after the battle of the Dryffesands, where, in 1593, seven hundred Maxwells fell beneath the spears and axes of her clan, is accused of dashing out the Lord Maxwell's brains with her own white hand, when she found that brave, humane, and courteous noble lying mortally wounded on the field, and when his silver locks were exposed by the loss of his helmet, which had been struck off in the *mêlée*; and this terrible deed she is said to have perpetrated with the ponderous iron key of Lochmaben Kirk, at the old thorn tree on the green holm of Dryffe. There was also that grim patriot, the old Marchioness of Hamilton, who, when her son entered the Firth of Forth, in 1639, at the head of six thousand Englishmen, rode to the beach with a pair of pistols at her saddlebow, vowing to God that she would shoot him as a traitor and a parracide, if he dared to land on Scottish ground under a foreign flag—a hint, which the recreant marquis, her son, fully understood and obeyed.

We believe few men now-a-days would relish having such fiery "and termagant Scots," as the partners of their bed and board; but the spirit and nature of these women were the development of the age in which they lived—an age when every house was a barred or moated garrison,—when every man was a trained soldier, and when a day seldom passed in city or hamlet without blood being shed in public fray or private feud; but these grim matrons, and such as these, were the mothers of the brave who led the line of battle at Ancrumford and Pinkey-cleugh, at Sark and Arkinhome, at Chevy Chase, Bannockburn, Haldenrig, and Northallerton, and on a thousand other fields, where Scottish men without regret—yea, perhaps, with stern joy—gave their swords, and lives, and dearest blood for the mountain-land that bore them.

It was this feudal and warlike spirit which made the resolute Lady Alison prosecute the quarrel against Preston with such determination and vindictiveness.

She wept in secret for her slaughtered son; but his death seemed to be only one other item in that heavy debt of hatred and thirst for vengeance which every drop of blood in the veins of Claude Hamilton could not assuage, even if poured out at her feet—a debt which she had no object in life but to pay with all the interest of her stern soul.

Tiger-like, she panted with eagerness for the return of her second son, Florence, doubting not that when the death of his father and brother were added to the old and inborn hatred of the House of Preston, his younger and more skilful hand could never fail in the combat to which she had resolved the slayer should be invited and goaded by every taunt, if he proved unwilling.

To her confessor, the old vicar of Tranent, who strove in vain to soothe this unchristian spirit, she would say fiercely,—"Peace! am I to forego my just feud at the behest of a book-i'-the-bosom monk? I trow not! I am a Kennedy of Colzean. Oh that this boy were back to me, that he might unkennel and slay the old wolf who bydes in yonder tower,—even as his ancestor slew the wolf of Gulane." "*He* has no son," she was wont to say with savage exultation, while grinding her strong white teeth and beating the floor with her cane; "his wife left him childless—he has no cub to transmit his blood with the feud to future times; so with him it must end. The sword of my Florence will end the strife with Preston's godless career and grasping race—black dool and pyne be on them!"

"But he has a niece," urged the white-haired vicar gently.

"A niece——" a

"His ward and heiress,—a ward of the crown, too."

"Mean ye that moppet the Countess of Yarrow, whose father drew the sword in pure wantonness on the day my husband fell?"

"Yes, Claude Hamilton's sister was an earl's wife."

"Why tell me that? what care I for his niece's coronet? We were belted knights and landed barons ere surnames were known in the North,—yea, a hundred years and more before a Hamilton was heard of. And this niece— what of her?"

"She may marry."

"Well—well."

"And her husband may—though Heaven forfend it—take up the feud."

"Had she a hundred husbands, we'll find cold iron for them all, priest— and in the sword is all my trust."

"Alas, lady! trust alone in God," replied the vicar, shaking his head; "He giveth much, and yet hath nought the less."

"Oh that my brave bairn were back. The French are skilful masters of the sword; and Anne of Albany promised me that Florence should have the best; that his hand should—if my Willie's failed—redress the wrongs of ages."

But, as already related, several days elapsed after the arrival of the ship, yet there came to Fawside tower no tidings of her son, whom, as he bears a part of some importance in our history, we must now introduce to the reader.

CHAPTER V
THE "GOLDEN ROSE"

Leo. —What would you have with me, honest neighbour?

Dog. —Marry, sir, I would have some confidence with you, that decerns you nearly.

Leo. —Brief, I pray you; for, you see, 'tis a busy time with me.

"Much Ado about Nothing."

The sun was setting in the westward—for in the year of grace 1547 it set in the westward just as it does now, though history omits to record the fact. Seven had tolled from the square towers of St. Mary and of the Commanderie of St. Anthony at Leith, on the evening of the first of August, the same on which we left a mother seated in the old tower upon the hills waiting anxiously for her son, when the latter—to wit, Florence Fawside— left the ship of the Sieur Nicolas de Villegaignon, knight of Rhodes, and admiral of the galleys of France, and landing with all his luggage, which consisted of three large leathern mails, found himself once more on *terra firma*, after a long but prosperous voyage from Brest; and, with a glow of satisfaction on his nut-brown visage, he stamped on the ground, to assure himself that it was not a planked deck, but the land—and good Scottish land too,—as he hurriedly approached the quaint wooden porch of "Ye Gowden Rois" (*i.e.* the "Golden Rose"), an hostel which bore that emblem painted on a huge signboard that swung between two wooden posts.

The latter were placed near the bank of the river, for although, to the eastward, there lay the charred remains of a wooden pier, burned by the English in 1544, Leith was destitute of a quay in those days; and thus a row of little gardens extended along the eastern bank between the water and the street of quaint Flemish-like mansions which faced it. These plots, or kailyards, were divided by privet or holly hedges, and among them lay fisher-boats, tar-barrels, rusty anchors, brown nets, and bladders, with other *débris* of the mercantile and fisher craft, which lay moored on both sides of the stream below Abbot Ballantyne's Bridge, the three stone arches of which spanned the Leith, where the pathway led to the church and burying-ground of St. Nicholas, and where stood a gate, at which a somewhat lucrative toll was levied by the monks of the Holy Cross.

Passing between the signposts and up the bank, Florence Fawside found himself before the "Golden Rose," a long irregular house three stories in height, built all of polished stone, yet having a front of elaborate timberwork forming two galleries, supported on carved pillars, and surmounted by three gables, whose acute apex sharply cut the sky-line, and gave the edifice a quaint and striking aspect. Cloaks of velvet and of camlet, horse-cloths, crimson saddles, belts of gold or buff leather, with one or two huge pieces of gaudy tapestry, were hung carelessly over the oak rails of the galleries, in which many persons were lounging, for the house and the stable-yard behind it were alike full of guests and bustle. The "Golden Rose" was the principal hostelry in Leith, and had been built for the accommodation of travellers, a few years before, by Logan of Restalrig, Lord Superior of the barony. Hence, the landlord, Ralf Riddel, being one of his vassals, was bound to give "up-putting to all the laird's retinue, man and horse, when they chanced to pass that way," a contingency which happened more frequently than the said Master Riddel, with all his inbred respect for the house of Logan, perhaps relished, especially as no overcharge could be made upon other visitors, for, by a statute of the late King James V., the bailies of royalties and regalities made a regular tariff of prices to be observed by all hostellers throughout the realm, and by this tariff the charges for corn, hay and straw, fish, flesh, bread, wine and ale, were all regulated and enforced under high penalties; but, by the same law, persons travelling with much money in their possession are wisely advised to reside with their *friends*. As Fawside entered, he observed a group of gentlemen, richly dressed, observing him narrowly from a dark gallery above the porch.

Though the arrival of a stranger, especially one on foot, did not usually excite much attention at the establishment of Master Ralf Riddel, the air and bearing, the handsome figure, and fine features of the young laird of Fawside, with his short-clipped beard and black moustache, *à la* François I., his magnificent crimson-velvet doublet, which was profusely embroidered with gold, and stiff as buckram and lace could make it, his enormous ruff and long sword, his little French cap of blue velvet, adorned by a long white feather, and diamond aigrette, the gift of Anne of Albany, his long black riding-boots, the tops of which joined his short trunk-hose, altogether caused the tapster and ostlers to make so favourable a report of his appearance that he was speedily waited on by the gudeman of the establishment in person.

He was conducted to an apartment the grated windows of which overlooked the stable-yard. The latter was full of pages, liveried lackeys, and armed troopers in iron-jacks, steel bonnets, and plate sleeves; horses, saddled and unsaddled, were led to and fro; and clumps of tall spears were reared here and there against the walls. The clamour of voices and clatter of hoofs, together with the neighing of steeds and barking of dogs, made the place instinct with life. The hostel was occupied by several of the noblesse and their retinues—for then no great lord could travel with out a troop of horse in his train; but, all unmindful of the bustle below, young Florence of Fawside, when the landlord returned, was gazing earnestly to the eastward, where, upon the crown of the high green eminence or sloping upland that overlooked the spacious bay of Musselburgh and stretched far away into Haddingtonshire, all bathed in gold and purple by the setting sun, he could discern, some ten miles distant, the outline of his old paternal home rising above the thicket of trees by which it was environed.

On turning, as he heard a step behind, he saw, on the roughly-hewn fir boards which formed the floor of the apartment, an ominous black stain, nearly a foot in circumference, to remind him that he dwelt in a land of swords and danger.

"I require a horse, gudeman," said he, divesting himself of his velvet mantle and rich sword-belt.

"A horse!—at this hour, sir?"

"Even so, my friend, for in less than an hour I must ride hence. You have, doubtless, a swift nag to spare?"

"Yea, sir, ten, if ye lacked them—ten, than whilk my Lord Regent hath none better in stall."

"'Tis well; and now for supper. I have been long in the land of kickshaws and frogs, where bearded men sup fricassees bedevilled with garlic and onions, in lieu of porridge and sturdy kailbrose; so, gudeman of mine, I long for a right Scottish dish."

"That shall ye have, fair sir, and welcome, with a stoup of Canary, Bourdeaux, or Alicant— —"

"Nay, I am no bibber, believe me."

"We get brave gude wine hereawa in Leith, sir, by our trade with the Flemings of the Dam."

"After seven years in a foreign land, gudeman," said Florence, slapping the hosteller kindly on the back, while his heart swelled and his eyes filled, "your Scottish tongue comes like music to my ear—yea, like the melody o' an auld song, man; and I snuff up my native air like a young horse turned out to grass; for, save once a year, by a letter given me by a passing traveller hastening Paris-ward, I have heard naught from home, or of aught that passed in Scotland here."

"Nocht, said ye?"

"Naught—so the term of my absence seems marvellously long—naught but evil," he added, with a darkening expression of face.

"Evil!"

"Yea; for I have returned to avenge the death of a dear kinsman."

"Such errands are nothing new in Scotland," said Ralf Riddel, sighing and shrugging his shoulders.

"No—in these hot days of feud and endless quarrelling. 'Tis a heavy task I have in hand, gudeman; but it must be done, when I have obeyed the behests of those I left in France."

"Belong you to hereawa, sir?"

"I do," replied Fawside, smiling.

"May I be pardoned for—for——"

"For what?" asked Florence, while the hosteller smoothed down his front hair, and twirled his bonnet on his fingers; "for what should I pardon you?"

"For speiring your name?"

"You may be pardoned, but not gratified, gudeman," replied Florence, laughing. "There are over-many under your rooftree to make it safe for me to utter my name aloud, alone as I am; for though I have been wellnigh seven years away, I have not forgotten the danger of rashly telling one's name in fiery Scotland."

"You are right, sir; yet my house is one without reproach."

"What says this dark stain on the floor?"

"That there I slew an Englishman, in the May of '44, when all Leith was in flames—houses, ships, and and piers—and ten thousand of his comrades, under the Lord Hertford, were on the march for Edinburgh. Yea, sir, I slew him there by one blow of my jeddart staff, for making his quarters good at sword's point. The 'Gowden Rose' is a house without reproach."

"But its visitors may not be so, despite their silken doublets and gilded coats of mail. Whose jackmen and lacqueys are these in the stable-yard?"

"The followers of the Earl of Glencairn, and of his son, the Lord Kilmaurs; of the Lord Gray and his son, the Master, with others whom I ken not; but they muster eighty horsemen in all."

"The English faction!" muttered Fawside. "By Heaven, 'tis high time I had the water of Esk behind my horse's heels. And these lords——"

"Are all on their way to Stirling, to keep tryste with the Lord Regent."

"Fool that I was, not to know at once the shakefork of the stable worn by the ruffians of Glencairn," said Fawside, referring to the cognizance of the Cunninghames, which is argent, a shakefork *sable*, granted to Henry of Kilmaurs, who was master stabler to King Alexander III.

"And those fellows in pyne doublets and cuirasses?"

"With the oak branch in their burganets, and morsing horns at their girdles?"

"Yes."

"They are the liverymen of the laird of Preston."

"Of Claude Hamilton of Preston!" exclaimed Fawside, instinctively assuming his sword.

"Yes."

"By St. Giles, I was right to speak below my beard, and utter not my name." Then, in a fierce whisper, he added, "Is *he* here?"

"No."

"So much the better. But get me supper and a swift horse. Sumpter nags will come anon for my leathern mails, which I leave in your care, gudeman. Beware how you let men handle them, though my *papers* and *valuables* I carry on my own proper person, where my sword can easier answer any kind friend who inquires after them."

"My house, I have said, is stainless and sakeless."

"And now for supper," said Florence impatiently.

"I can let you have a pie of eels, from Lithgow Loch; a hash of Fife mutton, yea, mutton from Largo, where they say every tooth in a sheep's head is worth a French crown."

"Good!—the supper quick, the horse quicker," said Fawside laughing;— for it was a superstition in those days, and for long after, that the teeth of the flocks which browsed on the conical hill of Largo were turned to solid silver by its herbage.

He then turned once more to the window, to gaze on his mother's distant dwelling,—on those hills from whence the last gleam of sunlight had now died away. He drew from a pocket in the breast of his beautiful doublet two letters, tied with white ribbons saltirewise, and sealed with yellow wax, impressed by three *fleur-de-lys*. One was addressed—

"A Madame ma soeur, la Seine d'Ecosse."

The other bore—

"For Monseigneur the Earl of Arran, Lord Hamilton, Knight of St. Andrew and St. Michael, Regent of Scotland."

The young traveller surveyed these important missives with a smile of satisfaction, and once more consigned them to the secret pocket of his doublet. While left thus to himself and his own thoughts, certain parties in an adjoining apartment were taking a particular interest in his affairs.

CHAPTER VI
CURIOSITY

"Who's he?
I know not—Duke Humphrey, mayhap;
But this I know, my sword will test it soon."

Old Play.

This apartment, which was next to that in which Florence Fawside was testing the merits of the eels of Linlithgow Loch (which are still much prized) and Ralf Riddel's Largo mutton and Alicant wine, opened off the shady gallery wherein we left a gaily-attired group, who had watched the traveller enter the "Golden Rose."

This group, which had also been observing a number of poor lepers, who, under a guard of men-at-arms, were on the sands waiting the boats which were to convey them to banishment on Inch Keith, and had made them the subject of various cruel and ribald jokes—this group, was composed of several men of better position than conduct, for it consisted of that Earl of Glencairn, who had slain one of his nearest relations under tryst; of the Earl of Cassilis; of Patrick Lord Gray of Kinfawns, and his son the master; John Lord Lyle of Duchal, and his son James the Master of Lyle, who had together slain Sir John Penny, an unarmed priest. Several gentlemen of their different surnames were with them—all men who had more or less shed blood in the private quarrels and open feuds of that wild and lawless time. All were richly dressed, for the age was one of profusion and ostentation; the splendour of the third and fourth James was yet remembered in the land, which had not as yet suffered by the civil wars and depression subsequent to the Reformation. Many of those to whom we are about to introduce the reader had their coats of arms embroidered on the breasts of their gorgeous doublets; but the greater number wore half armour, gorgets, breast-plates, and plate sleeves; and all, without distinction, had long swords, Scottish daggers, and Italian pistols or calivers at their girdles; and they were all, in secret, members of the anti-national or English faction—of which more anon.

"I have a presentiment that yonder young galliard in the crimson velvet bravery bodes us no good," said the Lord Kilmaurs in an undertone. He was a stern and reckless noble, whose brown-velvet hat had already been perforated by two bullets in a brawl that day.

"Why think you so, son?" asked his father the earl, whose cold grey eye ever suggested the idea that his lordship said one thing while thinking another.

"He came from yonder gilded galley of the Sieur de Villegaignon—and see! here come the admiral's own bargemen, with the lilies of France upon their pourpoints, bearing his mails. By my soul, sirs, this spark is served like a king's ambassador!"

"And may he not be the envoy of Henry of France?" asked some one.

"Nay, for he is only young Florence Fawside of that ilk, as I understand," said the Lord Kilmaurs, to whose right eye a savage glare was imparted, together with a spasmodic contortion of that side of his face, by a dreadful sword-wound, which he received at the defeat of the English at Ancramford.

"*Only!*" reiterated his father, with an accent upon the word; "Mahoun! art thou sure of this?"

"Sure as I am a living man."

"But men say he is still in France," urged the Lord Lyle.

"Nay, my lord," began the Master of Lyle, "for the old beldame his mother——"

"She is a Kennedy of Colzean, and my near kinswoman," interrupted Lord Cassilis haughtily.

"I crave your pardon, though fortunately we are not of Carrick, where all men court St. Kennedie," replied the other, bowing with a smile on his lip and a sneer in his eye; "but Dame Alison hath written letters into France to the Duchess Anne of Albany and Vendome, desiring her to send back the youth, that he might avenge the death of his brother, whom Claude Hamilton of Preston slew at the king's barresse, and in fair fight, as we all can testify."

"Ay, old Preston's sword hath been reddened alike in the blood of father and son, a strange but not uncommon fatality."

"Consanguinity, my Lord Lyle, should make that quarrel ours too," said the Earl of Cassilis; "but fortunately, I have no wish to embroil myself with Preston, and the old dame Alison hath ever disdained our aid and alliance."

"If that bedizened spark be really Fawside her son, he has been long in the service of Anne de la Tour of Vendome, widow of the late Regent

Albany," said one who had not yet spoken, and whose accent marked his country as England, though he wore the badges and livery of the house of Glencairn; "and rede me, sirs, he hath some other mission to Scotland here than his mother's feud with the Prestons."

"Thou art right, Master Shelly," said James Master of Lyle, as a sudden gleam shot athwart his sinister visage; "in these days, when trusty messengers are scarce and bribes high, falsehood dear and fidelity dearer, I doubt not he hath letters from Henry of Valois to the Queen-Mother, and from the grasping princes of the house of Guise to the Regent Arran—and these letters must be inimical to us. Is it thus thou wouldst say, my valiant captain of the Boulogners?"

"It is," replied the disguised English soldier, whose steel salade was worn well over his handsome face, for concealment.

"Such letters would let us see their game, which 'twere well to know ere they can learn ours," said Glencairn. "But if they are concealed in the lining of his doublet, in the scabbard of his sword, in the quills of his feathers, or perhaps indited with invisible necromantic ink by Catherine de Medicis— for I have known all these plans resorted to—we may kill the poor knave for nothing, and raise a pestilent hubbub in the burgh to boot."

"Kill him here, then," said Kilmaurs, his son.

"What, in the hostel?" said his father, starting.

"Yes," was the brief and fierce response.

"'Twould embroil us with Logan, whose property it is. But every thread of his garments shall be searched. 'Twas a shrewd thought of thine, Master Edward Shelly, for time presses in the matter of our baby-queen's marriage to thy baby-king."

"If we find such letters on him," said Kilmaurs with a ferocious glance at each of his companions in succession, "by the five wounds of God he shall swallow them ere he die. I made an English spy eat five on the night before the battle of Ancramford."

"And how fared he after?" asked Shelly laughing.

"Ill enough, I trow."

"How?"

"He straightway swelled up like a huge ball, and burst, whereby I opined that the letters had been written with poisoned ink."

"And these letters——"

"Were all anent the ransom of a friend of mine, who shared in England the exile of Mathew of Lennox, and whose lands had been gifted by the late James to me."

"Let us see to this man at once," said Lord Lyle; "for I assure you, sirs, that if this fellow beareth letters out of France to mar our lucrative plans, by my father's soul I will slay him, even as I slew that shaveling mass-priest Penny!"

"And how slew ye him?" asked Master Shelly, an Englishman of pleasing countenance and good presence, who seemed amused by the quaint ferocity of these Scottish lords.

"I slew him like a faulty hound, because I liked him not," replied Lyle with a fierce grimace; "and hewed off his shaven head with my whinger. Then my son reminded me that a soothsayer, the prior of Deer, who now sleeps in Roslin chapel, had foretold by his cradle that in days to come his head should be the highest in Scotland. In sooth, it shall be so, quoth I; and, fixing it on my spear, which was six Scottish ells in length, I rode home with it thus through all the Carse of Gowrie to my castle of Duchal, where you may yet see the bare pyked bones of it grinning on the bartizan wall."

"And what answer made you to the law?"

The other drew himself up with ineffable hauteur, and briefly replied—

"I am the Lord Lyle!"

"Hush, sirs," said Glencairn; "our man is in the next room, perhaps, and may overhear us."

"Let us see to him," said Kilmaurs, loosening his dagger in its sheath.

"Stay, sirs," said Shelly the Englishman; "and excuse me if I am less reckless in bloodshed than you; for, under favour, and with all due deference be it said, I came from a more peaceful land, where if the sword is drawn, it is usually for some weightier reason than because one man wears a dress striped with red and another wears it striped with green, or because one man wears a tuft of heather in his steel cap and another sports a sprig of laurel; and so, ere you proceed to violence in this matter, I would pray your lordship to be well assured of who this stranger is."

"If we suspect this knight of the crimson suit of being a spy of the Valois or the Guises, what matter is it who he is?" replied the master of Lyle impatiently. "But there is the landlord in conference with one of Preston's followers, so, let us inquire of him."

"Ralf Riddel!—gudeman, come hither," said Kilmaurs.

Thus commanded, Riddel ascended to the gallery, with several low bows, while the man with whom he had been conversing, and who was no other than Symon Brodie the butler of Preston, an unscrupulous and bloodthirsty swashbuckler, remained, bonnet in hand, on the steps a little lower down, to listen greedily to all he might overhear from a group so gaily attired.

"Did not yonder gay galliard come from a ship in the roads?" asked Lord Kilmaurs.

"Who?" responded Riddel, with evident reluctance.

"He of the crimson-velvet doublet and long French boots."

"Yes, sir," replied Riddel, with increasing hesitation, for he read mischief in the eyes of all.

"From the galley of Nicolas de Villegaignon?"

"Yes, my lords."

"He hath come from France, then!" said Kilmaurs sternly.

"It would seem so."

"Seem! Speak to the point," continued the fiery heir of Glencairn, "or, by the horns of Mahoun! we will burn thy house to the groundstone. It is so!"

"Yes—my lords,—yes."

"Speak out, cullionly knave," thundersd the Lord Kilmaurs, the long scar on whose visage became purple as his anger increased; "his name——"

"I ken it not."

"How—ye ken it not?"

"No."

"Why!"

"He conceals it."

"Hah! that betokens secrecy!" exclaimed Lord Lyle.

"And as we have secret projects," added his son, "we must suspect all of having the same; so doubt not that he hath letters. All who come from the vicinity of the Louvre, or the Hotel de Guise, bring dangerous letters to Holyrood, dangerous at least to us, and we must have them."

"He *has* come from France, my lords,—from France direct," said Symon Brodie, approaching and speaking in a whisper, as the abashed landlord withdrew. "Mairower, he is Florence Fawside of that ilk."

"You know him, then?" said several.

"Yea, and a' the race; I ken their dour dark look, and wha but he could wear on his breast, *gules*, a fess between three besants *or*?"

"Right, by Heaven!" said the master of Lyle.

"A follower of Anne of Vendome must have letters from which we may glean what France or the Lorraine princes mean to do," said Shelly bluntly; "cut him off if you will, but not here,—it must be done secretly."

"To horse, then," said Glencairn hoarsely, as if, wolf-like, he already scented blood on the soft evening breeze that came from the glassy river; "to horse, and beset all the roads—Leith-loan, the Figgate Muir, and every path to the southward and the east,—for if he passes the brig of Esk to-night our cause perhaps is lost. He bears, doubtless, letters to the Regent and Queen, with promises of war with England and succour from France. Pietro Strozzi, the Marechal Duke de Montmorenci, or the Comte de Dammartin, with twenty thousand arquebusiers and gendarmes, thrown into the scale against us, would leave our cause and the boy King Edward's but a feather-weight. To horse, sirs, and away; for this August gloaming darkens fast, and night will be on us anon!"

As the earl spoke, they all hurried to the stables, and proceeded to saddle and mount their horses for the deadly purpose in view, and none were more active than Symon Brodie and seven other armed lackeys of the Laird of Preston, who joined in the affair, with no other interest or intention than to cut off the poor youth, in prosecution of the wretched quarrel between their master's house and his; for men joined in such deadly things in those days, as readily as now we go to see a horse-race, a fire, or an election row.

Master Edward Shelly, the Englishman, who was disguised as a follower of the House of Glencairn, joined in the plot also, but with some unwillingness; for he ran considerable risk. By the laws of James II., any Englishman found in Scotland became the lawful captive of the first man who discovered him; and any Scottish subject who met an English man under tryst, as these noblesse were doing, was liable to imprisonment during the king's pleasure, and to the forfeiture of all he possessed.

Such was the law passed by the parliament at Stirling, in 1455.

CHAPTER VII
THE BRAWL

My sword, my spear, my shaggy shield,
   They make me lord of all below;
For he who dreads the lance to wield
   Before my shaggy shield must bow;
His lands, his vineyards must resign,
For all that cowards have is mine.

Dr. Leyden.

Being a married man, Ralf Riddel went straightway to his spouse, and in whispers—lest the panelled walls might have ears—he communicated his suspicions of the deadly intentions of his titled guests. A landlady of the nineteenth century would instantly, on learning such tidings, have made an outcry and summoned the police; but Euphemia Riddel received them with the coolness incident to those days, when every other morning a man slashed by sword or dagger was found dead or dying somewhere in the streets of Edinburgh.

"And what mean ye to do, gudeman?" she asked.

"Leave the event to Providence, gudewife."

"To Providence and their whingers!" she exclaimed.

"Hush, or the hail hive will be on us!" said he in a terrified whisper.

"Foul fa' ye, Ralf Riddel, if ye permit this wicked slaughter of a winsome young man!"

"But they would ding their daggers into me in a trice."

"What of that?" she asked sharply.

"A sma' matter to you perhaps, but mickle to me; and if I was pinked below the ribs by these bullies, Symon Brodie, that bluidthirsty and drunken butler o' auld Preston's would soon be drawing in his chair at the ingle. That chield is ower often here, gudewife, and I dinna like it. It is no aye for ale and up-putting he comes to the 'Golden Rose.' But what shall I do anent Fawside?"

"Gowk! do that whilk is right."

"And that is — —?" queried Ralf, scratching his head —

"To send a saddled horse to the Burgess close, and let the young laird out by the back yett while these lords and loons are busy in the yard. Take the horse round by your own hand while I see to the puir gentleman."

The matter was thus arranged at once; and while the gudeman of the hostel led the nag through a narrow by-lane to the place indicated, an old and narrow alley of dark and lofty houses which opened eastward off the bank of the river, his better half acquainted the young traveller with the danger which menaced him. With the boldness of his race, he at first refused to fly, and resolved to confront these men and fight them. Then he thought of his mother, and yielded to the entreaties of the good woman, his preserver.

"I will owe you a brooch of gold for this, gudewife," said he, kissing her hand and buckling on his sword.

It was the first time so brave and handsome a gentleman had done her this courtesy, and the heart of the woman swelled anew with pride and sympathy.

"Away! away!" she exclaimed, "lest dool and wae light on thy house and home to-night!"

"I thank you, gudewife — thank you kindly; I would not for worlds, were they mine, be maimed in a night-brawl by swashbucklers such as these, for I have greater and nobler work to perform than crossing my sword with such a rabble rout."

"Ay, the defence of our holy Kirk of Rome?"

"Nay; I shall not be slow in defending that if the time come; but I have a beloved father's murder under tryst and a tender brother's death in mortal combat to avenge, with the wrongs of centuries, upon the Hamiltons of Preston!" replied Florence, who, instead of having his ardour cooled by the fate of his relatives, longed with intense eagerness to see unsheathed against him the same sword by which they fell, that he might slay its wielder without mercy or remorse.

"And now, fair sir, away!"

"And the horse — —"

"Is at the Burgess Close foot, nigh unto the loan-end. Ride straight for Edinburgh, lest the eastward road to the Abbey Hill be beset."

"Thanks, madam," replied Florence, with a low French bow, as he loosened his long sword in its sheath, left the inn by a private door, and piloting his way in the twilight between hedgerows and low thatch-roofed cottages, reached the place where Riddel stood, holding the horse by its bridle. The hosteller would not listen to a word of thanks from Fawside, but urged him to "ride swiftly;" and assuredly time pressed, for he was barely in the saddle when at least forty armed and mounted men issued with scabbards, petronels, and hoofs clattering, from the stable-yard, and, separating into parties, proceeded at a rapid trot to beset the paths in every direction.

Fawside gave his horse the spur, and Riddel saw the sparks of fire fly from the flinty road as it sprang away towards the city.

When again the hosteller of the "Golden Rose" saw his fair roan nag, it was pierced by bullets, half-disembowelled, and lying drowned in the lake which then formed the northern moat of Edinburgh.

The darkness had now completely set in; and, save where a few trees, turf fences, or low dykes of stone and earth inclosed the fields, the whole country between the city and its seaport was open, but varied by many undulations and eminences covered by furze, tufted broom, and dark-green whin, or broken by hollows that were swampy, where the coot squatted in the oozy pools and the heron sent up its lonely cry from amid the thick rushes and masses of the broad-leaved water-dock.

Leaving Leith, which was then without those strong walls and iron gates by which it was engirt during the stormy regency of Mary of Lorraine, Fawside, after tracking his way almost instinctively through narrow alleys of thatched cottages and kail-gardens, ascended the brae above the Abbot's Bridge, and reached the road that led by the Bonny-toun (or Bonnie-haugh), a little hamlet where, in after-years, old Bishop Keith wrote his "History of the Scottish Church;" but the hum of the river, which there poured over a ledge of rough rocks, had scarcely died away in his rear, when swiftly and furiously he heard the clatter of iron hoofs upon the dusty bridle-road he was traversing.

At that moment the near hind shoe of his nag gave way, but by adhering to the hoof by a nail or two for some paces, nearly brought the animal down on its haunches, and even this trivial occurrence served to lessen the distance between Fawside and his pursuers, who cared not to disguise their purpose, as they shouted, hallooed, and taunted him by all the epithets and scurrility incident to the vulgar of the time; and foremost of all this rout, who were becoming excited with a thirst for blood and all the ardour of a hunt or race, rode Symon Brodie, the butler of Preston, mounted on a blood horse which belonged to his master, and had more than once borne at its neck the *silver bell*, the prize of the winner at Lanark races.

"Come on! come on!" he was exclaiming; "and look, lads, to your whingers and spur-whangs, for we win on him fast! Turn ye, Fawside! turn ye! and face, if ye dare, the same men that slew your kinsmen! Through! through!—a Hamilton! a Hamilton!"

These taunts made Fawside's blood boil within him, and a storm of hatred at these enemies of his family now tracking him with the most deadly intentions, gathered with stern ferocity in his heart: but the odds were too many against him; and though his cheek glowed and every pulse quickened with passion, he held on his way towards the city without swerving or casting a single glance behind. His pursuers were now so close, that he could hear them encouraging each other and laughing at those whom they distanced.

"Spur on—spur on!" cried the butler; "this gay galliard has nine golden targets at his velvet hat."

"They will blink brawly at our bonnet-lugs in the morning sun!" exclaimed another, goring his horse on hearing this fabricated incentive to blood and robbery. "I have plundered Dame Alison's eel-arks in the Howmire for a month past, and grazed my nowte on Birsley brae, but I must e'en change a' that if the laird win hame."

"The auld devil in the tower will burst her bobbins wi' spite if we slay her son!" said a third.

"On, on," cried others, "ere he gain the town-gates, for then the watch and the craftsmen will be raised like a hornet's nest on us, and the provost has but one word for brawlers—the *Wuddie!*"

"Sooth ay!" panted Brodie, pricking his horse with his dagger to increase its speed; "beware o' the Buith-holders and armed burgesses, for he is a landed man, and if we slay him——"

"Aver that we took him for a brawler, a dustifute, or fairand man."

"Havers!" exclaimed the savage butler; "wit ye, lads, 'tis our master's just feud. The young wolf hath come from France to slay our master. Preston is auld now, while he is lithe and young; no battle could be fair between them, so let us cut him off ere we ride homeward to-night—cut him off I say!"

"By my father's hand!" exclaimed another horseman who came abreast of them, and panted as he spoke, "I will venture both craig and weason to drive my dagger in his brisket. I will teach Scottish men to become the spies of France."

"Or the paid hirelings of England," retorted Fawside, now turning for the first time, and with his wheel-lock petronel discharging a flying shot at haphazard among his pursuers. One by the side of the last speaker, who was the Lord Kilmaurs, fell prone with a loud cry on the narrow path. Whether he was killed outright, or merely wounded, his comrades never tarried to inquire; but with a shout of rage and defiance, continued the race for death and life in the dark.

This episode occurred near a mill belonging to the monks of Holyrood—a quaint old edifice, having enormous buttresses, and in which King Robert I., when well stricken in years, is said by tradition to have found shelter on a stormy winter night, when the path to Edinburgh was buried deep under the drifted snow.

Skirting a little loch, the waters of which turned the mills of the canons of Sanctæ Crucis, the fugitive continued his flight towards the city, up the undulating slope now covered by the New Town of Edinburgh, but then a wilderness of furze and broom, till he reached the North-loch, which formed a moat or protection for the capital of the James's; for on that side there was no other defence than this artificial sheet of water, which the magistrates could at all times deepen by closing the sluice at the eastern extremity, between the Dow-Craig, or Calton, and the Craig-end gate.

Before Fawside the long and lofty ridge of the ancient city on its steep of rock and hill, upreared its rugged outline against the starry sky, broken into a hundred fantastic shapes, and terminating at the westward in the black and abrupt bluffs, crowned by the ancient castle, which then consisted of four huge donjons or masses of mason-work, the towers of King David, of St. Margaret, of the constable, and the royal lodging; but all were black and grim, for neither in the guarded fortress nor the walled city did a single ray of light shine out to vary the dusky gloom of the scenery. Our fathers went to bed betimes in the year 1547.

In the bosom of the long and narrow loch which spread before him, the reflected stars were twinkling, and headlong down its grassy slope he rode, and, without a moment's hesitation, plunged in his panting horse, with knee and spur, voice and bridle, urging it to gain the opposite bank; then plunge after plunge resounded on both sides, as nearly a score of horsemen leaped in after him, dashing the waters into a myriad foamy ripples, and resolved to follow him to the last; while others, less determined, or less interested in his destruction, or the capture of the supposed French missives, reined up their chargers on the bank, and fired their wheel-lock petronels at him, as his roan horse breasted the dark water bravely, and snorted, swimming with its head aloft and flanks immersed. Ere it was mid-way across, the poor animal uttered a wild cry, writhed under the rider, and by throwing back its head in agony, announced that it was mortally wounded, for it sank almost immediately, leaving Fawside to disentangle his feet from the stirrups and strike out for the opposite bank. Fortunately he had learned to swim expertly in the Loire, when at Vendome; thus he soon gained the opposite bank, but not without considerable difficulty, as its steep slope was covered by rushes, slime, and weedy grass.

The wheel-lock, or pistol, used by the men-at-arms of those days, was an invention of the Germans, and we have a minute description of it in Luigi Collados' treatise on Artillery, published at Venice in 1586, when it was deemed a firearm as perfect as now we deem our boasted Enfield or Lancaster rifle. The lock was composed of a solid wheel of fine steel revolving on an axle, to which a chain was attached. On being wound, this wheel drew up a strong chain, which, on the trigger being pulled, whirled the wheel with such velocity that the friction of its notched edge struck fire from a flint screwed into a cock which overhung the priming-pan. The wheels took some time to wind up or span, as it was technically termed, by a spanner or key, which the pistolier carried by a ribbon at his neck; but after all this preparation, like many better inventions of a more modern time, this weapon occasionally hung fire, and refused to explode at all.

However, on the present occasion, the wheel-locks of Florence's pursuers did their duty fatally for the poor horse he rode, and, boiling with a fury which he could no longer restrain, panting and breathless with his rapid ride, his recent immersion and present danger, he unsheathed his sword, determined to kill the first who came ashore, ere he turned once more to fly.

The first who came within his reach proved to be a follower of the Lord Glencairn, Hobbie Cunninghame, or Hobbie of the Kuychtsrig, who, in the preceding year, had been nearly hanged for abstracting "the provost's ox"—a fat bullock presented annually by the town-council to their chief magistrate,—and whom he cut down by a single backhanded stroke. The second he slew at the third pass, and he felt, as he ran him through the body, something of a shudder when the man's hot blood poured through the cut-steel network of his swordhilt, and mingled with the cold water of the loch which dripped from his doublet sleeves. But he thought, perhaps, little more about it, as he turned and rushed up the nearest close or alley, pursued by a dozen of his untiring enemies, who abandoned their horses and, with an ardour which their recent swim in the water failed to cool, followed him on foot up the steep slope, with swords and daggers drawn.

To quote a French writer when describing a similar incident—

"Let not our readers have the least bad opinion of our hero, who, after having killed a man, feared the police, but not God; for in 1547 all men were alike in this. They thought so little in that age of dying, that they also thought little of killing. We are brave now; but they were rash. People then lost, sold, or gave away their lives with profound carelessness."

Remorse or regret has nothing to do with this kind of killing; and any man who enjoyed a day or two shooting during the siege of Lucknow, or in the rifle-pits at Sebastopol, will tell you the same thing.

Fawside's blood was now fairly up, and he felt that with fierce joy he could make mince-meat of them all. The struggle was not merely a life for a life, but twelve lives for his—twelve swords against one! He reached the High Street, which traverses the crest of the lofty ridge occupied by the ancient city: it was involved in almost total darkness; for though in the reign of the late king the citizens had been ordained to hang out oil lanterns at certain hours, under the weaker rule of the Regent Arran they preferred alike to save their oil and the trouble. A vast breadth of opaque shadow enveloped this great thoroughfare, which was then encumbered by piles of timber and peat-stacks for fuel, as each citizen had one before his door; and there also—as in the streets of London and Paris at the same free-and-easy period—were huge mounds of every kind of household *débris*, amid which the pigs occupying the sties under fore-stairs and out-shots, revelled by day, as the kites and gleds did in the early morning before the booths were unclosed and the business of the day began; for these sable tenants of the adjacent woods swarmed then in the streets of Edinburgh, just as we may see them still about sunrise.

Between these piles of obstruction the skirmish continued, and Florence Fawside, finding that nearly all the arches of the various closes and wynds were closed and secured by massive iron-studded doors, which had been hung upon them as a security since the late invasion of '44, was compelled to continue his retreat through the Landmarket towards the Castle Hill; and then, having distanced several of his pursuers, he turned in wild desperation to face three who were close upon him, and whose swords there was no avoiding.

"They seek my letters or my life," thought he; "but my letters are more precious than my life—ay, more precious to Scotland and her little queen than the lives of fifty brave men. My mother—oh, my mother! what will be her thoughts if these assassins succeed in destroying me—hunting me thus to death like a mad dog. Oh, what a welcome home to my country!—the first night I tread again on Scottish ground. Hold your hands, sirs!" he exclaimed aloud. "I am on the queen's service, and the Lord Regent's too. Hold!—this is stoutrief, open felony and treason!"

"Fellow, thou makest a devil of a noise!" said the young Lord Kilmaurs, making a deadly thrust, which Florence parried, and almost by the same movement cut one of his companions across both legs, and for a moment brought the ruffian down upon his knees; but he started up and thrust madly at Fawside, whose back was now close to the wall of a house on the northern verge of the street, which there became narrow, as it approached the spur-gate of the Castle.

"Fie! armour—armour fie!" he exclaimed, using the cry of alarm then common in Edinburgh.

"Ding your whingers into him," said Kilmaurs furiously, as he paused for a moment to draw breath and let his companions' swords have full play, while his livid visage seemed by the starlight pale and green, as that of one who had been a corpse many days, and his dark eyes glittered like those of an incarnate demon. "At him to the hilt," he continued, "lest he rouse the burgh on us; for the common bell will be rung in five minutes, and then every bloated burgess and rascally booth-holder will be at the rescue, with halbert, jack and steel bonnet. At him, I say!"

"Are you Egyptians or thieves," said Fawside tauntingly; "if so, take my purse among ye and begone, in the name of the devil your master."

"No thieves or Egyptians are we," said Kilmaurs, again handling his sword with a savage laugh; "but Scottish gentlemen, who would fain know what paper news you bring out of France."

"From the three princes of the League," added Glencairn.

"The bloody Cardinal de Lorraine, and that foul kite of Rome, the Duc de Guise."

"And the Duc de Mayenne," added others, falling on with their swords.

"Ah!—'tis my letters rather than my life they seek," muttered Fawside. "Let me be wary—oh, let me be wary, blessed Heaven!"

He had now his single blade opposed at least to four; but, thanks to his own skill and the improvements made by a French master-at-arms on the earlier tuition he had received from old Roger of the Westmains, he kept them all in play, though his wrist began to fail and his sword-arm tingled to the shoulder. There shot a sharp and sudden pang through his left side, and on placing his hand there he felt the warm blood flowing from a wound. The sword of his first adversary, Lord Kilmaurs, had glanced along the ribs, and at the same moment a Cunningham gave him a stab between the bones of the sword-arm with a species of dagger, then named a Tynedale knife. There is an old saying that a Scotsman always fights best after seeing his own blood. Be that as it may, Fawside, on finding the current of his life now pouring from two wounds, that he was becoming weary, that there was a singing in his ears, a cloud descending on his eyes, and that the men with whom he fought seemed opaque shadows whose numbers were multiplying, and whose sword-blades his weapon sought and parried by mere instinct rather than by efforts of vision and skill—and, more than all, that many other merciless adversaries were coming clamorously and hastily up the street, a wild emotion of despair gathered with fury in his heart, at the prospect of never seeing his grey-haired mother more, and of being helplessly butchered on the first night he had set foot in the streets of Edinburgh after an absence of well-nigh seven years—butchered by men whom he knew not, and had never offended. Yet, with all this, he now disdained to cry for aid, but fought in silence and despair.

"He sinks at last!" said Symon Brodie with savage exultation. "A Hamilton! a Hamilton! Fawside, ye shall die!"

"Be it so. Then I to God and thou to the devil, false cullion!" he exclaimed, and by two well-directed thrusts he ran the half-tipsy butler and another knave through the body; but their steel caps had scarcely rung on the causeway when five or six other swords flashed before his eyes, and he received a third wound in the breast. On this a cry of agony, which was received by a shout of derision, escaped him.

"Kilmaurs, is not this fellow killed yet?" asked the Master of Lyle, who was one of the new-comers. "Devil bite me! is this French trafficker to keep twelve swordsmen in play and kill them all at his leisure!"

"Upon him now, his guard is down!" exclaimed the ferocious Kilmaurs, exasperated by the taunt of his compatriot, as he rushed forward to despatch the poor lad, whose head and hands were drooping as he reclined against the wall of a dark shadowy house, and felt that life and energy were alike passing away from him; when suddenly a tall man mingled his voice in the combat, and being armed with one of those poleaxes which all citizens were bound to possess for the purpose of "redding frays" within the burgh, he beat them back, shouting the while,

"Armour! armour! fie—to the rescue—fie!"

"What villain art thou?" demanded Glencairn imperiously, grasping his right arm.

"Fie! gar ding your whingers into him!" cried the others. "What matters it who he is?"

"Speak, rash fellow, lest I kill thee!" said the lofty noble. "I am the Lord Glencairn!"

"And I am Dick Hackerston, a burgess and free craftsman—a hammerman of Edinburgh. Fie!—have at ye a'! Is this fair play or foul, my lords and masters?" he exclaimed, as he swept them aside by describing a circle vigorously with his poleaxe.

At that moment blindness came upon the eyes of Florence, and a faintness overspread his limbs. The stone wall against which he reclined seemed to yield and give way; he felt the atmosphere change: a red light seemed to shine before his half-closed eyelids; and voices, gentle, softly modulated, and full of tender commiseration, floated in his ears.

He sank down—down he knew not, recked not where. .... He heard a door closed violently .... A stupor like death came over him, and he remembered no more! ....

CHAPTER VIII
THE REGENCY OF ARRAN

Yet if the gods demand her, let her sail, —
Our cares are only for the public weal:
Let me be deem'd the hateful cause of all,
And suffer, rather than my people fall.
The prize, the beauteous prize, I will resign,
So dearly valued, and so justly mine.

Iliad, i.

It has already been stated that the Regent of Scotland at this time was James Hamilton, Earl of Arran, better known amid the civil wars and woes of future years as the Duke of Chatelherault, a fief in Poitou, and formerly capital of the duchy of Chatelheraudois. His father was the first who obtained the earldom of Arran, and his mother was Janet Beaton, of Creich, niece of the unfortunate cardinal who was slain in the Castle of St. Andrew's. The French dukedom he received for the spirit with which he maintained Scottish and French interests against the valour of England and the machinations of that degraded and anti-national party the Scottish peers of King Henry's faction, a few of whom have already been introduced to the reader in the preceding chapter.

The little queen was a child in her fifth year; and Henry VIII., that wily and ferocious monarch, during his latter days left nothing untried, by subtle diplomacy, by open war, by hired assassins, and by bands of foreign *condottieri* leagued with his own troops, to remove from his path all obstruction to a marriage between his son Edward and the young queen of Scotland. He proposed to Arran, if he would deliver her person into his blood-imbrued hands, to assist him with all the power of England and Ireland to make for himself a new kingdom beyond the Forth, and to give his daughter Elizabeth, the future queen of England, in marriage to Arran's heir, the young Lord James Hamilton, then captain of the Scottish Archers in France; but the Regent knew how little Henry's boasts would avail him at the foot of the Grampians, or had patriotism enough to reject a proposal so wild and so disastrous with the disdain it merited; and so, in time, the English Bluebeard was gathered to his wives and to his fathers, bequeathing to the

Duke of Somerset, Protector of England during the minority of Edward VI., the pleasant task of arranging, by fair means or foul, a matrimonial alliance between that prince and the little queen of "the rugged land of spearmen."

Cardinal Beaton, long a faithful and a formidable enemy to Scottish treason and to English guile, had perished by the hands of assassins, whose secret projects were better understood at Windsor than at Holyrood. The invasion of Scotland, and the almost total destruction of Edinburgh—the burnings and the devastations in the fertile Lothians by Lord Hertford's army, with the rout of the English at the bloody battle of Ancrum—ended for a time all hope of Somerset ever accomplishing the perilous work so rashly bequeathed to him by his grasping and imperious master; yet, being a brave and high-spirited noble, he still continued the attempt in secret, as he could never despair of having the nation ultimately betrayed while that faithless class, its nobility, existed.

The Scottish peers were now, as usual, divided into two factions, one who adhered to the old treaty with France, and the other—the basest, most venal, and corrupt—composed of those who urged the advantages of the matrimonial alliance between the infant Queen Mary and the boy King Edward. These men, though bearing names of old historic memory, the

"Seed of those who scorn'd
To stoop the neck to wide imperial Rome,"

were mean enough to receive in secret sums of money, first from Henry of England, secondly from the Protector Somerset, and by written obligations to bind themselves to further the selfish and aggressive schemes of both; while, in the same spirit of political perfidy, they gave to the Scottish Regent Arran the most solemn assurances of their entire concurrence with him, in his conservative measures for obeying the will of the late King James V.—whose noble heart they broke,—and in defending the realm of his daughter against all foreign enemies, more especially their ancient foemen of the south. On one hand they openly announced their resolution to support the Church of their fathers, and the faith that came from Rome; on the other, they secretly leagued with those who slew the primate of Scotland in his archiepiscopal castle at St. Andrews, and plotted for the plunder of the temporalities.

The noble Earl of Huntly, with Arran and the more patriotic—the unblemished and unbribed,—looked towards France for a husband for their queen, and for troops to enable them to resist the combined strength of Cassilis, Glencairn, Kilmaurs, and more than two hundred titled Scottish traitors, when backed by the military power of England, and those Spanish and German mercenaries under Don Pedro de Gamboa and Conrad Baron of Wolfenstein, whom the Protector maintained in Norham, Carlisle, and other strongholds near the border.

The weakness of Arran's government, the feeble power of the newly-instituted courts of law, the licentious lives of a hierarchy whose Church and power were nodding to their fall, the gradual declension of an ancient faith, and the dawn of a new one divested of all that was striking or attractive to the imagination, and which, from its grim novelty, the people neither loved nor respected at heart,—all tended to arrest the rapid progress which Scotland had made in art and science, music and poetry, architecture, literature, printing, and commerce, under the fatherly care of the six last kings of the Stuart race. Hence there was generated, about the epoch of our story, a greater barbarism among the feudal aristocracy and their military followers, all of whom were ever but too fierce, turbulent, and prone to bloodshed. Thus outrages, feuds, raids, and combats, the siege and storm of castles and towers, were mere matters of every-day life; and a fight of a few hundred men-at-arms a side, with lance and buckler, sword and arquebuse, in the streets of Edinburgh, Perth, or Aberdeen, occasioned less excitement among their warlike citizens than an election row, a casual fire, or a runaway horse, in these our jogtrot days of peace societies and Sabbatarian twaddle.

The more ancient laws of Scotland, by which a man's life might be redeemed for nine times twenty cattle, or when for shedding blood south of the Scottish Sea (*i.e.* Firth of Forth) a penalty of twenty-five shillings was levied, or when, for committing the same offence north of the same sea the value of six cattle was exacted—had now been succeeded by a regular code of stricter statutes, to be enforced by regular courts of law and justice. Yet blood was shed and life taken more often than before, in sudden quarrel and old hereditary feud, daily—yea, hourly,—without other punishment or remedy than such as the nearest clansman or kinsman might inflict with the sword and torch—and these were seldom idle.

The times were wild and perilous!

All men wore arms, and used them on the most trivial occasions. Even James V., so famous for his justice and lenity, when a boy in his eleventh year, with his little Parmese dagger, stabbed a warder at the gate of Stirling Castle, because the man would not let him out to ramble in the town.

Hence such outrages as the murder of Cardinal Beaton in his own castle, the slaughter of Sir John Fawside by Claude Hamilton of Preston, on the skirts of Gladsmuir. The besieging of John Lord Lindesay, sheriff of Fife, when in the execution of his office, by the lairds of Clatto, Balfour, and Claverhouse, with eighty men-at-arms, while at the same time the

Grants amused themselves by sacking and burning the manor-house of Davy, in Strathnavern, and making a clean sweep of everything on the lands of Ardrossiere. Even the king's artillery, when *en route* from Stirling to Edinburgh, in 1526, were attacked, the gunners killed or dispersed, and the guns taken, by Bruce of Airth, who required a few field-pieces for his own mansion. Hence the slaughter of the Laird of Mouswaldmains by Bell of Currie, and of the Laird of Dalzel by the Lord Maxwell. Hence the abduction of Lady Margaret Stewart, daughter of Matthew Earl of Lennox, by her lover, the young Laird of Boghall, and the death of her husband John Lord Fleming, great chamberlain of Scotland, by the sword of John Tweedie, Baron of Drummelzier, who slew him when hawking, on the 1st November, 1524. Hence the slaughter of the Laird of Stonebyres by the rector of Colbinton; of two gentlemen named Nisbet, in the king's palace and presence, by Andrew Blackadder of that ilk; the murder of the Laird of Auchinharvie by the Earl of Eglinton; the assassination of that fine old priest and poet, Sir James Inglis, abbot of Culross, by the Baron of Tulliallan, in 1531, and the firing of the thatched kirk of Monivaird, in Strathearn, by the Drummonds, who destroyed therein "six score of the Murrayes, with their wives and childraine, who were all burned or slaine except one."

These little recreations of the Scottish landed gentry and their retainers were occasionally varied by branking scolding wives with iron bridles, or ducking them in ponds; burning witches and Lollards; hanging gipsies, and boring the tongues of evil-speakers with hot iron;—so that seldom a day passed, in town or country, without some stirring novelty of a lively nature.

One tract of land, where, in the year of Flodden, one thousand and forty-one ploughs had usually turned up the teeming soil, was now, as the Lord Dacre says, "clearly wasted, and had no man dwelling therein,"—wasted by his wanton inroads; and this desolated tract lay in the middle Marches, on the banks of the Leader, the Euse, and the Ale—the lovely border-land,—the land of war and song—of the sword and lyre; but there grew little grass, and less corn, where the hoof of the moss-trooper's steed left its iron print in the soil.

Superstition was not wanting to add to the terror of warring clans and those English devastators who, in 1544, laid Edinburgh in blazing ruin, and swept all the fair Lothians, as if the land had been burned up—tree, tower, and corn-field, hamlet, church, and hedgerow—by the fire which fell of old on the cities of the plain. Lady Glammes, a young and beautiful woman, was burned alive at Edinburgh, for treason, and some say sorcery; and in the year of our story, 1547, there was buried in the beautiful chapel of Roslin,

Father Samuel, the prior of St. Mary of Deir, who was deemed a wizard so terrible that all the sanctity of the place could scarcely keep his bones from rattling in their stone sarcophagus.

Wonderful things were seen and heard of in those quaint old times.

In 1570, a monstrous fish, having two human heads, each surmounted by a royal crown of gold, swam up Lochfyne; and seven years after, a swarm of fish, each having a monk's hood on its head, came up the Firth of Forth. In Glencomie, a gentleman of the house of Lovat slew a veritable scaly dragon, which vomited fire like that encountered by St. George of old, and set the purple heather in a flame. The northern sky was nightly brightened by ranks of glittering spears and waving pennons. In the woful year of Pinkeycleugh, a calf was brought forth with two heads, on Robert Ormiston's farm, in Lothian; and if other omen of evil to come were wanted, on the Westmains of Fawside, a huge bull which belonged to our friend Roger the Baillie, and was the pride of the parish, when browsing on the green brae-side, turned suddenly into a black boulder-stone, which may yet be seen by those who take the trouble of inquiring after it; while a "fierce besom" or comet that blazed o' nights in the southern quarter of the sky, portended evil coming from England, and made old men and grandmothers cower with affright in their cosy ingles beyond the fire, and tell their beads as their minds became filled with forebodings of dolor and woe: for though hardy and brave, they were simple souls—our Scottish sires, three hundred years ago.

Such was the state of the kingdom in the year of our story, and during the regency of Arran.

CHAPTER IX
MISTRUST

It will be great, thou son of pride!—I have been renowned in battle; but I never told my name to a foe.—*Ossian.*

Consciousness returned slowly to Florence Fawside, and when his eyes unclosed, he saw first the huge misshapen figures of a large green-and-russet-coloured tapestry, which covered the walls of a dimly-lighted room, the four carved posts of a bed, the magnificent canopy of which spread its shadow over him, and the soft laced pillows whereon his head reposed. Then he became sensible of the presence of persons moving about him on tiptoe, speaking in gentle whispers.

There were two women, young, beautiful, and richly dressed; and with them was a man whose white beard flowed over the front of his long and sable robe. Then came again the sensation of faintness—the sinking sensation of one about to die,—with the agony of his sword-wounds, which felt like the searings of a red-hot iron, when the hands of his fair attendants—soft, kind, and "tremulously gentle" hands they were—unbuttoned his doublet, untied his ruff, drew aside the breast of his lace shirt, and a handkerchief which he had thrust under it when first wounded, and which were now both soaked with blood. This caused his wounds to stream anew. He felt the current of his life gush forth, and while a faint cry of pity from a female voice came feebly to his ear, the sufferer, when making a futile effort to grasp the pocket which contained his fatal letters, became once more totally insensible.

The early dawn of a clear August morning was stealing through the iron-grated windows of the apartment in which he lay, when Florence awoke again to life, and, raising himself feebly on an elbow, looked around him.

He was in a chamber the walls of which were hung with beautiful tapestry; the ceiling was painted with mythological figures, and the oak floor was strewn with green rushes and freshly-cut flowers—for carpets were yet almost unknown in Britain. From a carved beam of oak, which crossed the ceiling transversely, hung a silver night-lamp, fed with perfumed oil, amid which the light was just expiring. In a shadowy corner of the room was an altar, bearing a glittering crucifix, before which were two flickering tapers, two vases of fresh roses, and an exquisitely-carved *prie-Dieu* of walnut-wood, inlaid with mother-of-pearl.

The hangings of his bed were of the finest crimson silk, festooned by gold cords and massive tassels. On one side, through the window, he could see the green northern bank of the loch which bordered the city, and through which on the night before he had striven to swim his horse; beyond it were yellow fields, green copsewood, and purple muirland, stretching to the shores of the azure Forth. On the other side were the quaint figures of the old tapestry which represented a Scottish tradition well known in the days of Hector Boece—that on the day when the battle of Bannockburn was fought and won, a knight in armour that shone with a marvellous brilliance, mounted on a black steed, all foamy with haste and bloody with spurring, appeared suddenly in the streets of Aberdeen, and with a loud voice announced Bruce's victory to the startled citizens. Passing thence to the north with frightful speed, over hill and valley, this shining warrior was seen to quit the land and spur his steed across the raging waves of the Pentland Firth, and to vanish in the mist that shrouded the northern isles. Hence some averred he was St. Magnus of Orkney, while the more aspiring maintained that he was St. Michael the Archangel.

"Where am I?" was the first mental question of the sufferer, as he pressed his hand across his swimming forehead. "My letters!" was his next thought. On a chair near him hung his doublet: he made a great effort to ascertain if they were untouched, but sank back upon his pillow, exhausted by the attempt.

Morning was far advanced when he revived again. He found something cold and sharp in flavour poured between his lips; it refreshed him, and on looking up he became inspired with new energy on seeing again the two ladies whose forms he believed last night to have been the portions of a feverish dream, or to have been conjured by his fancy from those upon the tapestry.

One was a tall and beautiful woman, of a noble and commanding presence, about thirty years of age; her forehead was rather broad than high; her nose, long and somewhat pointed, might have been too masculine, but for the charming softness of her other features, especially her clear hazel eyes, which were full of sweetness, and expressed the deepest commiseration. That her rank was high, her attire sufficiently announced.

She was dressed in a delentera of cloth-of-gold, the opened skirts of which displayed her petticoat of crimson brocade; her sleeves were of crimson satin tied by strings of pearl; her girdle was of gold surrounded by long pearl pendants; while a cross of diamonds sparkled on her breast.

Her companion seemed fully ten years younger: her stature was rather less; her complexion was equally fair; but her hair was of that deep brown which seems black by night; her features were so regular that nothing prevented them from being perhaps insipid; but the darkness of her eyebrows, with the vivacity of her deep violet-coloured blue eyes; and as she bent over the sufferer's bed, the rose-leaf tinge in her soft cheek came and went rapidly. She wore a loose robe of purple taffeta, trimmed with seed pearls; and among her dark hair there sparkled many precious stones; for the attire of people of rank in those days was gorgeously profuse in quality of material and elaboration of ornament.

"Mon Dieu!—he faints again!" said the former lady, in a soft but foreign accent, and with a tone of alarm.

"Nay, he only sleeps," whispered the other; "and see—now he wakens and recovers!"

"Saint Louis prie pour moi! but the pale aspect of this wounded boy so terrifies me!"

"Am I still in France?" murmured Fawside.

"Oh, he speaks of France!" exclaimed the elder, drawing nearer.

"Where am I, madame—in Paris?" asked Fawside faintly.

"Nay, you are safe in the city of Edinburgh."

"Safe! And who are you who condescend to treat me so humanely, so tenderly? Oh! I cannot dream. Last night—I now remember me,—I left the ship of the Sieur de Villegaignon, and was pursued by armed men,—by men who sought to murder me, and Heaven and they alone know why, for unto them I had done no wrong. I fell, wounded, I remember; but how came I here?"

"You must not speak, fair sir," replied the elder lady, placing her white and faultless hand upon the hot and parched mouth of the youth. "But listen, and I shall tell you. We heard the clash of swords (nothing singular in Edinburgh), and cries for 'help' beneath our windows; from whence we saw a man beset by many, who beat him down at last, though he fought valiantly with his back to the postern door of our mansion."

"A door!—methought it was a stone wall.

"Nay, sir, fortunately it was *not* the stone wall, but a door: my servants opened it; you fell inwards. It was instantly shut and barricaded, by nay orders, and thus we saved you."

"And this was last night?"

"Nay," replied the beautiful lady, smiling, and using her weetest foreign accent, "it was three nights ago."

"Three!"

"I have said so, monsieur."

"You are of France, dear madame?"

"So are many ladies at the Scottish court."

"And I—I——"

"Have been in sleep under the opiates of my physician, or at times delirious; but now, thanked be kind Heaven, and his judicious skill, all danger of fever is past."

"Three days and nights! Oh! madame, to how much inconvenience I must have put you."

"Say not so. To have saved your life is reward sufficient for my friend and me."

"Thanks, madame, thanks; not that I value life much, but for the sake of one I love dearly, and for the task I have to perform."

"One!—a lady, doubtless?" asked the younger, smiling.

"My mother!" replied Fawside, as his dark eyes flashed and suffused at the same moment!

"And your task is probably a pilgrimage?" continued she with the violet-blue eyes.

"Nay, lady, nay; no pilgrimage, but a behest full of danger and death, and inspired by a hate that seems at times to be a holy one—for the blood of a slain father inspires it."

"Madame," began the younger lady uneasily, "may it please your——"

"*Stay!*" exclaimed the other, interrupting the title by which she doubtless was about to be addressed;—and then they whispered together.

Fawside now remarked mentally that this was the third occasion on which she had been similarly interrupted.

"Here lurketh some mystery," thought he, glancing at his doublet, in the secret pocket of which his letters were concealed, "so let me be wary."

"These are exciting thoughts for one so weak and so severely wounded as you are," resumed the matron, for such she evidently was. "Know you who those outrageous assailants were?"

"Too well!—the men who slew my father under tryst, and my brave brother too, by falsity and secrecy, as 'tis said."

"And they?" faltered the lady.

"Who?"

"Your father and brother?"

"Were good men and leal."

"I doubt not that, sir. But their names?"

"Were second to none in the three Lothians."

"You are singularly wary, fair sir," said the elder lady proudly, and with an air of pique.

"And your father fell——," began the younger in a tremulous voice, as if the young man's vehemence terrified her.

"He fell so many years ago that the interest of my debt of blood and vengeance——"

"Is, I doubt not, doubled!"

"Yea, madame, quadrupled; and I shall have it rendered back duly, every drop."

"Oh! say not so," said the young lady, shuddering. "Think of all you have escaped, and how, on that fatal night, kind Heaven spared you."

"To avenge my family feud on those who would have slain me."

"And you have been in France?" said the lady in the cloth-of-gold, to change the subject.

"Yes, madame."

"And came from thence with Nicholas de Villegaignon?"

"Yes, madame."

"Ah, *mon Dieu!*—dear, dear France!" she exclaimed; "and you were there how long?"

"Seven happy years, lady."

"In the army, of course?"

"No."

"At the court of Henry of Valois?"

"No—with Anne de la Tour."

"The Duchess of Albany—a proud and haughty old widow."

"But a mistress kind and gentle to me. I had the honour to kiss King Henry's hand on my way home through Paris."

"Had you any letters or messages for Scotland?" asked the lady anxiously.

"Nay, I had no letters," he replied gloomily and briefly; "but tell me, pray, your names, your rank, ladies—in pity tell me!"

"Pardon us, sir," said the elder, patting his forehead kindly with her soft white hand; "in that you must hold us excused. We tell not our names lightly to a stranger—a wild fellow who fights with every armed man, and, for aught we know, makes love to every pretty woman, and who, moreover, shrouds in such provoking mystery his own name and purpose. So adieu, sir—a little time and we shall be with you again."

"Stay, madame—stay, and pardon me," he exclaimed, as they retired through the parted arras, and disappeared when its heavy fold closed behind them. Then he sank upon his pillow, exhausted even by this short interview.

"I am right," he muttered, as he lay with his eyes closed, in a species of half-stupor, or waking dream; "my name shall never pass my lips until I have the barbican gate of Fawside Tower behind me. And yet—and yet—how hard to mistrust that lovely girl with the dark-blue eyes and deep-brown hair!"

Rendered cautious by his late adventure, he tore off and defaced the armorial bearings, which, in the French fashion, he wore on the breast of his beautiful doublet, and resolved studiously to conceal alike his name, his purpose, and his letters, to say no more of whence he had come or whither he was bound, lest those two charming women, who so kindly watched and tended his sick couch, and who so sedulously concealed *their* names and titles, might be the wives, the loves, or kindred of his enemies.

Such were his resolves. But how weak are the resolves even of the brave and wary, when in the hands of a beautiful woman!

CHAPTER X
IN WHICH THE PATIENT
PROGRESSES FAVOURABLY

His qualities were beauteous as his form,
For maiden-tongued he was, and thereof free;
Yet, if men moved him, he was such a storm
As oft twixt May and April we may see.
A Lover's Complaint.

Aided by his youth and strength, and doubtless by his native air, which blew upon his pale face through the northern windows of his chamber, when the breeze waved the ripening corn and wafted the perfume of the heather and the yellow broom-bells across the North Loch, Florence recovered rapidly. His wounds soon healed, under the soothing influence of the medicinal balsams applied to them, and of the subtle opiates which he received from the hands of his two fair attendants, and from those of the white-bearded physician, who, with a pardonable vanity, cared not to conceal *his* name, but soon announced himself to be Master Peter Posset, chirurgeon to the late King James V. of blessed memory (whose deathbed he had soothed at Falkland Palace), and deacon of the chirurgeon-barbers of Edinburgh—a body who, in virtue of their office, were exempted by their charter from serving on juries, and from the duties of keeping watch and ward within the city.

Master Posset was a man of venerable aspect, with a voluminous white beard. He was measured in tone, pedantic in manner, and bled and blistered, according to the rule of the age, only when certain stars and signs which were believed to influence the human body, were in certain mansions of the firmament,—for he was a deep dabbler alike in alchemy and astrology. Yet in 1533 he had studied and practised at Lyons as hospital physician under Rabellais, and been the medical attendant of Jean du Bellay, Bishop of Paris, when that distinguished prelate travelled to Rome concerning the divorce of Henry VIII. of England in 1534. The residence of Master Posset was at the head of a forestair in the Lawn-market, where his uncouth sign,—a dried alligator, swung from an iron bracket, exciting fear and awe in the heart of country folks who came to buy or sell, and where the armorial cognizance of his craft,—*argent*, a naked corpse fessways *proper*, between a hand with an eye in its palm, the thistle and crown,—informed all that it was the domicile of the Deacon of the Chirurgeon-Barbers.

By his pedantry and prosy recollections of MM. Rabellais and Jean du Bellay, this worthy leech proved an intolerable bore to his patient; but he had evidently received due instructions to be reserved; for by no effort of cunning, of tact, and by no power of entreaty, could Fawside draw from him the secret of whose house they were in, and who were these two women so highly bred, so courtly, and so beautiful who attended him like sisters, and to whom he owed his life and rapid recovery. From a French valet who also attended him he was likewise unable to extract a syllable; for M. Antoine, though an excellent musician on the viol, made signs that he was dumb.

"Master Posset, good, kind Master Posset," said Florence one day, "I have exhausted all offers of bribes such as a gentleman in my present circumstances might make, and you have nobly rejected them all. Now I cast myself upon your pity, your humanity, to tell me who and what those two kind fairies are!"

"Who they are I dare not tell; *what* they are I may," replied the cautious leech.

"Say on, then. What are they?"

"A widow and a maid."

"The widow?" asked Florence impetuously.

"Is she with the hazel eyes and chestnut hair."

"The maid?"

"Of course the other, she with the darker hair and violet-blue eyes, and who, violet-like, secludes herself from all."

"The loveliest, thank Heaven!"

"Why thank you Heaven so fervently?" asked Master Posset with surprise.

"Ask me not!—ask me not!" exclaimed Fawside, in whose heart every glance, every action, and every trivial question or remark of the younger lady had made a deep impression.

"Their rank?"

"I may not, must not tell you," interrupted the physician hastily.

"It is high?"

"Few are nobler in the land."

"Ah! Master Posset, each looks like a queen."

"Perhaps they are so,—queens of Elfen," replied Master Posset, with a smile which his heavy white moustache concealed.

"You are most discreet, Master Apothecary," sighed Florence with impatience.

"To be discreet was one of my chief orders, and I am in the mansion of those who brook no trifling; and, as the great Rabellais was wont to say, discretion to a physician was as necessary as a needle to a compass."

"All this mystery seems rather peculiar and unnecessary; but thus much I can discern, that the younger gentlewoman treats the other with such deference and respect, that her rank must be inferior, though her beauty is second to none that I have seen even at the court of France."

"You are an acute observer, sir," replied the leech, reddening, and with some alarm; "but may not such deference and respect arise from her junior years?"

"Scarcely; for I can perceive that the elder is barely thirty years of age."

"Yet she has buried a second husband and at least two children."

"I shall soon discover *her* if you give me but one or two more such other details," said Florence laughing. "You will not attempt it, I hope," said Master Posset, with growing alarm, and preparing to withdraw.

"Most worthy doctor, what is that which succeeds best in this world?"

"I know not."

"Shall I tell you?"

"Yes."

"*Success.* I have great faith in it."

"The very words of the great Rabelais!"

"The devil take Rabelais!" said Florence with annoyance.

"Shame on you, young sir!" said Master Posset, who considered this rank blasphemy.

"Pardon me; but by this faith in success I shall never fail," replied Fawside laughing. "I shall soon be gone from here, where I have played the owl too long, and when well enough I shall soar like the lark. Ah! good Master Posset, most worthy deacon, dost think I have spent seven years of my life between Paris and Vendome without being able to discover a pretty demoiselle's name when I had the wish to do so. She cannot conceal herself long from me, be assured of that."

"Is it gallant to talk thus of those gentlewomen whose roof shelters you, and from whom you also conceal your own name?" asked Posset angrily.

"It is not; and yet, by my faith, *three* sword wounds have given me more reason for caution than I ever thought would fall to my lot. But I will take patience, for time unravelleth all things."

"As I have heard the divine Jean de Bellay preach in Notre Dame at Paris many a time—yea, sir, verily time unravelleth all things."

"Yea, and *avengeth* all things," said a soft voice on the other side of his couch; and on turning, Fawside met the bright eyes of the lady and her friend fixed upon him.

The young man was very handsome. His features were regular, but striking and marked; his hair was cut short, but was black and curly; his nose was straight, with a well-curved nostril; his chin was well defined, and fringed by a short-clipped French beard. His shirt-collar being open, displayed a muscular chest, white as the marble of Paros, but crossed by the ligatures and bandages which retained the healing balsams on his wounds. His features had all the freshness and charm of youth, but over them was spread the languor of recent suffering and loss of blood; thus his fine eyes were unnaturally bright and restless. Finding that the noble lady had overheard his heedless remarks, Fawside made efforts to rise to bow, and, reddening deeply, said,—

"Pardon me, madam, I knew not that you were so near; nor *you*, sweet mistress," he added in a tremulous voice, as he addressed the younger and more beautiful of those striking women, in whose charming society he had been thrown, and to whose care he had found himself confided for more than a week.

Long conscious of the power of her beauty, it was impossible for this young lady not to perceive and feel pleased with the interest she was exciting in the breast of Florence, the expression of whose dark eyes and the tone of whose voice too surely revealed it.

This morning her sweetly feminine face was more than usually lovely in an ermined triangular hood, trimmed with Isla pearls from Angus, and these were not whiter than her delicate neck and ring-laden fingers; she seldom spoke, save when addressed by her friend, and her replies were always brief.

"I heard you mention Paris and the Vendomois," said the latter to the patient, as she bent her clear hazel eyes upon him, and as Master Posset respectfully withdrew from the chamber by retiring backwards through the arras. "I know the latter well, and every bend of the beautiful Loire, with the old castle of the Comtes de la Marche and the ducal mansion of Charles of Bourbon——"

"And the great old abbey of the Holy Trinity, with its huge towers, its pointed windows, and the reliquary——"

"Where the Benedictines keep in a crystal case the Holy Tear——"

"Wept by our Blessed Saviour over the grave of Lazarus."

"Ah, I see we shall have some recollections in common," said the proud lady, smiling; "and fair Paris—how looketh it?"

"Gay and great as ever, forming, to my eyes,—in its life, bustle, and magnitude,—a wondrous contrast to our grim Scottish burghs, with their barred houses, their walls and gates, and steep streets encumbered by stacks of peat and fuel and heather."

"*Mon Dieu*, yes; one may caracole a horse along the Rue St. Jacques or the Rue St. Honore without meeting such uncouth obstructions as these. Is the Hotel de Ville finished yet?"

"Nearly so."

"Are those four delightful monsters of M—M—oh, I forget his name—completed on the tower of St. Jacques de la Boucharie?"

"Yes, madam, and grin over Paris all day long."

"You see, I know Paris, sir."

"Madame is doubtless only Scottish by adoption."

The lady smiled sadly, while her friend laughed aloud.

"I can see it before me now, in fancy," said she while her fine eyes dilated and sparkled, "smiling amid the plain that is covered with golden corn, and bounded by the vine-clad hills that spread from Mont l'Hery to Poissy; Paris with its busy streets of brick-fronts and stone-angles, of slated roofs and many-coloured houses—the huge masses of the *cité*, the *ville*, the great Bastile, and the double towers of mighty Notre Dame! I see them all glittering in the cloudless sun of noon, as one day my little daughter shall see them too!"

"A daughter—you have a daughter, madam," said Fawside with growing interest, "and are a widow; in pity tell me who you are?"

"We two have our little secrets, fair sir," she replied, holding up a slender finger with a waggish expression.

"By the cross on my dagger, I swear to you, madam——"

"But your dagger is lost."

"I regret that deeply, for it was the present of a noble dame."

"Since we are so bent on fruitlessly questioning each other, may I ask *her* name?" said the younger lady.

"Diana de Poictiers, the Duchess of Valentinois; it bears her three crescents engraved upon the hilt; but I left it in some knave's body on the night of the brawl. If he lives, the diamonds in the pommel may perhaps prove a salve for his sores; if he dies, a fund for his funeral—but a pest on't! my brave dagger is gone."

"Accept this from me," said the taller lady, taking from an ebony buffet that stood near, a jewelled poniard, and presenting it to Florence.

"A thousand thanks, madam—a lady's gift can never be declined; but what do I see? The cipher of James V.—of his late majesty."

"'Twas his dagger," said the lady gloomily, "and with it he threatened to stab Sir James Hamilton of Finnart, the inquisitor-general of Scotland; but I arrested his hand and took away the weapon; for the gentle King James would never refuse aught to a woman, a priest, or a child."

"And so you were known to the fair mistress of Francis I.?" asked the young lady with a slightly disdainful pout on her pretty lip.

"Nay, madam, I cannot say that she knew me; but once when she and her royal lover quarrelled, I bore a letter from her to Francis, and at a time when no other person would venture to approach him, his majesty being furious on the arrival of tidings that his fleet before Nice had been destroyed by the galleys of Andrew Doria."

"This was three years ago."

"I was loitering one day in the gallery of the Louvre, when she approached me, 'M. le Page,' said she, placing a little pink note in my hand, 'will you do a service for me?'

"'I belong to Madame la Duchesse d'Albany,' said I; 'yet I shall gladly obey you, madam.'

"'Then you shall have ten golden crowns.'

"'Ten crowns! Ah, madam,' said I, gallantly, 'I would rather have ten gifts less tangible.'

"'You shall have both, boy,' said she, laughing merrily; 'the crowns now and the kisses hereafter.'

"Her note to Francis proved successful: in less than ten minutes that princely monarch was at her feet. But with her kiss, she gave me a Parmese dagger, which she wore at her girdle, the gift of her present lover, Henry of Valois, and which you, madam, have so nobly replaced by this."

As he spoke, Florence, with the true loyal devotion of the olden time, kissed the cipher which was engraved on its hilt.

At that moment Master Posset reappeared, and whispered in the ear of the lady of the mansion.

"Excuse me, sir," said she; "there are those without who would speak with me."

And on her retiring suddenly with the physician, Florence, somewhat to his confusion, found himself for a time left alone with the younger and, as we have more than once said, more attractive of his two attendants, and in whom, though as yet nameless, we have little doubt the sagacious reader has already recognized the heroine of our story.

CHAPTER XI
THE OPAL RING

Late my spring-time came, but quickly
   Youth's rejoicing currents run,
And my inner life unfolded
   Like a flower before the sun.
Hopes, and aims, and aspirations,
   Grew within the growing boy;
Life had new interpretations;
   Manhood brought increase of joy.
                 Mary Howitt.

After a pause their eyes met, and the lady's were instantly averted; the cheeks of both were suffused by a blush, for they "were so young, and one so innocent," that they were incapable of feeling emotion without exhibiting this charming, but, at times, most troublesome symptom of it.

The lady spoke first.

"And so, sir, you are still resolved to preserve your *incognito*—to maintain your character of the unknown knight?"

"Yes, madam," said he in the same spirit of banter, "while in the castle of an enchantress—for here, indeed, am I under a spell. And, more than all, my wounds have made me cautious to the extent, perhaps, of ingratitude."

"So you actually mistrust us!" exclaimed the lady colouring deeply, while her dark-blue eyes sparkled with mingled amusement and surprise.

"I will risk anything rather than lie longer under an imputation such as your words convey," replied the young man impetuously: "I am Florence Fawside of that ilk. And, now that you know my name, I pray you tell not my enemies of it, for I might be slaughtered here perhaps, without once more striking a gallant blow in my own defence. I have told you my name," he added, lowering his voice to an accent of tenderness, while attempting to take her hand; but she started back; "and now, dear lady, honour me with yours."

But the lady had grown deadly pale; her fine eyes surveyed the speaker with an expression of gloomy and startled interest, mingled with pity and alarm. Florence, on beholding this emotion, at once detected that he had made a mistake by the sudden revelation of his name, and a vague sense of helplessness and danger possessed his heart.

"I shall never forget the kindness, the humanity, and the tenderness with which you have treated me, lady; but why all this strange mystery — for *you* cannot be unfriended and alone here, as I at present am? Why have I been concealed even from your servants? None have approached me but Master Posset the leech, and a Frenchman, Antoine, who pretends — as I suspect — to be deaf or dumb. All betokens some mystery, if not some pressing danger. Oh, that I were again strong enough to use my sword — to sit on horseback and begone!"

"To all these questions I can only reply by others. Why all these complaints — whence this alarm?"

"I must begone, lady," said Florence with a tremulous voice; for though dazzled and lured by the beauty of the speaker on one hand, he dreaded falling into some deadly snare on the other; "I long to see my aged mother — and I have letters — —"

"*Not* for the Regent, I hope?" said the young lady, coming forward a pace.

"Probe not my secrets, lady. I have told you my name — I am the last of an old race that never failed Scotland or her king in the hour of need or peril. I shall be faithful to you — —"

"To *me!*" reiterated the beautiful girl in a low voice, while blushing deeply. "I need not your faith, good sir?"

"To you and to my royal mistress; but I long to leave this — to see once more the aged mother who tended my infant years — —"

"A harsh and stern woman, who, if men say true, will urge you to the committal of dreadful deeds!"

"Say not so — she was ever gentle and loving to me, and to my brave brother Willie, who now, alas! sleeps in his father's grave."

"Gentle and loving! — so are the bear or the tigress to their cubs; but their fierce nature still remains."

"Remember that she you speak of is my mother, lady," said Florence, colouring with vexation.

"Pardon me — I speak but from report."

"I long, too, to see honest old Roger of the Westmains, with his white beard and hale nut-brown visage—my tutor in the science of defence, he who taught me to handle sword and dagger, arquebuse and pike, as if I had come into the world cap-a-pie; and next there is Father John of Tranent, the kind old vicar, who was wont in the long nights of winter to take me on his knee, and tell me such wondrous tales of Arthur's round table, of William Wallace, of Alexander, and of Hector—the prophecies of Thomas the Rhymer, and how they never fail to be fulfilled—the story of Red Ettin, the giant who had three heads, and of the Gyre Carlin, the mother-witch of all our Scottish witches, till my hair stood on end with terror of men so bold and people so weird and strange. I long to see my old nurse Maud, who was wont to rock me to sleep in the old turret, and sing me the 'Flowers of the Forest,' or the sweet old song of 'Gynkertoun;' and I long once more to find myself under the moss-covered roof of the old tower, where my mother waits and, it may be, weeps for me—that grim old mansion, with its barred gate, its dark loopholes, and narrow stairs, whose steps have been hallowed by time, and by the feet of generations of my forefathers who are now gone to God, and whose bones sleep under the shadow of His cross in the green kirkyard of Tranent."

"In short," said the lady, with a very decided pout on her beautiful red lips, "you are tired of dwelling here, and long to be gone."

"Here—ah, madam, say not so! Here, here with you, could I dwell for ever; but I have beloved ties and stern duties, that demand my presence elsewhere."

The dark-haired girl smiled and drooped her eyelids, while her confusion increased; for affection soon ripened in young hearts in those old days of nature and of impulse, before well-bred folks had learned to veil alike their hatred and their love under the same calm and impenetrable exterior.

The ice was now fairly broken, but their conversation became broken too.

After a pause, during which Florence had succeeded in capturing the little hand of the unknown, and kissing it at least thrice.

"You mean still to conceal your name from me!" said he with a tone of tender reproach.

"I act under the orders of another——"

"Another!—to whom do you yield this obedience? To me you seem inferior to none on earth."

"To none, I trust, in your estimation," said she, coquettishly.

"But to esteem, to love you as I do—to have intrusted you with my name, and yet to know not yours, is unkind, unfair, and subjecting me to torture and anxiety."

"I cannot give you my name—oh, pardon me, for in this matter, be assured, I am not my own mistress," said she, in a trembling voice.

"This is most strange, and like a chapter of Amadis, or some old romance. Then how shall I name you?"

"'Urganda the unknown,'[*] or aught you please," she replied, smiling to conceal her confusion as she withdrew her hand; and, taking from one of her fair and slender fingers a ring, she dropped it on the pillow of Florence, adding, "take this trinket—it has a *secret* by which one day you may know me. Take it, Florence Fawside, and wear it in memory of one who will never cease to regard you with most mournful interest, but who can never even be your—friend!"

[*] A famous enchantress in *Amadis de Gaul.*

"In memory—as if I could forget you while life and breath remained?" exclaimed Florence, bending over the jewel (an opal) to kiss it.

When he looked up the fair donor was gone. A tremulous motion of the arras in the twilight—eve had now closed in—indicated where she had vanished, before he could arrest her by word or deed, and implore an explanation of the strange and enigmatical words which had accompanied a gift so priceless to a lover.

She was gone; and, exhausted by the excitement of the interview, by the sudden turn it had taken, and the mutual revelation of a mutual interest in each other's hearts, Florence fell back upon his pillow, and lay long with his eyes closed and his whole being vibrating with joy, while the sober shadows of evening deepened in the tapestried room around him.

He was filled with a new happiness, his soul roved far away in the land of sunny dreams, his whole pulses seemed to quicken, and, with the conviction that this beautiful unknown loved him, he suddenly discovered there was in the world something else to live for than feudal vengeance.

"To-morrow I shall see her again," thought he; "to-morrow I shall hear her voice, and see her dear dove-like eyes assure me that she loves me still; and her name—oh, she must assuredly reveal it to me then. But are this interview and this ring, her gift, no fantasies of mine? Oh, to solve this strange mystery and concealment!"

As he thought thus, and gave utterance to his ideas half audibly, a red light flashed across the tapestried walls of the room. It came from the outside, and on raising himself he saw the wavering gleam of several torches on the well-grated windows, while the voices of men, one of whom, uttered hoarsely several words of command, the clatter of horses' hoofs, and the clank of iron-shod halberds and arquebuses, rang in the adjacent street. What did all these unusual sounds mean?

A vague emotion of alarm, filled his breast; he glanced round for his sword, and kept it in his hand in case of a sudden attack; but anon the gleam of the torches faded away, and the clatter of hoofs and spurs seemed to pass up the narrow street, and to lessen in distance.

Then all became still in the mansion and around it; and a foreboding, that portended he knew not what, fell upon the heart of the listener.

CHAPTER XII
MASTER POSSET

I am thy friend, thy best of friends;
  No bud in constant heats can blow—
The green fruit withers in the drought,
  But ripens where the waters flow.

Mackay.

The morrow came with its sunshine; but the two fair faces which had been wont to shed even a more cheering influence over the couch of the wounded youth were no longer there. Hour after hour passed, yet they did not come; and Fawside recalled with anxiety the too evident sounds or signs of a rapid departure on the preceding evening.

So passed the day. Dumb Antoine alone appeared; but from his grimaces nothing could be gathered. Night came on, and with it sleep, but a sleep disturbed by more than one dream of a fair face, with dark-blue eyes and lashes black and long, deep thoughtful glances and alluring smiles.

At last there came a sound that roused the dreamer; a ray of light flashed through the parted arras from another room.

"She comes!" was the first thought of Florence. "At this hour, impossible!" was the second.

There was a light step. Dawn was just breaking; but the good folks of that age were ever afoot betimes. At last the arras was parted boldly, and Master Posset, bearing a lamp, with his long silvery beard glittering over the front of his black serge gown, which hung in wavy folds to his feet, approached, bearing on a silver salver the patient's usual breakfast of weak hippocras, with maccaroon biscuits. He felt the youth's pulse, looked anxiously at his eyes and wounds, pronounced him infinitely better, and added that he "might on this day leave his couch."

"And the ladies?" asked Florence, unable to restrain his curiosity longer.

"What ladies?" queried the discreet Master Posset.

"Those who for so many days have watched my pillow like sisters—the hazel-eyed and the blue-eyed—for, alas! I know not their names. Where were they all yesterday, and where are they to-day?"

"Gone!"

"*Gone!*" faintly echoed Florence;—"but whither?"

"To Stirling."

"But why to Stirling?" asked Florence impetuously.

"Because they have business with the Lord Regent."

"I will follow them. My doublet—my boots and hose. Good Master Posset, your hand. Ah! great Heaven! how my head swims, and the room runs round as if each corner was in pursuit of the other!" exclaimed Florence, who sprang from bed, and would have fallen had not the attentive leech caught him in his arms.

"We must creep before we walk; and you must walk, sir, before you can ride a horse."

"When may I sit in my saddle?"

"In three days, perhaps."

"In three days I shall be in Stirling!" said the other impetuously.

"You had better go home," said Posset bluntly. "'Tis the advice of a sincere friend, who would not have you ride to Stirling on a bootless errand."

"Why bootless, Master Possett, when I tell you that I love, dearly love, one of those who have so abruptly forsaken me."

Master Posset's face, at least so much of it as his voluminous beard and moustache permitted one to see, underwent various expressions at this sudden announcement—-astonishment and perplexity, alarm, and then merriment.

"Fair sir," said he, laughing and shrugging his shoulders (a habit he had probably acquired from M. Rabelais), "you forget yourself."

"Wherefore, forsooth? Are they so high in rank above a landed baron?"

"In Scotland few are higher."

"Do not say these discouraging things, but tell me their names; for the hundredth time I implore you."

"I dare not."

"If I used threats, what would you say?"

"As my friend Rabelais said to a French knight at Lyons, when similarly threatened."

"And what said your devil of a Rabelais?"

"That threats ill became a sick man, when used to his friend; and worse still from one of your junior years, to a man in whose beard so few black hairs can be reckoned as in mine."

"Most true—forgive me; but when once free of this house, I shall soon solve the mystery. A woman so lovely as the younger lady must be well known, and must have many lovers."

"Doubtless."

"Thou art a most discreet apothecary, Master Posset—yea, a most wonderful apothecary!" said Fawside, gnawing the end of his moustache, and continuing to attire himself during this conversation; "and you really think she has *many*?"

"Yes; yet from her strength of character, I am assured she is a woman who in her lifetime will have but *one* love."

"One; come, that is encouraging!"

"Though little more than a girl in years, she is a woman in heart, in soul, and in mind. Do you understand me?"

"Yes—truss me those ribbons—thanks, Master Posset—I understand you, but only so far that if I am not the love referred to, I shall pass my sword through the body of the other who may occupy that position. Her faintest smile is worth a hundred golden crowns!"

"A sentiment worthy of Rabelais; but as your friend, Florence Fawside— one your senior in life and experience by many years—cease to speak or think of her thus."

"Why, if I love her?" demanded the young man, with a mixture of sadness and that impetuosity which formed one of the chief elements of his character.

"Because there are (as I call Heaven to witness!) barriers between you— —"

"Grace me guide! mean you to say she is married?"

"No; but still there are barriers insuperable to the success of such a love."

"To the brave?" asked Florence proudly.

"Yea, to the bravest."

"God alone knoweth what you all mean by this cruel enigma; but in three days I will set forth to solve it—to solve it or to die!"

The old doctor smiled at the young man's energy, and kindly offered the assistance of his arm to enable him to walk about the chamber, after obtaining from him his parole of honour, that without permission duly accorded he would not attempt to leave it or penetrate into other parts of the mansion.

The evening of the third day had faded into night, and night was passing into morning, when Master Posset appeared and said,—"Come, sir, horses are in waiting; we leave this immediately."

"In the dark?" asked Florence, with surprise.

"'Tis within an hour of dawn."

"A fresh mystery!—for whence—Stirling?"——"No."

"Whither then?"

"Fawside Tower—have you no ties there?"

"My mother—yes, my mother," said Florence, with a gush of tenderness in his heart, as he hastily dressed; "but once to embrace her, and then for Stirling—ho!"

"You may spare yourself the toil of such a journey; for I assure you, on the word of an honest man, that in less than three days perhaps those you seek will be again in Edinburgh."

To this the sole reply of Florence, was to kiss the opal ring, the secret of which he had as yet failed to discover.

"You must permit me to muffle your eyes."

"Wherefore, Master Posset? this precaution savours of mistrust, and becomes an insult."

"Laird of Fawside, I insist upon it; and she whose orders we must both obey also insists upon it."

"She—who?"

"The giver of the opal ring," whispered the doctor.

"Lead on—I obey," replied the young man, suddenly reduced to docility; "all things must end—and so this mystery."

Posset tied a handkerchief over the eyes of Florence, and taking his hand led him from the chamber, wherein he had suffered so much, and which he had now occupied for more than thirteen or fourteen days. He became conscious of the change of atmosphere as they proceeded from a corridor down a cold, stone staircase, and from thence to a street, evidently one of those steep, but paved closes of the ancient city, as they continued to ascend for some little distance. Then an iron gate in an archway (to judge by the echo) was opened and shut; then they walked about a hundred yards further, before Posset removed the muffling and permitted Fawside to gaze around him. On one side towered the lofty and fantastic mansions of the Landmarket[*] rising on arcades of oak and stone. Near him the quaint church of St. Giles reared its many-carved pinnacles and beautiful spire. Within its lofty aisles scarcely a taper was twinkling now; for already the careless prebendaries were finding other uses for their money than spending it in wax for its forty altars. Even the great brazen shrine in the chancel was dark; the money gifted so vainly by the pious and valiant men of old, to light God's altar until the day of doom—for so they phrased it— had been pounced upon by Lollard bailies for other purposes, and thirteen years later were to behold the shrine itself fall under the axe and hammer of the iconoclast, with the expulsion of the faith and its priesthood.

[*] An abbreviation of *In*land-market.

The wide and lofty thoroughfare was dark. Here and there an occasional ray shot from some of the grated windows, pouring a stream of light athwart the obscurity, which the stacks of peat, heather, and timber, already referred to as standing before almost every door, according to common use and wont, made more confusing to a wayfarer. Fawside recognized the spot where Kilmaurs and his pursuers on that eventful night first overtook him, where he received his first wound, and where he made his first resolute stand against them, before he was beaten further up the street.

On a signal from Master Posset, a groom leading two saddled horses came from under the stone arcade of a lofty mansion, then occupied by Robert Logan of Coatfield, who in 1520 was provost of Edinburgh, and was the first official of that rank who had halberds carried before him. This groom, whom Fawside suspected to be no other than the Frenchman Antoine, lifted his bonnet respectfully and withdrew.

"Fawside, the white or grey nag is yours," said the physician; "mount, and let us be gone, for the morning draws on apace, and my time is precious."

Almost trembling with eagerness, if not with weakness, Florence leaped into the saddle of the white horse, which was a beautiful animal, as he could easily perceive by the amplitude of its mane and tail, by the action of its proud head and slender fore-legs; and as he vaulted to his seat, without even using a stirrup, he felt all his wounds twinge, as if they would burst forth anew, for they were merely skinned over.

In ten minutes more they had left the city, after tossing a gratuity (a few *hardies*, *i.e.* liards of Guienne, worth three halfpence each in Scotland, where they were then current) to the warder at the Watergate, and were galloping by the eastern road towards the tower of Fawside. The stars were still shining brightly, and their light was reflected in the glassy bosom of the estuary that opened on the north and east, beyond a vast extent of desert beach and open moor. The steep and ancient bridge of Musselburgh was soon reached, and then Master Posset drew his bridle, saying,—

"Here, Fawside, I must bid you farewell."

"Farewell! you who have treated me so kindly, so generously—farewell, when we are within three Scots miles of my mother's hearth! Nay, nay, good Master Posset, this can never be."

"It must—I repeat. Entreaties and invitations are alike needless. I obey but the instructions of those I serve, and they are dames who brook no trifling."

"Bethink you, dear sir, of the danger of being abroad at this early and untimeous hour, when broken men, Egyptians and all manner of thieves, beset every highway and hover in every thicket."

The physician smiled, and, opening the breast of his furred cassock, showed beneath it a fine shirt of mail, which was flexible, and fitted him closely as a kid glove. "I *have* thought cf all that," said he, "and I have, moreover, my dagger and a pair of wheel-lock petronels at my saddle-bow. So now, adieu."

"But my fees to you, and this horse, Master Posset——"

"You will find it a beautiful grey, though he looks milky-white under the stars."

"To whom am I to return it?"

"To none—it is a free gift to you."

"To me—a gift," said Florence with astonishment; "from whom?"

"The lady——"

"Who—which lady?"

"The taller, with the hazel eyes and blonde hair; and you must accept; for 'twere ungallant to refuse."

"All this but bewilders and perplexes me the more. Would it had been the gift of the other! Ah, Master Posset, I have but one dread."

"Come," said the physician, laughing, "that is fortunate—lovers usually have many."

"One ever present dread, common to every lover—that she does not love me in return, but may be playing with my affection to prove the power of her own charms."

"Take courage—you have seen no rival."

"No; yet she must have many admirers of her beauty, and more aspirants to her hand and wealth; and one of these might soon become a formidable rival."

"Then you have your sword."

"In such a case a poor resource."

"But one that never fails," responded the warlike apothecary, turning his horse; and, after reiterating their adieux, they separated, and in a short space Florence Fawside found himself cantering up the steep crowned by the church of St. Michael, and thence by a narrow bridle-road that led up the hill-side to his mother's tower.

Fourteen nights had elapsed since last we saw her sitting lonely by her hearth; and now she had long since learned to weep for her only son as for one who was numbered with the dead.

CHAPTER XIII
HOME

Hail, land of spearmen! seed of those who scorn'd
To stoop the proud crest to imperial Rome!
Hail! dearest half of Albion sea-wall'd!
Hail! state unconquer'd by the fire of war,—
Red war that twenty ages round thee blazed!

Albania.

Some thoughts such as these which inspired this now forgotten Scottish bard filled the swelling heart of Florence Fawside, as he urged his horse up the winding way which led to his paternal tower. The morning sun had now risen brightly above the long pastoral ridges of the Lammermuir, and he could see the widening Forth, with all its rocky isles, and the long sweep of sandy beach which borders the beautiful bay that lies between the mouth of the Esk and the green links of Gulane, whereon, in those days, there stood an ancient church of St. Andrew, which William the Lion gifted unto the monks of Dryburgh. The blue estuary was studded by merchant barks and fisher craft, with their square and brown lug-sails, beating up against the ebb tide and a gentle breeze from the west.

The sky was of a light azure tint, flecked by floating masses of snowy cloud, which, on their eastern and lower edges, were tinged with burning gold.

The hottest days of the summer were now gone, the pastures had become somewhat parched, and the shrivelled foliage that rustled in the woods of Carberry seemed athirst for the rains of autumn. Amid the coppice, the corn-craik and the cushat dove sent up their peculiar notes. The corn-fields were turning from pale green to a golden brown; and, as the morning breeze passed over it, the bearded grain swayed heavily to and fro, like ripples on the bosom of a yellow lake. The white smoke curled from the green cottage roofs of moss and thatch; the blue-bonneted peasants were at work in the sunny fields—the women with their snooded hair, or their white Flemish curchies (that came into fashion when James II. espoused Mary the Rose of Gueldres), were milking the cattle, grinding their hand-mills, or busy about their little garden-plots; and to Florence all seemed to illustrate his country, and speak to his heart with that love of *home*, which *then*, even more than now, was the purest passion of the Scottish people, and which, in all their wanderings, they never forget, however distant the land in which their lot in life may be cast.

Florence felt all this as he spurred up the green braeside, and heard the people in his mother-tongue cry, "God him speed;" for though they knew him not, they saw that he was a handsome youth, a stranger, nobly mounted and bravely apparelled.

Every step he took brought some old recollection to his heart. The gurgling brooks in which he had fished and the leafy thickets in which he had bird-nested, the old trees up which he had clambered, were before him now, and the days of his boyhood, the familiar voices and faces of his slaughtered father and brother, came vividly to memory. The song of a farmer who was driving his team of horses to the field, the lowing of the cattle, the barking of the shepherds' collies, the perfume of the broom and the harebell on the upland slope, all spoke of country and of home. But with this emotion others mingled.

With all the genuine rapture of a boyish lover, he kissed again and again his opal ring, the gift of that beautiful unknown, who had filled his heart with a secret joy and given life a new impulse.

"What can its secret be? Oh! to unravel all this mystery!" he exclaimed to himself a hundred times; but the ring baffled all his scrutiny and ingenuity.

He had now four projects to put in force immediately after his return home.

First, to deliver his letter to the Regent, Earl of Arran.

Second, to deliver the other missive of Henry of Valois to the queen-mother, Mary of Lorraine.

Third, to discover his unknown mistress.

Fourth, to avenge his father's feud and fall by ridding the world of Claude Hamilton of Preston, the Lord Kilmaurs, and a few others; after which he would settle soberly down in his mother's house, and, for a time, lead the quiet life of a country gentleman—at least, such a life as they led in those days, when their swords were never from their sides.

And now, as he surmounted the long ridge of Fawside, the landscape opened further to the south and eastward, and he saw the old square keep of Elphinstone, in which George Wishart had been confined in the preceding year by Patrick, Earl of Bothwell, and the wall of which had rent with a mighty sound—rent from battlement to basement, as we may yet see it, at the moment of his martyrdom before the castle of St. Andrews.

The heart of Florence beat six pulses in a second as he drew nearer home, and saw the huge column of smoke ascending lazily from the square chimney of the hall, and the black crows and white pigeons fraternizing together on the stone ridge of the copehouse; and now he passed old Roger's thatched domicile, the Westmains or Grange, from whence the inmates of the castle were supplied with farm produce. It was all under fine cultivation save one wild spot named the Deilsrig, which was set aside, or left totally unused, for the propitiation of evil spirits; and none in the neigbourhood doubted that cattle which strayed or grazed thereon were elf-shot by the evil one, for they were frequently found dead within the turf boundary of this infernal spot, as their huge bones whitening among the dog-grass remained to attest; and there, too, lay the unblessed graves of certain Egyptians, who, despite the protections granted by James IV to "Anthony Gavino, Lord and Earl of Little Egypt," had been judicially drowned in the river Esk by Earl Bothwell, the sheriff of Haddington.

Florence glanced at the place, which had so many terrors for him as a child, and dashed up to the arched gate of the tower, where his emotion was such, that it was not until after three attempts he could sound the copper horn which hung by a chain to the wall; for such was the fashion then, when door-bells and brass knockers, like gas and steam and electricity, were still in the womb of time.

In a minute more he had sprung from his horse and rushed up the stair to the hall, where his mother, with a cry of mingled fear and joy, clasped him to her breast, and wept like a true woman rather than the stern and Spartan dame she usually seemed. Then old Roger of the Westmains, in the exuberance of his joy, flung his bonnet in the fire and danced about the hall table; and the grey-haired nurse, Maud, contended with the vicar, Mass John of Tranent, for the next and longest embrace of the returned one; for all welcomed him back to his home as one reprieved from the dead; for surmise had been exhausted, and all ingenuity had failed to afford a clue to his mysterious disappearance after landing at Leith from the galley of M. de Villegaignon.

After the first transports of her joy had subsided—and, indeed, they subsided soon, for her natural sternness of manner and ferocity of purpose soon resumed their sway in her angry and widowed heart, his mother kissed him thrice upon the forehead, held him at arm's length from her breast, surveying his features with an expression of mingled love, tenderness, anxiety, and anger.

"Thou hast been ill, Florence; thy cheeks are pale, wan, and hollow. Thou hast been suffering, my son—yea, suffering deeply. How came this about? Say!—thou hast no secrets from thine old mother!"

"Ask these wounds, dear mother; they have kept me for fourteen days a-bed and absent from you," he replied, as he tore open his crimson doublet, and shirt, and displayed on his bosom the sword-thrust, which was scarcely skinned over.

"Kyrie eleison!" muttered the white-haired vicar, lifting up his thin hands and hollow eyes.

Roger of the Westmains uttered a shout of rage and grasped his dagger.

"My bairn—my braw, bonnie bairn!" exclaimed the old nurse with tender commiseration.

"Florence," said his mother through her clenched teeth, "whose sword did this?"

"Can you ask me, mother?"

"*His!*—would you say?" she asked in a voice like a shriek, while pointing with her lean white hand to Preston Tower, the walls of which above the level landscape shone redly in the morning sun.

"Nay, not his, but the swords of his followers."

"Of Symon Brodie and Mungo Tennant?"

"Even so; I heard their names in the *mêlée*."

"Accursed be the brood; for their swords were reddest and readiest in the fray in which your father fell!"

"They and others dogged me close on the night I landed. I fought long and bravely——"

"My own son!—my dear dead husband's only son!"

"But what could one sword avail against twenty others? Struck down at last, I would have been hewn to pieces but for the stout arm of a friendly burgher and the kindness of——of——those who salved my wounds and tended me—yea, mother, kindly and tenderly as you would have done," he added, while the colour deepened in his face, and he sank wearily into the chair in which his slain father had last sat, and which since that day none had dared to occupy, as his widow would have deemed it a sacrilege.

It required but the description of this last outrage to rouse the blood of Dame Alison and of all her domestics to boiling heat.

"Be calm, dear mother, be calm," said Florence, pressing her trembling hand to his heart. "In three days I shall be well enough to handle my sword, and then I shall scheme out vengeance for all I have endured."

"Thou hearest him, vicar?" exclaimed Lady Alison, striking her hands together, while her dark eyes shot fire. "The spirit of my buried husband lives again in his boy!"

"Lord make us thankfu' therefor!" muttered the listening servants, who shared every sentiment of their mistress.

"Be wary, madam!" said the tall thin priest. "Whence still this mad craving for revenge?"

"In the presence of this poor lamb, who has so narrowly escaped a dreadful death, weak, pale, and wounded, dost thou ask me this, thou very shaveling?" she exclaimed with scornful energy. "My husband's feud and fall!—Oh, woe is me!—and my winsome Willie's death——"

"Demand a fearful reprisal!" said Florence, with a vehemence increased by his mother's presence and example; "and fearful it shall be!"

"Vengeance," replied the priest firmly, but meekly, "is ever the offspring of the weakest and least tutored mind."

"Father John!" exclaimed the pale widow.

"I say so with all deference, my son, and with all respect for our good lady your mother. In her thirst for vengeance, like the last stake of a gamester, she will risk you, her only son—risk you by invading the province of God; for to Him alone belongeth vengeance. Remember the holy words, Dame Alison: 'Vengeance is mine, saith the Lord, and I will repay it.'"

"So priests must preach," said Florence; "but, under favour, father, laymen find forgiveness hard to practise."

"So hard," hissed Lady Alison through her sharp and firm-set teeth, "that for each drop of Preston's blood I would give a rood of land—yea, for every drop a yellow rig of corn! 'Twas but three weeks ago, come the feast of Bartholomew, he followed a thief with a sleuth-hound of Gueldreland within the bounds of our barony."

"He dared?" said Florence, sharing all his mother's anger.

"He or some of his people; and without asking our license, took and hanged him on a thorn-tree at the Bucklea. Did not his swine root holes in the corn on our grange, destroying ten rigs of grain and more, and he scornfully refused our demands to make the damage good? Yet he burned the byres of our kinsman Roger for taking a deer in his wood at Bankton, though any man may hunt in any forest—even a royal one—so far as he may fling his bugle-horn before him; yet he broke Roger's bow and arrows, took away his arquebuse, and hanged all his dogs. And wherefore? Because he was a Fawside and a kinsman of thine. And now they would have slain thee, my son—thee, in whom my joy, my hope, my future all are centred!" she added, embracing Florence, the expression of whose handsome face had completely changed to gloom and anger under her influence. "But while fish swim in yonder Firth, and mussels grow on its rocks, our hatred shall live!"

The vicar, a priest of benign and venerable aspect, smiled sadly, and shook his white head with an air of deprecation.

"I fear me, madam," said he, "that the fish and the mussels are races that bid fair to outlive alike the Fawsides of that Ilk and the Hamiltons of Preston, their folly, feuds, and wickedness."

"On Rood-day in harvest, a year past, as I sat here alone by my spinning-wheel, my husband's armour clattered where it hangs on yonder wall,—and wot ye *why*? Preston was riding over the hill, and near our gate. Preston! and alone! Could I have got the old falcon ready on the bartizan, he had been shot like a hoodiecrow, as surely as the breath of heaven was in his nostrils!"

"Fie! madam—fie! I cannot listen to language such as this!" said the vicar, erecting his tall figure and preparing to retire.

"The wrongs I have endured in this world, yea, and the sorrows, too——"

"Should teach you to look for comfort in that which is to come," said the priest, with asperity.

"Not till I have had vengeance swift, sure, and deep on the house of Preston. No, friar! preach as you may, Alison Kennedy will never rest in the grave where her murdered husband lies, but with the assurance that Claude Hamilton lies mangled in his shroud—mangled by the sword of her son Florence! And he may slay him in open war; for so surely as the souls and bodies of men are governed by stars and climates, we shall have war with the English ere the autumn leaves are off the trees, and so surely shall that traitor Hamilton join them, for he was one of those whom Henry took at Solway, and feasted in London, to suit his own nefarious ends—like Cassilis, Lennox, and Glencairn."

Roger of the Westmains heard with grim satisfaction all this outpouring of bitterness of spirit; for he shared to the full her animosity to the unlucky laird of Preston. To Roger, old Lady Alison was the greatest potentate on earth. Had the Regent Arran, or Mary of Lorraine, commanded him to ride with his single spear against a brigade of English, he might have hesitated; but had Lady Alison desired him to leap off Salisbury Craigs, he would probably have done so, without the consideration of a moment, and had his old body dashed to pieces at the foot thereof.

In joy for her son's return, the lady of the tower ordered the bailie to distribute drink-silver (as it was then termed) to all her servants and followers; largesses to the town piper and drummer of Musselburgh, and to the poor gaberlunzies who sat on the kirk styles of Tranent and St. Michael. She then directed all the harness and warlike weapons to be thoroughly examined, preparatory to commencing hostilities against the grand enemy, who, as we shall shortly see, was in his tower of Preston, thinking of other things than the mischief she was brewing against him.

A few days slipped monotonously away.

After Paris—the Paris of Francis I. and Henry II.,—and after the busy chateau of the Duchess of Albany at Vendôme, the quiet and gloom of the little tower of Fawside soon became insupportable to its young proprietor. Thus, instead of remaining at home, attending to the collection of his rents in coin and kain, conferring with old Roger anent green and white crops on the mains of the Grange, listening to the stories of his nurse, holding bloodthirsty councils of war with his mother, concerning the best mode of invading with fire and sword the territories of a neighbour, only separated from his own by a turf dyke, or weaving deadly snares for cutting him off by the strong hand, he spent his whole days in Edinburgh, caracoling his beautiful grey horse up and down the High-street, through the courts of the palace, before the house of M. d'Oysell, the French ambassador, in the Cowgate, in the Greyfriars' Gardens, in the royal park, and in every place of public resort, with a plume in his velvet bonnet and a hawk on his left wrist, as became a gallant of the time, in the hope of discovering, even for a moment, his lost love, the donor of the opal ring. Daily he visited the dwelling of Master Posset, at the sign of the Stuffed Alligator, in the Lawnmarket, to prosecute his inquiries there; but either from accident or design, that most discreet of apothecaries was never at home. Thus daily the young Laird of Fawside was doomed to return disappointed, weary, and dispirited to his gloomy antique hall, or to his gloomier old bed-chamber in the northern portion of the tower—a portion concerning which the following tradition is related by Father John:—

Sir Thomas de Fawsyde, who, in 1330, married Muriella, daughter of Duncan, Earl of Fife, when quarrelling with her one day about a favourite falcon, which she had permitted to escape in the wood of Drumsheugh, in the heat of passion, drew off his steel glove and struck her white shoulder with his clenched hand. Muriella, though tender and gentle, was proud and high-spirited. She felt this unkindness and affront so keenly and bitterly, that, without a tear or reproach, she retired from his presence and secluding herself in the northern chamber, never spoke again, and refusing all food and sustenance, literally starved herself to death. Upon this Earl Duncan, before King David II., accused the rude knight of having slain his daughter.

"And because it was notour and manifest," says Sir John Skene of Curriehill, in his quaint "Buke of the auld Lawes," printed in 1609, "that he did not slae hir, nor gave hir a wound of the quhilk she died; bot gave her ane blow with his hand to teach and correct hir, and also untill the time of hir death dearly loved hir, and treated hir as a husband weill affectionate to his wife, the king pronounced him clene and quit."

But the spirit-form of this lady, dressed in quaint and ancient apparel, of that rustling silk peculiar to all ghostly ladies, with her long hair dishevelled, weeping and mourning, was averred, for ages, to haunt the room where now her descendant lay nightly on his couch, dreaming of the secret love he was more intent on discovering, than of pursuing the hereditary quarrel of his race, and oblivious of delivering to the Regent Arran and Mary of Lorraine the letters with which he was charged from the court of France.

The reason of the last remissness was simply this; he believed his fair one to be in Edinburgh, while the queen-mother was occasionally at Stirling, and the regent was at his country castle, in Cadzow Forest, in Clydesdale.

CHAPTER XIV
PRESTON TOWER

Then the Count of Clara began in this manner: "Sirs, it is manifest that men in this world can only become powerful by strengthening themselves with men and money; but the money must be employed in procuring men, for by men must kingdoms be defended and won." —*Amadis of Gaul.*

On the evening of the same day when Florence Fawside returned home, and his mother, like a spider in its hole, sat in her elbow-chair in the grim old tower upon the hill, weaving plots to net and destroy her feudal adversary, that detested personage in his equally grim old tower upon the lea, was forming plans of a similarly desperate, but much more extensive description.

The paved barbican of his residence was filled by nearly the same horses and horsemen, liverymen and pages, wearing the oak branch in their bonnets or the shakefork sable on their sleeves, and by many men-at-arms in helmet, jack, and wambeson, whom we formerly saw in the courtyard of the Golden Rose, at Leith, and whom we left in hot pursuit of Florence. As the shades of evening deepened on the harvest fields and bordering sea, the narrow slits and iron-grated windows of the old castle became filled with red light, for it was crowded by visitors; and the echoes of voices, of laughter, and shouts of loud and reckless merriment rang at times under the arched vaults of its ancient chambers.

Near Preston, a burgh of barony, composed of old houses of rough and rugged aspect, that cluster along a rocky beach of broken masses of basalt, denuded long ago of all earthy strata, stands this high square donjon tower of the Hamiltons of Preston, in later years a stronghold of the attainted Earls of Winton. The adjacent beach is now covered with shapeless ruins of redstone, from which, ever and anon, the ebbing sea sweeps a mass away; but in the time of our story these ruins were the flourishing saltpans of the enterprising monks of St. Marie de Newbattle, who, since the twelfth century, had pushed briskly the trade of salt-making; and nightly the broad red glares of their coal-fed furnaces were wont to shed a dusky light upon the rocky land and tossing sea—hence its present name, of the Priest-town-pans; though in days older still, when King Donald VII. was pining a blind captive in his prison, the locality was called Auldhammer. In 1547, its church was an open ruin, having been burned by the English three years before.

As a double security, within the barbican gate, this tower is entered by two arched doors on the east. One leads to the lower vaults *alone*; another, in the first story, reached by a ladder or bridge, gives access to the hall and sleeping apartments. Those who entered here, drew in the long ladder after them, and thus cut off all means of access from below. The vast pile of Borthwick, in Lothian, the tower of Coxton, near Elgin, the tower of Half-forest, near Inverurie, and many other Scottish castles of great antiquity, are constructed on this singular plan, where *security* was the first principle of our domestic architects. Preston had additions built to it in 1625; and a huge crenelated wall of that date still surmounts the simple machicolated battlements of the original edifice, making it one of the most conspicuous objects on the level land on which its lofty mass is reared. The original tower was one of the chain of fortresses garrisoned by Lord Home in the 15th century, and having been burned by the English army in 1650, after all the rough vicissitudes of war and time, it presents a mouldering, shattered, and venerable aspect.

The arched gate on the east was surmounted by the three cinque-foils pierced ermine of Hamilton; and on each side of it a large brass gun called a basilisk peered through a porthole, to "hint that here at least there was no thoroughfare." In short, Preston Tower is a mansion of those warlike, but thrifty and hearty old times when, by order, of the Scottish parliament, it was "statute and ordained that all lords should dwell in their castles and manors, and expend *the fruit of their lands in the counterie where the said lands lay."*

It had other tenants besides old Claude Hamilton and his cuirassed and turbulent retainers; as it was alleged to be haunted by a brownie and evil spirit; and for the latter Symon Brodie, the castle butler, nightly set apart a cup of ale. If Symon failed to perform this duty, the spirit, like a vampire bat, sucked the blood of one of the inmates. The little squat figure of the brownie, wearing a broad bonnet and short scarlet cloak, had been seen at times, especially on St. John's Night, to flit about the kitchen-door, watching for the departure of the servants, who always left to him, unmolested, his favourite haunt, the warm hearth of the great arched fireplace, where the livelong night he crooned a melancholy ditty, which sounded like the winter wind through a keyhole, as he swung above the *griesoch*, or gathering peat, from the iron cruik whereon by day, as Father John of Tranent records, "the mickle kail-pot hung."

The merriment was great in the old hall; for the supper, which had been a huge engagement or onslaught of knives and teeth upon all manner of edibles, was just over. People always fed well in those old times, if we may judge of the abundance which filled their boards three times per *diem*; yet what were they, or the Saxon gluttons of an earlier age, when compared to the youth who, unrestrained by the silly fear of civilized society, discussed before the Emperor Aurelian a boar, a sheep, a pig, and a hundred loaves; with beer in proportion; or to his imperial majesty Maximus Caius Julius, who—long live his memory—ate daily sixty-four pounds of meat, and drank therewith twenty-four quarts of rare old Roman wine!

The supper, a meal taken at the early hour of six in 1547, was over in Preston Hall. The long black table of oak had been cleared of all its trenchers and platters of silver, delft, tin, and wood; but a plentiful supply of wine— Alicant, Bordeaux, and Canary,—with ale and usquebaugh for those who preferred them, was substituted, in tall black-jacks which resembled troopers' boots, being made of strong leather, lined with pewter and rimmed with silver. Each of these jolly vessels held two Scottish pints (*i.e.* two quarts English); and drinking-vessels of silver for the nobles, horn for gentlemen, and wooden quaichs, cups, or luggies for their more favoured retainers, were disposed along the table by Symon Brodie (who had partly recovered from his sword-wound): we say more favoured retainers, for, as the drinking bout which succeeded the supper in Preston was a species of political conclave, a gathering of conspirators, the doors were carefully closed, and not a man, save those on whom the Scottish lords of the English faction could thoroughly rely, was permitted to remain within earshot; and hence, at each massive oak door of the hall stood an armed jackman, with his sword drawn; and on the dark pyne doublets, the dinted corslets and burganets, the brown visages and rough beards of these keen-eyed and listening sentinels, the smoky light of ten great torches which were ranged along the stone wall, five on each side, near the spring of the arched roof, flared and gleamed with a wavering radiance.

Nor were the party at the table less striking and picturesque.

In his elbow-chair old Claude of Preston occupied the head of the long board. His voluminous grey beard flowed over his quilted doublet, and concealed his gorget of fine steel; his bald head glanced in the light, and his keen, bright basilisk eyes surveyed the faces and seemed to pierce the souls of the speakers, as each in turn gave his suggestion as to the best mode of subverting that monarchy for the maintenance of which so many of their sires had died in battle.

There were present the Earl of Cassilis, he of abbot-roasting notoriety; the Earl of Glencairn and his son Lord Kilmaurs; the Lord Lyle and his son the Master; the Lord Gray; with two others whom we have not yet fully introduced to the reader; to wit, Patrick Hepburn Earl of Bothwell, abhorred by the Protestants as the first captor of George Wishart (and father of that Earl James who wrought the destruction of Mary Queen of Scots), and William Earl Marischal, the constable of Kincardine, both peers of a goodly presence, clad in half-armour, and wearing the peaked beard, close-shorn hair, and pointed moustache of the time.

Bothwell wore one of those curious thumb-rings concerning which bluff Jack Falstaff taunts King Hal. It was a gift from Mary of Lorraine, whom he once vainly believed to be in love with him, and whose slights had now driven him into the conspiracy against her. He had a golden girdle, which glittered in the light, and thereat hung the long sword which had been found clenched in the hand of his noble grandsire,

"Earl Adam Hepburn—he who died
At Flodden, by his sovereign's side,"

and which was popularly believed to have been charmed by a wizard, the late prior of Deer, in suchwise that the wielder of it should never have his blood drawn nor suffer harm, a spell which the wizard priest performed by kissing the hilt four times in the name of Crystsonday. Bothwell had been two years a prisoner in a royal fortress, for assisting in the raids and rapine of the late Earl of Yarrow; and after being many years banished from Scotland, had lived at Florence and Venice, where his natural turn for mischief and deep-laid plotting had been developed to the full.

Among these intriguers were two men of a very different kind, clad as followers of that master of treachery and statecraft, the fierce Earl of Glencairn, viz., Master Patten, who afterwards wrote the history of Somerset's hostile expedition into Scotland, and Master Edward Shelly, a brave English officer, whom we have already mentioned, and who was captain of a band of English soldiers known as the Boulogners. He had been at the capture and garrisoning of Boulogne-sur-Mer in 1544, where he superintended the rebuilding of the famous *Tour de l'Ordre*, a useless labour, as Edward VI. restored the town to France six years after. These two Londoners were still disguised in the livery of the Cunninghames, and, further to complete the imposture, wore peasants' coarse blue bonnets and those cuarans, or shoes of undressed hide, which obtained for our people the sobriquet of rough-footed Scots.

"Symon, ye loon, attend to the strangers," said Claude Hamilton. "Fill your bicker from the jack of Alicant, Master Shelly; or like you better a silver tassie, my man? I trust that you and worthy Master Patten, your secretary or servitor (we style such-like both in Scotland), have supped well?"

"Well, yea, and heartily sir," replied Shelly, wiping his curly beard with a napkin. "But Master Patten was whispering that he must teach your Scots cooks to make that which he loves as his own life—a jolly Devonshire squab and white-pot."

"Hah! And how make ye such, Master Patten?"

"With a pint of cream," replied Master Patten, "four eggs, nutmeg, sugar, salt, a loaf of bread, a handful of raisins, and some sweet butter. Then boil the whole in a bag, and seek a good tankard of March beer to wash it down with."

"God willing, sir, we shall learn your southern dishes, among other things, when, haply, we bring this marriage about with little King Edward VI. Each royal alliance hath brought some unco' fashion among us here in Scotland. Furred doublets came in with Margaret of Oldenburg; the Flemish hood with Mary of Gueldres; the velvet hat with Margaret Tudor; the French beard with Magdalene of Valois— —"

"And please heaven, worthy sir," snuffled Master Patten, "accession of wealth and strength with his majesty Edward VI."

"Right!" said Glencairn gruffly; "and your Devonshire squab to boot. And now, my lords and gentles, to business; for the night wears on, and we must keep tryst with my Lord Regent betimes at Stirling, for you know that he would confer with some of us previous to a convention of the estates. Let Master Shelly speak; for Master Patten hath brought new letters and tidings from the Lord Protector of England."

"Well, sirs," said Shelly bluntly, "to resume where we last left off. The Protector of England pledges himself to invade Scotland with an army sufficient to bear down all opposition, provided you and your armed adherents cast your swords into the scale with him."

"Agreed!" said Claude Hamilton, glancing round the table.

"Agreed!" added all, in varying tones of approval.

On the table lay a map of Scotland,—one of those so quaintly delineated by M. Nicholas d'Arville, chief cosmographer to the most Christian king; and to this reference was made from time to time by members of the worthy conclave, who sat around it or lounged in the hall.

"How many fighting-men can you raise in that district named the Lennox, to aid our cause?" asked Shelly, placing a finger on the part which indicated that ancient county.

"Its hereditary sheriff, Matthew Earl of Lennox, is one of *us*," replied Bothwell; "and he can bring into the field eight thousand soldiers."

"And then there are the Isles," began Glencairn.

"Yea, my lord," said Shelly, with an approving smile, "of old a very hotbed of revolt against the Scottish crown."

"And the place wherein our Edwards readily fermented treason," added Patten, "and stirred their lords to war against your kings, as independent princes of the Hebrides."

"Trust not to the islesmen," said Bothwell; "the vanity of their chiefs was crushed a hundred years ago, on the field of Harlaw."

"But haply the spirit lives there yet," said Shelly, making a memorandum; "and if we sent a few war-ships through the Western Sea under the Lord Clinton or Sir William Wentworth, our two best admirals, it might be no difficult task to rouse it once again to action."

"You deceive yourself," said Lord Lyle coldly; "the sovereign of Scotland is now, both by blood and position, hereditary Lord of the Isles, and the chiefs remember with love and veneration the chivalry of James IV., and patriotism of his son, who died at Falkland."

"Now, my lords, to the terms of your adherence with England," said Shelly, unfolding a parchment, to which several small seals were attached by pieces of ribbon; and after hemming once or twice, he arose and read aloud:—

"It is covenanted and written between us, Edward Duke of Somerset, Earl of Hertford, Viscount Beauchamp, Lord Seymour, uncle to the king our sovereign, lord high treasurer and earl-marshal of England, captain of the isles of Guernsey and Jersey, lieutenant-general of all his majesty's forces by sea and land, governor of his highness's most royal person, and protector of all his domains and subjects, knight of the most illustrious order of the Garter, and certain lords and barons of the realm of Scotland—to wit—Gilbert Kennedy, Earl of Cassilis——"

"Enough of this," said Cassilis bluntly, and with some alarm depicted in his face; "there are other peers who take precedence of me in parliament; so why not in this parchment of thine? moreover, we care not to hear our titles so rehearsed."

"In so dangerous a document as this," added some one.

"How, my lords," exclaimed Shelly with astonishment and something of scorn; "you dare not recede——"

"Dare not?" reiterated Cassilis, with a fierce frown.

"No," replied the Englishman bluntly.

"And wherefore, sirrah?"

"Because the Protector of England holds in his hand a document which, if sent to the Regent of Scotland, would hang seven among you as high as ever Haman hung of old."

"A document," repeated Kilmaurs, the gash on whose pale cheek grew black, while his eyes flashed fire; "is there another bond than this!"

"Yea, one written by Master Patten, and signed in the Star-chamber at London, by seven Scottish lords, then prisoners of war, after the field of Solway."

"And *they*—" queried Lyle, with knitted brow and inquiring eye.

"Bound themselves to assist King Henry VIII., of happy memory, in all his secret designs against their own country, promising to invest him with the government of Scotland during the little queen's minority; to drive out Arran and Mary of Lorraine; to admit English garrisons into all the fortresses; and, in short, to play the old game of Edward Longshanks, Comyn, and Baliol over again, in a land," added Shelly with an ill-disguised sneer, "that is not likely to display another Wallace, or to boast another field of Bannockburn."

"And those seven—" asked Lyle impetuously.

"Are the Earls of Cassilis and Glencairn, the Lords Somerville, Gray, Maxwell, Oliphant, and Fleming."

"Englishman, thou liest!" exclaimed the Master of Lyle, grasping his dagger; "the Lord Oliphant is my near kinsman."

"Peace, he lies not," said Cassilis; "I signed that bond, and by it will I abide."

"Yea, Master of Lyle," said Shelly blandly, with a glance of sombre scorn and fury in his eye; "and other documents there are, which, if known, would raise in Scotland such a storm that there is not an urchin in the streets of Edinburgh but would cast stones at you, and cry shame on the betrayers of his queen and country!"

"Silence, sirs," exclaimed old Claude Hamilton with alarm, "the conversation waxeth perilous."

"I am here on the crooked errand of the Duke of Somerset," said Shelly, rising with an air of lofty disdain, "no soldier's work it is, and rather would

I have been with my stout garrison at Boulogne, than clerking here with worthy Master Patten."

"Thrice have you come hither on such errands, Master Shelly, and they seem to pay well," said Kilmaurs tauntingly.

The Englishman clenched his hand and blushed with anger, as he said imprudently,—

"Thrice I have ridden into Scotland since that red day at Ancrumford, and each time have I gone home with a prouder heart than when I crossed the northern border."

"Prouder?" reiterated the fiery Kilmaurs, coming forward with a resentful expression in his lowering eye.

"Yes," replied the Englishman boldly, and grasping the secret petronel which he wore under his mantle; "for each time I asked myself, for *what sum* would an English yeoman sell his fatherland, his father's grave, or his king's honour, even as these Scottish earls, lords, and barons do, for this accursed lucre?" With these words, Shelly tore the purse from his girdle and dashing it on the table, continued: "When I bethink me of the truth and faith, the unavailing bravery and the stanch honesty of the stout Scottish commons I am here to betray through those whom they trust and honour, my heart glows with shame within me! Assuredly 'tis no work this for an English captain; so do thou the rest, in God's name, good Master Patten."

As Shelly sat sullenly down, and twisted from side to side in his chair, as if seated on the hot gridiron of St. Lawrence, it was high time for the more politic Patten to speak; for savage glares were exchanged on all sides of the table; Kennedies and Cunninghames closed round, each by his chieftain's side; swords and daggers were half-drawn, and Shelly's life was in evident jeopardy; for his taunts, alike unwise and daring, had found an echo in the venal hearts of those at whom they were levelled.

"Whence this indignation, most worthy emissary?" asked Kilmaurs, whose insolence and hauteur were proverbial.

"I am an *envoy*—not an emissary," replied Shelly, eyeing him firmly from his plumed bonnet to his white funnel boots; "I am a soldier, and have the heart of a soldier—I thank God, not of a diplomatist. I know more of gunnery and the brave game of war, than the subtlety of statecraft. I am here to obey orders: these are to confer with you on what your lordships consider a salable matter—your allegiance; had it been, as it may one day be, to cut your throats, 'twere all one to Ned Shelly."

"Hear *me*, my most honourable and good lords," began Master Patten, in his most wily and seductive manner; "you cannot recede, so allow me to go on. The promises of the English Protector must naturally meet the fondest wishes of all. Listen to our indenture. Patrick Earl of Bothwell promises, on the faith of a true man, to transfer his allegiance to the young king of England, and to surrender unto English troops his strong castle of Hermitage, on condition that he receives the hand of an English princess — —"

"Princess?" muttered several of the traitor conclave inquiringly, as they turned to each other.

"Who may *she* be?" asked Claude Hamilton with surprise.

"Katherine Willoughby, widow of Charles Brandon, Duke of Suffolk," continued Patten, reading.

Bothwell smiled proudly, as he thought of his triumph over Mary of Lorraine.

"But," said the Earl of Glencairn, "what sayeth this dainty dame to be sold thus, like a bale of goods?"

"What she may say can matter little," replied Patten.

"'Tis said she affects one named Bertie."

"My lord, the Duke of Somerset will amend that."

"A worthy successor to the poor Countess Agnes Sinclair of Ravenscraig!" said the Master of Lyle with something of scornful commiseration.

"My first countess sleeps in the kirk of St. Denis, at Dysart," said Bothwell coldly, "so I pray you to proceed, Master Patten; this espousal is *my* matter."

"The Lord Glencairn and Claude Hamilton of Preston," continued the scribe, "offer to co-operate in the invasion of Scotland, and at the head of three thousand men, their friends and vassals, to keep the Regent Arran in check until the English army arrive; the former to receive a hundred thousand crowns in gold on the day the infant queen of Scotland is delivered into Somerset's hand, and the latter to obtain a coronet, with the titles of Earl of Gladsmuir and Lord Preston of Auldhammer."

"Agreed!" said Preston, glancing round with an air of satisfaction and curiosity to see how the announcement was received.

"On that day, sirs," added Master Patten, "the infant queen of Scotland shall share the glory of being joint sovereign of a realm containing the English, Irish, and Welsh, the Cornishmen, and the French of Jersey, Guernsey, and Calais."

"But," said Glencairn, "what if our devil of a regent, with a good array of Scottish pikes, standeth in the way of all this?"

"Then, by heaven, sirs, black velvet will be in demand among the surname of Hamilton!" exclaimed Kilmaurs.

"How?" asked Claude of Preston angrily. "Would you dare— —"

"Exactly so!" interrupted Kilmaurs with his deadly smile.

"And the said Claude Hamilton, laird of Preston," continued poor Master Patten, reading very fast to avoid further interruptions, "hereby binds and obliges himself to bestow in marriage upon Master Edward Shelly, captain of the King of England's Boulogners, in reward for his services touching these state matters, the hand and estates of his niece, the Lady Madeline Hame, Countess of Yarrow, now his ward, and according to law in his custody as overlord, by the will of her late father the earl, who bound her to remain so until the age of twenty-one years."

"Thou art in luck, Master Shelly," said Kilmaurs, "for the lady is said to be beautiful."

"But suppose she will not have me?" suggested Shelly, who now smiled and played with the feather in his bonnet.

"Dare she refuse!" growled Claude Hamilton, gnawing his wiry moustache.

"We can get thee a love philtre from Master Posset," said Bothwell, laughing.

"As men say thou didst for Mary of Lorraine, what time she wellnigh died at Rothesay," whispered Glencairn.

"Then I philtred her with small avail," said the High Admiral, grinding his teeth, for he had really loved the widowed queen, while she had tolerated his addresses solely for political purposes of her own.

"But, Master Shelly, I know of one (a witch) who deals in love-charms, and who— —"

"Nay, my Lord Glencairn," replied the English soldier laughing, "I will have none of this damnable ware. A pretty Scots lass is witch enough for me. And now that we have concluded this paction, to which also the Earls of Athole, Crawford, Errol, and Sutherland have given their adhesion on the promise of being *honestly entertained,* I will drink one more tankard to its final success."[*]

[*] The political villany of which this chapter is descriptive is authentic. See Tytler, and particularly "Acta Regia," vol. iii.

"I have no heirs male," said Preston, almost with sadness; "and if this alliance be happily concluded, I will give away to the husband of my niece my lands of Over-Preston, if, during my lifetime, the said Edward Shelly shall give to me, as chief lord of the feu, a pair of gilt spurs and three crowns yearly at the feast of St. Barnabas."

"More luck still, Master Shelly!" said Bothwell.

"And I will grant to God and the church of St. Giles at Edinburgh, and to the monks serving God therein, for the health of my own soul, the souls of all my ancestors, the souls of the two Fawsides whom I slew, and for the souls of all the faithful dead, my wood and lands of Bankton for the yearly payment of a rose in Bleuch Farm."

"'Tis well!" said Shelly, with a singular smile, for he was alike indifferent to the old creed and the new. "But *remember* that by proclamations the Scottish people must be everywhere informed that we, the army of England, are coming to free them from the tyranny of the bishop of Rome—from the exorbitant revenues demanded by his church, whose meadows and pastures are to become the property of the barons, and that money shall no longer be levied among the poor by full-fed bishops and shorn shavelings for the celebration of masses and marriages, for burials and holy-bread, for wax and wine, vows and pilgrimages, processions, and prayers for children and fair weather, or for curses by bell, book, and candle, and all such Roman superstition. Say everywhere that we come with the sword, not to woo your queen, but to crush at once the falling hierarchy of Rome, even as we have crushed it in England! You understand me, sirs. And now, Master Patten, get your waxen taper ready. My lords, your seals and signatures to the bond; and remember, that a month hence the bridge of Berwick will be ringing to the tramp of armed feet on their northern march; and ere that time I shall have exchanged this Scottish bonnet for the steel burganet of my sturdy Boulogners."

The seals and the signatures of the few who could accomplish the (then) difficult task of affixing their degraded autographs to this rebellious *bond* were soon completed, and Master Shelly was consigning it to a secret pocket of his dagger-proof doublet, when Master Patten whispered waggishly,

"In sooth, sir, methinks a fair dame should have been also provided for *me* in this parchment."

"In good faith, Patten," said Shelly, laughing, "I love a lass at home in England—a fair jolly dame, who lives near Richmond; I have other two, who are as good as wives to me, at Calais and Boulogne; to wed a fourth, in Scotland here, were but to act King Harry over again, save that I don't shorten them by the head."

At that moment Symon Brodie, the butler, entered hastily, and whispered in the ear of his master, who exclaimed, while his nut-brown cheek grew pale,

"Fawside of that ilk has come home, say ye?"

"This morning our herdsmen on the Braehead saw him ride into the tower just as Tranent bell rang for the first mass."

"The devil!—Sayst thou so?" cried Kilmaurs, starting up. "Hath that fellow come alive again?"

"It wad seem sae, my lord," replied Symon, rubbing his half-healed sword-wound.

"Then we must have his French letters, even should we sack his house."

"Nay, sirs," said old Claude of Preston, "no such work as *that* shall be hatched here. I have had enough of the auld feud, and of Dame Alison, too—enough, and to spare. Not content with setting her husband and madcap eldest son upon me to their own skaith, she pays that auld gowk, Mass John of Tranent, to curse me daily, and consorts with witches and warlocks nightly for my destruction. Oh, 'tis a pestilent hag, this Dame Alison of Fawside!"

"A witch-carlin!" muttered the butler. "I hope some fine day to see the iron branks on her jaws."

"'Tis said she rambles about in the likeness of a brown tyke, to work evil on us," added Mungo Tennant. "If I had her once in that form, within range of my arquebuse——"

"Silence!" said the laird sternly; "the blood of her house is red enough upon my hands already!"

"Well, well. But the letters—the letters!" urged Kilmaurs impatiently; "are we to lose them?"

"If he ever had any, he must have delivered them long ere this," said Shelly.

"Under favour, sir," said Glencairn, "he left not Edinburgh (for the gate-wards are in our pay) until this day at dawn, or late last night, when one answering to his description rode through the Water-gate on a white horse. Word came tardily to the warder at the Brig of Esk; we had killed or taken him else at the Howmire."

"Let the tower of Fawside be watched narrowly," said Kilmaurs; "for these letters we must have ere we meet Arran and the Queen at Stirling, to know *their* plans as well as our own; for men should play warily who risk their heads in a game like ours, my lords."

"And now once more to the black jack, sirs," exclaimed the laird of Preston; "see to the wine-bickers, Symon, and fill—fill, while we drink thrice to the three fair brides whom this bond will soon make wedded wives—the Queen of Scots, the Countesses of Bothwell and Yarrow!"

That night the rebel lords and their retainers drank deep in Preston Tower; but tidings of an irruption of certain feudal enemies into Carrick, Kyle, and Cunninghame, giving all to fire and sword in these fertile districts, compelled Cassilis, Glencairn, Kilmaurs, and others, to depart on the spur ere mid-day; and hence it was that, as related in the preceding chapter, Florence Fawside found himself at such perfect liberty to ride daily to the city in his gayest apparel, and almost without armour, to prosecute a futile search for his fair unknown; while his fiery mother chafed and scoffed at his delay in commencing hostilities with the Hamiltons of Preston.

CHAPTER XV
THE LETTER OF THE VALOIS

Madame, I was true servant to thy mother,
    And in her favour aye stood thankfullie,
And though that I to serve be not so able
    As I was wont, because I may not see—
Yet that I hear thy people with high voice
    And joyful hearts cry continuallie—
Viva! Marie, tre noble Reyne d'Ecosse!
SIR RICHARD MAITLAND.

For seven consecutive days our hero traversed the streets of his native capital, poking his nose under the velvet hood of every lady whose figure or air resembled in any way those of his fair *innmorata*; and in these seven days he ran at least an average of eight-and-twenty risks of being run through the body for his impudence; but his handsome face, his suave apologies and brave apparel, obtained him readily the pardon of those he followed, jostled, or accosted. One evening he was just about to leave the city by the gloomy arch of the Pleasance Porte, above which grinned the skulls of those who had abetted the Master of Forbes in his wicked attempt upon the life of James V., when the booming of Mons Meg and of forty other great culverins from the castle-wall made the windows of the city shake; while the clanging bells in every church, monastery, and convent, gave out a merry peal.

He asked one who passed him, "What caused these signs of honour and acclaim?"

"The return of the Queen-Mother from Falkland," replied this person, a burgher, who was hastening from his booth, clad in his steel bonnet and jazarine jacket, with an arquebuse on his shoulder.

"The Queen-Mother!"

He paused, and, with an emotion of alarm; he remembered his dispatches from Henry of Valois to Mary of Lorraine and the Regent Arran, and resolved on the morrow to atone for his delay. As the armed citizen left him and mingled with the gathering crowd, the tone of his voice, and something in his air, brought to Fawside's memory that man of the stout arm and long axe who had so suddenly befriended him on that night, the desperate events of which seemed likely to influence the whole of his future career. Here was a key, perhaps, to the name and dwelling of his unknown beauty; but the chance was scarcely thought of ere it was gone!—already the armed stranger was lost amid the crowd that hurried up the adjacent close, to mingle, in the High Street, with the masses who greeted Mary of Lorraine with shouts of applause. She entered in the dusk, surrounded by torch-bearers and guarded by a body of mounted spearmen, led by Errol, the lord high constable of Scotland, a peer who was secretly in league with England against her. She was preceded by a long train of merchants, wearing fine black gowns of camlet, lined with silk and trimmed with velvet, according to the rule for all above ten pounds of stent; by the provost in armour, and the city officers and piper wearing doublets of Rouen canvas, and black hats with white strings, and all armed with swords, daggers, and partizans.

Arrived in the city on the morrow, Fawside rode at once to the residence of the Queen-Mother. He was well mounted, carefully accoutred, and armed to the teeth; for in those days no man knew what manner of men or adventures he might meet if he ventured a rood from his own gate.

His armour was a light suit of that species of puffed or ribbed mail which was designed as an imitation of the slashed dresses of the age. On his head was one of those steel caps known as a coursing-hat, adorned by a white feather. The mail was as bright as the hands of the first finisher in Paris (M. Fourbisser, Rue St. Jacques, armourer to the Garde du Corps Ecossais) could render it; and the cuirass was inlaid in gold, with a representation of the Crucifixion, as a charm against danger—a style introduced by Benvenuto Cellini, and named *damasquinée*; and Dame Alison, who, with a deep and deadly interest in her louring but affectionate eyes, had watched her son equipping himself and loading his petronels, sighed with anger that it was only for the city he was departing again.

"Edinburgh," she muttered; "ever and always Edinburgh! What demon lures thee there? Is it but to prance along the causeway, or flaunt before the saucy kimmers at the Butter Tron and Cramers-wives, thou goest with all this useless iron about thee?"

"Useless?" reiterated Florence with surprise.

"Yes—-useless to thee, at least!" she said, almost fiercely.

"Speak not so unkindly to me, dear mother; I am going elsewhere than to Edinburgh."

"Hah—whither?" she demanded, with some alarm.

"To the regent, on the business of the King of France; and in the wilds of the Torwood, or of Cadzow Forest, I may not find this *iron*, as you stigmatize the best of Milan plate, perhaps so useless a covering."

For the first time, the mother and son parted with coldness on her side; for the delay he exhibited in challenging Preston to mortal combat, or assaulting and sacking his farms, if not his tower, filled her angry heart with doubt and with disdain; for her long-cherished hope seemed on the eve of being dissipated.

These bitter emotions gave place to anxiety when, about nightfall, she heard news of the enemy. Roger of the Westmains hurriedly entered the hall, and, after paying his devoirs as usual to the ale-barrel, announced that, while driving a few stirks home from Gladsmuir—the fatal land of contention,—he had seen Claude Hamilton depart at the head of an armed train of at least twenty mounted men, by the road direct for Edinburgh.

"And my son is *there* alone!" was her first thought; for, in his anxiety to depart, and that he might with more freedom prosecute the search after his unknown, he had galloped westward from Fawside, without other friends than his sharp sword and his stout young arm.

"By this time—yea, long ere this," said Roger, looking at the sundial on the window-corner, "he will be far on the way to the Lord Arran's house of Cadzow, and not a horse in the barony could overtake him."

"Pray Heaven he may be so," replied the grim mother, crossing herself thrice; "he will be here to-morrow."

But many a morning dawned, and many a night came on, before she again saw her son, whose adventures we will now rehearse.

He soon ascertained that her majesty the queen-mother was at her new private residence (on the north side of the Castle-Hill Street), which, with its little oratory and guard-house, she had erected after the almost total destruction of Edinburgh by the English army in 1544. Holyrood Palace was burned on that occasion. Thus, at the time of our story, many of its southern apartments were in ruin; and hence Mary of Lorraine was compelled to find a more secure habitation within the walls of the city, and in the vicinity of the fortress, of which the gallant Sir James Hamilton of Stain-house was governor, until he was slain in a bloody tumult by the French.

Several persons, apparently of good position, were loitering near this little private palace, and to one of these—a page apparently—Fawside addressed himself; and on receiving a somewhat supercilious answer, he exclaimed angrily,—

"Quick, sirrah—announce me, for I must speak with the queen ere I ride for the lord regent's."

These words were overheard by two gentlemen richly dressed and brilliantly armed in gorgets and cuirasses of fine steel, with their swords and daggers glittering with precious stones. They were each attended by two pages, and jostled so rudely past Fawside, who had now dismounted, and held his horse by the bridle, that, had he not been amply occupied by his own thoughts, he would have called them severely to account, as an insult was never tolerated in those days.

"Bothwell!"

"Glencairn!" were the exclamations, as these worthies recognized and cautiously saluted each other.

"'Tis our man Fawside," whispered the latter; "doubtless he goes now to deliver his missives. Accursed folly that spared him; but 'tis too late now; let the queen receive hers."

"And he goeth hereafter to Arran. I heard him say so."

"He shall never pass through Cadzow Wood alive. I have a thought— stay—get me a clerk to write. Where lodges Master Patten?"

"At the upper Bow Porte—not a pistol-shot from this."

"This way, then," said Glencairn, twitching his friend's mantle; and they hurried away together, while the unfortunate Fawside, without the least idea that he was watched so narrowly, approached the Guise Palace, as it was named by the citizens.

This edifice, which was built of polished stone, was three stories in height; the access to it was by a turnpike stair, above the carved doorway of which were the cipher of the queen, "M.R.," and the pious legend, *Laus et honor Deo*, to exclude evil. On the opposite side of the narrow close was the guard-house, where a party of thirty men-at-arms, under Livingstone of Champfleurie, an esquire, all equipped by the queen, and brought from her own lands as private vassals, furnished sentinels for her modest dwelling. These men were armed with sword, dagger, and arquebuse, and bore on their doublets—which were of the royal livery of Scotland, scarlet faced with yellow—the arms of the queen-dowager, *or* bendwise *gules*, charged with the three winglets of Lorraine, and quartered with the Scottish arms,— *sol* a lion rampant within a double treasure, flory, and counter-flory, *mars*.

In those simple times, people of rank were easily accessible; thus, there was not much ceremony observed by royal personages. In a very brief space of time, Fawside found himself treading the oak floors of Mary of Lorraine's dwelling, as he was ushered by a page into a large apartment, the sombre tapestry of which was rendered yet darker by the narrow and ancient alley into which its three tall windows opened. This room was furnished with regal magnificence. The arras, which had formed a portion of the dowry of Yolande of Anjou, depicted the career of Garin the Wild Boar, who figures in the romance of "Gaharin de Lorraine." The chairs were covered with crimson velvet fringed with silver, and all bore the royal crown and cipher. The door and panelling, some of which are still preserved, were all of dark oak exquisitely carved, and in each compartment was a device, an armorial bearing, or a likeness of some member of the royal family; James V., with his pointed moustache, and bonnet smartly slouched over the right ear, being most frequently depicted. The ceiling, which is still preserved at Edinburgh, is of wood, and very singularly decorated. In the centre is the figure of our Saviour, encircled by the legend, —

Ego sum via, veritas, et vita.

In each compartment is an allegorical subject, such as the Dream of Jacob, the Vision of Death from the Apocalyse, &c., and one representing the Saviour asleep in the storm, with a view of Edinburgh, its castle and St. Giles's church in the background, His galley being afloat, *not* in the Sea of Galilee, but, curiously enough, in the centre of the North Loch.

Within a stone recess, canopied like a Gothic niche, and secured thereto by a chain of steel, stood the famous old tankard known as the *Fairy Cup* of King William the Lion.

Delrio relates, from Gulielmus Neubrigensis, that a peasant, one night, when passing near a rocky grotto, heard sounds of merriment; and on peeping in, beheld a quaint-looking company of dwarfish elves dancing and feasting. One offered him a cup to drink with them; but he poured out the bright liquor it contained, and rode off with the vessel, which was of unknown material and strange of fashion. It became the property of Henry the Elder, of England, and was presented by him to King William the Lion, of Scotland; after whom it became an heirloom of our kings,[*] and was now in the custody of Mary of Lorraine.

[*] "Discovrse of Miracles in the Catholic Chvrch." Antwerp, 1676.

Florence Fawside had barely time to observe all this, to unclasp his coursing-hat, glance at his figure in a mirror, and give that last and most satisfactory adjust to his hair, which every man and woman infallibly do previous to an interview, when the arras at the further end of the apartment was suddenly parted by the hands of two pages. Two ladies in rich dresses advanced, and our hero knew that he was in the presence of the widow of

James V. He sank upon his right knee, and bowed his head, until she desired him to rise and approach, with a welcome, to her mansion, in a voice, the tones of which stirred his inmost heart, by the emotions and recollections they awakened.

Mary of Lorraine was the sister of Francis, Duc de Guise, and widow of Louis of Orleans, Duc de Longueville, before her marriage with James V. of Scotland. She was beautiful and still young, being only in her thirty-second year. She was fair-complexioned, with a pale forehead and clear hazel eyes, which were expressive alike of intelligence, sweetness, and candour. Her red and cherub-like mouth ever wore the most charming smile; her hair was partly concealed by her lace coif; her high ruff came close round her dimpled chin; and on the breast of her puffed yellow satin dress, which was slashed with black velvet, and trimmed with black lace, sparkled a diamond cross, the farewell gift of her sister, who was prioress of the convent of St. Peter, at Rheims, in Champagne.

"Rise, monsieur—rise, sir," said she, smiling; "it seems almost strange when a gentleman kneels to me now."

"Alas, madam, that the widow of James V. should find it so in the kingdom of her daughter."

"Or a daughter of Lorraine; but so it is, sir—treason and heresy are spreading like a leprosy in the land; nor need I wonder that those decline to kneel in a palace, who refuse to do so before the altar of their God! *Mon Dieu*, M. de Fawside; but we live in strange and perilous times. You tremble, sir—are you unwell?"

Mary of Lorraine might well have asked this, for Florence grew pale, and tottered, so that he was compelled to grasp a chair for support, when, in the queen who addressed him, and in the lady her attendant, who remained a few paces behind, holding a feather fan partly before her face, he recognized those who had tended, nursed, and cured him of his wounds—she of the hazel, and she of the dark-blue eyes:

To the beautiful queen, and her still more beautiful friend and *dame d'honneur*, he was already as well known as if he had been the brother of both. In this bewilderment he gazed from one pair of charming eyes to the other, and played with the plume in his coursing-hat, utterly unable to speak; till the queen laughed merrily, and said,—

"Monsieur is most welcome to my poor house in l'Islebourg,"—for so the French named Edinburgh, from the number of lakes which surrounded its castle; "so our little romance is at an end—monsieur recognizes us, Madeline—all is discovered!"

"Madeline!" whispered Florence in his heart; "that name shall ever be a spell to me."

"Well, Laird of Fawside—so you have business with us. But first, I pray you, be seated, sir; your wounds cannot be entirely healed. I remember me, they were terrible!"

"Ah, madam!" said he, in a voice to which the fulness of his heart imparted a charming earnestness and richness of tone, as he again knelt down, "how shall I ever repay the honour you have already done me? The services of a life—a life of faith and gratitude—were indeed too little. But whence, came all this mystery?"

"For reasons which I disdain to acknowledge almost to myself," said the queen, with an inexplicable smile, which, whatever it meant, prevented the bewildered young man from saying more.

This royal lady seemed never to forget her lofty position when among those whom she knew to be the most uncompromising of the Scottish peers;—every graceful gesture, every proud glance of her clear and beautiful eyes, seemed to say,—

"I am Mary of Guise—Lorraine, Queen of Scotland! I cannot forget that I am the widow of James V., and the mother of Mary Queen of Scots."

But a gracious condescension, with a sweet gentleness of manner, to those whom she loved and trusted, made her wear a very different expression at times, and imparted to her features that alluring loveliness which, with her sorrows, became the dangerous inheritance of her daughter.

Like that unhappy daughter, her tastes were refined and exquisite; she was as passionately fond of music and poetry as the late king her husband, and maintained a foreign band of musicians and vocalists. Among the latter were five Italians, each of whom received from her privy purse thirteen pounds yearly, with a red bonnet and livery coat of yellow Bruges satin, trimmed and slashed with red,—the royal colours. M. Antoine (our pretended dumb valet), a Parisian, and her most trusted attendant, was master of this band, which included four violers, four trumpeters, two tabourners, and several Swiss drummers.

Danger, and the desperate game of politics as played by the Scottish noblesse, compelled this fair widow to use her beauty as a means of strengthening herself. Thus she pretended to receive the addresses of Lennox, Argyle, and Bothwell, luring them all to love her, while she deceived them all with hopes of a marriage, to gain time, till armed succour reached her court from France. She was fond of card-playing, and frequently lost a hundred crowns of the sun at one sitting to Bothwell, to Arran, and other peers; and now the former, filled with rage on discovering the emptiness of his hopes, had joined the faction of Somerset, who flattered his spirit of revenge and cupidity to the full by offering him the hand and fortune of the beautiful Katharine Willoughby.

His half-mad love for Mary of Lorraine was well known in Scotland, where, after his return from Venice, it prompted him to commit a thousand extravagances. It is yet remembered how, when sheathed in full armour, he galloped his barbed charger down the steep face of the Calton Hill, and made it leap, like another Pegasus, the barriers of the tilting-ground, that he might appear to advantage before her and the ladies of her court, when patronizing a great tournament near the old Carmelite monastery of Greenside.

But amid these historical details, which, as the Scots read all histories but their own, will no doubt be new to them, we are forgetting the bewildered young gentleman, who has just kissed the white jewelled hand of Mary of Lorraine, and risen to his feet by her command.

"And now, fair sir, that you have discovered us, you are no doubt come to proffer us your thanks for being your leeches and nurses," said the queen, laughing; "but we must insist upon sparing you all that; for, be assured, sir, we were performing but an act of simple Christian charity."

"I swear to your majesty, that until this moment I knew not who had so honoured me with protection and hospitality. I came but to place in your hands a paper——"

"Monsieur!"

"A paper, the possession, or supposed possession, of which, on the night that first brought me here, so nearly cost me my life; though by what means those ruffians guessed I was intrusted with it, I know not."

"'Tis a notice of some conspiracy, perhaps?"

"Nay—'tis a letter from his majesty the King of France."

"A letter from the Valois!" reiterated Mary, starting, while her eyes flashed with expectation.

"From Henry II.," replied the youth; and, drawing from his doublet the missive of the Most Christian king, he knelt again on presenting it to Mary of Lorraine.

"Thanks, sir, thanks. How droll, to think that I might have had this letter weeks ago, but for our little romance," she said merrily, while her hazel eyes seemed to dance in light, as she cut open the ribands by the scissors which hung at her gold chatelaine. She hastily read over the letter, the envelope of which, was spotted by the bearer's blood.

"If it please your grace—the news?" said the young lady, her attendant, in a soft voice.

"Countess, approach!" said the queen.

"She's a countess!" said Fawside inaudibly, and his heart sank at the discovery.

"'Tis brave news," exclaimed the queen with a tone of triumph; "Henry of Valois promises me succour; so my daughter shall never wed the son of English Henry—the offspring of a wretch who lived unsated with lust and blood, who put to death seventy-two thousand of his people, and who died at enmity with God and man. Read, Madeline, *ma belle! ma, bonne!* —read for yourself."

The lady read the letter, and presented it to the queen, who, ere she could speak, turned to Florence, saying,—

"Sir, as a faithful subject and true Scottish gentleman, it is but polite and just that you should know the contents of a letter with which you have been intrusted, and the defence of which has cost you so dear. But I rely on your honour—be secret and wary. Our schemes are great, for we are opposed to powerful and subtle schemers."

"Oh, madam, who would not die for your majesty?" exclaimed Florence in a burst of enthusiasm; for the beauty and condescension of the queen filled his soul with joy and pride, kindling within it a fervour which he had never known before.

The letter of Henry II. ran thus:—

"*Madame ma Soeur, la Reine d'Ecosse:*

"None in our kingdom of France can be better satisfied than we are with the good-will you have shown in the cause of our holy faith and common country; and knowing well the great need you have of assistance to further the great project of uniting our dear son the Dauphin to our kinswoman, your royal daughter the Queen of Scotland—to crush treason within and enemies without her realm, and ultimately to make you what you ought to be, Regent thereof, a portion of our valiant French army, veterans of the war in Italy, under wise and skilful captains, shall ere long land upon your shores. We would beseech you to keep in memory our notable plan of stirring up Ireland against the government of Edward VI., by supplying the O'Connors with arms, and proposing your young queen as a wife to Gerald, the youthful Earl of Kildare, to lure him to revolt against the aggressive English; though ere long the Sieur de Brezé, hereditary grand seneschal of Normandy, and M. le Chevalier de Villegaignon, admiral of our galleys, will be in the Scottish seas to convey her to France, of which—when I am borne by my faithful Scottish archers to my fathers' tomb at St. Denis—she shall be queen. Beseeching our Lord to give you, madame my sister, good health, a long life, and all you desire, we remain, your good brother,

"*From St. Germain-en-Laye*, "HENRI R.
"10 *April*, 1547."

"With ten thousand good French soldiers, united to the vassals of Huntley and other loyal peers, I shall be able alike to defy the power of England, of Arran, whom Somerset seeks to corrupt, and of those false Scots whom we have no doubt he has already corrupted," said the queen. "I must write at once to Arran, though he suspects me of aiming at the regency. A queen, a mother—I shall triumph! I will teach those rebel peers that Mary of Lorraine will struggle rather than stoop, and perish rather than yield! Champfleurie!—where is M. Champfleurie?"

"He is with the guard, madam," said the countess. "Shall I send for him?"

Now Livingstone of Champfleurie was a West-Lothian laird, who enjoyed the reputation of being one of the handsomest, but at the same time most dissipated men in Scotland; and on hearing him spoken of by the beautiful young countess, Florence experienced an unaccountable uneasiness; so he said hastily,—

"Madam, will you intrust me with your letter? I am on my way to the lord regent at Cadzow."

"A thousand thanks, sir; you shall be its bearer. And pray accept from me this chain in memory of your good service."

With these words, Mary of Lorraine, with an air of exquisite grace, took from her slender neck a chain of fine gold—the same chain which René II. of Lorraine wore in his famous battle with Charles the Bold,—and threw it over the bowed head of Florence.

"And you were presented to King Henry?" she asked.

"In the gallery of the Louvre, madam."

"By whom?"

"The Lord James Hamilton, captain of the archers of the Scottish Guard; and by M. le Comte d'Anguien."

"Ah! that brave old soldier, with his face of bronze and heart of steel! He is still alive?"

"Alive, and hale and well, madam; and most likely will command the troops destined for Scotland."

"The victor of Cerizoles, the conqueror of the Marquis del Vasto in Piedmont. And who else is to lead the troops that succour me?"

"M. le Comte de Martigues, say some; M. d'Essé d'Epainvilliers, say others."

"A brave soldier is d'Essé. According to the astrologer of Francis I., Mars was the shining lord of his nativity. Thus it was his destiny to lead the armies of France."

"Ah, madam," said the young countess, "is not this heathenish, like the preaching of the Lollards?"

"Of course; yet it was believed at the court of the Most Christian King. And what say they of our lord regent in France?"

"That he is true to French and Scottish interests, and hostile to the English alliance."

"That I well believe; but truer to his own interests than either."

"But they suspect him of wishing to secure the entire power of the kingdom, so that ere long Scotland may be governed by Hamiltons and nothing but Hamiltons; for already they hold the archbishopric of St. Andrew's and other sees; they govern half the royal castles, and hold priories and abbeys innumerable."

"That I know too well," said Mary, curling her proud red lip.

"And that, while printing the Bible in the Scottish tongue, and thus defying the bishops and disseminating heresy in Scotland, at Rome he seeks a cardinal's hat for his brother John, the archbishop of St. Andrew's."

"So—so; he would keep well with his Holiness there and well with the Lollards here! Has he yet to be taught that a man cannot serve two masters? Mon Dieu! poor M. l'Archevêque de Saint André should consider well what he seeks. Since Kirkaldy of Grange and the Melvilles slew David Beaton, the red barretta is a perilous cap for a Scot to wear. But when do you ride for Cadzow Castle?"

"The moment I am honoured with the missive of your majesty."

"That you shall shortly be, sir," replied Mary, sweeping up her train with one hand, while she joyously waved the other. "Oh, 'tis brave news this, of succour from France! I shall crush these traitors at last, and defy this insolent duke of Somerset. Dares he think that Mary of Scotland and Lorraine would peril her daughter's soul for his kingdom of England, with its lordship of Ireland to boot? Queen of Scotland she is, and queen of France and Navarre she shall be! I would rather don armour and die in the field by the side of d'Essé than yield up my child to the paid traitors of Henry VIII. and his successor, this boasting duke of Somerset. A queen, a mother, a woman, I shall appeal to all the gentlemen of Scotland; and if they fail me, I have still the noble chivalry of France!"

As the queen spoke, with a gesture of inimitable grace she withdrew through the arras, leaving Florence and the young countess together.

CHAPTER XVI
THE COUNTESS

Thy voice—oh, sweet to me it seems,
  And charms my raptured breast;
Like music on the moonlit sea,
  When waves are lull'd to rest.
The wealth of worlds were vain to give,
  Thy sinless heart to buy;
Oh, I will bless thee while I live,
  And love thee till I die.

Delta.

The young man was pale, mortified, and sick at heart; for the sudden discovery of the exalted rank of one whom he had learned to think his friend, and of the other whom he fondly believed to love him, made him lose all hope at once. He stood silent and embarrassed; but he remembered the opal ring, and gathering courage with that memory, he turned his eyes on the beautiful donor.

They filled with the soft light of love and tenderness as he gazed upon her. She caught, perhaps, the magnetic infection from his glance, for her long lashes drooped and a flush crossed her cheek; so from her confusion he gathered courage.

"Lady—Lady Madeline,—you see I have learned your name," began Florence, who knew not what to say.

"Well, sir, I am glad you have spoken; for our pause, to say the least of it, was very embarrassing," replied the young lady, playing with the point lace which edged the sleeve of her dress.

"If you will permit me, I have a question to ask."

"Say on," said she, laughing.

"What was the origin, or whence the purpose, of that strange mystery in which you enveloped me when I had lost the happiness of being here? Why did you conceal from me your rank—your name? and why was I conducted hence blindfold, like a spy from an enemy's camp?"

"Fair sir," said the countess, smiling, "I gave you permission to ask but one question; you have already run over four."

"And I implore you to answer me."

"All was done by order of her majesty the queen."

"But wherefore such foolish mystery?" asked Florence almost impetuously.

"Foolish!" reiterated the other, holding up a taper finger. "Oh, fie!—Said I not it was the queen's desire?"

"Pardon me; but I cannot resist emotions of mortification and deep sorrow."

"The queen-mother has many enemies in Scotland," said the countess, with a pretty little blush,—"Lollard preachers and disaffected peers, men who live by trafficking in court scandal and the circulation of wicked rumours: thus seeking to undermine her influence and to do her evil among the people. Do you understand me?"

"Under favour, I do not."

"Had these men, or such as these, known that a gentleman of your age and appearance was wounded or slain under her windows, all Scotland had declared him to be a lover, attacked by a rival or by the queen's guard; and, believe me, the spies of Somerset and the adherents of Bothwell and Lennox would readily multiply the fatal rumour. Had they learned that a poor wounded youth whom she had rescued from destruction was concealed in her chamber for many days, then still more had he been reputed a lover, and a man devoted to die a cruel death. Do you understand me now?"

"Oh, yes; and feel deeply her most generous clemency, which perilled her reputation for me."

"Mary of Guise and Lorraine was not reared at the court of Catharine de Medicis, nor was she wife of Louis de Longueville, without acquiring the virtues of patience and prudence," said the lady, smiling.

"But you, lady—you, at least, had no such reason for concealment."

"My secret involved that of my mistress; moreover, I had most serious reasons for greater secrecy."

"A jealous husband, perhaps?"

"Nay," said she, laughing, and showing the most beautiful little teeth in the world; "thank Heaven, I have no husband."

Florence began to breathe a little more freely.

"A lover, perhaps?" said he, affecting to smile.

"Nay, nor even a lover."

"St. Giles!—in what did your secrecy originate?"

"In yourself."

"You are a beautiful enigma," faltered Florence, taking her hands in his, while his heart trembled; "but—but whatever be the result of such an avowal, believe me from my soul when I say, that I had not been here three days before I learned to love you, Lady Madeline—love you dearly, fondly, truly!" he continued, in an almost breathless voice.

She grew very pale, abruptly withdrew her hands, and averted her face; for she felt that the voice of Fawside, like the voices of all who have a sincere and impassioned heart, had a powerful effect upon her.

"Speak to me—speak!" he urged; "do not, for pity's sake, look so coldly, or turn from me."

"I do not look coldly; but spare me the pain of hearing this avowal," she replied, while trembling.

"Spare you the pain—oh, Madeline! my love for you——"

"Is futile," she replied, with her eyes full of tears.

"Futile!"

"Yes."

"Why—oh, what mean you, Madeline? Who are you, that it should be so?"

"I am—I am——"

"Who—who?"

"One whom you must ever know for your deadly enemy," she replied, in a voice half-stifled by emotion.

Had a bomb exploded at the feet of Florence, he could not have been more astounded than by this strange relation.

"She is a kinswoman of Glencairn or Kilmaurs," thought he; "well, I can forgive her even that."

For a minute he was silent, as if overwhelmed by sadness and astonishment. At last he said,—

"My enemy—you?"

"By the solemn truth which I tell you, by the words I have said, we are separated for ever!"

"For the love of pity, say not so, I implore you!"

"What I say can matter little," she replied in a low broken voice; "I do love you, dear Florence; but our fate is in the hands of others."

"Others!" he exclaimed impetuously.

"Yes."

"What can control us, who are free agents?"

"Fatality. Thus our paths in life, like our graves in death, must lie far apart. But never, while breath remains, shall I forget you, Florence!"

"Oh, 'tis insanity or a dream this!" he exclaimed, and struck his forehead with a bewildered air; and, after bowing his face upon her hand, had barely time, to withdraw, when the heavy folds of the arras parted again, and the queen-mother stood before him, with a letter in her hand, and a smile almost of drollery on her beautiful lip; for she saw plainly, in the confusion of both, that a scene had taken place.

"You will convey this to my lord regent. It tells that I will meet him at the Convention of Estates in Stirling."

"Thanks for this high honour, madam," said Florence, kneeling for the double purpose of kissing the seal of the missive and veiling the deep colour which he felt was too evident in his face.

"And now, sir, ere you go, I shall have the pleasure of presenting you to the Queen of Scotland. I trust her majesty's noonday nap is over by this time."

The young man felt his eyes and heart fill at these words, for the loyalty of the olden time was a passion, strong and enthusiastic as that of a lover for his love.

Mary of Lorraine, with her white hand, drew back the tapestry, and revealed the inner apartment, the walls of which were hung with yellow Spanish leather stamped with crowns and thistles, and the oak floor of which was covered by what was then a very unusual luxury—a Persian carpet. Passing in, Florence found himself in the royal nursery.

In a cradle of oak, profusely carved, and having a little canopy surmounted by a crown, lay a child—a little white-skinned and golden-haired girl, in her fifth year, asleep, with her dark lashes reposing on a cheek that bore the pink tint we see at times in a white rose-leaf.

This child was Mary Queen of Scots!

The nurse, Janet Sinclair, wife of John Kemp, a burgess of Haddington, arose at their entrance.

The young man knelt down, and, with reverence and affection, pressed his lips to the child's dimpled hands, which were folded together above its little lace coverlet. The emotions of his heart would be difficult alike to analyze or portray.

How little could those four persons who stood by the cradle of that beloved and beautiful little one, foresee the dark shadows which enveloped her future!

"The little bride of the son of France!" said Mary of Lorraine; "she sleeps, alike oblivious of crowns and kingdoms."

At that moment the child opened her dark-grey eyes, and smiled to her mother.

"If this should be, how strange shall be her destiny!" said the countess thoughtfully.

"How?" reiterated the queen-mother anxiously.

"Yes—for what said True Thomas of Ercildoun more than three hundred years ago?"

"What said he?"

Then the countess replied,—

> "A queen of France shall bear a son,
>   Britain to brook from sea to sea;
> And she of Bruce's blood shall come,
>   As near as to the ninth degree."

"I pray that Heaven may so shape out the future that your verse shall prove better than an idle rhyme," said Mary of Lorraine, clasping her delicate hands; "for the royal child of my dead husband is the *ninth* in descent from the hero of Bannockburn."

Future events, in the birth of James VI., fulfilled this old prophecy, which, in the days of our story, was in the mouths of all the people.

"And now, until I have the honour of again paying my devotion to your majesty, perhaps at Stirling, farewell," said Fawside.

"Adieu, monsieur—may God keep you!"

A glance full of sad meaning from the countess was all the adieu he received from her; and next moment he found himself in the narrow alley, where a soldier in the livery of the queen's guard held his grey horse by its bridle.

CHAPTER XVII
A SNARE

Oh what a tangled web we weave,
When first we practise to deceive.

Scott.

In a preceding chapter we left two right honourable lords—to wit, the earls of Bothwell and Glencairn—in search of Master Patten, the scribe or secretary to Edward Shelly, the captain of the Boulogners. These gentlemen, as supposed followers of the house of Glencairn, resided in a quaint old-fashioned stone house, then known as Cunninghame's Land, which had been galleried and fronted with timber in the time of James IV. It was situated above the Upper Bow Porte, and there they were found readily enough by the two nobles, who had free entrance at all times. On this occasion, however, the earls, on coming in, hurriedly and unannounced, found the Englishmen seated at a table, immersed among letters, dockets of papers, maps, and manuscripts: they were both busy writing. Glencairn, who had a supreme contempt for such work, gave a hasty and impatient glance at Bothwell, whose only literary efforts had been to make his mark or fix his seal to a notary's deed; for, like Bell-the-Cat, of whom we read in "Marmion," or his majesty King Cole of the popular ditty, this untutored lord

"Quite scorn'd the fetters of four-and-twenty letters,
And it saved him a *vast deal of trouble.*"

On their abrupt entrance, Patten and Shelly started in alarm from their work. The former spread his hands over the papers, as if to protect them; but the valiant captain of the Boulogners drew his sword, with the first instinct of a soldier, to protect his compatriot and himself.

"Uds daggers! what new plot art thou hatching, worthy scribe, to put men's weasons in peril?" asked Glencairn; "how many human souls are bartered in these piles of scribbled paper—eh?"

"Up with thy sword, Master Shelly," said Bothwell, laughing, and twisting up his large black moustache. "Did you think we were the provost halberds or the queen's guard come to arrest you?"

"Either had found me ready, my lord. But I knew not what to think," replied Shelly with some displeasure, as he dropped his long straight sword into its scabbard, swept the papers into a drawer, and locked it. "Master Patten and I were deeply engaged——"

"Plotting—eh?"

"Nay, my Lord of Bothwell; I have had enough of that," replied the soldier coldly. "We were simply reducing the bulk of our correspondence to suit the compass of our cloak-bags, committing some papers to the flames, and selecting others for conveyance to England, for whither we set out——"

"Not before the convention at Stirling, I hope?"

"No."

"When?"

"Immediately after. Our work will then be completed, for peace or for war—for good or for evil."

"But time presses, and our man is not yet gone," said Glencairn, glancing anxiously from the window.

"What would your lordships with us?" asked Shelly; "and to what do we owe the honour of this visit?"

"To our lack of skill in the perilous art of clerking like worthy Master Patten," replied Glencairn.

"And to our zeal in the young king your master's service," added Bothwell, with his quiet mocking smile.

"To the point, my lords!" said Shelly haughtily, while he drew tighter, by a hole or two, the silver buckle of his sword-belt.

"Florence Fawside, the French envoy, spy, or what you will, is even now with Mary of Lorraine!"

"Art sure of this?" asked Shelly in a low voice, full of interest, as he gazed through the barred window.

"Sure as my name is Patrick Hepburn, Earl of Bothwell; we both saw him enter her residence; and a soldier of her guard holds the bridle of his grey horse at the door—a soldier, who says he departs thereafter for Cadzow—dost thou see, *for Cadzow!*"

"To the lord regent. This must not be!" said Master Patten, starting up.

"Let us follow and cut him off—'tis the simplest plan," said Shelly.

"Nay—nay!"

"Why, thou, Bothwell, art not wont to be wary!"

"Our trains are scattered abroad throughout the city, and if we fared ill——"

"Four to one?"

"He might still cut his way through us; and, if once he reaches Arran, with promises of French succour, the Hamiltons in the west and Huntly in the north will take the field at once against all malcontents: thus, the sooner we begin our *Miserere mei Dominus*, and commit our neckverse to memory, the better."

"If a long sword will not keep me from having a long neck, or my head from rolling among the sawdust, I shall e'en submit; I were not my father's son else!" said the grim Earl of Glencairn, frowning till his black eyebrows met over his fierce nose.

"But what can I do in this matter, my lords?" asked Shelly with impatience.

"Simply this. Desire Master Patten to write, with all speed, a note to a friend of mine. This note Champfleurie, captain of the queen's guard, a gentleman in our interest, will prevail upon Fawside to deliver, as he rides westward, to a friend of mine, mark you; and this friend will place him in sure ward till we arrive. Then, after investigating his cloak-bags and pockets to our hearts' content, if we do not find what will satisfy us, we can roast him over the potcruicks and baste him well with grease till his tongue tells us all he knows of the Guises and their desperate game."

"Agreed!" said Shelly, with a disdainful smile. "And this friend——"

"Is Allan Duthie, laird of Millheugh, whose tower, a strong but sequestered place, standeth near the highway that leads through Cadzow Forest. Quick!—indite me this note. We have no time to lose, for every moment I expect to see him come forth and betake him to horse, and then our plot will fail."

Patten with great deliberation selected a sheet of the coarse brown-tinted paper then used, and dipping his quill in the ink-horn, wrote to Bothwell's dictation the following note:—

"RIGHT TRUSTY FRIEND,—I greet you well and heartillie. It will be for the furtherance of our great cause if the bearer hereof, a spy of the Guises, who is on his way to Cadzow, be detained at your house until such time as I and my friends arrive. These with my hand at the pen,

"BOITHWELLE."

"For the Right Hon. the Laird of Millheugh. *These*."

"Can your friend read?" asked Shelly.

"Like Duns Scotus himself," replied Bothwell; adding, "Master Patten, I thank you. When I am the husband of Katharine Willoughby, I will requite this and other services as they deserve. And now for our messenger, who must receive this from the hand of Champfleurie to lull all suspicion."

"Fawside is quite unsuspecting," said Glencairn.

"And therefore, the more open to guile and to attack, poor fellow!" added Shelly with some commiseration, though not much afflicted with tender scruples at any time.

CHAPTER XVIII
THE DEATH-ERRAND

My lord hath sent you this note; and by me this farther charge, that you swerve not from the smallest article of it, neither in time, matter, or circumstance.—*Measure for Measure.*

Florence, with his heart beating wildly, from the conflicting revelations of his late interview, had placed his foot in the silver stirrup of his saddle, and was in the act of grasping his horse's flowing mane preparatory to mounting, when a gauntleted hand was laid bluntly on his shoulder, and on turning he met the dark and handsome, but somewhat crafty, face of John Livingstone of Champfleurie, captain of the queen's guard, a man who had been long enough about courts and among Scottish and French courtiers to acquire the habit of veiling every emotion of life under a bland and well-bred smile, from which nothing could be gathered. Though faithful enough to the queen, as faith went at court, he was also disposed to be not unfriendly to his kinsman the Earl of Bothwell, and, heedless whether the missive given him by the latter purported good or evil to the bearer, he undertook that Fawside should deliver it. It was a favourite proverb of this time-serving soldier, "as long as one is in the fox's service, one must bear up his tail."

"Under favour," said he, "I would speak with you, laird."

"Then speak quickly, for I am in haste," replied the young man, gathering up his reins.

"Pardon me, sir, but 'tis said that a traveller should carry two bags,—one of patience and one of crowns."

"I carry neither; so to the point, sir."

"I believe I have the honour of being known to you."

"Yes; John Livingstone of Champfleurie, captain of the queen's guard," replied Florence, bowing.

"'Tis said you ride westward."

"True. But how know you that?"

"My sentinels overheard it from the pages of the queen."

"Well?"

"Pass you by the tower of Millheugh, in Cadzow Wood?"

"Perhaps; but the country thereabout is strange and new to me," said Florence impatiently.

"There are wild bulls, broken men, sloughs, pitfalls, and swamps in plenty. But will you do a fair lady of the court a favour?"

"That will I blithely," replied Fawside, whose heart beat quicker at the request.

"She is in sore trouble, and lacks a messenger to her kinsman, the laird of Millheugh. As you pass his tower, will you please to deliver this little letter, and tarry a moment to refresh?"

"And the lady?—her name?—who is she?"

"Inquire not, as a gallant man."

"Mystery again!" thought Florence, as he took the note, and his mind immediately reverted to the lady he had just left.

Who was this fair woman, so beautiful, so graceful, so gentle in breeding and manner, that avowed herself his enemy, and yet admitted that she loved him; who gave him an opal ring in token of that love, and yet repelled further advances; and who now, he fondly believed, intrusted him with a letter?

"Champfleurie," said he, "I presume you know all the great people about the queen-mother's court?"

"Ay, from the great Earl of Huntly down to yonder little foot-page, who is clanking his spurs at the Close-head; for your court page is a great man too."

"Then pray tell me who are the queen's ladies?"

The captain smiled; for, if court scandal could be trusted, he stood high in favour with more than one of them; so he said evasively,—

"You seek to discover of whose letter you are bearer?"

"Nay, on my honour I do not!"

"Her ladies?" queried the cunning captain, pausing for a reply.

"Yes, what countesses has she about her?"

"There are the countesses of Huntly, Monteith, Mar, and Crawford."

"Pshaw! all these are old, or well up in years."

"Well, I said not otherwise," replied the arquebusier, laughing.

"The young and beautiful?"

"Are Errol, Orkney, and Argyle."

"Nay, 'tis none of these I ask for. I am assured, Laird of Champfleurie, that you are a most discreet man; but fare you well, sir—so now for Cadzow ho!" and putting his Ripon spurs to his impatient horse, he rode hastily off.

Champfleurie looked after the fated young man, who trotted his grey charger through the time-blackened arch of the Upper Bow Porte, and disappeared down the winding descent of the ancient street which lay beyond, and athwart the picturesque mansions of which the meridian sun was pouring its broad flakes of hazy light, that varied its mass of shadows.

"Poor fool!" said the captain of the guard with his crafty smile; "he rides on his *death-errand*."

The dawn of the next day was breaking, when a mounted man reined up his horse at the turnpike-stair, which gave access to a quaint tenement on the Castle-hill, known as the *Bothwell Lodging* (not far from where Master Posset's dried aligator swung daily in the wind), and demanded, at once to see his lordship on business of importance. In a scarlet gown trimmed with black fur, under which he carried his unsheathed dagger as a safeguard, the earl, who had just sprung from bed, appeared in his chamber of dais before the messenger, who was a rough and weather-beaten fellow, in a morion and plated jack, and who seemed half-trooper, half-brigand, and wholly desperado.

"Well, varlet," said the earl angrily, "you rouse us betimes! What the devil is astir? Have the English taken my castle of Hermitage, or are the Lord Clinton's war-ships off Dunbar Sands—eh?"

"Neither, lord earl," replied the man, in a strong Clydesdale accent; "I hae come in frae the west country, and been in my stirrups since twa past midnight."

"From Millheugh?"

"Direct."

"The spy— —"

"Bound hand and foot, is safely lodged in Millheugh Tower, where the laird bade me say he shall bide in sure ward until ye come west; or if ye wished it, he would bind him to the pot-cruicks ower the low in the kitchen, and smeik his secret out o' him by dint o' green-wood boughs, and wet bog peats."

"Right—I shall reward him for this, and thee too," said the earl, with fierce triumph. "Thank St. Bryde of Bothwell, or the devil more likely, we have nailed this knavish messenger at last. Get thee a horn of Flemish wine, my man, a fresh horse, and order all my train; I shall ride for Millheugh, and leave the West Porte behind me, ere the sun be up!"

Bothwell made such expedition, that in reality, ere the sun rose above Arthur's Seat, he and Glencairn, with Millheugh's messenger and a train of twenty well-armed horsemen, had galloped through the western gate of the city, skirted the hill of Craiglockart, the ancient manors of Meggatland and Red Hall, and taken the old Lanark road, direct to the country of the Hamiltons.

Meanwhile, let us see how fared it with the solitary messenger of Mary of Lorraine.

CHAPTER XIX
CADZOW FOREST

Mightiest of the beasts of chase,
    That roam in woody Caledon,
Crashing the forest in his race,
    The mountain bull comes thundering on!

Scott.

The evening of the day on which he left the metropolis was closing, when, after a ride of many miles, Florence found himself, with a sorely jaded horse, on the borders of the ancient forest of Cadzow, in that district which was named of old Machinshire, from the chapel of St. Machin.

The nature of the roads, which in those days were mere bridle-paths, narrow, rough, and stony, being carried straight over hill and through valley, irrespective of all local obstacles, and were rendered dangerous by the uncultivated morasses and lonely wastes they traversed, and by the fords or deep and bridgeless torrents which intersected them—the nature of such paths for travelling from Lothian to Lanarkshire, had impaired the energies of the fine charger which had been the gift of Mary of Lorraine; and, in a wild and solitary place, near which no dwelling could be perceived, and where, on all sides, nothing was visible but the great gnarled stems of the oak forest, Florence dismounted, just as the solemn gloaming drew on; and while his foam-flaked horse cropped the herbage that grew deep and rich under the shade of the trees, he sat down for a time, to consider in which direction he should seek the Tower of Millheugh, where he was to deliver the pretended court lady's letter, and wherein he mentally proposed to remain until the morrow, when he could choose a more fitting time to appear before the Regent of Scotland, one of whose country residences, the Castle of Cadzow, was but a few miles distant.

At this time the town habitation of the Hamilton family was in the Kirk-of-field Wynd at Edinburgh, a steep, narrow, and ancient street, the name of which has since been changed.

A sensation of lassitude came upon Florence, who felt weary after his long and rough ride; and as the red flush of the August sun faded away behind the purple hills, and its warm tints grew cold on the rugged stems and crisping leaves of the Druid oaks of Cadzow, his mind became impressed by the sylvan beauty and intense solitude of the scenery, and reverted to those whose faces he had that morning left behind him; and, like all who have travelled, far and rapidly, he felt the difficulty of realizing the extent of distance that actually lay between him and them. With the last light of evening lingering on his glittering coat of mail, and the bridle of his white horse drooping over his right arm, he sat under a shady oak, like a knight errant of old, waiting for adventures; but though witches and fairies remained in Scotland, the age of giants and dwarfs and genii had passed away.

He thought of his mother, pale, austere, and reproachful; loving him well, fondly,—yea, madly,—and yet, withal, so ready to peril his life in maintaining her old hereditary feud, in the fulfilment of her savage vow, and for the gratification of her morbid vengeance—a life which might yet be useful to her queen and country—a young life, which the possessor of it had suddenly found to be invested with a new charm, a hitherto unknown value; and here, drawing off his long glove, he gazed on the opal ring of Madeline—Madeline *who*?

"Oh, perplexity!" he exclaimed; "'tis a romance with which our coquettish French queen is amusing herself, and of which she wishes to make me and this beloved girl the hero and heroine."

And, sunk in one of those reveries so natural to a lover, when he seems to talk to, and have responses from, the object beloved; when a thousand things are said that were omitted when last with her,—for when the heart is full, thoughts come quicker than language, Fawside remained in the twilight and in the forest, with the gloaming deepening around him, heedless alike of the outlaws who were averred to make their haunt there, and of the ferocious white bulls (*Bos sylvestris*), the famous red-eyed, black-horned, black-hoofed, and snowy-maned mountain bison of old Caledonia, herds of which have frequented the Forest of Cadzow from pre-historic days, long anterior to the Roman invasion, down to the present time.

On every hand spread the vast wilderness of oaks, some of which still measure twenty-five and twenty-eight feet in circumference, and are of an antiquity so great that they must have witnessed the rites of the Druids; being the last remains of that immense forest which anciently covered all the south of Scotland, from the waves of the Atlantic to those of the German Ocean.

In the wildest part of this wild wood—the Caledonia Sylva—stood the tower of Allan Duthie of Millheugh, in a little dell near a ruined and mossgrown mill, the fragments of which were overshadowed by an oak of stupendous dimensions, known as King Malcolm's Tree, from the following little legend, which (as we dearly love all that pertained to Scotland "in the brave days of old") we will take the liberty of inserting here.

A few years after the fall of Macbeth and the destruction of his castle of Dunsinane, Queen Margaret, Evan, the chancellor and Christian bishop of Galloway, revealed to King Malcolm III. a design which Duthac, one of his thanes, on whom he had bestowed many favours, had formed against his life, and which he resolved to put in execution as soon as he came to court.

"Be silent," said the king, "and leave me to deal with this matter in my own way."

Ere long, the accused noble came to court with a numerous train of half-savage warriors, barelegged and barearmed, from the wilds of Galloway, and on the day thereafter, Malcolm, who was residing in the Castle of Stirling, proclaimed a great hunting-match, and set forth for Cadzow Forest to hunt the mountain bull. In the most secluded part of the wood, he contrived to separate Duthac from the rest of the royal party, and drawing him into a gloomy little dell, under the shadow of a mighty oak, he leaped from his saddle and said,—

"Thane, dismount!"

Duthac at once alighted from his saddle, which, like his bridle, was hung with little silver bells.

"Draw!" said the king sternly; but Duthac hesitated.

"Draw, lest I kill thee, by the holy St. Kessoge!—kill thee defenceless!" exclaimed the brave king, unsheathing his long cross-hilted and double-edged broadsword, which was of a fashion then, and for long after, worn by the Scots, and the guards of which were turned down for the purpose of locking in and breaking an adversary's blade.

Duthac grew pale on hearing the vow of Malcolm; for St. Kessoge was then in great repute, so much so that in the sixth century his name was the war-cry of the Scots and Irish. Casting on the ground his green hunting-mantle, which had been embroidered by the white hands of his Saxon queen, St. Margaret, the king exclaimed,—

"Thane!—behold, we are here alone, and armed alike, with none to give one aid against the other. No ear can hear, nor eye can see us, save those of God! If you are still the brave man you have approved yourself in battle against the English and the Normans, and have the courage to essay your secret purpose, attempt it now! If you deem me deserving of death, where can you deal it better, more manfully, or more opportunely, than *here*, in this secluded forest? You linger—you falter—*you*, Duthac the Thane! Hast thou prepared a poison for me?" demanded the king, with increasing energy;—"that were the treason of a woman. Wouldst thou murder me in my sleep, as Malcolm II. was slain at Glammis?—an adultress might do that. Hast thou a hidden dagger, to stab me in secret?—'twere the deed of a coward and slave; and, Duthac, I hold thee to be neither. Fight me here, hand to hand, like a soldier—like a true Scottish man, that your treason at least may be freed from a baseness that will consign you and your race to future infamy!"

Struck to the soul by this valiant and magnanimous spirit, Duthac presented his sword-hilt to Malcolm, and, kneeling before him (as Mathew Paris relates), implored pardon.

"Fear nothing, Thane," said Malcolm III., taking his hand; "for, by the Black Rood of Scotland, thou shalt suffer no evil from me. Henceforward we are comrades—we are friends, as in other days we were soothfast fellow-soldiers."

From that hour Duthac became a most faithful subject. He received from Malcolm the land whereon they stood, and in confirmation thereof his charter was touched by the silver battle-axe which our kings carried before sceptres were known (and which was long preserved in the Castle of Dunstaffnage); and from this episode the vast oak by the brook was named King Malcolm's Tree.

Duthac was slain by his side at the siege of Alnwick, and was buried in the chapel of St. Machin; but his descendants, bearing the name of Duthie, inherited the lands of Millheugh, in Cadzow, for long after the period of our story: but to resume— —

The reverie of Fawside was broken by a sudden shout that rose from the dingles of the forest.

It was evidently a cry for succour; there was a rushing sound, and a riderless horse came galloping wildly past, but stopped near the grey of Fawside, who adroitly caught the bridle which was trailing on the ground, and thus arrested the steed, by skilfully securing the rein to one of its fore legs.

Again he heard the cry, and it had a strange weird sound, being like that of a man in terror or in mortal agony. Florence hastened towards the place from whence it seemed to come, and by the dim twilight, which the thick foliage of the oaks rendered yet more dusky, he perceived a man stretched on the ground, and one of the wild bulls of the district plunging at him with his wide-spread horns, which the victim strove to elude, by rolling from side to side, so that the bull beat his armed head against the earth or the roots of the trees.

"Help! for God's love and St. Mary's sake—help!" cried the dismounted man.

On seeing Florence approach, the bull, which was of vast height and bulk, and of milk-white colour, with its muzzle, horns, and hoofs of the deepest jet-black, uttered a species of grunting roar, and tossing his lion-like mane, which was white as the foam on the crest of a wave, lowered his broad head to attack this new enemy. Like that bull which bore away the fair Europa,—

"Large rolls of fat about his shoulders hung,
And to his neck the double dewlap clung;
His skin was whiter than the snow that lies
Unsullied by the breath of southern skies;
Huge shining horns on his curled forhead stand,
As polish'd and turn'd by the workman's hand."

This formidable enemy turned all his wrath on Florence; but the latter unhooked the wheel-lock petronel from his girdle, and, by a well-directed bullet shot right into the curly forehead of this king of the forest, laid him bleeding and powerless on the turf, where he lolled out his long red tongue, beat the air wildly with his hoofs for a moment, and then stretching his great bony limbs with a convulsive shudder, lay still and lifeless.

"Kind Heaven sent you just in time, fair sir; by my father's bones, 'tis the narrowest of all narrow escapes!" said the rescued man, staggering up. "That foreign firework engine of thine hath done me gude service."

Florence could now perceive that the speaker was a gentleman, apparently well up in years. His face was partly concealed by the aventayle of his helmet, which had become twisted or wedged, as he stated, by his horse having stumbled on seeing the bull, and thus thrown him against the root of a tree; but this protection for the face being partly open, Florence could perceive that his eyes were keen and fiery, and that his beard and moustache were white as winter frost.

Like all who travelled or went to any distance, however short from their own doors, in these ticklish times, he wore a suit of half-armour that reached to the knees, below which his legs were encased in long black riding-boots, which were ribbed with tempered iron.

"In the wood I outrode and missed my train, of nearly a score of horsemen," he continued; "and as the neighbourhood has an indifferent reputation for honesty, I shall be glad to remain with you, sir, till we find a place of shelter for the night; but may I ask your name?"

"You may," replied Florence, "but under favour, sir, in these times of feud and mistrust, is it safe for me, a stranger, who has no friend near but his single sword, to mention *his* name to one who speaks so freely of having some twenty horse or so within call?"

"You have somewhat of a foreign accent?"

"Perhaps so—I have been these seven years past in France."

"France—umph! Hence your mistrust."

"Exactly so. The land of Catholics and Huguenots, bastiles and gendarmerie, was exactly the place to teach prudence to the tongue and patience to the hand."

"Then I claim the same right to mistrust and reserve," said the stranger haughtily; "though when only man to man I see but little reason for it, especially as I am an auld carle, and thou art lithe and young."

Florence felt a glow of anger at this remark; but he thought of his letters, his recent wounds, of Bothwell, Glencairn, &c., and merely replied evasively,—

"Your horse awaits you here—so let us mount."

"Whither go you; or is that a secret too?"

"Nay—I ride for Cadzow."

"To the house of my lord regent?"——"Yes."

The stranger muttered something in the hollow of his helmet, and it was to this purpose,—

"From France, and for Cadzow! Cogsbones! can this be the Guise messenger our party wot of?"

"Go you so far?" asked Florence.

"Nay, I am only on my way to visit the house of a remote kinsman—the Laird of Millheugh."

"Indeed! I am bound for the same mansion, could I but find it. We may proceed together, and I shall trust me to your guidance."

"With pleasure."

"I have a letter for the laird from a kinsman of his, a great lady at court, and I propose to leave it at the tower to-night, that I may reach Cadzow at a more suitable hour on the morrow."

"Now, this sounds passing strange to me," said the old gentleman, peering keenly at Fawside under the peak of his helmet, and endeavouring to scan his features closely. "Millheugh hath no kinswoman at court. From whom had you the billet?"

"Champfleurie, captain of the queen's guard."

"Hah! A master in the art of intrigue, I warrant him! Let me see this note, if it please you?"

Florence placed it in the right hand of the stranger, whose left now grasped his horse's bridle.

"It bears on the seal the anchor and chevrons of Bothwell."

"Of Earl Patrick?" exclaimed Florence, changing colour.

"Yea; and his coronet, as I can see plainly enough, even by this twilight. Herein lies some mystery, but no evil, I trust; for the Lord Bothwell is my assured friend. So let us forward, for yonder are the lights in Millheugh Towershining, about a mile distant."

"A *mystery*, say you, sir?" reiterated Florence angrily. "I have nothing to do with court secrets; and if this laird of Champfleurie has trepanned me into one, I shall read him a severe lesson, were he the last Livingstone in Scotland. And now, sir, as I have no intention of further concealing my name, know that I am Florence Fawside of Fawside and that ilk in Lothian, and fear no man breathing!"

The stranger, with a startled air, drew back a pace, and after a pause said, in a low and changed voice,—

"I have heard of you, and of your old feud with Claude Hamilton of Preston anent the right of pasturage and forestry."

"Then you have only heard that which all in Scotland know, and that I am under vow to slay him!"

"Has this old man—for he is old, this Claude of Preston, ever given you personal cause for hatred?"

"Personally none," said Florence, with hesitation.

"And yet you hate him?"

"Yea, with an impulse that fiends alone might comprehend!" was the impetuous reply.

"Wherefore?"

"Ask my suffering mother, who reared me from infancy in this deadly hate! Ask my dead father, and ask my dead brother, who sleep together in the old aisle of Tranent Kirk, and they might tell you why! They died—those two brave and faithful ones—by Preston's bloody hands, bequeathing to me, as the chief part of mine inheritance, hatred—and well have I treasured it! This sword was my father's; this dagger was poor Willie's; and in Preston's blood I am bound by a hundred vows to dye them both!"

"He is old," said the other gravely; "I tell thee, old."

"Then Scotland can the better spare him," was the stern response.

"Enough of this," said the stranger haughtily. "I am a Hamilton; and here in Cadzow Wood, in the heart of the country of the Hamiltons, bethink you that your words are alike unwary and unwise. Here is your letter for Millheugh; and now let us proceed. I have quarrels enough of my own, without adding yours to my care."

The elderly stranger restored the sealed note to Florence, and on mounting was about to speak again, when his horse, which was still restive and unruly after the late occurrence and report of the pistol-shot, on being touched by the spur reared wildly back, and snorted as it cowered twice upon its haunches and tossed up its head; then throwing forward its fore feet, it sprang away like an arrow from a bow, and vanished with its rider in the darkened vista of the forest. Fawside's first impulse was to hallo aloud, and, for a time, to search after his new acquaintance; but this proved unavailing, for the echo of each far-stretching dingle alone replied.

"This stranger spoke truth," thought he. "I have been both unwary and unwise in disclosing my name and my feud to one I knew not—to one who proves to be a Hamilton,—and here in Cadzow Wood, too! So-ho for Millheugh; fortunately yonder are the tower lights still glinting through the foliage."

Directing his horse's steps by the red stripes of vertical light which shone through the narrow windows of the tower that had been indicated by the stranger as the fortalice of Millheugh, Florence threaded his way along the narrow dell the leafy monarch of which was the giant oak of King Malcolm, and soon reached the outer gate of the barbican.

CHAPTER XX
MILLHEUGH

"Without principle, talent, or intelligence, he is ungracious as a hog, greedy as a vulture, and thievish as a jackdaw." —*Humphrey Clinker.*

Such, indeed, was the character of the person upon whose rustic privacy Fawside now intruded himself. The tower, though built four centuries before, by Duthac the Thane, was indicative of the character of Allan, his descendant. It was grim, narrow, and massively constructed. The walls were enormously thick; the windows were small, placed far from the floors of the chambers they lighted, and were thickly grated without and within. The stone sill of each was perforated, to permit the emission of arrows or arquebuse shot for defence; and these perforations, when not required, were, as usual in Scotland, closed temporarily by wooden plugs. A high barbican wall enclosed the court of the tower on all sides save towards the brook, the waters of which were collected to form a moat that was crossed by a drawbridge directly under the base of the keep.

The laird was coarse in manner, rough and unlettered, but subtle in spirit, strong of limb, hardy by nature, keen-eyed, and heartless. In his time he had perpetrated many outrages, but always in form of raid; and secluded in the fastnesses of Cadzow Wood, under the wing and authority of the House of Hamilton, to whom—though a fierce tyrant to others—he was a pretended slave, and (while in the pay of its enemies) a most obsequious and useful vassal, he had long eluded and braved the feeble power of the newly-created courts of law,—Scotland's last and best gift from James V. He had barbarously treated, for years, a poor girl to whom he had been handfasted, and to be rid of her, had her accused of sorcery and drowned in the Avon; nor had he even pity for her children, whom he was accused of bestowing on Anthony Gavino, chief of the Egyptians, to be made vagrants and thieves. But the greatest outrage in which he was concerned was the assassination of the gentle priest and poet, Sir James Inglis of Culross. When his accomplices fled to the Hill of Refuge at Torphichen, and claimed the sanctuary of the Preceptor and Knights of St. John of Jerusalem, he sought a safer shelter in his own barred tower, where he lurked night and day, surrounded by pikes and arquebuses, until the clamour occasioned by the sacrilege died away, or some new outrage in other quarters attracted the attention of the people.

His gatekeeper and butler, his valets and stablers, had all the aspect of brigands, gypsies, or broken troopers. Their manners were coarse and sullen, or boisterous; patched visages, blackened eyes, and broken noses, were common to them all; and when Florence, in his rich suit of half-mail, with his jewelled poniard, his inlaid petronel, and glittering spurs, was ushered into the dimly-lighted hall, they surveyed him askance, with unpleasant but meaning looks that seemed to say,—"If time and place fitted, by St. Paul, we would soon ease thee of all this bravery!"

The stone walls of the hall were lighted by four large and coarse yellow candles, that flared and sputtered in sconces of brass; but more fully by an ample fire of pine-roots and turf that blazed on the hearth under a wide-arched mantelpiece, from whence the flames cast along the paved floor a lurid glow, as from the mouth of an opened furnace. The grated windows of this hall were arched, and sunk in recesses whose depth was lost in shadow. Several old weapons, covered with rust and cobwebs, with a few tin and wooden trenchers of the plainest description, were the only ornaments or appurtenances on the walls of this rude old dwelling, while the furniture, which consisted of a table, a few forms and tripod stools, was all of common wood. The floor was strewn with dried rushes, and eight or ten men, retainers of the tower,—fellows rough, unshaven, and uncombed in aspect, clad in shabby doublets, were lounging around two who were engaged in a game of tric-trac.

They started up at the entrance of a stranger, and two others who had been asleep on the stone seats within the glowing fireplace now came forward, and cast aside the grey border plaids in which they had been muffled.

They—the latter—wore gorgets of black iron, with pyne doublets, swords, and Tyndale knives. Their steel caps and bucklers lay near. They were hardy and weatherbeaten men, but of brutal aspect; and one whose visage was rosy-red, and whose nose was like a thick cluster of red currants, proved to be no other than Symon Brodie, the drunken butler of Preston Tower, while his companion was Mungo Tenant, the warden of the same distinguished establishment. Some recollection of their faces—for Florence, when a boy, had once been unmercifully beaten by this same butler,—or of their livery and badges, caused him to be at once upon his guard, and to beware of what might ensue.

"Laird—laird Millheugh! a stranger would speak wi' ye," said several voices officiously; and on one of the tric-trac players rising up, with an oath and a growl on the interruption, Fawside found himself confronted, rather than received, by the master of this free-and-easy mansion.

"God save you, sir," said he, with a blunt country nod, and a leer in his eye, as he surveyed the bright arms and gay apparel of his visitor with an expression in which contempt and covetousness were curiously blended; "whence come you?"

"From Edinburgh— —"

"Ay, ay, I thought sae; a braw gallant—one of the galliards o' Holyrood or Falkland Green—or of the regent, eh? I have seen muckle bravery o' this kind about Arran's house in the Kirk o' field Wynd."

"Nay, sir, you mistake," was the haughty reply of Florence, to whom this bearing proved very offensive; "I have no connection with the court, neither have I the honour to hold any post or place about the person of the regent, but am a plain country gentleman of Lothian; and being on my way to Cadzow, the captain of the queen's guard asked me to deliver this letter here, where he was pleased to add, I should be welcome to tarry and refresh."

"Welcome you are, and welcome are a' who like better to byde in Millheugh than in the forest for a night; but what, in the black devil's name, can the captain of the queen's guard, a painted and scented loon like Champfleurie, have to say to me?"

"'Tis from a lady of the queen dowager's court."

"Whew!" said the laird, with a roar of laughter; "let me see the letter, friend."

As Florence presented the note, the laird rudely and impatiently snatched it from his hand, broke the seal, and proceeded to make himself master of its contents. But this mastery was a process by no means speedily accomplished by this country gentleman of the year 1547. He drew close to one of the wall-sconces, scratched his head, viewed the writing from various points, and, after much delay, perplexity, and muttering, under his ragged moustaches, many maledictions on the writer and himself, he succeeded in deciphering the few lines it contained. On this, a smile of mingled cunning and ferocity spread over his massive and vulgar face.

During this delay, Fawside, whom he had permitted to stand, had an ample opportunity of observing him.

He was tall and, we have said, strongly formed. His complexion was pale and sallow, though his hair was black as jet. His dark eyes had ever a malicious twinkle, and a villanous expression was impressed on his whole face by a wound received at the battle of Linlithgow, where the sword of the bastard of Arran—the same ignoble steel that slew the good and gentle Earl of Lennox—had laid his left cheek open, at the same moment completely demolishing the bridge of his nose, which had never at any time been very handsome. His attire consisted of a dirty and greasy doublet, formed of what had once been peach-coloured velvet, discoloured in several places by perspiration, slops of wine, and the rust of his armour. It was rent under the arms, torn at the slashes, and, in lieu of buttons, was tied by faded ribbons, and, where these had failed, by plain twine. His russet sarcenet trunk hose were in the same condition. He wore cuarans of rough hide on his feet, and had a long horn-hafted dagger of butcherly aspect in his calfskin girdle. Add to all this black masses of elf-lock hair, a shaggy beard and moustache, and we hope that the reader sees before him Allan Duthie of the Millheugh.

A deep quiet laugh stole over his features on making himself master of the contents of this letter, with the purport of which our seventeenth chapter has made the reader familiar. He gave a meaning glance at his ruffianly and unscrupulous retainers, who were intently eyeing the stranger as a prize or prey. Then he surveyed the latter, the aspect of whose lithe, stalwart, and well-armed figure made him resolve that a little policy would be wiser than an open and unprovoked assault, before securing him. Moreover, he feared that in a scuffle the gay suit of French plate armour, which he meant to appropriate, and which, he flattered himself, would exactly fit his burly figure, might suffer damage; and this he by no means desired, especially when this unsuspicious visitor, who had brought his own death-warrant, might be much more easily killed or captured without it. All this passed through his subtle mind in a moment. Then he turned to Florence, saying with an artful smile,—

"Ye are right welcome, fair sir, to the poor cheer o' Millheugh Ha'; but will ye no unstrap this braw harness, and draw nearer the ingle; for though the month be August, the cauld wind soughs at the lumheid, as if some wrinkled hag were byding there, on her way hame frae the moon or the warlock-sabbath."

"I thank you," replied the young man; "and if one of your servitors will so fer favour me as to undo the straps of this steel casing——"

"That will I, mysel', do blythely, Fawside," said the laird, who with great readiness unfastened the various buckles of some portions of the beautiful suit of mail, and removed them, with the shining and embossed coursing-hat, to a side buffet, muttering while doing so,—"By the deil's horns, he has a pyne doublet under a'; but a dab wi a dirk may soon make a hole in that. Look weel to this harness, lads,—as if it were mine ain," he added aloud, with a wink to some of his people, who seemed quite to understand the hint. "And so ye have come from Edinburgh——"

"Last," said Florence, laughing; "but a month since I was in Paris."

"Oho!—and what new plots are the bloody Guises hatching—for they are aye up to some develrie anent us, eh?"

"I know of none, laird," said Florence with reserve; "I have come from France certainly, but I have not the honour to be ranked either as a friend or confidant of the Cardinal de Guise or the Duc de Mayenne. Indeed, I never saw them but once, for a few minutes, in the gallery of the Louvre."

"Yet Bothwell styles you a spy of the Guises!" thought Millheugh. "Well, well, sir," he added aloud; "'tis no matter o' mine. Serve up the supper quick; but, ere sitting down, sir, would ye take off your braw belt and sword?"

"Nay, Millheugh," said Florence smiling, though certain undefined suspicions occurred to him; "I am never unarmed even in my own house; and you, I see, wear your belt and Tynedale knife."

"Oh, it matters nocht to me," said the laird with a cunning laugh; "but I thocht ye might sup the easier without your lang iron spit and braw baldrick."

A repast of the plainest kind, but great in quantity, consisting mainly of brose, haggis, sowons, and porridge with prunes in it, was now served up, with cold beef, and venison hams; and, while the two retainers of Claude Hamilton sat somewhat apart, darting covert scowls from under their shaggy brows at their master's feudal enemy, they, as well as Millheugh's hungry foresters, made great havock among the contents of the piled platters and ample cogies with which the table was furnished—viands which were washed down by a river of ruddy-brown ale, flowing from a large cask set upon a bin, in a stone recess, the Gothic canopy of which showed that in the days of the present proprietor's father therein had stood a crucifix and holy-water font, wherein all were wont to dip their fingers before sitting down to meals;—but the times were changing fast, and the minds, manners, and morals of the people were changing with them.

When supper was over, Florence, weary with his long and rough ride of so many miles, and heartily sick of the laird's coarse, if not brutal conversation, retired to rest; and believing himself in perfect security, divested himself of his attire, and was soon in a profound and dreamless slumber—so profound, that he heard not at midnight three very decided attempts which were made by certain parties without to force his door, the many locks and bars of which, however, fortunately stood firm and were his friends. Soundly he slept, though his couch was made only of soft heather, packed closely in on an oblong frame, with the points uppermost, and a sheet spread over it, in the old Scottish fashion. But towards morning— all unconscious that he was a prisoner—sounds of distant merriment came floating to his ear, and awoke him for a time.

That night, and for hours after midnight had passed, Millheugh and his men drank deeply in the rude and ancient hall, and their songs and boisterous laughter, came to the ear of Florence by fits, upon the weird howling of the morning wind. One drunken ditty, composed by some West Lothian (and long forgotten) song-writer, on Preston's never sober butler, seemed an especial favourite, and a score of voices made its chorus shake the vaulted roof of the old tower. It ran thus:—

"Symon Brodie had a cow:
　When she was lost, he couldna find her;
But he did a' that man could do,
　Till she cam' hame wi her tail behind her.
　　Honest bald Symon Brodie,
　　Stupid auld doitit bodie!
　　　Gin ye pass by Preston Tower,
　　　Birl the stoup wi Preston Brodie.

"Symon Brodie had a wife,
　And wow! but she was braw and bonnie;
A clout she tuik frae off the buik,
　And preened it on her cockernonie.
　　Honest bald Symon Brodie,
　　Stupid auld drunken bodie!
　　　For Claude, the laird o' Preston Tower,
　　　Has kiss'd the wife o' Symon Brodie."

Florence awoke late—at least, *late* for 1547; the time-dial indicated the hour of eleven; when he rose, dressed himself, and descended to the hall, with his purse in his hand to scatter a largess among the servants, to breakfast, and then begone with all speed.

By various pretexts, the laird procrastinated the time for his departure, till Fawside was at last compelled to order his horse peremptorily. Then Allan Duthie threw aside all disguise, and laughed outright at him.

Florence started from the table, and with his hand on his sword approached the door of the hall.

Then the laird snatched up an arquebuse with a lighted match, and at the head of several domestics, variously armed, prepared to dispute his exit, by completely barring the way; at this critical stage of their proceedings the sound of a hunting-horn, blown loudly at the gate, made even the most forward of the brawlers pause to a time.

"Is that thy master's horn, Symon?" asked the treacherous laird.

"I dinna ken, Millheugh," replied Symon, arming his right hand with a tankard, the contents of which he had just drained, and the creamy froth of which covered all his Bardolph nose and grizzly-grey moustache; "but he must be here ere midday pass."!

"Claude Hamilton here!" thought Florence, as the blood rushed back upon his heart; "one house can never hold us—with these people, too! Oh, mother! to-morrow you may say your mass-prayers for my butchery. Millheugh must know of our feud, and yet he told me not he was expected here!"

"If he come not speedily," continued the jesting ruffian, "woe worth all the breakfast he is likely to get; but the loss o' it will be a just punishment, as I ken he eats beef and mutton in Lenten-time, instead of kail and green herbs, for the gude o' his soul."

"What the deil hae our souls to do wi' kail, or beef, or mutton, Millheugh, whate'er our appetites may?" asked Symon Brodie; "a gude appetite is a sign o' a gude conscience. There sounds the horn again!"

"A Lollard, hey?" exclaimed Millheugh; "thou hast heard Friar Forest preach, I warrant."

"I heard him preach, and saw him burned at a stake on the Castle Hill."

"Take ye care then, Symon, for there are faggots for those who speak like thee; and a butler will burn as well as a friar."

"Indubitably."

"Make way, fellows!" exclaimed Florence, lunging at Millheugh with his sword; "make me way, or your lives are not worth a dog's ransom. 'Tis well for thee, and such as thee, Symon Brodie, that the terror of the scoffer and the impious, Cardinal Beaton, is in his grave!"

"His eminence," said Millheugh, "aye deemed himself on better terms with Heaven than other men."

"Weel, weel," said the impudent butler, "he hath since, peradventure, discovered his mistake in that matter."

"Thou saucy varlet," exclaimed Fawside, making at him a blow, which he eluded by leaping on one side, "darest thou speak of him so in the presence of a loyal gentleman?"

"Peace, I command you," cried Millheugh; "for, by the hoof of Mahoun, here come more visitors!"

As he spoke the jangle of spurs was heard on the stair that gave access to the upper stories of the tower. Several gentlemen, well armed, and richly clad in riding-coats, with long boots of Spanish leather, and having, mostly, helmets, cuirasses, and gorgets, hurriedly thronged into the hall; and Fawside felt a momentary emotion of alarm on recognizing among them the voices and figures of Patrick Earl of Bothwell, the Earl of Glencairn, and the sinister visage of his son, the Lord Kilmaurs.

CHAPTER XXI
A BOTHWELL! A BOTHWELL!

Yet might not Aquilante's spirit fail,
Though shivered was his shield, and gashed his mail!
Cautious but firm he struck; no sign of dread,
His aspect or his manly port displayed.

Roncesvalles.

With a burst of laughter these turbulent nobles and their armed followers, who were numerous, unsheathed their swords; and Florence boldly confronted them all, while his heart beat rapidly,—-for he knew that entreaty or concession would avail him nothing. He knew, too, that he had been foully ensnared. He found himself in a perilous predicament, for he soon recognized the voices, if not the faces, of nearly all the same men by whom he had been so sorely beset on the first night of his landing from the galley of M. de Villegaignon.

"So, so! Our worthy Millheugh has brought the boar to bay!" exclaimed Kilmaurs, the wound on whose sinister visage grew purple in his excitement as he pressed forward.

"Ha-ha! Fawside, most worthy messenger," added Bothwell; "thou art quite alone, eh!"

"Alone; but not as St. John was, in the Isle of Patmos; for he is with his betters and much good company," said Glencairn.

"Do cease with this irreverence, Glencairn," said Bothwell, who, like all that still adhered to Rome, was nervously sensitive of all that appertained to the faith of his forefathers.

"Ye haver, my lord," was the surly rejoinder. "That whilk our forbears of auld deemed reverence we now term but rank idolatry, and an abomination in the nostrils of the Lord."

"Like loyalty to the crown and faith to our country—folly, eh? But enough of this," said the selfish and blood-thirsty Kilmaurs. "And now for the matter in hand. Worthy Master Florence Fawside——"

"A spruce young cock o' the game, my masters!" said Symon Brodie. "I warrant ye will find him tough enough."

"We should keep him for fighting on Fasterns e'en," added Millheugh, who was not quite sober.

"Silence!" cried Kilmaurs. "We have other ends in view for him, and need not this ribaldry."

"What am I to understand by all this studied insolence, and by my being thus beset?" demanded Florence, standing on his guard, sternly eyeing them all, and waving his sword in a circle around him. "Speak, sirs, lest I slay the most silent man among you."

"You have brought letters," began Kilmaurs.

"One to the laird of Millheugh, most certainly. That letter I delivered."

"Oh, yes; of a verity we doubt not that," continued his chief tormentor Kilmaurs;—"the letter from a fair court lady—a countess, at least, who was in sore trouble, and lacked a messenger to her dear kinsman here. We mean not that. Ha-ha! Champfleurie played his cards well!"

"I have been snared and deluded!" said the poor youth, while his heart beat like lightning; and he glanced round him vainly for means of escape, or, at least, for a desperate and protracted resistance.

"Precisely so; you have been deluded. Champfleurie——"

"Like each one of you, is a villain, whom, will God, I shall yet unmask and slay!" exclaimed their victim.

"By St. Bride! poor devil, I almost pity thee!" said Bothwell. "Thou'lt fare hardly enough at the hands of Millheugh and his ragged Robins."

"Florence Fawside," said Kilmaurs, "we know thee to be a spy of the Guises and bearer of their letters to Mary of Lorraine and the Regent Arran. We can easily slay thee, and obtain such papers as may be concealed in secret pockets; but we care not, by cracking the nut, to gain the kernel so hastily. Ye may be the custodier of other and more important secrets than men care to commit to paper, especially such men as the Cardinal de Guise and Monseigneur the Duc de Mayenne: and these secrets we must have!"

"Sirs, I swear to you, as a gentleman and a true Scottish man, I am the depositary of no such secrets as you suppose," said the unfortunate youth, with great earnestness; for though brave, even to temerity, he thought of his old mother and his young love, while all their swords seemed to glitter death before him, and his sinking heart grew sad.

"A cock-laird like thee may swear to anything," said Kilmaurs insolently.

"Thou, Kilmaurs, art an empty boaster, and a coward. My race is among the oldest in the land."

"Being descended, in the male line, direct from Adam."

"Despite this insolence, I repeat, my lords, that I tell you—truth!"

"Knave, thou dost not tell the truth," exclaimed Kilmaurs, who became pallid with fury; "so, beware, lest we have thy tongue torn out by the roots and nailed on Hamilton cross, to feed the gleds and hoodicrows. I have seen such done ere this."

"If he lieth, the event shall prove," said Glencairn; "let him be disarmed, and bound to the iron cruick above the hall fire; then pile on wetted wood and green boughs, till we smoke the secrets out of him."

A shout of fierce and derisive acclamation greeted this suggestion of an impromptu mode of torture not uncommon in those old lawless times; and the tone of defiance assumed by the victim was lost amid the bantering laughter and insults of more than thirty voices. Surrounded on all hands, he had only power left to run one assailant through the body, and before he could withdraw his sword to repeat the thrust, a score of heavy hands were laid upon him, those of his host, Allan of Millheugh, being among the most active. His sword and poniard were at once rent away, and he was dragged over the blood-stained floor towards the large arched fireplace. In the lust of blood, the feudal, or political, or religious rancour which animated those at whose mercy he was now so completely cast, they struggled with each other for who should give him a blow or a buffet, and contended vehemently for the office of binding him to the iron beam that swung over the blazing fire.

Florence struggled also—but in vain. The united strength and the iron hands of his numerous enemies, noble and ignoble, were irresistible and overpowering.

He strove to cry aloud, but whether for mercy or in defiance, in his bewilderment, he knew not; his voice was gone, and he could scarcely gasp for breath: then how much less was he able to articulate.

"A rope—a rope!" cried Millheugh; "weel wetted, too, lest it burn when we birsel him. Quick, ye loons, quick!"

"Heap damp boughs and green peats on the fire," said Glencairn. "Quick—lest instead of only *smoking* the secret out of him, we roast him before the right time."

Bruised, bleeding, pale, and powerless, Florence now found himself under the rough arch of the yawning fireplace and the flame of the large pile of blazing fuel that lay heaped on the hearth was already scorching him to the quick! Above his head swung the smoke-blackened bar of the cruick whereon occasionally large pots and cauldrons were hung, and which moved outward or inward, in sockets, like a crane.

His hands were roughly forced behind him by the united strength of several men, and held thus while Mungo Tennant, the warder of Preston, proceeded to tie them. Meantime others were piling green boughs on the flame, partially to quench its heat, and to fill the vast tunnel-like chimney with black smoke, amid which they seemed like demons superintending infernal orgies. While this was proceeding, there was a snaky glare in the glistening and triumphant eyes of Kilmaurs. This fierce young lord was popularly believed to possess an *evil eye*, and that his gaze had the power of blighting whatever it fell upon. Friend or foe, horse or sheep, were averred to wither away. In Cunninghame, it was said that corn died in the ear, and the leaves of a tree shrivelled and dropped off, if he looked at them fixedly; and this dangerous attribute made him a source of terror to all—even to the irreverend Reformer, his father.

All was nearly complete: the fire, half suppressed by the damp fuel, now emitted a dense column of black smoke, and a well-wetted rope was already made fast to the iron bar.

"Up wi' him, now, to the cruick, by craig and heels," said Glencairn; "and then let him sneeze in the reek, like a carlin in the mist."

"God have mercy on me; for men will have none!" was the mental prayer of Florence, with a half-stifled groan, as he felt himself lifted off the floor and held over the smoke:—but ere the principal cord was made fast, a powerful man burst through the crowd around the vast fireplace, and, forcing them asunder, commanded all, "on pain of death, to hold their hands!"

"A Bothwell! a Bothwell!" cried Earl Patrick, in a voice of thunder. "Who dares cry hold, when I command to strike?"

CHAPTER XXII
THE SCORNED AMITY

Chieftains, forego!
I hold the first who strikes, my foe.
Madmen forbear your frantic jar!
Lady of the Lake.

"Hold all your hands," exclaimed the new comer; "or by Heaven's vengeance, I will run the foremost of you through the body!"

"Who dares to lift his voice thus under my roof-tree?" demanded Millheugh savagely, forcing a passage, dagger in hand, through the throng.

"I dare!—I, Claude Hamilton of Preston," replied the stranger, in whom Florence (now released, and though reclining faint and feebly on a bench) recognized, to his astonishment, the grey-bearded man whom, in Cadzow Forest, he had rescued from mutilation and a dreadful death.

"And think you, carle, that we will obey you?" demanded the Earl of Bothwell contemptuously.

"Perhaps not, were I alone; but when I tell you, lord earl, that I have now a train of thirty horsemen, armed with jack and spear, in the tower court, and that I have but to sound this horn to bring every man to my aid, the face of affairs may be changed. I lost my train in the forest; but fortunately, it would appear, we have reached this place together at a very critical time."

"Hark you, Laird of Preston," said Glencairn angrily; "what are we to understand by all this? Would you attempt to deprive us of a lawful prisoner, whom we have captured at last, and after no small trouble, too? He—this Fawside—is your feudal enemy, and our political opponent, being an emissary of the bloody-minded Guises. Will you, then, dare to befriend him?"

"Ay, even he will I befriend," replied the old man sternly.

"This is rank insanity," exclaimed the Earl of Bothwell; "does one of our own party turn against us thus? And have we ridden five-and-thirty miles or more to find ourselves defrauded of our prey by the mere bullying of an auld carle like this? Forward! again, my men, and string me yonder poppinjay up to the cruick with the rope—not at his waist, but round his knavish neck! Or, if you will make still shorter work, let two take him by the hands, and two by the heels, and by one fell swing dash out his brains against the stone wall! I have seen such done in Venice ere this. I am Patrick Hepburn, Earl of Bothwell, and high sheriff of Haddington—who shall dare to gainsay me?"

"Stand back, I command you," thundered the resolute old laird of Preston, grasping his silver-mounted bugle with one hand, while menacing all with one of those long and ponderous two-handed swords then worn by the Scots;—"back, I say; or, by the arm of St. Giles and all that is holy in heaven, I will make hawks' meat of the first man who advances! 'Tis scarcely twelve hours since, when in Cadzow Wood, this youth, though mine enemy, saved me from a frantic white bull, when lying half stunned by a fall from my horse; and blessed be God, who hath enabled me to come hither in time to prevent a deed so foul as you, my lords, contemplate. And now I tell ye, sirs, that were he laden with a horse-load of letters from the Guises, from the Cardinal, the Duke de Mayenne, and from Henry of Valois to boot, he shall ride forth on his way, sakeless and free, escorted by my own followers; and if thou, Allan o' Millheugh, (for weel do I ken thee for a bully and a knave of auld, man!) restore not to him all of which he has been deprived, I will light such a fire in Millheugh Tower as Cadzow Wood hath never seen since its tallest oaks were acorns!"

All present knew that Hamilton of Preston was a resolute man, who would adhere to his word. Defrauded of their prey, the three lords muttered vengeance, and sheathing their swords, retired sullenly into a corner of the hall. The laird of Millheugh attempted to string together a few awkward and absurd apologies, while restoring to Fawside his much-coveted arms and armour, which he hastily put on in silence, and with the sombre fury that filled his heart expressed in every lineament of his agitated face, which was now deathly pale, and marked by more than one wound or bruise, received in the recent struggle.

"Drink, sir; you look faint and ill, after all this rough handling," said Claude of Preston, handing a cup of wine to his young feudal enemy, whose handsome features he scrutinized with an expression of sadness and interest,—for Florence was said to be the living image of his father Sir John, whom Preston slew.

The youth drank the wine, and returned the cup, saying briefly,—

"Sir, I thank you: you, at least, are an honourable enemy—and brave and humane as honourable."

"And such, young man, the Hamiltons of Preston ever found each gentleman of your house to be."

"For that compliment, again I thank you."

He had now completed his arming, in which Preston courteously assisted him; and on drawing his sword, he could no longer restrain the rage and indignation with which his heart was bursting, and in this tide of wrath he included his preserver with his enemies.

"Allen Duthie of Millheugh," said he sternly, while his eyes glared under the peak of his helmet, "I brand thee as a false coward and foul thief; and such I shall prove thee to be, in the face of all men, at a fitting time. I am now ready to depart; and gladly will I do so," he added, with a furtive glance at Preston; "for, of a verity, the air of this place suffocates me."

"Ere ye go," said Preston, drawing off his glove, "Florence Fawside, in presence of these lords and gentlemen, for the good offices that have passed between us, last night and to-day, I offer you my friendship and alliance, to the end that our feud be stanched, and committed to oblivion."

"You ask me this," said the young man with rising anger, "while wearing at your side the same sword that slew my poor father and my brother Willie!"

"Nay, if that be all, though with this sword, my forefather, with his Scots, held the bridge of Verneuil, in Anjou, against Duke Clarence's English billmen, I will shiver the blade to atoms——"

"Keep your sword, Preston," replied Florence; "ere long, you will require it for other purposes. Friendship cannot exist with hatred,—alliance with mistrust."

"You will never live to comb a beard as grey as mine, if you speak thus rashly through life," said Preston grimly.

"I speak like my father's son; and I care not for dying early, if I die as my father lived and died—with honour!"

"'Tis said like the brave son of a brave father; but once more, Fawside, remember you gave me life last night—to-day I give you life and liberty."

"Taunt me not with the service, old man. 'Tis well we are still, I thank God, equal! My blood boils hotly, Preston; and, despite the good you do me, I must remember my vow. Our fathers' feud is but renewed: draw—a life I have given—a life I will peril again, even here; so, come on!"

"In this hostile hall?"

"Where place so fitting as this foul den of would-be murder and robbery?"

"Rash fool! If I am slain, your life will be forfeited," replied the baron, drawing back a pace.

"I care not," replied the youth wildly and mournfully—for the events of the morning had filled his soul with a fury which required an object whereon to expend itself; "at my mother's knee as a child, at the altar of God as a man, I have sworn a thousand times to slay thee, even as ye slew my father under tryst, wherever and whenever I met thee—and now the hour is come!"

During this new dispute, the three lords, and the group around them, looked on and listened with approving smiles; for to them it seemed that Preston had merely come in time to save them the trouble of killing their prisoner.

"If he escape," said Glencairn, "we can beset the paths from Cadzow, and watch for his departure. Our squire-errant rides alone, and must fall an easy prey."

"But," said his son, "if the letters be delivered, what then shall we have?"

"Vengeance!"

"Preston changes colour," said Bothwell, with a sardonic smile; "there will be such a raid in my sheriffdom, as Lothian hath not seen since Sir Ralf Evers, the Englishman, knocked with his gauntlet on the Bristo-gate, at Edinburgh."

"And thereafter had his brains knocked out at Ancrumford," said Kilmaurs, who slew him there; "but, hush, the storm grows apace."

At Fawside's last remark, Preston's wrinkled cheek grew deathly pale.

"Bairn, begone," said he loftily, "lest I send thee to thy mother in a colt's-halter. Go—I scorn the accusation, as I scorn your anger. If I took your father's life in feud, 'twas fairly done in open fray, and *not* under tryst; and that life I saved twice at Flodden, from the Lord Surrey's band of pikemen. Go—go, I say, and God bless thee;—the wish may be all the better, that it cometh from the lips of a man whose years are wellnigh three score and ten."

"The murderer of my father and my brother! Draw, lest I smite ye where ye stand!"

"Never! your blood is owre red on my hands already."

"Hah, 'tis a coward I am confronting."

"Shame on thee, Fawside, to say so," exclaimed the Earl of Bothwell, who began to watch this strange scene with new and more generous interest.

Preston became fearfully pale, and trembled with emotion, while his staunch henchmen, Mungo Tennant and Symon Brodie, uttered a shout of anger, and drew their swords.

"Recal that bitter word, boy?" said Hamilton, hoarsely.

"Coward, coward!" continued Florence, menacing his throat with the point of his sword.

Preston struck it contemptuously aside with his bare hand, and gasped for breath. He then made an attempt to draw his sword; but relinquishing the hilt, by a violent effort mastered his emotion.

"Boy," said he, "my pride and my spirit are passing away from me. There was a time when, by a glance, I had almost slain thee for an insult such as this—but that day is gone, yea, gone for ever! A coward, I?" he continued, with a wild, choking laugh, while the tears started to his reddened eyes; "rash fool! thy brave father, whose spirit may now witness this meeting, would never so have taunted me; but I am old enough to bear even this from thee. Go, I say, in peace; for on this right Land of mine there is already more than enough of the blood of your family."

In five minutes after this, Florence had left the tower of Millheugh, and found himself riding through the green glades of Cadzow Forest, the upper foliage of which was glittering in the noonday sun.

Mentally he rehearsed his late meeting with Preston, and now his own heart—as his better passions resumed their wonted sway—began to accuse him of acting harshly, and without grace or generosity. Despite himself, his cheek began to redden with a glow of honest shame, for the taunts he had hurled upon a gentleman whose years were so many, and whose high valour had been so often and so undoubtedly proved in battle; but these thoughts were immediately stifled, as the tall form, and grave, resentful face of his stern mother seemed to rise before him, and gave rise to other ideas; then, lest he might be followed by the men of Bothwell or Glencairn, he spurred his fleet grey to a gallop, and pushed on rapidly for the residence of the regent.

CHAPTER XXIII
CADZOW CASTLE

When princely Hamilton's abode
Ennobled Cadzow's Gothic towers,
The song went round, the goblet flow'd,
And wassail sped the jocund hours.

Scott.

The Avon, a tributary of the Clyde, flows through a beautiful valley, the sides of which are clothed with magnificent timber of great size and age. Embosomed amid the thickest part of this forest, surrounded by trees which were planted during the reign of David I., and overhanging a rushing torrent, the rocks of which are covered by masses of dark ivy and luxuriant creeping-plants, stands the castle of Cadzow, now an open ruin, having been dismantled in the wars of Queen Mary's time, but which, at the epoch of our story, had banners on its ramparts and cannon at its gate, being in all the strength and pride of a feudal stronghold as the residence of a princely and powerful chief, James Earl of Arran, who, by his position as regent, was the first subject in the realm.

This castle is about a mile distant from the town of Hamilton, where Florence was informed that the regent, though at Cadzow, was preparing, with all his train, to depart for Stirling. This venerable fortress once gave a name to the whole district, and both were anciently the property of the crown of Scotland, as there are yet extant charters granted by Alexanders II. and III. dated at "our Castle of Cadzow;" but David II. gifted to Walter, the son of Sir Gilbert of Hamilton, his lands of Cadzow and Edelwood, in the county of Lanark; and thereafter on the whole territory was bestowed the present name of Hamilton, the castle and forest alone retaining their ancient designation.

Many horses, saddled and richly caparisoned, held by grooms, liverymen, pages, or men-at-arms, were grouped under the trees of the park; and the bustle of preparation previous to departure was evident in and about the castle as Florence rode up to the gate, where his arrival attracted but little attention amid the throng of nearly a hundred gay cavaliers, who were waiting for the appearance of the regent.

After some inquiry, our new-comer found a page wearing the livery of the house of Hamilton, and desired him to say that a gentleman from Edinburgh requested the honour of an audience.

"You cannot see the regent," replied the page bluntly, while switching a few specks of dust from his white leather boots with a fine laced handkerchief.

"Why so?"

"His grace is at dinner," was the brief reply.

"He sits long; 'tis one by the dial."

"Kings are pleased to be hungry sometimes, and a regent may be so, too."

"Thou saucy jackfeather, say instantly to the captain of the guard, the usher, or whoever is in waiting, that I, Florence Fawside of that ilk, bearer of letters from the queen-mother and the king of France, am here at his castle gate, or, by the furies! I will scourge you with my bridle, were you the last, as I verily believe you are the first, of your race in Scotland!"

This imperious speech crushed even the proverbial insolence of the court page, who was a son of Hamilton of Dalserfe. He reddened with anger, and frowned; then he gave a saucy smile and withdrew, saying, —

"I shall do your bidding, sir."

In a few minutes after, the messenger found himself ushered into a stately hall, and in the presence of the Regent of Scotland.

James, second earl of Arran and tenth in descent from the founder of his house, who rose to favour under King Alexander II., was a peer of noble presence. He had been the loyal friend of the late King James V., whom he accompanied in his expedition to the Orcades and Western Isles in 1536, and with whom, in the September of that year, he embarked for France, and was present at his nuptials with Magdalene de Valois, the eldest daughter of Francis I., in the church of Notre Dame at Paris. She died soon after, a young and beautiful queen of twenty summer days; and the king, about a year after, espoused the daughter of René of Lorraine, Mary, whom we have already had the pleasure of introducing to the reader. As regent of Scotland, Arran passed many patriotic laws, one of which, sanctioning the issue of the new Bible which Father William, a Dominican, had translated into the Scottish tongue, procured him, on one hand the affection of the Reformers, and on the other the hatred of those who adhered to the Church of Rome.

He was above the middle height; he had that peculiar length and gravity of visage which the shorn hair and peaked beard imparted to the faces of all the great and noble of his time, as we may see in the portraits of Francis I., Philip II., James V., of Raleigh, Morton, Murray, and others; his eyes and hair were dark; when he smiled, it was haughtily, with his lips closed; while the troubles incident to his time and government gave him a saddened and preoccupied look. He wore a hongreline of blue velvet laced with gold braid, and so called from the pelisse of the Hungarians. This species of doublet was buttoned close under the chin, but was open below, to display a cuirass of the finest steel inlaid with magnificent carving. It had been presented by Christian II. of Denmark to his father, who had led five thousand Scots to succour that monarch in the war of 1504.

He was attended by four pages, all sons of barons of the surname of Hamilton—to wit, the young lairds of Dalserfe, Broomhall, Allershaw (who in manhood and in after years fought at Langside "for God and Queen Mary"), and Bothwellhaugh, a grave and resolute boy, who twenty years later was to slay the regent Maray. Clad in cloth-of-gold, with gold chains at their necks, they had his armorial bearings embroidered on the breasts of their doublets, and, though mere boys, they were armed like men, with swords and daggers.

"Welcome to Cadzow," said the regent, presenting his hand, which Fawside kissed respectfully. "You have come from France, I am informed?"

"With M. le Chevalier de Villegaignon."

"Villegaignon!" reiterated the regent coldly, but with surprise. "He hath come and been gone again these several weeks. How comes it to pass, young sir, that I have only now the honour of seeing you?"

"The honour is mine, Lord Arran. As regent of Scotland, all honour must, after our young queen, flow from you."

Arran gave a cold smile, and replied,

"This is well-timed flattery, and proves that you have not spent seven years, as I have heard, with the Duchess Anne of Albany without benefit."

Fawside bowed, and presented the letter of Henry II.

"What spots are these on the cover?" exclaimed Arran. "Blood! You have been fighting, sir—been wounded! Where was this? And you have delayed——"

"Three swords in one's body are likely enough to cause delay; and I, my lord, have had these, with a stroke or so, from a partizan to boot. Hence the delay of which your grace complains."

"Indeed! I must inquire into this. But such brawls are now of hourly occurrence. Retire, gentlemen," said he to the four pages; who at once withdrew to resume their game of primero in the antechamber.

Florence briefly and modestly, but with an indignation that grew in spite of himself, related the dangers he had undergone, first in the streets of Edinburgh and latterly in the tower of Millheugh, to which he had been snared by the letter given from the hand of Champfleurie; and as he proceeded, the broad brow of Arran grew black as a thunder-cloud, and his whole face assumed a sombre expression.

"Now, heaven grant me patience!" he exclaimed, striking his sword on the floor; "there is more than a mere brawl in this: treason lies under it— treason and a conspiracy; and, by my father's soul, I shall hang them all!"

"Hang nobles?"

"Well, the more titled rascals shall have the perilous honour of having their heads sliced off by an axe,—the grim privilege of nobility; but the more common rogues I shall hang high and dry, like scarecrows in a cornfield."

"My lord regent, I beseech you not to embroil yourself with powerful peers like Cassilis, Bothwell, and Glencairn, for a small matter like my three sword-cuts."

"Knaves who are at faith and peace with England, as I am told," continued Arran, pursuing his own thoughts.

"True, my lord; but when we find among them a man like Hugh Earl of Eglinton, who is constable of Rothesay, bailie of Cunningham, and chamberlain of Irvine, to attempt punishment would embroil your whole government, and peril the Queen's authority."

"And both are so weak, that no later than last year, without the assistance of the prior of Rhodes, and his galleys, I could not dislodge a few sacrilegious rebels from the castle of St. Andrew's! Yet we are strong,—we Hamiltons," continued the regent loftily; "the blood of our house has mingled with that of our kings, and run over Scotland in a thousand channels; but you counsel well and wisely, Fawside; for there are times when I fear that the envy of these malcontent lords will destroy me, and level even the throne."

"Fear them not, my lord; that man is worth little who excites not envy."

"Faith, thou art right, boy!" said the regent cheerfully; "and though those who wronged thee are perhaps too numerous and powerful for me to punish at present, a time shall come; and meanwhile, I will not the less reward your worth and bravery; and now, sir, for the letter of the Valois."

As he read it, the contents seemed to please him; his eyes sparkled; a glow suffused his cheek, and an expression of triumph spread over all his features.

"We are to have auxiliaries from Henry II. to strengthen my government, and enable me to resist the wiles and wishes of the English protector, so that our young queen shall wed the heir of France, and *not* the son of the last Tudor! Good—good! Monsieur d'Essé d'Epainvilliers is to be lieutenant-general; Monsieur d'Andelot, colonel of two thousand French men-at-arms," he muttered, reading the names of those soldiers who served at the siege of Leith, and in the campaign of 1548; "the Rhinegrave will bring three thousand Almayners armed with pike and arquebuse; Monsieur Etanges is to be colonel of a thousand gendarmes on horseback; Signor Pietro Strozzi will lead a thousand Italian veterans; M. le Chevalier de Dunois is to be general of the ordnance; and the Sieur Nicholas de Villegaignon, knight of Rhodez, and admiral of the galleys of France, shall bring twenty-two war-ships, and sixty-two transports, all bearing the red lion of Scotland. 'Tis good, 'tis noble of King Henry, and worthy the spirit of the old alliance with France.

'Fall—fall, whatever befall,
Our Lion shall be lord of all!'

If we have war with England,—and hourly I expect a declaration of it, the sooner these succours arrive the better, for there are many men in Scotland so foully corrupted by English gold, that I tremble at the prospect of leading a Scottish army to the field, lest it crumble by the very corruption of our peers."

"The galleys and transports were lying in the harbour of Brest, where I saw them when I sailed; and they wait— —"

"Wait—for what?"

"The arrival of the troops, who are all chosen men, and are now on their march from the frontiers of Italy; but I have yet another letter for your grace."

"From whom?"

"Her majesty the queen-mother."

The brow of Arran darkened for a moment, as he opened and read the missive.

"She exults at the prospect of having so many French men-at-arms to fence her daughter's throne, and fight the English; but let me be wary, lest they fight with Scottish men as well. Sir, if you love me— —"

"Oh, your excellency!"

"And wish to serve me," resumed the regent, grasping the arm of Fawside, and bending his keen dark eyes upon him, "you must avoid that dangerous Frenchwoman."

"Who, my lord?" stammered Fawside.

"The widow of the late king; for she plots deeply to deprive me of the regency, which is the darling object of her ambition, and the hope of the Guises; and this I know so well, that I dare scarcely lay my head on its pillow at night, for fear that a hand with a dagger is concealed behind the arras,—avoid her, I say; avoid her!"

Florence coloured deeply as the beautiful face and form of the royal widow seemed to rise before him, with the dearer image of her friend. Arran now insisted on his visitor being seated; and the purport of King Henry's letter having put him in the best of humours, he became more conversational. He walked about the room, and as he did so, or stood with his back to the fire, he said,—

"I presume, sir, that you know how hard a task the loyal and faithful have to perform here in Scotland, to maintain the national league with France, in the face of secret treaties, formed, or *said* to have been formed, by certain of our lords, who were the prisoners of King Henry after the field of Solway, and whose plots, by the seven pillars of the house of wisdom, a wise man will be needed to unravel."

"In France, I heard such things talked of openly; and that Henry VIII. had the audacity to propose, if you would put the little Queen Mary into his murderous hands, to give his daughter Elizabeth in marriage to your son, now captain of the Scottish guard, and, with an army, to make you king of all Scotland beyond the river Forth."

"You heard rightly, sir," said Arran, with a scornful laugh; "'twas a knave's hope—a madman's project; and then he tried gold; but had he offered all the precious metal that Michael Scott cheated the devil of, he would have failed with James of Arran!"

"And how did wise Sir Michael cheat the devil?"

"Know ye not the story?" asked the earl, smiling.

"No, my lord."

"The Evil One was as marvellously overreached as when Michael employed him to make ropes of sea-sand. He cut a hole in the crown of his bonnet, and here, in Cadzow wood, holding it over the mouth of a coalheugh, which the devil saw not, so curiously had the wizard concealed it, he tauntingly offered to barter his soul for the said bonnet full of gold-dust."

"And the devil——"

"Was outwitted, as he had to fill the pit ere he could fill the bonnet. So had Henry of England offered me all the gold which the infernal pit of Michael of Balwearie contained, he had failed to tempt me; though I fear that a less bribe has tempted many others, who pretend to be merely averse to the residence of our queen in France; but, after our conference at Stirling, I have resolved that she sail for Brest; for I would rather see the daughter of James V. lying by his side at Holyrood than wedded to son of him who, three years ago, carried fire and sword into Scotland, and who broke the gentle heart of Catharine of Aragon!"

"But what of the Protector Somerset?"

"He may meet us again in battle, when and where he will; and now, sir, if you will accompany me to Stirling, whither I set forth in a few minutes, you must refresh; for on my faith you look both weary and worn."

Florence, in truth, felt and looked as the regent said; for after his long ride from Edinburgh, and the adventures of the past day and night, he was becoming faint and pale. The regent sounded a silver whistle, which lay on the table, and was then used in lieu of a hand-bell. The young laird, of Dalserfe, the senior page, appeared; and to him Arran remitted the duty of attending to the wants of his visitor. The latter, though he would have preferred returning to Edinburgh, *felt* that the wish of Arran to have his company so far as Stirling implied a command, obedience to which became more palatable when he discovered that Mary of Lorraine and the ladies of her court would be present at the intended conference.

The regent, a man of great penetration, though too quiet and well-meaning to govern a people so turbulent as the Scots, saw in Florence a young man, travelled, brave, intelligent, of good position, of high spirit, and—what was much more remarkable in 1547—of education. He felt that such a man might prove invaluable to his household and government, and was anxious to attach him to his person.

This idea proved fortunate; for, by accompanying the regent to Stirling, he eluded the followers of Bothwell and Glencairn, some twenty or so of whom, with loaded arquebuses, were at that moment lurking in the forest of Cadzow, for the express purpose of cutting him off, if he came forth from the castle alone.

CHAPTER XXIV
THE JOURNEY

Right hand they leave thy cliffs, Craigforth!
And soon that bulwark of the north,
Grey Stirling, with its tower and town,
Upon their fleet career look'd down.

Scott.

On the way from Cadzow to Stirling, though frequently honoured by the society of the regent, who requested him to ride near his person, Florence was sad, sombre, and abstracted; for his heart was full of fiery and bitter thoughts. In Arran's train there rode a hundred horse, mostly gentlemen, all well mounted, richly apparelled, and splendidly armed. As many of these were Hamiltons, they viewed with some jealousy and mistrust the sudden familiarity which seemed to exist between the stranger and their chief. The events which had taken place since the night of his landing at Leith had almost soured his heart against his own countrymen; at least these events had filled it with a thirst for vengeance on all who were in league against the regent Arran; for with those, and such as those, he correctly classed the men who had laid such deadly snares for his destruction, and had pursued with such rancour one who had done them no wrong.

Champfleurie he had resolved to slay, without much preface or ceremony, on the first available opportunity. He had similar benevolent views regarding the laird of Millheugh, the Lord Kilmaurs, and so many others, that, had he possessed the hands of Briareus, and had in every hand a sword, he would not have found them too many to fulfil his mental and hostile engagements. His old inborn and hereditary hatred of Preston was still unwavering, though tinged with compunction; for he could not but remember and acknowledge the generosity of the old man on whose grey hairs he had hurled his scorn, his obliquy, and defiance.

And then came to memory his love—his unknown love—so beautiful and so playfully mysterious—a countess, yet one whose name he had failed to discover among the many countesses who, by the policy or loyalty of their husbands, clustered about the person of Mary of Lorraine; for it was becoming evident to all, that if a false move in the great games of war and politics were made by Arran, she, when supported by the Guises, a French army under D'Essé d'Epainvilliers, and those Scottish lords who adhered to her, would not fail to obtain for herself that which she prized more than life—the regency of Scotland.

The train of Arran rode rapidly, to reach Stirling in time, lest the train of the queen-mother, who was coming from Edinburgh, might enter the town before them; and on this journey Florence could perceive, from incidents that occurred, how the people and the times were changing.

The wild white bulls were seen in great numbers about the woods of Cumbernauld, and the gentlemen of the regent's troop pursued and shot one of great size and beauty for mere sport, while it was grazing on the wild furzy heath of Fannyside-muir. They assigned the carcass to three of the Queen's bedesmen, or blue-gown beggars, who were passing, and then rode heedlessly on their way; though on an oak by the wayside there hung the festering and hideous remains of two poor Egyptians, who had been put to death by Malcolm Lord Fleming of Cumbernauld for having slain one of these useless white oxen for food.

At Templar-denny, they crossed the Carron by an ancient bridge of four pointed Gothic arches, built by the Knights of the Temple in the reign of David I.; and there, as the glittering train of Arran rode through the village, the whole population were assembled on the bank of the river, in wild commotion, to duck a woman accused of witchcraft, while the air was rent by shouts of—

"A witch! a witch!—banes to the bleeze, and soul to the deil!"

The victim was a hag, old enough, and ugly enough, to support the character. She had dwelt apart from all in a wretched hut upon the haunted Hill of Oaks, and was accused of working much evil to a man who once mocked her years. By one spell she had stopped his mill for nine days and as many nights; thus, though the Carron swept through the mill-race with the fury of a summer flood, the old moss-encrusted and wooden wheel stood still and immovable; but when it *did* turn, it was with a vengeance indeed! It whirled with such velocity that the mill took fire and was soon reduced to ashes; and all this she had achieved by the simple agency of burying a black cat alive, and casting above it three handfuls of salt.

She shrieked piteously for aid and for mercy, as Arran's glittering train swept past; but the age of chivalry was gone—vile superstition had taken its place; and all these hundred lords, knights, and gentlemen, rode on their way, abandoning this unhappy being to the fury of a mob, who soon ended her sufferings in the waters of the Carron, which swept her body to the Firth.

The Reformation, with the superstition of witchcraft, grew and flourished side by side in Scotland.

As the regent's train traversed the district famed still as the Scottish Marathon, a proof was seen of the progress the whole kingdom was making towards a universal apostasy from Rome. Though a body of Cistercian nuns, on a pilgrimage from the priory of Emanuel, on the Avon, were heard singing the *sexte*, or noonday service of their order, in the chapel of St. Mary at Skoek, and the harmony of their sweet voices came delightfully on the soft wind that swayed the masses of wavy grain, and rustled the foliage of the Torwood at Bannockburn, one of those crosses which piety of old had placed in almost every Scottish village, had been overthrown in the night; the arms of this symbol of redemption had been shattered, and the effigy of the Great Martyr was dashed to fragments, which were strewed over the roadway.

Florence was neither devout nor bigoted, yet, like many of the regent's train, he felt that there was something in this new spectacle and sacrilege which deeply wounded his heart, and all the old traditions—if we may so name the solemn faith in which his mother reared him, and in which so many of his ancestors had died—rushed like a flood upon his soul. Several gentlemen checked their horses, and frowned or muttered; others smiled heedlessly and covertly, for the day was coming when all reverence for the cross and triple crown of Rome would be lost amid the stern opposition of one portion of the Scottish nation and the apathetic indifference of the other.

CHAPTER XXV
THE PROCESSION

And many a band of ardent youths were seen,
Some into rapture fired by glory's charms,
Or hurl'd the thundering car along the green,
Or march'd embattled on in glittering arms.

Beattie.

The Regent Arran, with his gay train—their armour, jewels, and lace all flashing in the sunshine—came at a gallop through the magnificent glades of the old Torwood, and entered Stirling by its lower gate, at the moment that the cannon from the lofty castle, under the orders of Hans Cochrane, the Queen's master-gunner, began to boom from the ramparts; and the bells of the Dominicans, in the Friar Wynd, and of the Franciscans, among whom King James IV. was wont to pass each Good Friday on his bare knees, "in sackcloth shirt and iron belt," rang merrily; and the vast silver-toned bell which King David hung in the great tower of Cambus Kenneth, on the green links of Forth, replied in the distance.

The steep and narrow High Street of Stirling was so densely crowded by the burgesses and population of the adjacent villages, by country farmers and bonnet-lairds on horseback, each with his gudewife cosily trussed on a pillow behind him—and also by the trains of the Queen and Queen-mother, that it was with difficulty Arran could approach, with his plumed hat in hand (he had given his helmet to young Dalserfe), to pay his proper respects and take his place on the right hand of Mary of Lorraine, while his retinue mingled with hers.

The day was beautiful, clear, and serene; and the charming purity of the air, with the lofty situation of Stirling, rising on its ridge of rock from a vast extent of fertile plain, curving hills, blue river, and green forest scenery, that spread for miles around it, till mellowed faint and far away in sunny mist and distance, might have made one think that it was on some such August day that King William the Lion, in his last sickness, when the prayers of the Church, and when the subtle medicines drained from his fairy goblet, failed to save him, thought of Stirling, and begged his courtiers to bear him there, that he might inhale its delightful atmosphere, and live yet a little longer.

Amid the ceaseless hum of conversation, the air rang with cries, laughter, the confused clamour, caused by the trampling of thousands of feet and iron hoofs in the narrow space, where this dense and dusty throng, like the waves of a human sea, seemed to be broken against the abrupt abutments of the houses, wynds, and alleys; the towers of turnpike stairs and out-shots, or at times by the lowered lance, the levelled arquebuse, or clenched hand of some exasperated man-at-arms who became incommoded by the pressure upon his mailed person.

Every window was full of faces, and every out-shot, fore-stair, and doorhead, every ledge, moulding, and even the tops of some of the houses, bore a freight of bare-headed and bare-legged urchins, who, excited by the cannon, the bells, the crowd, the music, and the general hubbub, waved their caps or bonnets, and lent their shrill voices to swell the great chorus of sounds by which the Queen-mother, her little daughter, and the Regent Arran, were welcomed into the loyal and ancient burgh of Stirling, whose noble castle was to our kings of old what Windsor was to the house of England, and Aranjuez to the line of Castile, a summer palace, and—if such could be found in stormy Scotland—a place for recreation and repose.

The Earl of Bothwell, outwardly still a loyal noble, with a troop of spearmen, all cuirassed, helmeted, and on horseback, led the van; then came the great officers of state, mounted on caparisoned horses, each with his train of grooms and lackeys, many wearing their robes or official insignia; thus Bothwell wore at his neck a silver whistle, and on his banner an anchor, in virtue of his office as Lord High Admiral of Scotland.

First came the Lord Chancellor, John Hamilton, archbishop of St. Andrew's, a mild and gentle statesman, of great presence and dignity, the *last* Catholic primate of Scotland. He was barbarously murdered in 1571, at the bridge of Stirling, and in his last moments was insulted by his enemies compelling him to wear his pontifical robes.

Then came the Lord High Treasurer, John Hamilton, abbot of Paisley, brother of the Regent; and the Comptroller of Scotland, William Commendator, of Culross, each in the robes of his order. Then followed the Lord Keeper of the Privy Seal, bearing it in a velvet purse embroidered with the royal arms. This statesman was William Lord Ruthven, of the fated line of Gowrie, and father of the stern Ruthven, who looked so pale and ghastly through his barred helmet on that night twenty years after, when David Rizzio was slain in the north tower of Holyrood.

The Secretary of State, David Panater, bishop of Ross, keen-eyed and shaggy-browed, bent his stern glance over the multitude. This was a learned prelate, poet, and statesman, who was once prior of St. Mary's beautiful isle, and for seven years was Scottish ambassador in France. Then came the laird of Colinton, who was Lord Clerk Register, but who handled his two-handed sword better than his pen, riding beside the bishop of Orkney, who was lord president of the Court of Session, and a dabbler in the literature of the day—a scanty commodity withal.

The Great Chamberlain of Scotland came next. He was Malcolm Lord Fleming of Cumbernauld, a brave and proud peer, who possessed a vast estate, having no less than twelve royal charters of lands and baronies in various counties. He was without armour, but wore a doublet of shining cloth of gold, with a chain and medal, also of gold, at his neck. Thirty gentlemen in armour, and as many servants in livery coats, armed with swords and petronels, and all bearing the name, arms, and colours of Fleming, rode behind him. Then, amid many other gentlemen, rode Claude Hamilton, of Preston, with his train of rough fellows, armed with helmet, jack, and spear, headed by his drunken butler, Symon Brodie, who had encased his portly person in a suit of remarkably rusty old iron, furnished with a capacious casque of the fifteenth contury, from the hollow depths of which he swore at the crowd as confidently as if he had been an arquebusier of the royal guard.

Preceded by many barons of parliament, wearing their crimson-velvet caps, which were adorned by golden circles, studded with six equidistant pearls, and by many bishops, abbots, and priors, in many-coloured robes, came M. d'Oysell, the ambassador of France, and Monsignore Grimani, patriarch of Venice and legate of Pope Paul III. A Venetian, feeble, nervous, sallow-visaged, and black-eyed, he had come to urge upon the Scottish hierarchy "the necessity for crushing the growing heresy, lest the church of God should fall." As if he had been a cardinal priest, two silver pillars were borne before him by two Dominican friars, between whom rode a Scottish knight of Rhodes or Malta, from the preceptory of Torphichen, armed on all points, wearing the black mantle of his order, and bearing aloft the Roman banner, on which were gilded the triple crown of the sovereign pontiff and the symbolical keys of heaven.

The clamour of the populace was hushed as this solemn personage approached; but it was no spirit of reverence that repressed them; for, sullen and contemptuous, the Reformers as yet muttered only under their beards, and scowled beneath their bonnets at the envoy of "the pagan fu' o' pride;" for the time was one of change—the old faith all but dead, and the new was little respected and less understood.

We have said that the train of the Regent Arran joined that of the Queen-mother. He felt something of pique and envy at its splendour, yet he courteously rode bareheaded by her side. In taking his place there, Fawside fell back, and, being pressed by the density of the crowd against the corner of a house, was compelled to remain there inactive on horseback while this glittering procession, amid which so many of his personal enemies—such as Preston, Cassilis, Glencairn, and Ealmaurs—bore a part, passed on. The sight of these in succession filled his heart with a longing for retributive justice upon them—a longing so deep and high, that the emotion swelled his breast till the clasps of his cuirass were strained to starting; yet, remembering that he was there alone—but one among many, common prudence compelled him to remain quiescent for a time.

Led by Champfleurie came the Queen's band of armed pensioners or arquebusiers, wearing the arms and livery of Scotland and Lorraine. These soldiers were first embodied by the widow of James V., and existed as a portion of the Stirling garrison, wearing the Quaint costume of her time until 1803, when they were incorporated with one of the garrison battalions formed by George III. On this day they were preceded by the Queen's Swiss drummers, her trumpeters, violers, and tabourners, all clad in yellow Bruges satin, slashed and trimmed with red, and led by M. Antoine, in whom Florence immediately recognized the pretended dumb valet of his mysterious habitation.

Then came the widowed queen herself, looking rather pale, but beautiful as ever. She was seated in a chariot, then deemed a wonderful piece of mechanism. It was twelve feet long by six wide, and rumbled along on four elaborately-carved wheels. It was drawn by six switch-tailed Flemish mares, each led by a lackey in scarlet and yellow, and was lined and hung with "doole-claith, or French black," as old Sir James Kirkaldy of Grange, her treasurer, styles it. Before it, an esquire bore her husband's royal banner, for the painting of which, in gold and fine colours, Andro Watson, limner to King James V., received the sum of four pounds.

By her side was a little girl, whose sweet and childlike face was encircled by a triangular hood of purple velvet edged with pearls. This girl, with the dimpled cheeks and merry eyes, which dilated and glittered with alternate delight, surprise, and alarm at the bustle around her, was the queen of all the land, the only child of James V.; and old men who had fought at Solway, at Flodden, and at Ancrumford—aged soldiers, who had carried their white heads erect in Scotland's bloodiest battles,—veiled them now, and prayed aloud that God might bless her.

The conventional smile upon the beautiful face of Mary of Lorraine was like the cold brightness of a winter sun, for many upon whom her smiles were falling she loved little and suspected much; and thus she smiled on

Arran when he bowed to his horse's mane to kiss her gloved hand. But the childlike Queen Mary laughed aloud, and held out both, her pretty hands to the bearded earl, with a smile so sweet and natural, that even the cold and politic noble was moved, for it was the simple greeting of youth to a familiar face; while with her mother he was on the terms of two well-bred people who are shrewdly playing a selfish game and quite understand each other. Yet, as he gazed on the clear bright limpid eyes and smiling face of the beautiful child, he more than half repented the departure from that treaty by which she was to have become the bride of his son, the Lord Hamilton, who was then a soldier in France—a treaty which would have placed the house of Arran on the Scottish throne. Mary's object was to obtain the regency, and with it the permanent custody of her daughter till she came of age; while Arran, as next heir to the throne, was resolved to hold both in his own hands, at all hazards and at all perils.

In the Queen's chariot were four ladies, who, like herself, wore the black velvet dool-cloak, the large hood of which, in the fashion of the time, was pulled so far over the face as to impart to the wearer the aspect of a mourner at a funeral.

While all his pulses quickened with eagerness and anxiety, Florence strove to pierce the crowd that stood between him and this great mis-shapen and slowly-moving vehicle, which contained the two queens and their ladies; but under their capacious hoods he failed to discover the face of her he sought.

Suddenly one raised her gloved hand and lightly threw back the front of her hood. The action gave Florence a start like an electric shock.

"'Tis she!" he exclaimed, on recognizing the soft features, the dark eyebrows and hair of his unknown. "And now I cannot fail to discover her, as many here must know the names and rank of the ladies of the tabourette."

He turned to a person who, like himself, was on horseback, but who, being completely wedged in by the crowd, sat in his saddle gazing passively at the pageant, which ascended the steep street towards the castle of Stirling. He was well armed, and wore the livery and badges of a trooper of the house of Glencairn, yet seemed, withal, to be a gentleman. In short, this person, who was gazing, apparently, with the vacant curiosity of a mere spectator, was one of the most enterprising actors in our drama—Master Edward Shelly, the Englishman. To him, all this affair was but one other feature in the perilous political game he had been ordered to play, and which, in his soul, he despised.

He knew that the beautiful, noble, and wealthy wife proposed for him by the Scottish malcontents, was among the attendants of the two queens;

and though, as a soldier, a Boulogner, tolerably indifferent on the subject of matrimony in general, and, as an Englishman of 1547, especially indifferent on the matter of a Scottish wife, he certainly had some curiosity again to see this lady, whom, as yet, he had never addressed, but whom he had repeatedly passed in the streets, or seen at mass, and once at a hawking-party on Wardie Muir, when in attendance on Mary of Lorraine, like whom, she was a graceful and expert horse-woman.

The eyes of these two men were lighted by smiles, and the colour in their cheeks heightened as they saw the fair young face, so suddenly revealed from the sombre shadow of the doole-cloak; but an examination of their smiles will prove that they resulted from different emotions.

Florence expressed in his moistened eyes all his soul felt of honest joy and love on beholding one so dear to his heart—a heart as yet unhackneyed in the ways of the world; and the warm flush came and went on his smooth boyish cheek, while every pulse beat rapidly.

The smile that spread slowly over the handsome and sunburned face of Edward Shelly, expressed only satisfaction, with (it might be) a dash of triumph, that she was all we have described her to be. Even in that age he was past the years of romantic or sudden attachments. Shelly was verging on forty; and his latter twenty years had been spent in Calais and other English garrisons in France: thus, in some respects, his morality, especially as regarded women, fitted him as loosely as his leather glove.

"So ho, my future wife!" he muttered, twisting his thick moustache up to his eyes, in the clear blue of which drollery was perhaps the prevailing expression.

"My love, unknown love!" whispered Florence in the depth of his heart, and then a sadness came over all his features and his soul, he knew not why.

These two persons, the man and the youth, the careless and the impassioned, the triumphant and the sad, conscious that the same face attracted them, now turned towards each other, and spoke.

"Worthy sir, can you favour me with the name of that lady who has just thrown back her hood?" asked Florence, in a voice that was almost tremulous, as if he feared the secret of his heart would be exposed.

"And who is now speaking to the little queen?"

"Yes."

"'Tis Madeline Home, the Countess of Yarrow."

"*Yarrow!*" reiterated Florence in a breathless voice.

"Yes, the niece, and some say, heiress, of Claude Hamilton of Preston, who hath just passed upward with a train of horse, and his butler, a drunken lout, like a huge lobster at their head."

Had a cannon exploded at his ear, Florence could not have been more astounded than by this revelation of a relationship so fatal to the romance and success of his love.

"She is beautiful, my friend," continued the Englishman, looking at her, with his head on one side, with the air of a connoisseur admiring a horse, a yacht, or a picture; "what think you of her?"

"That one so fair, so noble, must have many, perhaps too many lovers," sighed the young man in a voice of bitterness, as he cast down his eyes.

His manner was so strange, that Shelly now turned sharply towards him, and from the expression of his face began to gather, or to fear, that there were in Stirling more lovers already than were quite necessary; but the Queen's great chariot passed on; the crowd collapsed in its rear; the two horsemen were roughly separated, and Florence, bewildered by what he had just heard, mechanically followed the Regent's train towards the Castle of Stirling. He had but one thought:—

"Countess of Yarrow; she is the Countess of Yarrow, whose father's sword was foremost on the day my father fell!"

This, then, was the reason why she and the Queen, with a tact and secrecy which thus defeated the end in view, had so studiously concealed her name from him. But what availed their tact and secrecy now?

To love the niece, the ward and successor, the nearest and only kinswoman of Claude Hamilton, the man whom, since infancy, he had been taught to abhor,—the slayer of his father, the slayer of his brave brother Willie; he whom he had registered a thousand impious vows to destroy whenever and wherever they met,—at church or in market, in field or on highway; he whose name in Fawside Tower had been a household word for all that was vile and hateful; he whose friendship he had so totally scorned, and on whose white hairs he had heaped obloquy and hurled defiance!

Alas! it produced a terrible chaos of thought and revulsion of feeling. Here Father John of Tranent would recognize the finger of Heaven, pointing a way to soothe the angry passions of men, and to a lasting peace between the rival races; but then Dame Alison, that stern daughter of the gloomy house of Colzean, would only recognize a snare of the Evil One, who was seeking to deprive her of her "pound of flesh," — of her just and lawful meed of vengeance!

Full of these distressing reflections, Florence followed the train of the Queen into the Castle of Stirling, and, dismounting within the arched gate, which is defended by round towers, that are still of great strength, and were then surmounted by steeple-like roofs of slate, he joined the Regent's suite, who were now all on foot. Hence the loud and incessant jingling of spurs of gold, of silver, and of Ripon steel, upon the pavement of the yard, the staircases, and the great hall, where the conference was to be held, proved how great was the number of men of distinction who followed Mary of Lorraine and the Regent to council.

As the former alighted from her chariot, there occurred (according to the narrative of the vicar of Tranent) one of those incidents, which were frequent in those simple times, when royalty was easier of access than now.

An aged woman, wearing a curchie and tartan cloak, threw herself on her knees, and lifting up her hands, exclaimed, —

"Heaven save your grace!"

"What seek you?" asked the Queen, pausing.

"Charity; — my gudeman died on Flodden Hill wi' his four sons and his three brethren."

"My poor woman," said Mary of Lorraine, detaching a purse from her girdle, and placing it in the hand of the mendicant, "then we have each lost a husband for Scotland."

The Countess of Yarrow led the little Queen Mary by the left hand.

The Regent Arran gave his right hand, ungloved, to her mother; their suites formed in procession; and, while the trumpets sounded shrill and high, they ascended to the hall, between ranks of pikemen and arquebusiers facing inwards.

The bells continued to toll; still the populace without shouted their acclaim; still the iron culverins and brass moyennes thundered in smoke and flame from the massive bastions and arched loopholes, wreathing the grey turrets with fleecy vapour, and waking the distant echoes of the Torwood and the Abbey Craig; while, that nothing might be wanting to swell the combination of noises, two old lions, pets and favourites of the late King James, to whom they had been sent by the Emperor Charles V., roused angrily from their lethargic noonday dose, were pawing, prancing, and bellowing in that small court, which, from their presence there, is yet named the Lions' Den.

CHAPTER XXVI
THE CONVENTION OF ESTATES

Oh, gentlemen of Scotland! oh, chevaliers of France!
How each and all had grasp'd his sword and seized his
angry lance, If lady-love, or sister dear, or nearer, dearer
bride, Had been like me, your friendless queen, insulted
and belied!

Bon Gaultier.

This meeting took place in that magnificent hall which was built by James III. for banquets and the meeting of parliament. It is one hundred and twenty feet long; and to the taste for architecture, which led him to embellish it in a style of the most florid beauty (long since destroyed by the utilitarian barbarism of the Board of Ordnance), with his love for painting, poetry, music, and sculpture, he owed much of that malignity which embittered his short life, and ultimately led to his fatal and terrible end in the adjacent field of Sauchieburn.

Unlike the rough, rude tower which crowns the tremendous precipice that overhangs the valley, and from the small windows of which our earlier monarchs, such as the four Malcolms, the three Alexanders, and the three Roberts, were wont to survey the mighty landscape of wood and wold, mountain and rock, through which the snaky Forth winds far away to sea, — with the giant Grampians, deep, dark, and purple, cut by the hand of God into a hundred splintered peaks, mellowing in distance amid the skies of gold and azure, — unlike this rude tower, we say, from the battlements of which men had seen Wallace win his victory, by the old bridge, and Bruce sweep Edward's host from Bannockburn, — the buildings of James III. in Stirling Castle are covered by quaint pilasters, deep niches, elaborate carvings, and rich mouldings; by columns and brackets, supporting statues of Venus, Diana, Perseus, Cleopatra, James V., and Omphale.

The hall had a lofty roof of oak, from which hung English, Moorish, and Portuguese banners, taken in battles at sea by the gallant Bartons; by Sir Andrew Wood, of Largo, in his famous *Yellow Frigate*; and by Sir Alexander Mathieson, the "old king of the sea." Its walls were covered by gaudy frescoes, or pieces of tapestry, the work of Margaret of Oldenburg and the ladies of her court. At the upper end stood the throne, under the old purple canopy of James IV., until whose reign the royal colour in Scotland had been purple; and on a table, before this lofty chair, lay the sceptre, the sword of state, and the crown, — that crown of thorns, and of sorrow, which more than one valiant king of Scotland has bequeathed to his son on the battlefield, — the fatal heritage of a fated line of kings.

During a flourish of trumpets, the little queen was placed upon the throne, where she gazed about her smiling, while a mixture of childlike wonder, alarm, and drollery glittered in her dark and dilating eyes. On her left hand sat Mary of Lorraine, a step lower down; on her right stood the Regent, in his shining doublet, leaning on his long sword. Behind the former were grouped the Countesses of Yarrow, Mar, Huntly, Errol, and Orkney, in their long dool-cloaks; behind the latter was a gay suite of lesser barons and gentlemen of the surname of Hamilton, gorgeously attired and armed.

With an emotion of irrepressible sadness, Mary of Lorraine gazed round the beautiful hall, and on the splendid but silent crowd which filled it; glittering in armour, lace, velvet, silk, jewellery, plumage, and embroidery. Then her fine eyes drooped on the child by her side.

To her, Stirling Castle was a place of many sad and stirring associations. There, her husband, the magnificent and gallant James V., was born, and crowned in the same year in which his father fell in battle. It was his favourite residence, and the scene of many of his merry frolics, as the gudeman of Ballengeich; and there their only surviving child, Queen Mary, had been crowned in 1543, when only nine months old, — crowned queen of a people who were to cast her forth as a waif upon the sea of misfortune; but on whose annals the story of her sorrows, and of their shame has cast a shadow that may never fade.

Many conflicting public and private interests were involved in the result of this convention of estates, or conference at Stirling.

The marriage of the young queen with the heir of France, or with the boy Edward VI.; and hence the great question of peace or war with England; involving the lives of thousands, who were doomed never to see the close of autumn.

Bothwell looked forward with confidence to the rejection of the French marriage, and to himself obtaining the hand of an English princess, when he could exult over Mary of Lorraine, who had trifled with his love, as with the love of many others, as already related, for reasons of her own, and slighted him in the end.

M. d'Oysell, the ambassador of Henry II., confidently anticipated the successful issue of that diplomacy which would ultimately make him a peer of France, knight of St. Michael, and perhaps lord of some forfeited Huguenot seigneurie.

M. Grimani, the patriarch of Venice, had also in view the maintenance of the ancient league between France and Scotland; that the hydra-headed heresy of the latter might be destroyed by fire and sword, if the power of the preacher failed.

Claude Hamilton, of Preston, already saw in imagination his coming patent of the earldom of Gladsmuir, as others of his faction—Cassilis, Glencairn, and Kilmaurs—did their pensions, places, and profits, if the English marriage was achieved.

Edward Shelly, somewhat to his own surprise, felt a combination of selfishness and delight, at the prospect of winning a rich and beautiful wife—a young countess, and perhaps an earldom, as the reward of *his* diplomacy; while poor Florence Fawside, ignorant of all these secret springs of action, which moved the wise and good, or the titled knaves around him, looked gloomily forward to the sequel of the feud he had yet to foster, and to the consequent loss, for ever, of a love that was all the more seductive and alluring because such a passion was new to his heart, and that she who was its origin, had thrown much that was romantic around it. Although the poor lad knew it not, on the decision of these lords and barons, loyal and true, or rebel and false, depended, perhaps, the sequel of his love; for the object of it was to be bartered, as Shelly phrased it, "like a bale of goods," to a foreign emissary, as the price of his services in assisting to subvert the liberties of Scotland. In his sudden grief, on discovering the abyss of old hereditary hate that yawned between himself and Madeline Home, he forgot even the wrongs he had to avenge upon the Laird of Champfleurie and others, who had plotted for his destruction. He forgot all but her presence, and that she was lost to him!

All Lowland Scotland stood on tiptoe, watching with anxiety the result of a debate that was to give her an English king, or was still further to cement the league of five hundred years, by placing the French dauphin on the throne of the Stuarts; we say *Lowland* Scotland, for the Celts, ever at war among themselves, viewed with disdain or heeded not whatever was done, beyond their then impassable boundary, the Grampians.

Arran looked forward to having the regency placed more securely in his hands, and resolving that, if it passed, as ultimately it did, into the firmer grasp of Mary of Lorraine, to resort at once to arms, and hoist the standard of revolt on his castle of Cadzow.

Let us see how all this ended.

The debate was stormy, for many of the speakers were rude and brief in speech, rough, unlettered, fierce, and turbulent. Frowns were exchanged, gauntleted hands were clenched, and more than once the pommels of swords and poniards were ominously touched, among both parties; for though the proud spirit and patriotism of many were roused to fiery action by the great event at issue, there were others, whom we need not name—the *Scottish utilitarians* of 1547—whose cupidity and selfishness alone were enlisted in the cause; but vain were their exertions. The letter of Henry of Valois, the production of which caused many an eye to lour on Florence, who, absorbed in his own thoughts, was all unconscious that he was observed at all,— the energy of his ambassador, M. d'Oysell, and the eloquence of Mary of Lorraine, when united to her own beauty and her husband's memory, bore all before them! Hence the proposals of the English Protector, Somerset, were abruptly rejected, with something very much akin to disdain. In his letters there was assumed a dictatorial tone, which could not fail to offend the loyal portion of the Scottish *noblesse*.

"By his holiness Pope Julius II.," said Arran with a kindling eye, "it was ordained in 1504, that at his court the king of Scotland should take precedence of the kings of Castile, of Hungary, Poland, Navarre, of Bohemia, and Denmark; and that he should recognize no superior but God and His vicegerent on earth: then whence this grotesque loftiness of tone from a regent of England?"

The patriarch of Venice and the French ambassador beheld this growing indignation with evident satisfaction; while glances of ill-concealed anger and dismay were exchanged by those whose names were affixed to the indenture which, at that moment, Shelly carried in the secret pocket of his jazarine-jacket. Cassilis, who had little patience and less politeness, openly insulted the legate by terming Pope Julius "a shaveling mass-monger and pagan priest."

"My lord, my lord!" exclaimed the Archbishop of St. Andrew's, growing pale with anger; "beware lest he excommunicate thee with bell, book, and candle!"

"I care not," replied the sullen earl, frowning at the primate under the aventayle of his helmet; "for I am ready to maintain, wi' the auld Lollards o' Kyle, that the pope is a pagan, who exalteth himself against God, and above Him; that he can neither remit sins nor the pains of purgatory by mumbling Latin, or scribbling on a sheep-hide; that the blessing of a bishop is worth less than a brass bodle, and that Paul III. is the head o' the crumbling kirk of Antichrist!"

The sallow Venetian trembled with horror and anger at these words, and raised his thin white tremulous hands to heaven.

"Sancta Maria!" he exclaimed; "silence, thou false peer, lest I have thee burned quick!"

Cassilis laughed aloud, till every joint in his armour rattled.

"I am Gilbert Kennedy," said he, "and can betake me to my auld house in the wilds o' Carrick; so send your faggots there; and, hark ye, sir legate, I, who have hanged a monk, may feed the crows with a patriarch."

Cassilis was a stern and ferocious lord, so none dared to reply. He was a tyrant over his vassals, who found his avarice insatiable; yet it was always exerted in form of feudal law. Thus, on the marriage of each of his daughters (he had two—Jean, married to the Earl of Orkney, and Catherine, to the Laird of Banburrow), or the knighting of his sons, the master, and Sir Thomas of Colzean; or for the maintenance of feuds with his neighbours, he had mulcted them heavily by the ordinance which made it "lesome to the lord to seek sic help frae his men conforme to their faculties and the quantitie of their lands;" in short, to tax them, and seize the best of the goods in stable, byre, roost, and cheese-room, whenever the lord pleased, or found an urgent necessity for so doing.

The arguments and energy of this avaricious peer, of Glencairn, Kilmaurs, and others, who were in secret the agents or adherents of Somerset, if they failed to convince the mass who heard them, of the advantages that might accrue from a nuptial and political union with England, succeeded at last in filling with undefined alarm the bosom of Mary of Lorraine, whose finely nervous and aristocratic, yet soft temperament, was as ill calculated to withstand the turbulence, cupidity, and savagery of these atrocious peers, as in after-times her daughter to withstand their sons. She knew the falsehood of those with whom she had to contend, and who were now collected in a gloomy group near the council-table. Her soft cheek, from having the pink tinge of a sea-shell, crimsoned; her beautiful eyes filled with light, and, with a hand white as marble, grasping an arm of her innocent daughter's throne, she rose to speak, and then all were hushed to silence, and every eye was turned towards her.

"My lords and gentlemen," said she, gathering courage from the emergency of the moment and the presence of M. d'Oysell and the patriarch of Venice, "the holy religion which was planted in this soil a thousand years ago, and which flourished so broadly and so well, yielding good fruit, has been all but uprooted! A cardinal priest, a prince of the Church, has been barbarously murdered in his own archiepiscopal palace, and, gashed by wounds, his naked corpse has been suspended from its ramparts in the light of noon! Already, by this tremendous act, the altar of God has been defiled and the temple shaken to its foundation. Through the dim vista of events to come, I look forward with fear and sorrow to the future reign of my little daughter, the child of the good King James V.—that King James whom Pope Julius made defender of the faith, and girt with a sword sharpened by his holy hand on the altar-stone of St. Peter, against all heretics, especially those of England,—that James V., whose young and noble heart was broken by the rebel spirit of his peers, by their treason to Scotland in the cabinet, and their cowardice at the battle of Solway. Nay, never frown on me, or rattle your swords, my lords of Cassilis and Glencairn," she added, waving her small white hand, on which the jewels flashed like the scorn that lighted up her eyes; "I am a woman, and claim a woman's privilege to speak; and thus I repeat again, that I anticipate the future of my daughter, a Stuart and a Guise, among you with grief and horror! The Earls of Bothwell and Glencairn have spoken well and plausibly; but apart from all, the Duke of Somerset's conditions, which are unworthy the Scottish crown and degrading to the Scottish people, what happiness could be my daughter's in wedding the son of the apostate Henry,—he who was the horror of all modest women,—he who espoused Anne Boleyn, knowing her to be his own daughter, and yet laid her head on the block; who violated his promises to Anne of Cleves, and sent her fair successor also to the block; who murdered the aged Countess of Salisbury, and sent more than seventy thousand of his subjects to await his appearance before the judgment-seat of God; he who, by his lusts, and by his treason to the Holy See, made all England turn, in one day, heretic! Yet it is to the son of this man you would wed her in helpless infancy; and to the custody of his creature Somerset you would yield her, the daughter of Scotland and of France!"

A deep silence succeeded this outburst. At last Arran spoke.

"Fear not, madam," said he; "being the next kinsman to the crown, I am, by the ancient custom of our mother country, the tutor or custodian of its infant sovereign, and, with God's will, I shall remain so!"

"None dare dispute this right, Lord Earl," said Mary.

"None, save the king of England or his representative," urged Glencairn; "and he does so by the right of a treaty for the marriage of Edward with the daughter of King James, a treaty——"

"Which we do not recognize," interrupted Arran.

"What cared Henry of England for treaties?" exclaimed Arran's brother, the Archbishop of St. Andrew's,—"he who trampled on all laws, human and divine?"

"He hath gone to the place of his reward, sir priest," replied the rude Glencairn; "and now we have to deal, not with a dead king, but with the Duke of Somerset."

"A heretic as stout," continued the incensed primate, "though perhaps less lecherous and lustful."

"Lustful enough of our Scottish blood," said the gallant Earl of Huntly, with a smile, "if we may judge of his campaign among us here in '44, when we knew him as Edward Earl of Hertford."

"The result of all this chattering will be that we shall have war," said Glencairn. "The English will come — —"

"With their Spanish and German auxiliaries — —"

"Well, let them come," retorted Arran. "Our hills are steep, our streams are deep and swift, our hearts, I hope, as stout, and the swords bequeathed to us by our sires from a thousand bloody fields, are sharp and sure as ever! Let Somerset come, with his English billmen, his German pikes, and Spanish arquebuses: when true to herself, Scotland is unconquerable!"

"Thou art right, my lord," added the patriarch of Venice; "her people are unconquerable. But among her nobles are men ever ready to bend their necks to any chain of gold, or sell their faith and honour to the highest bidder!"

Perceiving that their design of having the English marriage accomplished was on the eve of being hopelessly frustrated, — that the proposals of the Valois were all but formally accepted by the regent and Mary of Lorraine, those who were in secret league with England became desperate, and Kilmaurs at last conceived the artful idea of embroiling Arran with the Queen-mother on a point concerning which he knew them to be remarkably sensitive. The smile of this crafty young lord was a mere twitch of the mouth, an unpleasant grimace at best; yet such a smile his visage wore when, during a pause in this strangely-conducted controversy, he said to Arran, in a low and stern voice, —

"Beware, my lord regent, lest this French marriage be not a plot of the Guises merely to involve us in a war with England."

"For that I care little. But to what end would it be?"

"An alteration in the regency."

Arran changed colour, and eyeing the young lord askance, asked, through his clenched teeth,

"That I may be succeeded by whom?"

"The Queen-mother, very probably."

"'Tis false, my Lord Kilmaurs!" exclaimed Mary of Lorraine, haughtily, "I say so—I, Mary, Queen of Scotland!"

"Under favour, madam," said Arran, reddening with annoyance, "you are neither Queen of Scotland nor the Scots, but simply queen-mother of the sovereign. There is a difference, you will pardon me. Henry of Valois is king of France; Edward VI. is king of England; but our monarchs have ever been kings of the Scots; for the SOIL belongs to the people."

"That whilk they soak so readily wi their gude red bluid, may weel be theirs," said the aged Earl of Mar.

"Bravade as ye may," urged Kilmaurs, "'tis all a plot of the Guises; and such I will maintain it to be."

"Now, grant me patience to scorn this base calumny!" said Mary of Lorraine, growing alternately red and pale with anger; for though she coveted this post in her heart, she knew too well the danger of making an enemy of Arran. "Good, my lords; I have made no struggle for the regency, nor have ever ventured to compete with my cousin Arran."

"Madam," said Arran coldly, "what right could you have pled?"

"Right enough," replied the Queen, veiling her anger by a smile; "nor am I quite without precedents either."

"Indeed!" said Arran, while Kilmaurs twitched the velvet mantle of Cassilis, and smiled to see the train on fire; "will you please to state this right?"

"A mother's right to rear her tender offspring; and Heaven knows that thought engrossed my whole heart, after the death of my two sons at Bothesay, and of my late husband and beloved king."

"God sain him! God rest him in his grave at Holyrood!" muttered the loyal old Earl of Mar, raising his bonnet; "he was the father of the poor."

"Lord earl, I thank you," said Mary, whose eyes filled with tears, and whose daughter, on perceiving this emotion, gently stole her little hand within hers; "after his death, I might have urged the parliament to remember that Mary of Gueldres, the widow of James II., and Margaret Tudor, the widow of James IV., were both regents of Scotland; then why not I, Mary of Guise and Lorraine, widow of their descendant, James V.? Yet, I asked you not for this. I love my kinsman Arran; but I better love my little daughter— the child your monarch left me. Is it not so, my good Lord Regent?"

"It is, madam; you speak most fairly and truly," replied Arran, whose smile belied the admission.

"I call God and His blessed Mother to witness, if I had then a thought in the world, but to rear my babe, as I was reared by my father, René of Lorraine, a good Catholic, and to guard her from the intrigues of those who would destroy the liberties of her country and her hope of salvation, by giving her in marriage to the heretic son of a heretic king."

"And while united to resist this object," said Arran, courteously kissing her white hand, "we are invincible; so long live the Dauphin of France, who shall one day be Francis I., king of the Scots."

A loud burst of applause shook the hall, while the malcontent lords exchanged glances of fury.

"Beware, my Lord of Arran, beware," said Glencairn; "last year, '46, Francis I. of France was glad to purchase a peace with England at the expense of eight hundred thousand crowns."

"We will purchase it at the expense of a few superfluous lives," retorted Arran, with a glance of stern significance, which made the sombre earl yet more grim and sullen; and now Bothwell began to fear that his chance of obtaining an English princess to grace his castle of Hermitage, was about as slender as Master Edward Shelly's hope of obtaining a Scottish countess, for better or worse.

The general result of this conference, or convention of the lords spiritual and temporal, was a unanimity of sentiment on the part of the regent and of the queen-mother to promote internal peace and public order. The former, for the common weal, formally renounced the contract of marriage between the young queen and his son the Lord Hamilton, in favour of the Dauphin of France, and annulled all the bonds given by various powerful peers, who pledged themselves to see that alliance effected.

The Earl of Angus and the Lord Maxwell, stung with shame, publicly and solemnly repudiated all promises of loyalty or fealty to England; and the peer last named was made warden of the western marches. Bothwell, Cassilis, and Glencairn, with others of their party, were left in a state of doubt, irresolution, and fear; for there was now at hand a crisis which would force them to arms, either for Scotland or against her.

The convention dissolved, and from that hour Scotland and England prepared for open war!

During the debate the eyes of Florence and of the countess met repeatedly, and each time she trembled, coloured deeply, and looked aside. Then, after a time, she durst not turn towards him. She knew that now he must have discovered her name, and who she was; and her heart seemed to shrink and wither up within her, in dread lest his love might turn to indifference, if not to hatred; for she knew the depth of abhorrence excited by the memory of the death-feud, inculcated by Lady Alison, in the two sons of Sir John Fawside.

Meanwhile, ignorant of what was passing in the minds of his niece and his soi-disant enemy, the old Laird of Preston had more than once surveyed the latter with somewhat of melancholy interest; for he knew the wild, stern spirit which this youth inherited from his father—and the ideas he had imbibed with the milk and blood of his mother; but poor Florence, overwhelmed by varied emotions, and by the secret he had so recently learned, avoided altogether the keen grey eye of Hamilton.

The queen-mother made a low reverence to the lords of convention, and while the sharp trumpets flourished bravely, withdrew with her daughter and ladies of honour. The eye of Florence followed sorrowfully the sombre group in their doole-cloaks (for Mary of Lorraine in public still wore the garb of mourning), and in imagination he seemed to be bidding adieu for ever to his love, and the hope it had kindled within him.

In presence of this beautiful girl the young man seemed to be alike without words or thoughts that had any coherence.

So absorbing was the emotion, that he was quite unconscious of the insolent and defiant glances levelled at him by Glencairn, by his son Kilmaurs, and others, as they brushed past and left the hall, to scheme further plots for vengeance or for safety; for these lords and their followers were only restrained by a knowledge of the locality, of its sanctity, and of the high powers of the Lord High Constable, from assaulting and slaying him, sword in hand, within the precincts of this royal castle and palace; for princely Stirling, in Scotland's earlier days, was both.

Within an hour after the convention broke up two horsemen were seen passing eastward, through the Torwood, at full speed, to lessen as much as possible the eighty Scottish miles or so that lay between them and the frontiers of England.

They were the valiant captain of the Boulogners and Master Patten, the emissaries of the Duke of Somerset, on the high-road for Berwick and London, to announce that England had no argument left her now but a sharp and dangerous one—the sword!

The loyal and true foresaw the evils to come with sincere sorrow; and, under their silvery beards, old men muttered that ancient prophecy so fatally and so frequently applicable to Scotland:—

Woe unto the land whose king is a child!

CHAPTER XXVII
MADELINE HOME

'Tis but thy name, that is my enemy;—
Thou art thyself though, not a Montague.
What's Montague? It is nor hand, nor foot,
Nor arm, nor face, nor any other part
Belonging to a man.

Romeo and Juliet.

Left almost alone in the king's hall, Florence retired from it with a heart that was alternately a prey to the emotions of sadness and mortification, bitterness and anger.

He had seen Madeline Home in her place at court as Countess of Yarrow, as maid of honour to Mary of Lorraine and as daughter of that brave Quentin Home, sixth Earl of Yarrow, who bore the king's standard at Flodden, and was warden of the middle marches—who was cupbearer to James V., and his ambassador to John III. of Portugal. Florence had seen the eyes of a hundred men surveying with admiration her beauty, which rivalled and at times outshone that of the queen she attended. The conference had lasted three hours. In all that time his eyes had scarcely seen another object than Madeline, and yet she had seldom turned her gaze towards him, and latterly not at all; for she felt oppressively conscious that she was in his presence, and that she had in some way wronged him.

She had become cold, he conceived; for it never occurred to him that, in her timidity, and lest other eyes might read their secret, she dared no longer trust herself to look upon him; and he knew not what this steadiness of averted gaze cost her poor little heart.

The dream which had filled his imagination with so much joy during the past few weeks—the dream of being loved by a woman young and beautiful—was now passing away; and the grim, armed figure of Claude Hamilton of Preston, with the warnings and incitements of his mother to bloodshed and hostility, seemed to loom darkly out from amid the shadows of the future.

In this sombre mood, and doubtful whether or not he ought to wait upon the regent before leaving Stirling, he wandered from the castle into the large tract of ground which lies south-west of it. Enclosed by a massive stone wall, this place is still known as the king's park, because there of old our monarchs kept tame deer. From thence he passed into the royal gardens, which lay at the east end of this park; and where vestiges of the walks and parterres, with the stumps of decayed fruit-trees, are still remaining amid the weeds and rushes of a marsh. In the centre of these parterres rises a mound of circular form, flattened on the summit, and named still the Round Table, from the games of chivalry played there by the princely Jameses and their knights of old, when a warrior spirit was strong in the land.

It was now one of the loveliest of August evenings. The green masses of the giant Ochil range, the columnar fronts of the Abbey craig, and of Craigforth, were basking in the sunshine; while the pale-blue or deep-purple summits of the mightier Grampians—Britain's ridgy backbone—stood sharply up against the clear glory of the golden sky; and chief of all arose the hill of God Benledi.

The terraces of the royal garden were balustraded with carved stonework, and were reached by flights of steps. They were decorated with vases of flowers, statues, and rosariums; and, in the old Scoto-French fashion, there were long grassy walks shaded by hedgerows of privet and holly, closely clipped, and compact and dense as a wall of leaves could well be.

As Florence wandered through these green alleys, oppressed by the thoughts we have described, at a sudden turn he met a lady, who carried upon her left wrist a hawk, the glossy pinions and plumage of which she was caressing. It sat upon a hawk-glove which was set with pearls, and with more than one ruby. Her other hand was bare, and of wonderful whiteness and beauty. She looked up as they drew near; and the heart of Florence beat painfully quick as his eyes met those of the promenader.

She was the Countess of Yarrow!

Flushing for a moment, she became very pale as she gave Florence her gloveless hand, which he kissed with a tremulous lip, ere it was hurriedly withdrawn; and then ensued one of those dreamy and painful pauses when, if doubt or fear exist in lovers, their eyes and hearts seem striving to analyse each other.

"At last I have learned your secret," said Florence sadly. "This day has discovered to me all—your rank, and, most sad and calamitous of all, your name and race; for my own peace, O lady, a double revelation most fatal!"

"Fatal!" she reiterated tremulously—her voice had a musical chord in it, which made every word she uttered singularly sweet and pleasing—"did you really say fatal?"

"Can the word excite your surprise?" he asked with a sadness amounting to bitterness; "when you knew that I was Florence Fawside, and the sworn enemy of your race—hating it and all its upholders—hating your blood and all who inherit it—even as the house of Preston have hated me and mine—with a rancour akin to that of devils; for in this faith my mother reared me.

"Yet, while knowing all that, I ministered unto you in your perilous illness, even as a sister—as a wife would have done," said the countess, in a low voice.

"And by that most gentle ministry—by your dazzling beauty and adorable manner, lured me to love you."

"Lured!"

"Oh, Lady Madeline! my heart is swollen to bursting. You said you loved me."

"And I love you still, dear, dear Florence!" she replied, in a voice broken by agitation.

"Alas! but yesternight I repelled the proffered friendship of your kinsman—repelled it as my dead father, as my dead brother would have done—with antipathy and scorn; and woe is me! the blood of both is on his sword and on his soul!"

The countess bowed her face upon her hands, and wept bitterly; her shoulders shook with emotion, and her bosom heaved with sobs. For a moment the heart of Fawside was wrung.

"Countess—Lady Yarrow—dearest Madeline—do not weep! Pardon me if I am rough of speech; your tears fall like molten lead upon my heart. My love—my dear love—look up and listen to me," he continued, taking her hands in his; while the hawk flew to the end of the cord which retained it, and screamed and fluttered its wings. "Oh, what shall I say to unsay the bitterness of words that should never have escaped me, and least of all to one so gentle and so tender as you!"

"And you saved the life of my kinsman, my uncle Claude, in Cadzow Wood?"

"And he mine——"

"In Millheugh tower?"

"Yes,—from Allan Duthie, and his vile marauders."

"He told me all, dear Florence, all, and did full justice to your truth and courage," said the young countess, looking up, while her bright eyes suffused with tears of joy; "after such services given mutually, this hatred, so wicked and unnatural, must surely lessen and die."

"Under favour, sweetest heart; these services so given and tendered, but placed us again upon an equality. Thought and action in each are still free. One cannot upbraid, or fetter the other's hand, by the bitter taunt, *to me thou owest life!*"

"Alas! here ends my dream; for if I find you thus stubborn and wilful to me, how shall I find my older, and sterner kinsmen?"

"Your dream, beloved Madeline,—of what?" asked the young man tenderly.

"Of peace and goodwill at least, if not of love and amity between us; for well do I know that so strong is your mother's hatred, that when we ding down Tantallon, and make a bridge to the Bass,[*] we may attempt to overcome it, but not till then."

[*] An old proverb, descriptive of an impossibility.

"Ah, speak not of my mother, Madeline," replied Florence, in an agitated voice; "the foreknowledge of all with which she may—nay, must taunt me, makes me think at times of bidding Scotland adieu for a season at least, and of returning to the Duchess of Albany, at Vendome; of joining the French army, now advancing into the Milanese; or, in short, of going anywhere, Madeline, save back to my father's old tower on Fawside Hill."

The eyes of the young countess were fixed on him sadly, sweetly, and with somewhat of reproach in them.

"You could not—" she began;

"At this crisis, no—when duty requires every loyal gentleman to lay his sword and service at the feet of Mary of Lorraine."

"Does no other sentiment than mere loyalty chain you here?" said the countess reproachfully; "could you——"

"Leave you—you would ask, beloved Madeline! ah, no—I am bewildered, and know not what I say."

He threw one arm round her, and pressed her to his breast, and his lip to hers.

When with her now, all the hopes and desires of life seemed to be gratified, and existence to have attained its culminating point, yet they were without words to express their emotion.

Each, to the full, had admitted or owned their love for the other. Then what more had they to say, for loverlike, their eyes were full of eloquence, though their tongues remained silent.

Suddenly a group of ladies appeared at the end of the long leafy alley. They were the queen-mother, the young queen Mary, and four ladies of honour. Florence had only time to whisper,—

"God mark thee, sweet one; adieu!"—to snatch one other kiss—a kiss never to be forgotten; and with a heart that beat joyously, and a head that seemed to whirl with delight, he quitted the royal garden with all speed, crossed the king's park, and ascended once more to the castle of Stirling.

CHAPTER XXVIII
CHAMPFLEURIE

Captain Swagger has ask'd me to wait on you, sir!—
Of course you remember last evening's transaction?—
And you, as a gentleman, cannot demur
At giving the captain the due satisfaction.

We have said that Florence left the countess with a tumult of emotion in his breast. He was full of joy that she loved him,—joy and honest triumph; but to what end was all this love? Circumstanced and separated as they were, by fate, by feud, and fortune, what could its sequel be, or how could a happy result ever be achieved?

At this perplexing thought, the tombs of his father and brother in the church of Tranent—those two quaintly-carved altar-tombs, on each of which lay the rigid effigy of an armed knight, his head upheld by two angels, his stony eyes gazing upward, and his mailed hands clasped in ceaseless prayer, as they lay with shield on arm and sword at side,—seemed to rise like the solemn barriers of death, between him and Madeline Home; for in each of these tombs lay the "blood-boltered" corpse of a near and dear kinsman, slain in feud and mortal fight, by the hand of Claude Hamilton. Florence still viewed the latter as the hereditary foe of his race; and with him, in the blindness of his anger, he identified those attempts by which his life had been so savagely and ruthlessly jeopardized of late.

The recollection of all he had undergone by wounds and indignity, filled him with a bitterness which even his successful love could scarcely soothe; and as he crossed the castle-yard to order his horse, on perceiving the captain of Mary of Lorraine's arquebusiers in conversation with a woman at one of the palace doors, he immediately approached him. The soldier was bravely apparelled in a red satin doublet and mantle, a white velvet hat with a red feather, white boots furnished with long gold spurs, which he clanked together, and apparently very much to his own satisfaction, as he pirouetted about, and laughed gaily with his female friend, while his delicately-gloved right hand played alternately with an amber rosary that dangled at his waist, and with a chain and medal of gold which hung at his neck. He wore a cuirass, which shone like a steel mirror; and had, of course, his sword and dagger.

Here Florence found a legitimate object whereon to vent his irritation; and, as he drew near, the woman, who was no other than Janet Sinclair, the little queen's foster-mother, retired hastily and shut the door, on which Champfleurie, with an air of annoyance which he was at no pains to conceal, turned, with a frown on his handsome but sinister face, and surveyed Florence from head to foot with the cool air of perfect assurance.

"I presume, sir, that you know me?" said the latter, sternly.

"I soon know every man who dares assume such a tone to me," replied the captain gruffly.

"Dares!"

"I have said so, sir," replied the soldier, shaking his plume.

"Ha! ha! You either mock yourself or me."

"Uds daggers, sirrah! What make you here?"

"That you shall soon learn. You remember giving me, in the streets of Edinburgh, a letter for the laird of Millheugh!"

"I have some faint recollection of doing so," replied Champfleurie, with an impertinent yawn.

"That letter was a deadly snare,—a lure for my destruction; and you knew it to be so."

"You—John Livingstone of Champfleurie!"

"How, laird of Fawside—how?"

"By the tenor of the letter, and by the message with which you accompanied it, you proved yourself to be——"

"What? Be wary, sir,—what?"

"A false liar!"

Livingstone grew pale with rage. He drew back a pace, and pressing the hilt of his sword against his heart for a moment, relinquished it with a gasp of anger. On this, his fiery opponent, who was his junior by ten years, smiled scornfully, and said,—

"You know the sensation of a sword-blade entering your flesh?"

"Cogsbones! I should think so!" replied the captain, with a smile equally proud and scornful. "I have, in my time, had a dozen of good swords in me; seven in duels, two at Ancrumford, and three at the rout of Solway."

"Then what is it like?"

"Do you wish practical proof, damned jackfeather?"

"What is it like?" reiterated Florence furiously.

"Hot iron."

"Then you shall enjoy that warm sensation again!"

"Indeed!" sneered Champfleurie.

"Yes!" replied Florence, unsheathing his sword with a fury no longer restrainable; for during this strange conversation he had gradually been drawing the captain towards the Nether Baillery, a secluded part of the fortress. "Defend yourself, villain, lest I kill you where you stand!"

"Stay!—stay!" exclaimed the other, defending himself only by his left arm, round which he quickly rolled his velvet mantle.

"Why stay? Would you confess? If so, the queen's chaplain——"

"Bah! Confession went out with the cardinal last year. But hold your wrath, sir, and put up your sword; remember where we are, and that our lands are forfeited to the Lord High Constable if we draw weapons within the precincts of a royal castle or palace, and must I remind you that the queen's fortress of Stirling is both. Moreover, my Lord of Errol, the constable, once caught me kissing his lady's hand; and husbands have troublesome memories sometimes."

"Sir, I thank you for the lesson; in my just anger I forgot where we were. But we need have no lack of a trysting-place."

"No sir, if you are thus stout and resolute," replied the captain, coming close, with a sombre frown on his face; for being as perfectly master of his temper as of his sword, he was the deadlier and more dangerous enemy. "At sunset I will meet you beside the Roman Rock, below the castle wall."

"Good! Till then——"

"Adieu."

And with a stern salute they both separated.

"Plague take thee for a ruffling bully," thought Champfleurie. "But, by the blessed pig of St. Anthony, I shall kill thee like a cur, or I am no true Livingstone!"

People thought little of risking life, and less of fighting, in those days. But as Florence remembered the young love he had just left, her sweetness, her beauty, and passionate nature; and then his stern mother, who loved and prized him as an only son, the prop of her years, the last of his line and the hope of its vengeance, the idea that he might for ever take up his abode in the burial-place of Stirling, filled him with a temporary sadness and gloom. Fortunately, however, but brief time was left him for sombre reflection, as he had barely parted from Champfleurie when the young baron of Dalserfe approached, cap in hand, to say that the regent desired to speak with him immediately.

Florence remembered the warning of Champfleurie, and believing they had been watched, his first idea suggested a rebuke, if not captivity, for drawing sword in a royal castle, as Arran was endeavouring, but in vain, to repress the lawless and tumultory spirit of the time. However, on being ushered into his presence, his smile and welcome at once relieved the young man from all apprehension on that score.

CHAPTER XXIX
THE DOUGLAS ROOM

Wist England's king that I was ta'en,
 O gin a blythe man he would be;
For once I slew his sister's son,
 And on his breast have broke a tree.

           Ballad.

The regent was alone, and seated at a table covered with papers, in a small chamber of the royal apartments, in the north-west corner of the castle. It was hung with tapestry, worked by the hands of Mary of Gueldres, as this closet had been a favourite study or resort of her husband, James II., whose name, "Jacobus Scotorum Rex," with the legend, *I.H.S. Maria Mother of the Saviour*, may still be distinctly traced in golden letters, amid the elaborate carvings of the cornice. In this closet hung two well-battered suits of armour, which had been worn in a single combat in the valley of Stirling, on a day in the Lent of 1449, by two noble Burgundians, named De Lalain, one of whom, Jacques, was esteemed as the best knight in Europe; but they were both slain, after a severe and bloody conflict, by two gentlemen of the house of Douglas, in presence of James II., who acted as umpire or judge of the lists. In this little room, the same monarch, by one stroke of his dagger, slew William, sixth Earl of Douglas, whom he knew to be in league with others against the throne, and whose bleeding body was flung over the window by the captain of the guard, into the Nether Baillerie, where his bones were found in the beginning of the present century.

From this terrible episode, which, though warranted in some respects, fixed an indelible stigma on the reign of the second James; the closet is still known by the name of *The Douglas Room*.

Arran looked weary and thoughtful; for after the irritating convention, he had a long interview with his brother John, who was Archbishop of St. Andrew's and lord chancellor; and with David, Bishop of Ross, the secretary of state, whom Florence passed in earnest conversation together on the staircase as he ascended.

"Fawside," said he, "after what has occurred to-day, you and every other gentleman in Scotland, may look to your harness, for we shall have war ere the next month be past."

"My harness is ever ready, and like my sword, is at the service of your grace."

"But the intrigues of our traitors will blunt the edges of the sharpest swords we possess."

"You mean — —"

"The malcontent nobles, and the more turbulent of our landed gentry. Can I have patience with them, when Heaven itself seems to have none, since it permits them to slay and decimate each other, in their endless feuds and quarrels?"

At this remark, the young man coloured deeply, as he thought the regent referred to the feud of his family with the Hamiltons of Preston.

"You change colour," said Arran, smiling; "believe me, I referred not to your father's ancient quarrel with my kinsman, Claude, for your father was a brave and leal Scottish man; none was there better than he, or more approved in arms, among the soldiers of James IV. He fought at Flodden. But by that blush, Fawside, I perceive you are not much of a courtier," added the regent, laughing.

"No, lord earl, though I have passed some time in the saloons of the Louvre and St. Germains; happily I am not."

"Happily?"

"Yes, my lord; kings can at all times find courtiers, but loyal subjects and true soldiers are less brittle ware."

"And you — —"

"Hope that I have the honour to be esteemed a loyal subject."

"And a brave soldier, too, young man."

"I have yet that name to win," said Florence modestly.

"At this perplexing time, when every avenue and antechamber of our palaces are thronged by traitors, who were in league with the late English Harry, and are now at faith with the protector, I do not deem it expedient to visit with condign punishment those men, of whose base intrigues I am, to some extent aware; yet, within the last hour, I have sent the Earl of Bothwell, deprived of his sword, spurs, and green ribbon, guarded by forty troopers, all Hamiltons, a prisoner to the castle of Edinburgh. There, in the sure ward of its governor, Sir James Hamilton of Stainehouse, let him await — through the iron bars of David's Tower—the coming of Dame Katherine Willoughby, his English bride; and there shall he remain in solitude and seclusion, while I consider the means of crushing his compatriots, after we have swept the foe back to their own country."

"Bothwell a prisoner!" exclaimed Florence; "I should like to hear my Lord Glencaim's opinion of this."

"What would his opinion be?"

"He is a lord of the Scottish privy council."

"But his opinion; what would it be?"

"He is a lord of council."

"Sir, what mean you by repeating that?"

"Because, as a royal councillor, he must not appear to think different from your grace."

Arran knit his brows, and then smiled.

"By my soul, young sir, you have picked up some wit in your travels; but it may provoke the exercise of a sharper weapon in Scotland. 'Tis dangerous here especially. The town is full of our malcontent lords and the gentlemen of their trains. They swagger in the streets, and jostle the queen's guards, impeding even the horse-litter of Mary of Lorraine. They say and practise a thousand insolences in public; their swords flash under the nose of any poor burgess body who dares but look at them; they are fine fellows—yea, brave fellows; but I hope to beat the dust from their jerkins, after we have used them to beat the Duke of Somerset." Arran laughed bitterly as he spoke thus, and then resumed more gravely: "To attempt to crush the hydra on the eve of a foreign invasion, would be an unwise policy. The friends and followers of my enemies would at once join the invader; and bethink you, the clothyard shafts of the English, or the balls of the Spanish arquebuses, may save our Scottish headsmen and hangmen some work in time to come, by sending our faithless ones to the place of their reward. But now to the point, concerning which I sent for you. Preparations are to be made on all hands for the defence of the country. A line of beacons is to be established from St. Abb's Head to the summit of the palace of Linlithgow, in order that due intimation may be given of the moment the English cross the Tweed or Solway; and in the old Highland fashion, the cross of fire shall be the warning to arms. You have done me good service, laird of Fawside; and this I mean to reward in the manner most pleasing to yourself—by taxing yet further your faith and loyalty."

"My lord regent, you read my thoughts like a wizard."

"To you, under a royal warrant, which will be sent to your tower, in Lothian, I remit the task of superintending the erection of those beacons, on the most available sites. As for the expense, the lord high treasurer must see to that; and each landed baron must furnish both workmen and material for the balefire in his own vicinity—as the landholders of Lothian furnished all that was requisite for the outer wall of Edinburgh, in the year of Flodden. You will see to this."

"At the hazard of my life I will perform any duty you may do me the honour to assign me," replied Florence, with enthusiasm.

The regent bowed, and when men in his position bowed, Florence knew that it was a hint, the interview was over. As he prepared to retire,—

"You must promise me, sir," said Arran, "to avoid all brawls, duels, and quarrels."

"As far as a man may do so, consistent with honour," replied Florence, as he retired and hastened to keep his appointment with Champfleurie.

Pleased that one of his foes was now in captivity and disgrace, proud of the high trust reposed in himself by the regent, and prouder that the young countess still loved him, no man ever went forth to kill or be killed in higher spirits than our hero, as he descended from The Douglas Room and called for his horse. It was soon brought; and as he rode between the four large towers which then guarded the arched porch of the castle, with the air of an emperor, and with the lavish generosity of a true gallant of the time, he put his hand into the embroidered purse which hung at his girdle, and scattered a glittering shower of its contents among the grooms, lackeys, and pages who lounged on the benches at the gate, and whose shouts of applause followed him as he rode hurriedly down the spacious esplanade.

CHAPTER XXX
THE ROMAN ROCK

Your love ne'er learn'd to flee,
    Bonnie dame—winsome dame!
Your love ne'er learn'd to flee,
    My winsome dame!

Old Song.

The sombre reflections mentioned at the close of the last chapter but one, again recurred to Florence, as he rode from the fortress and sought the winding path which led to the place of his hostile meeting. Then for the first time he remembered that he was without a second, and there was no man in Stirling whom he knew sufficiently to implicate in such an affair; indeed, he was totally without acquaintances. Checking his horse and looking around, he perceived, at the head of the Broad Wynd, a man about to mount a stout nag. This person wore a brown doublet of Flemish broadcloth, with long red sarcenet hose; he had on an open helmet, cuirass, and a grey border plaid. At his belt hung a long dagger, and at his saddlebow a Jedwood axe, locally known as a Jethart staff. His burly figure, rough beard, and open, honest expression of face, aroused the interest and won the favour of Florence, who for some time past had been forced to study the physiognomies of men; and by his equipment believing him to be a respectable burgess or yeoman, he at once addressed him,—

"May I ask, gudeman, if you are a burgher of Stirling?"

"Nay, sir; I come frae the gude town——"

"Edinburgh?"

"At your service, fair sir."

"'Tis well—I am from that quarter, or a matter of ten miles east of it, myself."

"In what can I serve you, sir? I am Dick Hackerston, a free burgess and guild brother, at the sign o' the 'Crossed Axes' in the Landmarket, where my booth is as weel kenned as St. Giles's steeple."

"Hackerston," reiterated Fawside, to whom his voice seemed familiar; "is such thy name, good fellow?"

"Sooth is it, sir; and my father's before me. Sae, wherefore sic marvel?"

"To you I owe my life, brave man!"

"To owe me siller is nae uncommon thing; but that a man—a braw gallant like you—owes life to me, is something new," replied the merchant, with surprise.

"Have you forgotten that night when on the Castle Hill a single swordsman was so sorely beset by the weapons of at least a score of swashbuckler knaves; and when, but for your Jeddart staff——"

"By my faith, weel do I remember that bluidy night," said he, warmly shaking the hand of Florence; "and how I was beset in turn by these foul limmers, ilk ane o' whom deserved a St. Johnston tippet, for they would have slain me on the open causeway, and burned my booth to boot, but for the timeous arrival o' the town guard and some burgess friends who heard the shouts under their windows, and came forth wi pyne doublet and axe to redd the fray. Wi some landward merchants I ride eastward in an hour, ilk escorting the other, as there are many uncanny loons in the Torwood at times; so, in what can I serve you, sir?"

"I am the laird of Fawside, and shall be right glad to ride eastward in your company."

The merchant touched the peak of his morion.

"I ken the auld tower on the braehead, above the Howemire o' Inveresk."

"I have to fight a false villain who hath wronged me; but am without a single friend to see fair play ensured. Gudeman, may I reckon on thee?"

"Command me, sir, if a gentleman will take the aid o' a plain burgess body."

"I thank you, gudeman, and may have some right to ask it of you; for my father, old Sir John of that ilk, led the burgesses of Edinburgh, when King James marched his host to Falamuir."

"And your enemy——"

"Is Livingstone of Champfleurie."

"Captain of the queen's guard?"

"The same."

"An impudent varlet—a scurvy arquebussier, who poked his nose under my gudewife's hood nae further gane than three days ago, as she was coming frae the Mass, by the north door o' St. Giles; and he wi' the Lord Kilmaurs were coming, drunk as pipers, frae an ale-browster's booth in the Crames. I am your man; and you meet him——"

"At the Roman Rock."

"When?"

"Within five minutes by the dial."

"Come on, laird—I am ready."

"I ask you but to see fair play, and if I am slain to bear this ring to the Countess of Yarrow, and my last message to—my mother."

"Yes," said Hackerston, grasping the hand of Florence, and giving his axe a flourish; "but ere I left the ground on sic a deevilish and dolorous errand, by the arm of St. Giles, the patron o' cripples, I'll hae smitten the head frae the shoulders o' Champfleurie as I would the neb frae a syboe; so, on, and without fear!"

"*Forth, and feir nocht*! 'Tis the motto of my house, gudeman; and your words are ominous of good fortune."

Hackerston mounted his horse, and rode by the side of Florence to the rendezvous, where they found the captain of the guard, accompanied by Lord Kilmaurs, awaiting them. Both wore the half-suits of light armour usually worn at that time by all Scottish gentlemen when walking abroad.

The scene of this encounter, of which we find a minute relation in the pages of a venerable diarist of the day, was the vicinity of the Roman Rock, which took its name from an inscription thereon. It was visible in that age, but has since been effaced by time and the action of the weather. The basalt had been smoothly chiselled, and bore on its face a Latin legend, cut by the soldiers of Julius Agricola, intimating that on the Rock of Stirling—the Mons Dolorum, or Hill of Strife—the second legion of the Roman army "held their daily and nightly watch," while on the Grampians the still victorious Scots barred the deep passes that led to the land of the Gael.

"So, sir," said the captain of arquebuses, loftily, "you have come *at last*!"

"I crave pardon if I have detained you one minute over the appointed time," replied Fawside, with gloomy politeness; "but I had to procure a friend."

"You have more to crave pardon for, sirrah," said Lord Kilmaurs roughly; "as it is said that, by the agency of letters——"

"Letters again! That word bids fair to be the bane of my existence."

"Yea—letters brought out of France by thee from those accursed Guises, the Lord Bothwell, my assured friend, hath been degraded—deprived of his green ribbon—and committed to the custody of a Hamilton—a parasite of the Lord Arran."

"I brought no letters out of France, but such as well became the queen's liege man to bear," replied Florence haughtily.

"Well, and how about your friend: is a burrowtown merchant—a mere booth-holder, as I take him to be,—a beseeming squire for a landed baron—a gentleman of that ilk?" asked Kilmaurs, with a lightning glance in his sinister eye.

"Some flesher of Falkirk or souter of Linlithgow, I warrant," added the equally insolent Champfleurie, laughing.

"I am a brother o' the merchant guild, my masters," replied Hackerston, unabashed by their overweening manner; "and ken ye, sirs, that nae souter, litster, or flesher, can be one of us, unless he swear that he use not his office wi' his ain hand, but deputeth it to servitors under him?"

"What the devil does all this mean?" asked Kilmaurs, shrugging his shoulders. "Do you know, Champfleurie?"

"It means, gentlemen," replied Florence, sternly, "that I—being too well aware there were assassins and bravoes here in Stirling, who, under the guise of nobility assault and murder in the night—thought that the aid of an honest man, stout of heart and ready of hand, as this brave burgess has before approved himself to be, might not be unnecessary; and so, in lack of other friend, I sought his good offices here."

"And I commend you to keep a civil tongue in your head, my Lord o' Kilmaurs; for my Jethart staff has ere this notched a thicker one than yours. I have gien mony an uncanny cloure in my time."

"Enough of this!" exclaimed Champfleurie, drawing his sword and dagger.

"Yea, enough and to spare," added Florence, unsheathing his rapier and the exquisite little poniard given to him by Mary of Lorraine, and closing in close and mortal combat. They fought with such impetuosity that at the third pass he ran Champfleurie through the left forearm, piercing his plate sleeve like a gossamer web, and inflicting a wound so severe that the blood dripped over his fingers. This wound, by almost paralyzing his left hand, rendered his dagger useless, either for stabbing or parrying, for which latter purpose this little weapon was more especially used by the sword-playing gallants of those days.

The bearing of Champfleurie, which previous to this had been cool, contemptuous, and defiant, now became furious and wrathful.

He lunged and thrust almost at random; and twice Fawside contrived to secure his blade by arresting it in the ironwork of his own hilt; he was thus enabled to retain it, and, locking in, to menace the throat of Champfleurie with his dagger; but twice he generously released the blade, which he might easily have snapped from its hilt; and thus the combat was twice renewed, after they had breathed a little, and glared into each other's pale and excited faces.

The skill and generosity of Florence excited even the admiration of Kilmaurs, who exclaimed, —

"Well and nobly done, Fawside! But that I am sworn to be thine enemy I could wish thee for a friend. Another such mischance, Champfleurie, and by Heaven thou art a lost man!"

On each of these occasions Hackerston uttered a stentorian shout of applause, which in some measure served to dissipate the little self-possession retained by Champfleurie, who soon became almost blind with passion and hatred. In this state he soon proved an easy conquest to his antagonist, who by one tremendous blow broke his weapon to shivers, scattering the shining steel as if it had been a blade of glass, and, closing in, with the large hilt of his own rapier, struck him to the earth, and pinned him there by placing a foot on his breast. The blood flowed copiously from the mouth of the fallen man, who lay completely at the mercy of the victor.

"Champfleurie, thou mansworn loon, ask life at my hands, lest I slay thee like a venomous reptile."

"Nay, I need not ask that which is beyond your power to grant me," groaned the other.

"How, sir—what mean you?"

"That—that I am mortally wounded."

"Impossible!" exclaimed Florence with astonishment; "I did but give you a buffet with the shell of my sword—a mere buffet, sirrah."

"Draw near—draw near," said Champfleurie, half closing his eyes; and Florence knelt beside him.

"Nearer still I have somewhat to say—something to give thee."

Florence, with no emotion now in his heart but the purest commiseration, stooped over the supposed sufferer, who, transferring his dagger from one hand to the other, suddenly grasped him by the throat, dragged him down, and strove to stab him in the heart; but the point glanced aside upon the polished face of Fawside's finely-tempered cuirass, and the attempt was futile, as the blade went under his left arm.

Sudden though the action, Florence, by pressing his arm against his side, retained the weapon there, and, with his sword shortened in his hand, again menaced the throat of Champfleurie; but changing his purpose, instead of killing him on the instant, as he deserved, he merely compressed his steel gorget until he was almost suffocated, and then wrenching away the poniard, snapped the blade in pieces and threw them in his face in token of contempt.

At that moment the Lord Kilmaurs came forward, with his sword sheathed and his right hand ungloved.

"Laird of Fawside," said he, "you are a gentleman brave and accomplished as Champfleurie is false and unworthy. Accept my hand, in token that never again will I draw sword on you in any feud or faction, save for her majesty the queen. You have converted me from a foe to a friend."

"Then," says the old diarist already referred to, "the laird of Fawside, a soothfast youth and gallant, took the young lord's hand in his for a brief space, saying, with a laugh,—

"'He has rent me a velvet doublet, that cost fifty shillings in the Rue l'Arbre Sec, and ruined my garsay hosen by two sword-thrusts; but I am without a scratch.'"

Then straightway mounting his horse, without casting another glance at his prostrate enemy, who was covered with shame, he left the burgh of Stirling, in company with three landward merchants on their way to Edinburgh. And so, for the present, ended his quarrel with the laird of Champfleurie.

CHAPTER XXXI
THE JOURNEY HOME

By my faith, there be thieves i' the wood!
Soho, sir,—straightway stand, and let us see
What manner of knave or varlet you be.

Old Play.

It was fortunate for Florence that he was accompanied by the three well-armed and well-mounted burgesses of Edinburgh, as several of the Lord Bothwell's friends or allies were loitering in the Torwood, as before they had lingered in Cadzow, with intentions towards him the reverse of friendly. Thus, though the conversation of his companions concerning imports and exports, tallow, flax, and battens from Muscovy, beer from Dantzig, wines from Low Germanie, fruits from France, and so forth, or the latest whim-whams or absurdities of the provost and council of Edinburgh, did not prove very interesting to him—a lover, a youth who had lately left the gaities of Paris, the court of France, and who, since then, had been so favourably noticed by Mary of Lorraine, the most beautiful queen in the world,—their burly forms in jack and morion, their long iron-hilted swords and wheel-lock calivers were of good service in protecting his passage through the wilds of the Torwood and past the Callender, the stronghold of the Livingstones, one of whose chief men, the laird of Champfleurie, had suffered so severely at his hands. One of those who accompanied him was John Hamilton, then a well-known merchant in the West Bow, a cadet of the house of Inverwick, who afterwards fought valiantly and fell at Pinkey.

From the green depths of the Torwood, Florence gazed fondly and wistfully back to Stirling, and his soul seemed to follow his eyes, till castle, rock, and spire melted into the dusk of eve.

The castle of Callender, the seat of Alexander fifth Lord Livingstone—a stern man, of high integrity, to whom Mary of Lorraine entrusted the custody of her daughter,—was a strong tower, surrounded by a deep fosse, and had a high wall forming the outer vallium of the place; and our travellers found themselves close to it about nightfall.

"The auld lord is a rough tyke," said Dick Hackerston; "so, after what has happened to that loon Champfleurie (as ill news travel fast), we had better abide elsewhere than in the Callender."

"The Lord Livingstone bears a high repute," said Florence, "and is greatly loved and trusted by the queen."

"Though somewhat of a courtier," said Hamilton, "he is keeper of the king's forest of Torwood, and, by living among trees and wild bulls his notions have become dark and fierce. I agree wi' you, neighbour Hackerston, we'll e'en find lodgings elsewhere, or lie under the gude greenwood."

"So be it," replied Florence. "And yet, sirs, 'tis somewhat hard that you, three honest burgesses, should be shelterless on my account. Think you that the Lord Livingstone, even if he heard ere morning, which is barely possible, of my open duel with his scurvy namesake, would make common cause with him against me?"

"I would fear to trust him," replied Hackerston; "for bluid is warmer than water."

"I little like lying a night in the Torwood," said John Hamilton; "preferring my snug bit housie at the Bowhead, wi my gudewife birling her wheel in the cosy ingle, and the bairns tumbling ilk owre the other on the floor; mairowre, I am a stranger hereawa. Johnnie Faa's gang o' Egyptians are abroad; and the saints forfend that I come not to harm!"

"Why you in particular! What fear you?" asked Florence.

"Gude kens! But this morning I put on my sark with the wrong side outwards, and placed my *left* shoe on the right foot."

"Let us ride on to the castle of the Torwood," said Hackerston. "I ken the good dame who bides there, and have got her cramosie kirtles from France, and vessels of delft and pewter from the Flemings of the Dam. She lost her spouse in a brawl wi' the Livingstones, and may make us a' the mair welcome that one of our company has the bluid o' one o' that name on his hands. She comes o' Highland kin—Muriel Mac Ildhui, and is the last o' the Neishes, a tribe extirpated by the Mac Nabs at Lochearn. Come on, sirs; I ken the way, and can guide you there."

Putting spurs to their horses, they turned aside from the fortalice of the Lord Livingstone, which stood on the side of a green and gentle slope, and skirting a morass named Callender Bog, penetrated into a denser part of the Torwood by a path which, though apparently familiar to Hackerston, was scarcely visible to his companions, for night had closed completely in, and the pale light of the diamond-like stars was intercepted by the thick foliage of the old primeval oaks, which tossed their rustling branches in the rising wind. The rich grass that covered the path muffled, to some extent, the sound of their horses' feet; thus, on hearing voices before them,—

"Hush!" said Florence in a loud whisper; "and look to your weapons, sirs; for the Torwood has but an indifferent reputation."

He had scarcely spoken, when a clear and jolly voice was heard singing merrily a song, the chorus of which was something to this purpose:—

> "Saint George he was for England,
>   Saint Denis was for France:
> Sing *Honi soit*, my merry men.
>   *Qui mal y pense!*"

"Englishmen, by this light!" exclaimed Florence.

"By this murk darkness, rather!" added Hackerston, unslinging his Jethart axe from his saddlebow. "And bold fellows they must be, to chorus thus in the Torwood!"

The four travellers now hastily put on their helmets, which hitherto had been hung at the bow of their saddles, and for which, during their ride from Stirling, they had substituted bonnets of blue cloth.

"Stand, sirs!" said Florence. "Who are you!"

"Strangers," replied a voice, and then two horsemen became visible amid the gloom of the interlaced trees,—"strangers, who have lost their way in this devilish forest."

"This devilish forest belongs to the queen of Scotland; and how come you to be singing here by night?"

"By the Mass! I knew not that it was a crime to sing by night any more than to sing by day," exclaimed the other, laughing; "I do so when it listeth me."

"'Twas something unwary, at all events," continued Florence, advancing so close that he could perceive the speaker, by his air and manner, to be undoubtedly a gentleman; "but, as your song discovers your country, say, my friends, what make you here, so far from your own borders?"

"We do not yet make war," replied the other; "be assured, fair sir, we have only lost our way, and sorely lack a guide."

"For whence?"

"The highway to Berwick, to which place we belong."

"A word with you."

"Marry! sir, a score—you are welcome."

"You are perhaps ignorant of the law by which, if any Englishman comes into the kingdom of Scotland, to kirk or market, or to any other place, without a safe assurance, the warden, or any man, may make him a lawful prisoner."

"Nay, fair sir, we are not ignorant of that law, and have here a special assurance from the Scottish earl who is lord-warden of the eastern marches."

"'Tis well,—then for this night at least, we are comrades," replied Florence, giving his hand to the strangers, who were no other than Master Edward Shelly, and his companion, Master William Patten, of London; who, having mistaken the way, and being wary of exciting suspicion by inquiries, had for some hours been completely astray in the Torwood. Hackerston, who had suffered severe pecuniary losses in the war of '44, when the Duke of Somerset (then Lord Hertford) set Edinburgh on fire in eight different quarters, grumbled under his beard at this accession to their party.

"Fawside," said he, "I am a man true and faithful to God and the queen. Praised be Heaven, I have never consorted with traitors, or made tryst or truce with Englishmen——"

"Yes; but to leave strangers adrift in this wild wood, where broken men and savage bulls, yea, and wolves too, have their lair, is what an honest fellow like you would never consent to; so, lead on."

In a few minutes more, the travellers found themselves close to a small square tower, surrounded by a fosse and wall—an edifice the ruins of which still remain, and present in their aspect nothing remarkable, or different from the usual towers of Scottish landholders of limited means.

"Hallo—gate, gate, ho!" shouted Hackerston, two or three times, before a man appeared on the summit of the keep, and after counting the number of men, by the starlight, disappeared. His inspection had evidently been unsatisfactory, for he presented himself again, but lower down, on the barbican wall, and immediately above the gate, where he thrust a cresset over the parapet, at the end of a long pole, and surveyed the visitors a second time. The species of light called a cresset, was formed of a loosely-twisted rope, dipped in pitch and resin, and coiled up in a little iron basket, which swung like a trivet between the prongs of a fork. It flared on the old walls of the tower, on the keen, peering eyes and waving grey beard of the old warder, as he shaded his grim face with his weather-beaten hand, and assured himself that those who came so late, and halloed so loud, were *not* Livingstones bent on stouthrief and hamesücken, but real and veritable travellers, lacking food and shelter for man and horse. Apparently this second and closer scrutiny, which the desperate nature of the times required and rendered common, satisfied his scruples; the flashing cresset was withdrawn, the gate was unclosed, and Florence, with his five companions, soon found himself in the hall or chamber of dais, in the little fortalice still known as the haunted castle of the Torwood.

CHAPTER XXXII
THE CHATELAINE OF THE TORWOOD

After riding about three leagues, they saw the castle, and a goodly one it seemed; for before it ran a river, and it had a drawbridge, whereon was a fair tower at the end.—*Amadis de Gaul.*

Florence now recognized the face of Edward Shelly.

"We have met before—to-day, I think, in the streets of Stirling?" said he.

"Exactly—and what then?" asked Shelly, bluntly and uneasily.

"Nothing, save that I am pleased to see in this solitary place a face that is in any way familiar to me."

Shelly bowed, and smiled pleasantly; for the errand which brought him into Scotland, and the dangerous papers with which he was entrusted—papers bearing signatures involving war, and death, and treason—kept him ever anxious, restless, and suspicious of all who approached him.

The chatelaine or mistress of the mansion—the Lady Torwood, as she was named, though but the widow of a landed gentleman, whose possessions lay principally amid the wilds of that once extensive forest, now approached. She wore a black silk dooleweed, with a cross of white velvet sewn on the left shoulder, in memory of her deceased husband (a mark of mourning which was introduced into Scotland by the late king, on the death of his first queen Magdalene of Valois); she was young, for her years were under six-and-twenty, pale and saddened in expression. Three little children, the eldest of whom was not over three years, all clad in black dresses, each with a little white cross on the shoulder, nestled among the ample skirts of her dooleweed, and peeped in mingled alarm and wonder at the strangers, whom the lady received courteously: for in those days the halls of the landholders and the refectories of the monasteries were the halting-places of all travellers, when, neither inns nor taverns could be found; and, indeed, prejudices against the latter ran so high that acts were passed by parliament, to enforce the patronage of hostelries.

Lady Torwood's manner of receiving her visitors was singularly soft and polite; yet it was not unmixed with anxiety, for her little tower stood in a lonely place, and six well-armed strangers were not quite the kind of people a widowed mother might wish to see in that lawless time. The extreme paleness of her complexion contrasted strongly with the blackness of her smooth shining hair and the darkness of her eyes and lashes, while her figure and bearing had all that fawn-like grace which is (or was) peculiar to the women of certain northern clans in Scotland.

"We crave your pardon for this untimely intrusion, madame," said Florence, courteously, "but we have been belated and astray in the forest; and as I have had a quarrel—one of those unpleasant things that will ensue at times among armed men,—a crossing of swords, in fact, with a Livingstone, you will readily understand that my vicinity to the Callender——"

"Sirs, you are welcome here, apologies are unnecessary," replied the lady, whose accent sounded somewhat like that of a foreigner, for she belonged to a Celtic tribe, and had acquired the Lowland language as that of another people. "You have had a quarrel with a Livingstone," she continued, while her quiet dark eyes were filled by a momentary light; "that name has cost me dear indeed! but let me not think of it now. Here you are safe, sir—your names——"

"Dick Hackerston, a burgess o' Edinburgh," replied the burly proprietor of the Jethart axe; "and my friends are also free burgesses and landward merchants like mysel'. My booth is nigh unto Master Posset's lodging,—an unco' strange man he is, my lady; he cured the sair eyne o' a bairn o' mine, by rubbing them thrice wi' a grey cat's tail."

"And you, sirs?" said the lady, smiling, and turning to Shelly and Patten.

"Englishmen, of Berwick," replied the former.

"Englishmen!" reiterated the fair chatelaine, colouring—for the laws against harbouring them were so severe as to involve the highest penalties.

"Be assured, madam," replied the confident Shelly; "we travel under the lord warden's especial protection."

"And I am Florence Fawside of that ilk, in East Lothian."

"I have heard of you—at least, of your family," replied the lady, while another gleam heightened her pale and pretty face, "and of their long feud with the Hamiltons of Preston. Dearly have such feuds cost me and mine! In one, my whole race perished, save myself; and in another, I lost my dear gudeman, his brother, and many brave friends and kinsmen, leaving me a forlorn widow, with these three sakeless bairns to rear."

"Live in hope, madam," replied Florence, with something of the spirit in which his mother reared him.

"Hope?" questioned the widow sadly, as she lifted her meek eyes to his; "what hope is there for me!"

"That these children may one day avenge you!"

"Oh, sir, speak not thus," said she anxiously, while one white hand and arm went involuntarily round the curly head of her eldest little one; "forbid it, God! I hope to teach them that not unto us, but to Him alone belongeth vengeance."

"Would that my mother had reared us as this gentle woman rears her little brood!" thought Florence, struck by her resigned spirit and Madonna-like aspect; "my brother had now been spared to us,—and Madeline, my love for her had then been no secret, like a deadly sin; but, alas! my father's blood is yet upon her kinsman's sword and soul!"

These and many similar ideas passed through his mind, while refreshments were placed upon the table; a cold chine of beef, manchets, and oat cakes, with flagons of Lammas ale; and the wants of the six guests were promptly attended to by the servants of the tower, while its mistress sat by the fire, in the only arm-chair in the hall, with her feet resting on a tabourette, and her three children nestling by her side, or playing and frolicking, with the lurchers and terriers that were stretched on the hearth, which was covered by a large straw matting, the work of those tawny outlaws the Egyptians, a tribe of whom had been lurking in the Torwood since the days of their patron James IV.

The usual evening meal had long been over in Torwood Tower; thus the lady sat apart from all, but conversed freely with her unexpected guests, more especially with Florence and Shelly: but the latter, though by nature the most frank and jovial of all jovial and frank fellows, felt the peculiarity, the delicacy and danger of his situation, and thus became singularly reserved. He therefore sought to turn the conversation as much as possible from subjects likely to lead to himself, to his companion Master Patten, or to their object in venturing into Scotland, whither Englishmen seldom came in those days of war and mutual mistrust, but with harness on their backs. In that age, before the invention of newspapers, the sole means of circulating current events (all of which were unusually marvellous) were passing travellers, pardoners, and begging friars, who gave their own version of "wars and rumours of wars," of battles, of fiery dragons, of spectres, devils, omens, and other wonders, which, with an occasional miracle in church, formed the staple topics of conversation in the middle ages, and for a long time after them, in Scotland. Thus, afraid that, as a stranger and wayfarer, he might be unpleasantly questioned by the inmates of this secluded tower, and lured to admit more than prudence suggested or patience brooked,

Shelly, with considerable tact, led the fair chatelaine to speak entirely of her own affairs.

"And did your husband fall in battle?" he asked, with affected sympathy.

"Nay, sir; but in one of these vile civil brawls which are socially and morally the scourge of Scotland; and which our kings have always striven, but in vain, to crush. He and his father had been long at feud with the Livingstones, about the right of forestry in the Torwood,—even as the Fawsides have been at feud with the Hamiltons anent the right of pasturage on Gladsmuir; and with the same rancour they and their armed followers fought whenever they met, afield, at market, at church, in burgh, and on highway. Many were wickedly slain, and many grievously wounded, on both sides, till once, when the late King James of blessed memory was hunting in the Torwood, and both were in attendance on him, he commanded my husband and Alexander Lord Livingstone to take each other's hands in token of perpetual amity,—and in case of refusal, he threatened to commit them to the Peel of Blackness. Slowly, unwillingly, and with no consenting souls they did so, and, with a glare of hate in their eyes, vowed a hollow friendship over a cup of wine; and merrily the good King James drained it; to them both, fondly believing, in the kindness of his heart, that he had stanched the feud for ever. A vain hope! The day was passed in the forest; many a wolf, white bull, and deer were slaughtered, and many a horse and dog were gored and disembowelled in the conflict. Night came on, and, flushed with the king's good wine, their good cheer, and the excitement of the chase, the hunters separated; and before the midhour had passed, my poor husband, when on his way home, was beset by the Livingstones, led by the laird of Champfleurie, and, failing to reach the sanctuary of St. Modan's kirk, was barbarously murdered at Callender Bog, where, three days after, his fair body, sore gashed by many a ghastly wound, and divested of baldrick, bugle, sword, and dagger, was found by our sleuth dogs;—and, woe is me! his winsome eyes had been plucked forth by the gleds or eagles. We buried him in St. Modan's kirk, and therein I founded an altar, where masses shall be said for his soul's repose so long as the world shall last, at ten marks the mass. Heaven guide that the feud may be forgotten in his early grave, for I have seen enough of such horrors in my time; and the memory of them, so far from inciting *me* to vengeance, like the stern lady of Fawside, fills me with dismay and woe."

"Would that my mother could hear this gentle woman speak!" thought Florence; "yet what would it avail me?"

"I come from the north country, sir," resumed the lady, her manner warming as she spoke; "from a district and of a race, where the blood of men, though shed more freely, waxes hotter than in the Lowlands here. My name is Muriel MacNeish, or MacIldhui; and I saw, in one night, all who bore my name and shared my blood, laid corpses round our hearth, as the closing scene of one of the darkest feuds that ever shed death and horror over the lovely vale of the Earn!"

To draw attention from his own affairs, Edward Shelly expressed some curiosity to hear her story; so, while Florence and his companions drew round, the Lady Muriel related the following legend, to which, from the resemblance borne by one of the characters to his mother, our hero listened with deep interest; and which, as it contains much that is private, as well as public history, we will take the liberty of rehearsing here, in our own words and in our own way.

CHAPTER XXXIII
THE NEISH'S HEAD

It fell about the Martimas time,
  When winds blow snell and cauld.
That Adam o' Gordon said to his men,
  Where will we get a hauld?
See ye not yon fair castle
  Stands on yon lily lea?
The laird and I hae a deadly feud,
  And the lady I fain would see.

Adam o' Gordon.

For ages, a feud had existed between the MacNabs and MacNeishes, two tribes of considerable strength and influence, who, without having any marked limits to their territories, possessed that wild and mountainous district which lies around Lochearn.

The former of these clans was a bravich of the Siol Alpin, and took its name (*i.e.*, the sons of the abbot) from the ancient head of the Kuldee Abbey of Glendochart; and, during the reign of James IV., they had successfully carried fire and sword into the land of their enemies, who possessed the district then known as the Neishes' Country, lying between Comrie and Lochearn, comprising the Pass of Strathearn, Dundurn, the Hill of St. Fillan, Glentiarkin, and part of Glenartney. Embittered by old traditionary wrongs, transmitted orally by sire to son, from age to age, the rancour of these two tribes was without a parallel, even in the annals of ancient Celtic ferocity and lust of vengeance; and fired by the memory of a thousand real or imaginary acts of aggression the boys of each generation, while sitting on their fathers' knees, longed to be men, that they might bend the bow or bear the tuagh and claymore against their hereditary enemies.

On one occasion, the MacNeishes had carried off the holy bell of St. Fillan, a relic of remote antiquity, which in those days stood on a tombstone in the burial-ground of the saint's church, and was venerated by all; but it was miraculously restored; for this bell, like the old bells of Soissons, in Burgundy, and of St. Fillan's, in Meath, had the strange power of extricating itself from the hands of the spoilers, and came back through the air to Strathfillan, ringing merrily all the way; but the circumstance of its abstraction greatly increased the hostility between the rival tribes.

In this petty war, the chief of the MacNabs fell, being slain by an arrow from the bow of Finlay MacNeish, his enemy; but he left twelve sons and his widow, Aileen, a daughter of the clan Donald (the race of the Sea) to carry on the feud; and animated by hate and fury, this woman, stern by nature and savage in purpose, seemed to have no thought, no hope for, or idea of, the future, but as they might serve "to *feed* her revenge," which aimed at the destruction of the Neishes, root and branch, and the ultimate capture of their territory.

By her instigation, gathering all their fighting-men for one decisive effort for the supremacy of the district, her sons marched from Kennil House, and the two clans met in battle with nearly a thousand swordsmen on each side, in a wild and pastoral vale, named Glenboultachan, between two high and solitary mountains on the northern shore of Lochearn. Each was led by its chief, and they rushed at once down the green slope to mingle in close and mortal strife, with wild yells, bitter epithets and invectives, while the war-cries rang and the pipers blew, as additional incentives to slaughter and enthusiasm. Plying their sharp broadswords or long poleaxes with both hands, for greater freedom in the work of death, they tossed targets and plaids, breastplates and lurichs of steel, aside; and so that work, ever so rapid and terrible in a Highland battle, went fearfully on.

This battle took place on St. Fillan's Day, 1522, and the MacNabs bore with them the crook of the saint to ensure victory. It was borne by the MacIndoirs, who were the hereditary standard-bearers of MacNab, and had been custodiers of the crook ever since the death of St. Fillan, in 649, an office in which they were confirmed by a royal charter of King James II., in 1437. It is of solid silver, twelve inches long, elaborately carved, and having on one side a precious stone; on the other, the effigy of our Saviour, and was the same relic which, with the saint's arm-bone, Robert the Bruce had with him at the field of Bannockburn.[*]

> [*] In 1818 the last of the MacIndoirs, a Highland emigrant, took this valuable relic with him to America, and it is now preserved, with the letters and charters of James II., in the township of MacNab, in Canada.

The morning sun, when pouring his light between the parted clouds athwart that gloomy mountain gorge, lighted up a terrible and bewildering scene, which Aileen MacNab, from the summit of a rocky peak, surveyed in gloomy joy, with her grey, dishevelled hair hanging over her shoulders, as she knelt on ashes strewn crosswise on the heather; and there, with a crucifix before her, and a rosary on her wrist, she implored God and St. Fillan to grant her children and her tribe a victory; and then she left her orisons, to shoot a shaft from her dead husband's bow, among the press of combatants that fought like a herd of tigers in the glen beneath her. Then she would again prostrate herself upon the ashes and before her cross, which was made of the aspen—for of *that wood*, saith old tradition, the true cross was made; hence the tree is accursed, and its leaves shall never rest.

Wedged together in a dense and yelling mass, the two clans were all mingled pellmell in wild *mêlée*, fighting man to man, scorning to seek quarter, and scorning to yield it. Heads were cloven through helmets of steel, bosoms pierced through lurichs of tempered rings, while hands and limbs were swept off as the sharp wind may sweep the withered reeds from a frozen brook in winter; and the long sword-blades, that flashed in the sun, seemed to whirl without ceasing, like a huge *chevaux de frize*, grinding all to death beneath them.

Conspicuous above all this fiery throng, like the Destroying Angel or the Spirit of Carnage, wearing three eagle's feathers in the cone of his helmet, and clad in a lurich of shining rings, which covered his whole bulky form from his neck to the edge of his kilt, towered the eldest son of Aileen, named *Ian Mion, Mac an Abba* (*i.e.*, smooth John, the son of the abbot), an ironical sobriquet bestowed upon him in consequence of the roughness of his aspect and the coarse, grim, unyielding nature of his character. He bent all his energies to capture the Neishes' banner, which bore their crest, viz., a cupid with his bow in the dexter, and an arrow in the sinister hand, with the motto, *Amicitiam trahit amor*. The tall and bearded bearer was soon cloven down by Ian Mion, and the embroidered banner became the trophy of his prowess and daring.

On the other side, Finlay MacNeish, a chief of great age, but of wondrous strength and activity, fought with unparalleled bravery; but John MacNab and his eleven brothers bore all before them, and repeatedly hewed a bloody lane through the ranks of their foemen. At last their followers began to prevail; and in wild desperation and despair at the slaughter of his people, on beholding three of his sons perish by his side, and on finding the disgrace of defeat impending, the aged chief of the Neishes placed his back to a large rude granite block, which still marks the scene of this conflict, and, poising overhead his two-handed sword, stood like a lion at bay. His vast stature, his known strength and bravery, as he towered above the fray, with his white hair streaming in the wind (the clasps of his helmet having given way, he had lost it); the wild glare of his grey and haggard eyes; the blood streaming from his forehead, which had been wounded by an arrow, and from his long, uplifted sword, which (like the claymore of Alaster MacColl) had a remarkable accessory, in the shape of an iron ball, that slid along the back of the blade to give an additional weight to every cut,—all this combined, made the bravest of the MacNabs pause for a moment ere they encountered him; but after a dreadful struggle, in which he slew many of his assailants, the brave old man sank at last under a score of wounds inflicted by swords and daggers; and as his grey hairs mingled with the bloody heather, and were savagely trampled down, the triumphant yell of the MacNabs made the blue welkin ring and the mountains echo; while his people were swept from the field, and perished in scores as they fled, being hewed down on all sides by the swords and axes of the MacNabs, or pierced by their arrows; and the red lichens which spot the old grey stone in Glenboultachan are still believed by the peasantry to be the encrusted blood of the chief of the Neishes.

With MacCallum Glas, their bard, about twenty of the tribe escaped, and took refuge on a wooded islet at the eastern end of Lochearn, where, in wrath and sorrow, they could lurk and plan schemes of revenge, which the all-but total extinction of their name and number rendered futile; while the victorious MacNabs, after sweeping their whole country of cattle, and destroying all their farms, cottages, and dwellings, returned to hold high jubilee in Kennil House, the fortified residence of their chief, which stands upon a rocky isthmus, near the head of Loch Tay, and to inter their dead in the old burial-place of the abbot's children, Innis Bui—a greenswarded islet in the Dochart, where their graves are still shaded by a grove of those dark and solemn pines which were always planted by the Celts of old to mark where the tombs of their people lay; and there the impetuous Dochart, after rushing in foam over a long series of cascades, under the shadow of the giant Benlawers, ends its wild career in the Tay.

The slain of the enemy were stripped by the victors, and, by order of the remorseless Lady Aileen, were left as food for the wolf and raven. A few were interred by Alpin Maol (*i.e.* the Bald), an old monk of Inchaffray, who officiated as priest of the church of St. Fillan. He came to survey that terrible field at the close of eve; and of all the stately men who lay there on the blood-stained heather, gashed by wounds, and with their glazing eyes upturned to heaven, or lying half immersed in a tributary of Lochearn, towards which, many had crawled in their thirst and suffering, he found only *one* who survived. The rest, to the number of hundreds around, were dead. They lay in piles, amid vast gouts of blood and broken weapons, and tufts of heather uptorn by the clutches of the dead in their death-agony.

The wounded man proved to be the aged chief of the Neishes, whom the priest, Father Alpin, with the assistance of his sacristan, bore to a place of concealment, and, when his wounds were healed, conducted him in secret to the islet in the loch, where the remnant of his people were lurking, and where he found his daughter Muriel—a child of two years of age— the sole survivor of all his once numerous household; for in their mad fury the fierce MacNabs had spared no living thing, but swept all the land from Comrie to the beautiful banks of Lochearn, killing even the house and hunting-dogs of the vanquished. In every dwelling the *clach-an-eorna*, or rude mortar, then used for shelling barley by means of a wooden pestle, was broken and destroyed. The creel-houses, or wicker-work edifices, used as hunting-lodges, and even every *baile mhuilainn*, or mill-town, was burned and ruined, that never more might the Neishes find shelter or food. All the land was veritably burned up, as when ferns were burned in autumn—a Celtic superstition long since forgotten.

The feeble old chief was received with tears by the relics of his tribe; and these tears spoke more than a thousand languages of all they had suffered, and were ready yet to endure, for him and the now tarnished honour of their fallen race.

In a roughly-constructed hut, or creel-house, so named from being formed of stakes driven into the earth, with turf and wattled twigs between, the remnant of the MacNeishes lived the lives of outlaws; and having secured the only boat that lay in Lochearn, they were wont to make sudden and hostile descents on all sides of the lake, and suddenly at night, when least expected, the cries of those they were slaughtering without mercy arose with the flames of blazing cottages amid the wooded wilderness, and marked where they were dealing out vengeance on the spoilers. Then by a sudden retreat to their boat, they would gain the shelter of their isle, and there, defying all pursuit, would subsist for days on the precarious plunder won in these midnight creaghs or forays.

Penury, privation, and the despair of retrieving what they had lost, or of ever being able to make any resolute stand against the conquerors, made them wilder, more desperate, and savage, than any other landless and broken tribe,—even than the MacGregors in the days of James VI. They subsisted entirely by plunder, winning their daily food by the sword and the bow; and, ere a year was passed, their garments consisted of little else than the skins of deer and other wild animals. Thinly peopled as that mountain district was at all times, the operations of Finlay MacNeish and his twenty desperate men rendered it more desolate than ever; for the MacNabs and their adherents, finding the vicinity of Lochearn so troubled and dangerous, removed their families, with their flocks and herds, to a distance from its shores; but still, while the outlaws on the isle kept possession of their boat, and destroyed every other that was set afloat in the loch, they were enabled to lead their lawless life in security; while the government of the regent, John Duke of Albany, who had never much power at any time beyond the Highland border, gave itself no concern whatever in the matter, for the duke resided principally in France.

From the residence of these outlaws, the green islet which is in the middle of the lower part of Lochearn is still named the Isle of the Neishes.

The future fate of the few stout men who adhered to him, their chief, cost him but little thought. He knew that they would, too probably, all die in detail, falling, as their forefathers fell, by the edge of the sword; but the future of his little daughter, the last of all his race, pressed heavy on the old man's soul, for he would rather have seen her in her grave than the prisoner, it might be the bondswoman, of the abhorred MacNabs. He would gladly have committed her to the care of Alpin Maol, the priest of St. Fillan, that she might be sent to the abbot of Inchaffray, and by him be placed in the charge of some noble lady or holy woman; but the priest abode where his church stood, far from the isle of bondage, in the very heart of the enemy's country, and the aged Finlay had no means of communicating with him by message or letter.

Muriel was now three years old, and her beauty was expanding as her days increased. She was pale and colourless, but her hair was jetty black, and her quiet dark eyes expressed only sadness and melancholy thoughts, for, child though she was, the *sauvagerie* which surrounded her, and the sombre gloom of her white-haired sire, a man whose whole heart and soul, whose every thought and plan and prayer were dedicated to retributive vengeance, impressed her with awe; and she shrank from all his grim followers save MacCallum Glas, or the grey son of Columba the citharist, the bard of the tribe, to whose care her mother had committed her on that night of horror in which she perished in their burning mansion, the night succeeding the defeat in Glenboultachan.

The darkness of Muriel's eyes contrasted powerfully with the dazzling purity of her skin, which the tribe believed to be the result of a charm given to her mother by a certain wise-woman, who advised her to dip violets in goat's milk and morning dew, and to bathe the child therewith; for, according to an old Celtic recipe, "Anoint thy face with the milk of goats in which violets have been dipped, and there is not a chief in the glens but will be charmed with thy beauty."

So said the citharist in his song; but MacNeish, as he made the sign of the cross on her pure and innocent brow, exclaimed, —

"Thou art but a fool, grey Callum, for, by the great stone of Glentiarkin! her beauty cometh from no other charm than the breath of her Maker."

And in every foray he sought to bring some gaud or trinket of silver or of gold to deck his daughter, the child of his old age, the last of his doomed race; the little idol who shed a ray of light upon his melancholy and desperate household in that wild and desolate isle.

So passed a year.

CHAPTER XXXIV
THE NEISH'S HEAD—STORY CONTINUED

Thus to her children Luisa speaks—she cries,
With you, my sons, my fate, my vengeance lies!
Live for that cause alone, with it to fall,
A bleeding mother's is a holy call.

Portugal: a Poem.

It was a year of danger, wounds, and rapine; still the MacNeishes, in their wave-surrounded fortress, defied all, and escaped every attempt to capture or destroy them; for still their boat was the only one whose keel ploughed the waters of Lochearn. And now approached St. Fillan's Day, 1523, the first anniversary of their disastrous defeat in Glenboultachan. In honour of this returning day of victory, Lady Aileen MacNab invited all the principal duine-wassals of her tribe to a great feast or festival; and to procure various accessories for the banquet and carousal MacIndoir, the standard-bearer, with other adherents of trust, were sent to the town of Grieff, which is situated on the slope of the Grampians. Having made all their purchases of provisions, wine and fruit, &c., they were returning with four laden sumpter-horses; but when crossing the Ruchil; at a place where it flowed through a thicket of pines, a shrill whistle was heard. Then followed shouts of wild fury and exultation, and MacIndoir found himself surrounded by Finlay MacNeish and his desperate followers, who by some means had obtained intelligence of his journey to Crieff. They were armed with rusty swords and battered targets, and were clad in little else than skins of the wolf and deer. Gaunt men they were; hollow-eyed, fierce and savage in aspect. Their long unshaven beards flowed over their breasts, and their matted hair, without covering or other dressing than a thong or fillet of deerskin, waved in the breeze or streamed over their naked shoulders like the manes of wild horses.

"The Neishes, by the arm of St. Fillan!" exclaimed MacIndoir, drawing his sword in anger and dismay.

"Yes, the Neishes, by the mass, the pope, and St. Fillan to boot!" replied the aged chief, with gloomy ferocity expressed in every lineament of his face, as he turned up the sleeves of his tattered doublet and grasped his two-handed sword; "we have long been supping the poorest of bruith,[*] but now we shall have the good cheer of those sons of the devil who oppress us. Come on, my children—come on!"

[*] Gaelic—hence the word *broth*.

A brief struggle ensued; and while defending himself bravely, MacIndoir vainly threatened the caterans with the "kindly gallows of Crieff," the power of William Earl of Monteith, who was then steward of Strathearn; and, more more than all, with the dreadful retribution which Lady MacNab and her sons would assuredly demand if their goods were plundered or spoiled.

Shouts of derisive laughter were his sole reply, and they mingled strangely with the cries of the wounded, the imprecations of the victors, and the clash of blades, which at every stroke scattered sparks of fire and blood-drops through the sunny air. In a few minutes MacIndoir was compelled to seek safety in flight; while his followers were all cut down, and the four sumpter-horses, with their burdens, captured. Using their swords and dirks as goads, the MacNeishes drove them at a furious pace down the hills towards Lochearn, in a solitary creek of which, under a shroud of ivy, willow, and waterdocks, they had concealed their boat, on board of which they rapidly stowed their plunder. The four horses were then denuded of their trappings, hamstrung, and left to limp away or die in the pine forest; while the MacNeishes, with a shout of defiance, shipped their oars, and as their long fleet birlinn cleft the clear waters of the lake and shot towards the little wooded isle, on the summit of which pale Muriel, with a beating heart, awaited them, the song of exultation raised by MacCallum Glas, as he sat harp in hand in the prow, and the chorus of twenty voices that joined his at intervals, reached the ears of the panting MacIndoir, when he paused on the brow of a neighbouring rock, and pressing the blade of his dirk to his trembling lips, swore to have a terrible revenge for the affront they had put upon him and the stern wife of his late chief, an affront which, to a Celt, seemed an outrage upon all laws divine as well as human.

On reaching Kennil House he related to Lady MacNab the events of his journey from Crieff, stating that the sumpter-horses with their burdens were gone, and that his whole party, consisting of six men, had been cut to pieces by caterans.

"By the Neishes?" she exclaimed in accents of rage.

"By the old wolf in the isle of Lochearn; and the blood of six of our people has soaked the heather."

"Yet *thou* returnest alive to tell the shameful story!" was her fierce exclamation, as she smote him on the beard with her clenched hand, and her twelve tall sons gathered round her, muttering threats and growls of anger, all the deeper that they knew them to be futile, as the deep lake rendered the isle impregnable. They formed a hundred fierce schemes of wholesale slaughter, and for the total destruction of the wasps' nest—for so they termed the retreat of the Neishes; but as the waters of the lake were too broad for armed men to swim them, and no boat could be procured, their projects ended in nothing but a settled wrath, all the deeper that it was without resource or vent; so night closed in, and they sat in moody silence in their mother's hall. Its windows overlooked Loch Tay, the waters of which were flushed in one place by the light that lingered in the ruddy west; and in others its deep blue was studded by the tremulous reflection of the stars. From the margin of the loch the beautiful and evergreen pines spread their solemn cones darkly over mountain and valley, as far as the eye could reach. Virgil praises their beauty in gardens; but the Mantuan bard never saw the wiry-foliaged and red-stemmed pine, that twists its knotty and tenacious roots round the basaltic rocks of the Scottish mountains, or he had found a fitter subject for his muse.

Aileen MacNab surveyed the darkening landscape with a gleam in her stern grey eyes, and turned from time to time to observe her surly and athletic sons, who were grouped near the large fire that blazed on the hearth, and which cast from its deep archway, a lurid glow on their bare muscular limbs, and floating red tartans; and then the idea that an insult had been offered to her on the first anniversary of their great victory,—that she had been obliged to despatch messengers to her friends announcing that the banquet had been put off,—and that at that very time too, probably, the wild caterans on the islet were feasting on the good cheer which MacIndoir had procured in Crieff, and were pouring her rare French and Flemish wines down their brawny throats, made her tremble with wrath.

Repeatedly she addressed Ian Mion, her eldest son; but on this night, John the Smooth, was unusually gloomy and abstracted, and made no response.

It was averred that once, when hunting near the well of St. Fillan, he had met and loved a beautiful fairy woman, who presented him with a ruby ring, the rich colour of which would always remain deep and bright while his love lasted, but would fade as his love faded, and death come nigh the donor. The well where he received this strange gift, is still considered alike weird and holy in Strathfillan; and there, even at this late age of the world, rags and ribbands are tied to the twigs near it, and small propitiatory oblations in the form of coin, are dropped into its limpid waters by the superstitious Celts of the district. Ian Mion had long ceased to visit the well, for the love he had vowed was a passing one, and the ring had been growing paler and more pale. On this night, as he surveyed it by the red glow of the bog-wood fire, the ruby had become white as snow, — a token that the fairy was dead, and that danger was near *himself*. He shuddered, and then the sharp, stern, voice of his mother roused him, as she clenched her trembling and uplifted hands above her grey head, and exclaimed bitterly, —

"A Dhia! oh that my husband was here, instead of lying in the place of sleep at Innis Bui, for this night is the night for vengeance, if his lads were but *the lads!*"

This significant mode of communicating a sentiment, — a mode strongly characteristic of the genuine Celt, was immediately understood by the twelve sturdy warriors at the fire.

"Taunt us not, mother," said Ian Mion, starting as if stung by a serpent, "the night is *the* night for a terrible deed, and your sons are *the* lads to achieve it, or may their bones never lie by their father's side under the dark pines of Innis Bui."

He took his long claymore from the wall, and placed it in his broad leather belt; he slung his target on his left shoulder, and grimly felt the point of his sharp biodag, or Highland dagger; and his eleven brothers followed his example, arming themselves with gloomy alacrity, while Ian, with a smile of fierce exultation, surveyed their stature and equipment.

"Now mother," said he, "we go to Lochearn."

"Achial! achial, am bata!" muttered his brother Gillespie. (Alas—alas, a boat!)

"Why not take our birlinn from Loch Tay?" exclaimed Lady Aileen.

"And sail it over the hills to Lochearn!" added her son Malcolm, who was somewhat of a jester.

"No—but carry it on your shoulders, my sons. There are twelve of you; and for what did I bear—for what did I suckle you, but to rear you to act as your father expected, like men!"

"Our mother speaks wisely," said Gillespie.

"'Tis well and bravely thought of," added Ian Mion; "so, now for vengeance on the Neishes, the accursed *ceathearne coille!*" (*i.e.*, woodmen, or outlaws.)

"Then go," exclaimed Lady Aileen, with uplifted hands; "and remember, *the Neish's head*, or let me never see ye more, and may the curse of your dead father dog ye to your graves!"

In a minute more the twelve brethren had left the castle, and rushed to a little jetty in Loch Tay, where their birlinn or painted and gilded pleasure-boat was moored.

It was soon beached, or drawn ashore, and raising it on their shoulders they proceeded (six brothers relieving the other six at every mile of the way) to ascend the steep, rocky, shelves of a mountain, and descended from thence into a narrow and gloomy gorge, that forms the avenue of Glentarkin. Unwearied and resolute, the twelve brothers bore thus the birlinn on their shoulders, over this rough and rugged tract of mountain, and down the stony bed of a steep and brawling torrent, which tore its way through a rift of marl and clay, and serving as a guide for miles, poured its waters into Lochearn.

"Quick, lads—quick," urged Ian Mion, pausing in a song by which he had sought to cheer the way.

"Hurry no man's cattle, Ian," said Gillespie, as he panted under his share of the burden.

"But hurry your lazy legs, for a storm is coming."

"How know you that?"

"This morning I came over Bendoran——"

"Aire Dhia!" exclaimed Malcolm; "an enchanted place, where storms are foretold."

"So was I foretold it," replied Ian; "for I heard the hollow voice of the wind sighing through the valley; the shepherds also heard it, and were collecting all their flocks in bught and pen. So, on, lads, on! And now by St. Fillan, I can see Lochearn gleaming in the starlight far down below us."

The moon, which had lighted them for some portion of the way, imparting by her pale radiance a ghastly aspect to everything, now waned behind the summit of Benvoirlich, and all became sombre, dark, and solemn, amid the pine-woods, and on the water of Lochearn, when, about one hour after midnight, the twelve MacNabs launched their birlinn, stepped on board, and without waiting a moment to rest or refresh, so resolute were they, and so determined to elude their mother's malison and to fulfil their vows of vengeance, they slipped their oars, and in silence shot their sharp-prowed vessel across the calm and lonely lake, and soon reached the Neishes' islet, which resembled a dense thicket or copsewood, as the stems of the trees seemed to start sheer from the water.

With muffled oars they pulled around it, and all seemed still in its woody recesses. No sound was heard—not even the barking of a dog, and so intense was the silence, that Ian Mion began to doubt whether the foes he had taken so much trouble to reach, were now in the isle or on the mainland, until he found their boat moored in a little creek. Driving his biodag again and again through its planks, he soon scuttled it, and shoved it into the loch, where it filled and sank, thus cutting off, for ever, all chance of flight for the foe, if defeated, and of communication with the mainland, if victorious. All this was performed in nervous haste, for, from this secluded islet, the diabolical water-horse had been frequently seen to dash into the lake; and it was long the abode of a *uirisk*, a being half demon, half mortal, whose piercing shriek before a storm could make all Lochearn echo. Mooring their birlinn under the lower branches of a large pine, the twelve brothers landed, braced on their arms their targets, which were formed of coiled straw-rope, covered by thrice-barkened bull-hide, and studded with round brass nails. Then, unsheathing their long and sharp claymores, they began warily to approach a red light, which they now detected in the centre of the isle, where it glimmered with wavering radiance between the stems of the trees. Advancing cautiously, they discovered it to proceed from the window—if an open unglazed aperture can be so termed—of the long and low-roofed creel-house or cottage built by the MacNeishes on the isle, and the turf walls of which they had carefully loop-holed for defence by arrows; but now, overcome by fatigue, very probably by the unusual quantity of good food and rich foreign wines they had imbibed, lulled too by the sense of perfect security, they kept no watch or ward; and thus, on peeping in, Ian Mion and his brethren beheld their enemies all asleep (save one) on the clay floor of the wattled wigwam (the hovel was little better), rolled in skins of deer, or coarse smoke-blackened plaids, the dull checks of which were the simple dyes of wild herbs and of the mountain heather.

Ian Mion ground his teeth, and his fingers tightened on the hilt of his claymore, when finding his hated enemies within arm's length at last, and, to all appearance, a prey so easy.

The fire from which the light proceeded, was formed of guisse-monaye, or bog oak from the morasses. It burned cheerily in the centre of the clay floor, from whence, in the old Highland fashion, the smoke was permitted—after curling among the bronze-like cabers—to find its way through an aperture in the roof. Seated by this fire, upon a block of wood, was the venerable Finlay MacNeish, of all that wearied band the only one awake. He was enveloped in a tattered plaid of bright colours. His white hair fell in curly masses around his bronzed visage, and mingled with his noble beard; his chin rested on his left hand, and his elbow was placed on his bare left knee. He was buried in thought; but a stern smile from time to time lit up his hollow eye; for, warmed by the generous wine of France and of the

Flemings of the Dam, which his good sword had that day won from the followers of his mortal enemy and oppressor, he was full of brilliant waking dreams; though his thoughts chiefly wandered to the little couch of furs and heath, whereon slept the pale child, Muriel, the last of all his race, the flower of that wild islet, and the hope and joy of all his desperate band. For her, he planned out future triumphs, and the memory of all he had lost in that one fatal battle, the wild pass of Strathearn, the green Dundurn, the lone hill of St. Fillan, and beautiful Glenartney; his ruined home; his plundered flocks and herds; his wasted fields and ravaged farms,—all now, even to the time-honoured burial-place of his fathers, the prey of the MacNabs,—filled his soul with rage; and he saw before him the things such stern dreamers only see, in the red, glowing and changing embers of the fire, on which his gaze was fixed.

His thoughts were suddenly and roughly arrested by a shout of triumph at the opening which served for a window. He turned sharply, and on beholding the face of a stranger, threw aside his plaid, and drew the sword which was never for a moment from his side.

"Who are you?" he demanded, in astonishment and alarm; "speak, and speak quickly!"

"Ian Mion Mac an Abba," replied the eldest son of Aileen, with a smile of scorn and triumph.

"Smooth John of the accursed race, in the island of the Neishes! What seek you, caitiff?"

"A just vengeance; so come on thou false cateran, or yield."

"MacNeish yields to the hand of the blessed God only; but never to a MacNab of woman born!" replied the aged Finlay, with that air of supreme grandeur which the old Celtic warriors could at times assume. "Up, up to arms!" he added to his people; but wine, weariness, and slumber heavily sealed their eyes, and he found neither response nor succour, while he and Ian met hand to hand.

Their swords crossed, and by the light of the bog-wood fire, their wild eyes glared into each other's faces; and while blade pressed and rasped against blade, ere they struck or thrust, MacNeish said,—

"I am old, and thou, John MacNab, art lithe and young. If I fall, for the sake of our blessed Lady of Pity have mercy on my child—my little Muriel; other boon than this have I none to ask."

"She shall have such mercy as brave men ever accord to women and children," replied MacNab.

"I thank you, Ian Mion——"

"But for *thee*, there is——"

"Only death. I know it—so come on! It may be that I shall die, yet I care not, if I can redeem my old life by having the best life among ye—ye sons of a misbegotten cur!"

A thrust which he made full at the broad breast of Ian Mion, was parried with such force, that his arm tingled to the shoulder; and now the poor old man felt the weakness of his many years, and the hopelessness of resistance.

"MacNeish, you fight without hope—a man foredoomed to evil," said Ian mockingly.

"True; to evil and vengeance!" exclaimed the other gloomily, for his mother had borne him on Childermas Day, 1467 (the 28th December) the anniversary of Herod's slaughter of the innocents; a day of especial ill omen in Scotland, for which it was deemed unlucky for a man to put on a new doublet, to clip his beard, or attempt anything in this world—then how much less to have the effrontery to come into it!

It was vain for the old man to contend with an antagonist so formidable as Ian Mion, who soon beat him to the earth by a mortal wound, trod upon his sword and broke it. Then, twisting his fingers through the silver locks of Mac Neish's ample beard, he dragged him to the block of wood on which he had been so recently seated, and there ruthlessly severed his head from his body by one slash of the claymore.

Ere the combat had ended, by a catastrophe so sudden and terrible, his eleven brothers had pierced and cut to pieces the whole band as they lay in their drunken slumber, and incapable of resistance. Of all the tribe of MacNeish none escaped, but Muriel, his child, and a little boy (the son of Grey Callum, the bard) who concealed himself under a creel, and lay there in deadly fear, and drenched by the warm blood which flowed more than an inch deep over the clay floor of this frightful hut.

The summits of Benvoirlich, and of the wooded hills that look down on lovely Lochearn, were tinged with gold and purple by the rising sun, as, with panting hearts and bloody hands, the twelve brothers rowed their birlinn from that isle of death towards the wooded shore, bearing with them the white head of MacNeish; nor did they rest for a moment until they reached the hall of Kennil House, where their pale, grim mother, who had never once closed her blood-shot eyes in sleep, awaited them.

"Mo mather—na biodh fromgh, oirbh!" ("My mother, fear nothing now!") exclaimed Ian Mion, as he held aloft the ghastly head by its silver locks; and from that hour the MacNabs took as their crest, "the Neish's head," *affrontée*, with the motto *Dreid Nocht*. Aileen embraced her twelve savage sons, with stern exultation, and ordered the head to be spiked on the summit of her mansion; while a banquet was spread, and the piper marched before the door, making every chamber ring to the notes of the clan salute, *Failte Mhic an Abba*.

Lady Aileen would not permit the slaughtered caterans to receive the rights of sepulture.

"There, on the Neish's isle, let them lie unburied," she exclaimed, "without aid from priest or prayer, torch or taper, mass-bell or mourner,— that their bones may whiten as a terrible memorial to all that would dare to withstand us!"

So said this fierce woman; but gentle Father Alpin Maol, the good old monk of Inchaffray, had them interred in one grave, over which he placed a cairn of stones, and one of those Celtic crosses of a fashion which is only to be found in Scotland and Ireland. On the island the ruins of the Neishes' dwelling may still be traced, and on Innis Bui there still stands a monument erected by the MacNabs in commemoration of their savage triumph.

The son of Grey Callum, the bard, when he grew to manhood, settled in Strathallan; and from him are descended all who at the present day bear the names of Neish or MacIldiu.

Little Muriel, who was almost inanimate with grief and terror, Father Alpin bore with him to Inchaffray, in Strathearn, where she chanced to meet the eye of James V., when on a hunting expedition; so she became the *protégée* of that good king, and when she grew to woman's estate, he bestowed her, with a portion in marriage, upon one of his esquires—the laird of the Torwood—and she was the pale, sad widow who, with her three children nestling about her skirts, related to Florence, to Shelly, and their companions, this barbarous tale of a Highland feud.

Florence listened to it with deep interest, and the narrative filled his mind with melancholy reflections; for in the character of Lady Aileen MacNab he too easily recognized a resemblance to his own mother,—stern, implacable, and revengeful.

Shelly looked at Master Patten as Lady Muriel concluded, and shrugged his shoulders, with an expression in his eye which seemed so much as to say that he cared not how soon the waters of the Tweed, and the Tyne and the Tees to boot, were between him and the land were such events were matters of not uncommon occurrence.

CHAPTER XXXV
A RIVAL

Cast off these vile suspicions, and the fear
That makes it danger!

Southey.

The limited accommodation of this small tower could only afford two chambers for the unexpected visitors. To Florence, as a gentleman of known degree, was assigned the best; to Shelly and his companion Master Patten, as strangers and travellers, was assigned the other; while worthy Dick Hackerston and his friends, as mere "burgess bodies," or landward merchants, were left to wrap themselves in their cloaks and plaids, and to sleep on benches in the hall, after the fire had been heaped with fresh fuel, bog-wood, peat, and coal; and after the pale chatelaine and her children had withdrawn to rest.

The chamber of Florence was sombre in aspect. On one side the arras tapestry bore a representation of the Crucifixion, and before it stood a prie-dieu and kneeling-stool of black oak; on the latter lay a missal, richly gilded. The bed had four twisted spiral columns; which supported a gloomy entablature and canopy, adorned by funeral-like plumes of black feathers.

Before retiring to rest, Florence for a time found a pleasure and employment with the opal ring of Madeline, and a flame from the lamp seemed to play amid its changing hues.

In the superstition of that and preceding ages, and according to the ideas of those who practised the occult sciences, a mysterious and malignant power was believed to exist in the opal.

"Malignant!" thought he, as the dark story of the Highland feud and the memory of his mother's revengeful character occurred to him; "if it really be, that this strange stone, in which the flames seem to glow and waver, possesses any power over me, it can only be that of irresistible fatality."

When he thus spoke, or rather reflected, he seemed to hear the name and title of Madeline uttered by some one near him; or could it be the imagined echo of his own unuttered thoughts?

He paused and listened. Voices were speaking in an adjoining room; and as it was only separated by an old wainscot partition, the joints and panels of which were frail and gaping from age, he raised the arras and placed his ear close to an opening. The voices came from the chamber of the two Englishmen, whom he could perceive through the fracture in the boarding. They had not undressed, but had merely thrown off their doublets, and seemed resolved to sleep half ready for any emergency with their drawn swords beside them.

"And so the prospect alarms you, my brave bully boy?" continued Shelly, who was twisting his moustache before a mirror, and seemed to be bantering his companion.

"It doth, of a verity," replied Master Patten; "so let us pray the glorious Virgin Mary, that she keep us from witches, the Scots, and the devil!"

"Thou hast no fear of the fires in Smithfield?" said Shelly; "cogsbones! in old King Harry's time I have seen two fat citizens, and a lean apothecary from Aldgate, all burning in one blaze for saying little more. But, worthy Master Patten, when I am the husband of yonder sweet lady of Yarrow, what shall I make thee—seneschal, comptroller, or steward of the household? or would you prefer a snug place at court, where clerkly skill would avail thee? But, by St. George, thou wouldst need to sleep in a suit of mail, well tempered and graven with saintly miracles; for the avenues of a Scottish palace are well beset by swords and daggers."

"Marry come up! Master Shelly, don't talk of such things," replied Patten gravely. "By my soul, if I ever set foot in this cursed country of rough-footed and blue-capped heathens again, but under harness, may I never more see London stone or hear the bell of St. Paul's!"

"We found it more pleasant when mounting guard at Boulogne, making love to the market wenches at Calais, and playing the devil in the wine cabarets, eh? Bluff King Harry's service had more pleasantries and fewer perils than his son's—the little King Edward."

"Ugh! think of that devilish story of the Red-shanks who live but a few miles off—those Nabs or Neishes, or whatever the barbarians style themselves. Why, 'twas like the tales that old mariners tell us, at Puddle Wharf and London Bridge, of black devils and savages who dwell beyond Cape Flyaway, in the kingdom of Prester John, or in the Island of the Seven Cities, which can only be found, once in every hundred years. Nay, I shall settle me down somewhere within the sound of Bow bells, and doubt not that, for what I have done in the young king's service here in Scotland, our Lord Chancellor, Sir William Paulet, now Lord St. John of Basing (and who is to be Marquis of Winchester), or Sir William Petre, our most worthy Secretary of State, will make me some honourable provision."

"If not, mine honest Bill Patten, thou hast still thy sword and the scarlet-and-blue livery of a Boulogner; but, as I was saying, when I am fairly wedded—ha! ha! droll, is it not?—to my sweet Lady Yarrow, as the reward of my service here in Scotland——"

Florence did not wait to hear what the heedless Englishman proposed to do after this happy event; but, dropping the arras, he took his sword, and leaving the chamber, knocked roughly at the door of the two strangers, who started to their weapons before they opened it.

"Sirs," said Florence sternly, "I have discovered you to be two spies of the Protector Somerset."

"Discovered! Then you have been listening?" said Shelly with admirable coolness, though his nut-brown cheek grew pale with anger.

"How I have come to know it, matters not; but the plain fact stands manifest—you are spies!"

"Spies?" reiterated Shelly, trembling with suppressed passion.

"I have said so."

"Be wary, sir—be wary; I wear a sword."

"Edward Shelly, captain of King Henry's Boulogners, need not remind any one that he wears a sword, and can use it too. His name has found an echo even in the chambers of the Tournelles and the Louvre, where I have heard him praised as a true and valiant soldier."

"I thank you, squire—I mean, laird of Fawside—for this compliment; but——"

"To be a spy!"

"*Tudieu!* as we used to say at Boulogne," exclaimed Shelly furiously; "do not repeat that hateful word!—well?"

"Is to deserve the gallows."

"You are deceived, sir,—I tell you, deceived. I am no spy, by all that is sacred on earth!" replied Shelly hoarsely; for he was striving to master his pride and passion. "Remember," he added, involuntarily placing his left hand upon the secret pocket which contained his perilous despatches—"remember that *you* were accused of being a spy of the dukes of Guise and Mayenne."

"But falsely so."

"As I may be of being an emissary of Edward Duke of Somerset."

"Then what meaneth all I overheard about your services in Scotland—of Sir William Petre and the Lord St. John of Basing, both of whom are well-known intriguers and favourers of the mad schemes of the late King Henry?"

"'Tis exceedingly probable that they are so," replied Shelly evasively; "for you must know that one is Lord High Chancellor of England, and the other is Secretary of State."

He spoke slowly, to gain time for thought, as he felt all the perils of their position, and glanced down the dark corridor without, surmising, if he suddenly slew Fawside, how he and Patten could get out of the tower, and escape into the forest. The project seemed too desperate; for it scarcely occurred to him, when he relinquished it.

"Now, hark you, sir," said he. "To make this matter short, is it your purpose to make us prisoners?"

"No; for I would not wittingly bring two unfortunate men to a public and infamous death, more especially he of whom I heard so much in France, the brave leader of the English Boulogners."

"'Tis well, sir," replied Shelly, in a voice that seemed to falter with honest emotion. "You act generously; though, had you resolved otherwise, you had got but two dead bodies for your pains."

"Dead bodies?" queried Master Patten anxiously.

"Yes," added Shelly firmly; "for I would have run *you* through the heart, my friend, to seal your lips for ever; and then I would have fought to the last—yea, to the very death-gasp; for never shall a pestilent Scot fix an iron fetter on this hand, which planted the red cross of England on the Tour de l'Ordre!"

"In this chamber you have more than once to-night mentioned the name of a lady," said Florence gravely.

"Exactly; the Countess of Yarrow—bonny Madeline Home," replied Shelly gaily, and with a most provoking smile. "But what then?"

"You actually aspire to her hand,—you, a stranger, a foreigner?"

"Cogsbones! yea, to more; and who shall dare to gainsay me?"

"I do," replied Florence, who felt himself growing alternately pale and red with the anger that gathered in his heart.

"You! On what pretence or principle?"

"As her accepted lover."

"Whew!" whistled Shelly. "The deuce and the devil! Dost thou say so? Then I suppose we shall come to blows, after all."

"Not here, at least," said Florence, with the calmness of concentrated rage in his tone, though his brow was crimson and his eyes were sparkling with light; "to fight here were to destroy you and your companion. I know not on what your presumptuous aspirations are based; but if we meet not in battle ere thirty days from this be passed, I shall send my cartel to the Marshal of Berwick, and challenge you to a solemn single combat."

"Good! I am easily found when wanted for such work; and so, until that pleasant meeting be arranged— —"

"Adieu, sirs."

"A good repose to you," said Shelly, closing the door of his room and carefully securing it.

"What think you of all this?" asked Patten, with some alarm and excitement in his face and manner.

"By St. John the Silent! I was beginning to think we were to prate at the door all night," yawned Shelly, with a tone of irritation, as he threw himself upon his couch, spread his mantle over him, and went to sleep with the readiness of a soldier—a readiness provoking to Master Patten, who, after their late visitor's departure, felt doubly anxious and wakeful.

In the morning, when Florence, with Hackerston, and the three burgesses, bade their farewell to Lady Muriel, and left the tower of the Torwood, they found that their two English friends (concerning whose names and purpose Florence observed a steady silence) had arisen by daylight, obtained a guide, betaken them to horse, and three hours before had disappeared by the eastern road through the forest.

CHAPTER XXXVI
THE RETURN

What is the worst of woes that wait an age?
What stamps the wrinkle deeper on the brow?
To view each loved one blotted from life's page,
And be on earth, alone, as I am now.

Byron.

As Florence and his companions took the same road that led towards Lothian, he reflected on all that he had heard pass between Shelly and Patten on the preceding evening; and though he humanely felt some satisfaction that they were gone, and consequently, he hoped, in safety, the circumstance of the English gentleman canvassing to his comrade so openly and confidently the prospect of his marriage with the Countess of Yarrow, occasioned ample food for reflection, and for those perplexing and annoying thoughts which suggest themselves so readily to the restless imagination of a lover.

"He has seen her, and knows she is beautiful, rich, and beloved by Mary of Lorraine," thought he; "and a mere spirit of empty bravado has made him speak thus. Madeline may be able to solve the mystery; if not, I have still my sword, and dearly shall Master Shelly pay for his empty boasting."

As they passed through Falkirk, they found the whole population of that place (then a little thatched burgh of barony) in the streets and thronging the porch of the ancient church of St. Modan, where the bell was being solemnly tolled in the old square steeple. The faces of all they met, were expressive of dismay and excitement. A dead body (of a recanted heretic, of course), which had been possessed by an evil spirit, was on that day cast thrice out of its grave, in the dark depth of which it could only be retained in peace at last by Father Andrew Haig (the *last* Catholic vicar of the church) placing the consecrated Host upon the coffin, and having the earth heaped over it.

This ghastly marvel furnished ample matter for conversation until the travellers passed the Almond by a boat at Temple-Liston. There the river, which is now spanned by a bridge of very ordinary dimensions, was then so broad that for centuries it was crossed by a regular ferry-boat; and as the current was swollen and rolling rapidly, some time elapsed before the little party of men and horses were safely transported to its eastern bank.

Near this ferry, upon the soft yellow moss of a long lea-rig, sat a party of ploughmen and shepherds, making a rustic banquet of rye and soft scones, with milk, curds, and clouted cream, or sourkitts, as it was named from the staved kitts in which it was held. Some of these peasants wore hoods of blue or brown cloth, buttoned under the chin, and all had the grey plaid, or one of dull striped tartan, thrown over the left shoulder. Each had a knife at his girdle, and, in the old Scotch fashion, a horn spoon, which dangled at his hood or bonnet lug. The peasant girls had their hair snooded, and were bare-legged, though their feet were encased in cuarans of untanned hide, tied with thongs above the ankle.

The morose gloom subsequent to the Reformation had not yet fallen upon the people, and this peasant group, while their herds and horses grazed near, before resuming labour in the fields, proceeded to amuse themselves with the buck-horn and corn-pipe, and danced to the music of these and the lilting of their own voices, for such were the simple manners and enjoyments of the peasantry in the olden time.

The quiet aspect of the landscape, which possessed all the tints of summer ripened and mellowed into autumn; the merry peasants dancing on the greensward; the blue river flowing in front, and the herds that dotted its banks basking in the sunshine; while on the steep beyond rose the grey turreted preceptory and Norman church of the Knights of St. John,—made Florence think with sorrow of the change a month of war and havock might work here; and full of such reflections and of his own affairs, his secret love, his hostile mother, and his unfinished feud, he listened with some impatience to the prosing of honest Dick Hackerston, who rehearsed the magnitude of his own commercial transactions, to wit, how for my lord the Abbot Ballantyne of Holyrood he sold the wool of all the sheep which ranged upon the abbey lands at Liberton and Coldbrandspath, and the skins and hides of all the animals slaughtered for the plentiful table of that great monastery; and how he bought, bartered, or procured in return, from the French, the Flemings, and the English, raisins, almonds, rice, loaf-sugar, love-apples, oranges, olives, ginger, mace, and pepper; for Master Peter Posset great boxes of dried herbs and apothecaries' stuffs; for the court ladies bales of French romances; for Ralph Riddle, of the "Golden Rose," cases of Rhenish, Malvoisie, and Gascon wines, and so forth; till our young gentleman of 1547, who felt just about as much interest in such matters as one of the present age might feel in scrip and railway shares, bank-stock and bonds, yawned with sheer weariness, when, at the west port of Edinburgh, he bade adieu to his mercantile companions, and, without halting to refresh his horse, took the road which, after passing the castles of Craigmillar and Brunstane, led direct to his own secluded home.

The shades of evening were deepening on the level but fertile landscape, on the distant hills, and on the darkening sea, when he drew up in the court of Fawside tower, and on dismounting hastened to meet his mother. With a stern lip and tearful eye she received him, and with a settled gloom, on her pale white brow; for, clad in her deepest dooleweeds, she had spent the day in prayer and meditation between the tombs Of her husband and her eldest son in the church of Tranent; and now, with a sigh of bitter impatience, she beheld poor Florence, who was oppressed by the sombre aspect of a home such as she made it, toss aside his sword and steel coursing-hat, and sink wearily and in silence into a chair near the hall fire.

"So, so, you are weary?" said she, supporting herself on her long cane with one hand, while with grim kindness she patted his head with the other. "While ye have been wandering like a fule-bairn between Edinburgh and Stirling, or Gude alane kens where, our tenants have neglected, for the first time in their lives, to bring their Lammas wheat into the barbican, whilk, as you ken, they are bound to send duly tied in a sack to you as their overlord."

"Oh, mother, heed not the Lammas wheat; anon we shall have other things to think of than the collecting of rent or kain."

"Hah!—say you so? Then the news at Edinburgh Cross— —"

"Is war?"

"'Tis well! Our men have been turning to women since the fields of Ancrum and Solway. And this war is, of course, anent the marriage of a boy king and a baby queen; a brave matter, truly, for bearded men to fight about!"

"It would seem so; and now I almost begin to agree with the Lord Huntly's view of this coming strife."

"Indeed!" said his mother, with more of scorn than curiosity in her manner; "and what may *his* view be?"

"That he dislikes not the match."

"The false Highland limmer!" she hissed through her set teeth; "so he dislikes not the match— —"

"But hates the manner of wooing."

"Now, by the souls of my ancestors who are in Heaven!" exclaimed Dame Alison, striking her long cane fiercely on the paved floor of the hall, "I love the manner of wooing, and thus may Scotland and England ever woo each other, with hands gloved and helmets barred; for I hate the accursed match, and would rather see the child Mary Stuart strangled in the cradle, and her sceptre become the heritage of Arran, than live to be the bride of the apostate Henry's son and the crowned queen of our hereditary enemies! And now, since we are talking of foemen, saw ye aught in your gowk-like rambling of the hell-brood who bide in the barred tower on yonder lea?"

"I did, mother," sighed Florence.

"Preston himself, perhaps."

"Yea, mother; thrice."

"Hath manhood gone out of the land! And ye parted, as ye met, sakeless and bloodless?"

"As you see me, mother," replied Florence, overwhelmed by the bitterness of thoughts he dared not utter.

"Saints of God!" she exclaimed, and raised her clenched hand as if she would have smote him on his sad but handsome face; then suddenly repressing the fierce impulse, she turned abruptly and left the hall.

Florence thought of the sweet merry eyes of Madeline Home; and all their memory was requisite to render life endurable with such a welcome to his mother's hearth.

CHAPTER XXXVII
LADY ALISON

Oh, get thee gone! thou mak'st me wrong the dead,
By wasting moments consecrate to tears,
In idle railing at a wretch like thee!
A mother rarely will with patience hear
A true reproach against a living son,
Far less a taunt directed at the dead.

Firmillian.

Preparations for war between Scotland and England progressed rapidly. Though the religious, and, in some degree, the political principles of the Regent Arran were unsettled, he evinced the utmost activity in his military arrangements; and in the south the Duke of Somerset was scarcely less energetic. Too well aware, by the history of the past, that the designs of England were other than merely matrimonial, that her inborn spirit of grasping ambition and aggression was abroad, and that her kings and governors had never respected truce or treaty, peace or promise, the Earl of Arran left nothing undone to attach the malcontent nobles to his own person. He ordered all the border castles to be repaired, strengthened, and garrisoned; he ordained the sheriffs of counties, the stewards of stewartries, the provosts of cities, and all the great barons, to train the people to arms, to the use of the bow and arquebuse, by frequent weapon-shows and musters. Old seamen who had served under Sir Andrew Wood, the valiant Bartons, and others, he encouraged to equip armed caravels and gallant privateers, with orders to sink, burn, and destroy; while on land he strove, by threats or entreaties, to crush the bitter feuds that existed between clan and clan or lord and laird, that all might reserve their united strength and sharpest steel for the common enemy.

Like the loyal lords, tue malcontents mustered and trained their vassels, but were secretly watching the current of events; while among the people, Catholic and Protestant, reformed and unreformed (*i.e.,* heretic and idolater, as they pleasantly stigmatized each other), all for a time merged their disputes in the common cause, and armed them side by side, for the defence of their mother country. The reformers were undoubtedly in the interest of Reformed England, and averse to Catholic France; hence "a miraculous shower of puddocks" (*Anglicè*, frogs) which fell about this time somewhere in Fife, tended greatly to perturb the souls of the pious and godly, as being forerunners of a French army, headed by the Cardinal of Lorraine, or "the popish and bloodie Duke of Guise."

Time passed, and the end of August drew nigh; but there came no tidings from Scotland's faithless ally, of that armed force so solemnly promised, by those letters which Florence had brought from the Louvre, and at last the Regent Arran began to find that he must trust to himself alone to crush traitors within, and face his foes beyond the realm.

So energetic were the measures of Florence, that within three weeks from the time of his leaving Stirling, a long line of such beacons as the regent desired was established upon all the hills near the coast of the German Sea, and from the high rocky bluff of St. Abb to the summit of the palace of Linlithgow. Another line of beacons was also placed along the borders from sea to sea, on the highest eminences, and on many of the castles and peels, which had been strengthened by the engineers who came to Scotland two years before, with the five thousand men-at-arms, sent over by Francis I., under George Montgomerie, laird of Larges, in Ayrshire—famous in history as that Comte de Larges who slew Henry II. of France in a tournament. As in the older time of James II., and by the ordinance of his twelfth parliament, Florence posted armed watchmen between Roxburgh and Berwick and on all the fords of Tweed, and built on Home Castle, the greatest balefire. One beacon was to be the warning that the enemy were in motion; two, that they had begun to cross the river; and four, "all at anis as foure candellis" (to quote Glendook) that they were in great strength, and on their march for the Lothians.

He left mounted guards composed of the vassals of the loyal border lords, whose sentinels were to convey instant intelligence of the foe's advance by day; then by the regent it was ordained that none should leave their residences, or remove their goods or cattle, as it was his resolution to defend every hearth and foot of ground to the last; and the cross of fire was to be the signal to arms! After completing these arrangements to the entire satisfaction of Arran, to whom he made his report at Edinburgh, Florence, on one of the last days of August, returned, with old Roger of Westmains, to his secluded little fortlet, to muster his retinue, and await the summons to the field.

Meanwhile, Glencairn, Cassilis, Kilmaurs, and other ignoble lords of their party, were absent at their own estates, superintending the fortification of their castles and array of their contingents, for the queen or against her, as the tide of events might make it suitable for them to act. Bothwell was brooding over his captivity in the castle of Edinburgh, and planning schemes of vengeance on Arran, on Mary of Lorraine, and on our hero, whom he conceived to be in some way implicated in his affairs. Shelly and Patten had reached London, from whence they joined the army of Somerset.

M. Antoine was composing a new piece of music, in honour of the intended nuptial alliance with France, and had resolved that it should rival the marriage ode or epithalamium of the servile Buchanan. Mary of Lorraine and her ladies were busy with a new tapestry, as a present for the dauphine. Champfleurie was salving his sores at Stirling, and taking new lessons in the science of defence ind destruction. Old Claude Hamilton was also preparing for war, by deepening the fosse of his tall, grim tower, and like other barons, was storing up the grain, fuel, and provender of his tenants, in its spacious vaults, and in the barns and granaries which stood within its strong barbican while ten brass drakes, imported for him from Flanders, by Dick Hackerston, peeped their round muzzles over the parapet of the keep.

On the first evening of his return from the borders, Florence was seated in the hall with his mother, who occupied her usual window bench, where she guided her spindle, which whirled on the floor; while he, dreading a recurrence to her everlasting topic, the Hamiltons of. Preston, and with his mind now, after an absence of three weeks, more than ever full of the image of Madeline, affected to be deeply immersed in the old black-lettered pages of "the Knightly tale of Gologras and Gawaine," from the quaint press of Chepman and Millar, printers to his late Majesty James IV., but his mother soon began to open the trenches, for he heard her muttering,—

"Yes, yes, 'tis a basilisk I must get. Let me see, Master Posset said that basilisks are hatched from dwarf eggs laid by old cocks; and that they grow to little winged dragons, whose eyes, as all the world knoweth, can slay by a single glance. I must get me one, if all things fail, and let it loose in Preston tower—that one reptile may destroy the others—yet Gude keep me from evil and witchcraft!"

While muttering thus, slowly and in a manner peculiar to all who live much alone, or are in the habit of communing with themselves, she glanced twice or thrice impatiently towards her son but he still read on. Finding her audible remarks produced no response, she addressed him.

"Wit ye now, my son, that Preston's niece, the daughter of that foul Earl of Yarrow, who drew his sword in the fray in which your father fell, is even now in Preston tower."

"Madeline!" faltered Florence, closing his book.

"Yea, Madeline Home; ye know her name it seems. So, when will there be a better time than now to form a plan for destroying the whole brood, root and branch?"

"A worse you mean, mother," said Florence, as the dark story of Aileen MacNab occurred to him.

"A *better*—I mean what I say; for in the war and tumult of an invasion, what matter a few lives more or less?"

"Mother, I dare not urge the feud at present," sighed poor Florence.

"Dare not—did I hear you aright? have two acts of common charity— it may be of merest courtesy that passed between ye in the Torwood, so blunted the keen resentment which hath lived for so many generations?"

"The regent——"

"Prate not to me of regents—nay, nor of kings," she persisted, whirling her spindle like lightning.

"And Madel—this countess, she came to Preston——"

"Last night, and this morning she rode forth over Gladsmuir, with a tasselled hawk on her dainty glove, and Mungo Tennant (oh that I had him within range of an arquebuse!) in attendance upon her, with a stand of birds, where a lash should be, on his knave's shoulders. And they hawked over the whole muir, though 'tis ours if the sword can fence what the king's charter hath failed to define. So I tell thee, son, that ere we lose men or harness in fighting the English, let us have one brave onslaught at Preston tower, and end this matter for ever."

"Its walls are high, its gate is yetlan iron."

"Pshaw! Hear me: Hamilton expects no attack; what, then, so easy as at midnight to surround the tower with forty resolute mounted men, each with a windlan of straw trussed to his saddle-bow; force the outer gate— John Cargill, the smith at Carberry, says he can ding it to shivers wi' his forehammer, so e'en take the loon at his word; kill the keeper; pile the straw at the tower doors, and fire it; set bakehouse, and brewhouse, and mautkiln in a flame; then kill, by push of spear and shot of arquebuse, all who seek to escape; smoke them to death, even as wight Wallace smoked the English at the barns of Ayr. You pause——"

"By an act of the secret council it was ordained that this matter should end, mother; for such is the law."

"Hear him, Westmains!" said she with scornful pity, as the ground-bailie entered, made a low bow, and, according to his wont, marched straight to the ale-barrel. "I talk of the feud in which his father and his brother Willie fell; and he quotes law to me like one of the ten sworn advocates, or a villanous notary of the new college of justice. I tell thee, malapert bairn, that all the secret councils in the world cannot alter the ancient law of Scotland, as written by David II., anent feuds. What says it, Roger?"

"That 'gif the king grants peace to the slayer without the consent of the nearest friends of him who is slain, these friends may seek revenge——'"

"Mark ye that, Florence—*may seek revenge!*"

"'Lawfully of him or of them who slew their friend.' Thus 'tis lawful to prosecute our feud to the death," added the ground-bailie.

"And in this faith I reared thee since thou wert but a wee bairnie, supping thy first porridge with Father John's apostle-spoon."

"Does not our Scottish law ordain that he who slays another shall be dragged to trial?" asked Florence.

"Law again! Oh, I shall go mad!" exclaimed Lady Alison, dashing her spindle from her, and pressing her hands over her grey temples, while her eyes flashed with fire. "When your father had a doubt in law, he consulted neither statute nor scrivener, but put his sword to the grindstone in the yard. Would you call it murder if we slew every man in yonder tower upon the lea to-night? I trow not. 'Twould be a righteous act in the eyes of Heaven; and it would be styled by men—even by those loons whose laws ye quote—a misfortune—a slaughter committed in *chaud-melle*—even as thy father was slain by the Hamiltons; and Willie—my brave, my true, my winsome Willie—how died he?"

"In upholding that which the lord regent justly terms a curse to Scotland—an hereditary feud."

"Oh, can it be God's desire that I should be driven mad!" exclaimed Lady Alison, lifting up her voice, her eyes, and hands, with mingled rage and pity.

"Mother, hear me," urged Florence, as the gentleness and beauty of Madeline, with the open, honest advances of Claude Hamilton, and those proffers of peace which were repulsed in an evil moment, and under the influence of her who now spoke, all came vividly before him.

"Never did one of this house or race talk thus, like a lurdane monk, like a mouthing abbot, or a craven wretch, but thee! He who slays by the sword, as Preston slew thy father, shall by the sword be slain; for so in Holy Writ the blessed hand of God inscribed it. Even Mass John of Tranent admitteth that!"

Florence felt the truth of what she urged, and something of the old traditionary hate made his cheek glow with red shame for a moment, while his heart was heavy with sadness.

"Then, if I slay this man with my sword, mother," said he gently, "am I in turn to perish by the steel of some one else?"

"Slave!" cried Lady Alison in a voice like a shriek; "did the brave father to whom, for our shame, I bore thee—did thy brother, who died in the feud like a true Scottish gentleman—reckon thus—how they lived or when they died? whom they slew or by whom they were slain? I trow not! Thou hast become white-livered in France. Anne of Albany hath deceived me, and made thee a maudlin fool! Out upon thee—fie! fie! Begone, lest I stain my old hands in blood by dinging my bodkin into thee!"

With these fierce words, and seeming to concentrate the whole energies of her wild spirit in a glance of combined scorn and fury, she struck her right hand upon her busk, swept up the long black skirt of her dooleweed with the left, and retired from the hall with the bearing of a tragedy queen.

Roger of Westmains, who had never before witnessed such scenes between Lady Alison and her son, or any of her family, gazed after her wistfully, and then surveying the young laird with a perplexed glance, he shook his white head in a way that might mean anything or nothing, just as one might choose to construe it, and withdrew after his fiery mistress.

Then, with the manner of one who had been thoroughly worried, Florence laid aside his book, took his mantle, sword, and coursing-hat; and ordering out his favourite grey, galloped from the tower at a furious pace, he knew not and cared not whither—anywhere to be rid of his mother's fierce taunts—of his own bitter thoughts and perplexities.

He had but one fixed wish as he cast his eyes to the green ridge of Soltra and the greener brow of Dunprender Law, that ere midnight the red blaze of those beacons he had so recently erected thereon might warn all Scotland of the coming foe! War itself would be a relief from the excitement or irritation he endured now.

CHAPTER XXXVIII
THE CHAPEL OF ST. MARTIN

With a graceful step and stately,
  Proud of heart and proud of mien;
With her deep eyes shining grayly,
  Cometh Lady Madeline,
    Trembling as with cold;
With cheek red-flush'd like daisy tip,
And full-ripe pouting ruby lip,
  And hair of tawny gold.

Household Words.

Plato asserted that hopes were the dreams of people waking; and Thales the Milesian affirmed that hope was the most lasting of all things; for when all seemed lost to man, it still remained. Thus our lover, like every other lover before the flood, or since, hoped on, though prejudice, fortune, and hostility had raised between him and Madeline Home barriers that seemed all but insurmountable.

Skirting the green hill of Carberry, he reached the banks of the brawling and beautiful Esk, then a deeper and a broader river than now. He boldly swam his horse through it near Edmondstone Edge, and spurred over the then open wastes known as the mains of Sheriff Hall, where on the purple muir lay the green ridges and trenches of a Roman camp, with a gallows-tree—an old and thunder-riven oak, on which hung the bony fragments of one malefactor and the recently-executed body of another, who had been doomed to death by the Douglasses of Dalkeith. Down the steep slope from Newton-kirk he rode heedlessly, and passed the grey and ancient Ramparts of Craigmillar, where, with beacon and culverin, barred gate and moated wall, old Sir Symon Preston of that ilk, was preparing for the coming strife; then giving his horse the reins, he let him wander on, or crop the grass by the solitary way; for Florence was buried in sad thoughts, yet his eyes failed not to linger from time to time on the distant outline of the capital, upheaved upon its ridge of rock, all rugged, broken, and fantastic; the castle, spires, and every clustered mass of building, like the beetling brows of Salisbury and Arthur's bare round cone, tinted by the deep red of the western sun—a tint that seemed the brighter when contrasted with the fields of yellow corn that swayed their full ripe ears in the foreground, and the green masses of oak foliage that covered all the burghmuir in the middle distance of that lovely landscape.

From the hill which is crowned by the ancient village of Kirkliberton, he rode slowly on till he reached Kilmartin, a little cell or chapel in a sequestered part of the eastern flank of the broom-covered hills of Braid. It was a plain edifice with lancet windows, and had a cross on its gable; it was of great antiquity, having been built by a baron of Mortonhall, who had gone to the Holy Land, and who, when lying wounded by a poisoned arrow, on the shore at Galilee, had made a vow to found a cell, if he ever saw his native land again. Two aged sycamores cast a sombre shadow over a few green graves which lay within the low, half-ruined wall that enclosed the precincts. Those grass-covered mounds marked the last resting-places of various hermits who had succeeded Father Martin, who though locally canonized as a saint, is now forgotten (at least his history is only known to ourselves), and who, like him, had occupied the little cottage close by the chapel, and had drawn the element of baptism from the spring of pure water that sparkled as it poured in the sunshine over a ledge of whin rock, and gurgled in torquoise-blue between the ripe corn-rigs, and under the yellow broom-bells, to join the Burn of Braid.

The story of Father Martin is somewhat singular. Among the five thousand military pilgrims from Scotland, who accompanied David Earl of Garioch to Palestine, there was a citizen of Edinburgh, named Martin Oliver. In the year 1191 he found himself with the army of Richard of England, then besieging Ptolmais. Having been guilty of some crime, Oliver, to avoid punishment, deserted to the Saracens, and became, outwardly, a renegade to his religion. Tormented day and night by his conscience, he endured the utmost misery, and on his knees vowed to atone to God for his crime. One day when posted as a sentinel on the outworks of the town, he perceived not far from him a Christian soldier, in whom he recognized a comrade, one of Earl David's band, named John Durward, whom he addressed in the Scottish tongue, telling him that he was weary of life, and longed to atone for his pretended apostasy. A communication was thus kept up from time to time, and on a certain night, Martin Oliver introduced the Scottish Crusaders "into a part of the city." The English followed, and Ptolmais was immediately captured. So says Hector Boethius, and Maimbourg, in his "Histoire des Croisades," adds, that assuredly the Christian princes had a sure intelligencer within the town. Oliver returned to his native land, and in a hermitage amid the lonely hills of Braid he passed his days in prayer and penance for his apostasy, and to atone for serving the enemies of God, in a city where the true cross was said to be destroyed.

Many little chapels like Kilmartin, and such as St. Catherine at the Balmwell, St. John the Baptist on the Burghmuir, and of our Lady at Bridge-end, studded all the fertile Lothians, and were each kept by an old priest, who derived a scanty subsistence from the pious, the charitable or the credulous; from farmers, for blessing their herds and crops, for baptising their little ones, or praying for fine weather,—even now, when Scotland was on the verge of that tremendous change the Reformation. To Florence, the calm seclusion of this old chapel, which was situated in a green hollow of those wild and barren hills, seemed soothing and inviting, and there he resolved to rest awhile, and if possible to give himself up to deeper thought, that under its calm influence he might discover some means of extrication from his present difficulties. Dismounting, he tied his horse to the chapel door, and entered without observing that under the sycamores there stood three richly-caparisoned horses, two of which were ridden by armed grooms, in the royal livery, while the third, whereon was a lady's pad of crimson velvet, was riderless.

A plain altar, with a stone step, well-worn by the knees of generations of peasantry who had prayed there; a rude crucifix of freestone, carved within a niche, and an old skull, which, if abstracted, was said to have the power of always returning to the chapel, were the sole features of the interior, unless we add a slab in the centre, marked by a cross, and inscribed *Mater Dei memento mei*. This marked the grave of Father Martin, the repentant soldier of Ptolmais, who lived to the age of ninety, and died when Alexander III. was on the throne of Scotland.

Florence had scarcely entered, dipped his fingers in the stone font at the door, and surveyed the bare, bleak little oratory, with the listlessness of a pre-occupied man, when the rustling of silk and the sound of a light step behind, made him turn, and lo! Madeline Home, wearing over her usual dress a long blue riding-robe of Flemish cloth, and having on her pretty head one of the prettiest of little Anne Boleyn hoods of purple velvet, stood before him, with her long skirt gathered up gracefully in her left hand, on which sat her favourite hawk (the same bird which had excited Dame Alison's indignation), and in her right she held a jewelled riding-switch.

On beholding a person in the little chapel, she paused; but when their eyes met, a bright flush passed over her sweet delicate face, with an expression of surprise and inquiry. Her half-opened lips revealed her little teeth, so white and closely set; and her dilated eyes seemed to ask an explanation, but Florence pressed her hand, and then they exchanged one of those long and tender kisses which are never forgotten.

"Dearest Florence," she whispered, "how came you here?"

"At a time so strangely opportune, you would ask?"

"You did not follow me!"

"Follow you? Heavens, no!—and yet had I known——"

"Then how came you here?"

"By fatality—happy fortune—which you choose. God alone knoweth how, for, my sweetest heart, I know not. I rode forth from Fawside to escape from a bitterness too deep for telling; and riding on, on—I knew not, cared not whither; my grey—the grey the queen gave me—tarried at the chapel-door, and so I am here."

"How strange—when I was here too!" said Madeline, whose fine eyes sparkled with pleasure and drollery.

"A fortunate coincidence!" said Florence, caressing her hands.

"To-day I was in Edinburgh with the queen, and being on my way home to Preston, she gave me an alms for the Franciscan at Kilmartin here, with that which the good man values more,—a fragment of St. Martin's garment, no larger than a testoon; but brought from her sister, Madame the prioress of Rheims, by Monsieur d'Oysell, the ambassador."

"And you are returning——"

"To Preston Tower."

"And to your uncle Claude?"

"Yes."

"When, so near—our residences being within view of each other,—may I hope to see you?" urged Florence; "may I hope that we shall meet, in some place where none can see or interrupt us?"

A pressure of his hand and a sweet smile were his assuring reply.

"Thanks, dear, dear Madeline; then I may escort you eastward?" said he anxiously.

"So far as Carberry you may. Fortunately, I have the queen's servants in attendance on me, and not my uncle's; so let us mount and go, for the evening is drawing on, and probably we shall not ride fast," she added, with a droll smile.

"I am with you so seldom, dearest Madeline, that I am loath to lessen the joy of our happy meeting; do tarry with me here a little longer."

"But the queen's grooms— —"

"Let them wait; for what do the varlets wear livery? I have a matter near my heart on which I must speak with you."

"That you love me," said Madeline playfully; "but you have told me that often already."

"Love you, Lady Yarrow! oh, I love you—love you dearly; but— —"

"But what?"

"My heart beats so fast, and love so bewilders me, that I know not what I say."

"To the point—you have some secret, Florence."

"Know you a gentleman named Shelly?"

"No;—but wherefore?"

"Edward Shelly?"

"No," she replied, her bright eyes filling with wonder.

"Edward Shelly, captain of the English band named the Boulogners?"

"No—I tell you no; but why all these questions?"

"It is most inexplicable!" exclaimed Florence; and he hastily told her what he had overheard Shelly saying to Master Patten, and the astonishment and perplexity of poor Madeline was great. Then she switched the skirt of her riding-dress impatiently, and said laughing,—

"'Tis the first time I have heard of this unknown lover. I hope he is handsome and gallant,—I should like much to see him; but—but 'tis impossible all this, dearest Florence; you dreamed it, or you but jest with me."

"Nay, 'tis no dream or jest, sweet Madeline, as I am to fight a solemn duel anent it, on the Border-side, with the same Edward Shelly, unless— —"

"What—what?" she asked, growing pale.

"We meet in battle before a month be past, and of that there is every probability."

"This cannot be; his falsehoods must be seen to! I shall know who this impudent varlet is, who dares to use my name even in empty jest!" said Madeline gravely; "but how truly spoke Mary of Lorraine this morning, when she said that love is more transient than friendship, for a lover is ever under delusions. But think no more of this saucy fellow, dear Florence. We need not add jealousy to the troubles that already environ our unfortunate passion. I am so happy when with you, that all existence seems a blank between each of our meetings. Poor dear Florence! I do love to read in your kind eyes the joy my presence excites in your bosom—the love of which I am the source!"

Her manner, so soft, so suave and winning, when contrasted to the harsh, stern, and imperious bearing of his mother, lent her a charm far surpassing all the attractions of mere loveliness. After a long pause, during which her hot cheek was resting on his shoulder, and his arm was pressed around her,—

"See," said she, "the sun has set, for the painted glass of the windows has lost all its brilliance; we must go, Florence, lest mischief befall us if we ride late,—and, of all things in the world," she added, with a merry smile, "let us avoid that fated place, the Elveskirk."

"What manner of kirk may it be?" he asked, as he led her forth.

"A place near this, where an ancestor of mine was borne away by a fairy; so, beware of a damsel in green, Florence," said Madeline merrily, as he lifted her to the saddle, and then, taking the bridle, led her horse along the narrow road that traversed the Braid Hills. He then mounted, and the two lackeys of Mary of Lorraine, dropping a little to the rear, followed them at an easy pace.

"You see yonder steep knoll, so thickly covered by waving broom," said Madeline; "below it is a round hollow, called the Elveskirk, where the grass is ever of the most brilliant and beautiful green, as it is said to be mowed and watered by the fairies who dwell there, and who, on the Eve of St. John, are wont to dance and hold their revels in it. Once upon a time, an ancestor of mine, a brave young knight, who was lord of the manor of Morton Hall— yonder moated tower among the dark old woods—had been dining with the abbot of St. Mary, at Newbattle, and was returning home, over the hills, near Kirkliberton. This was long ago, in the days of James I.

"The night was clear, and the moon shone brightly, when he met by the wayside a fair-skinned and golden-haired lady in green, whom he addressed in the language of gallantry, and who beguiled him to spend a few hours with her in the green hollow of the Elveskirk. Swift flew these hours, when love and pleasure chased them! and when the moon was sunk behind the Pentlands, and the east was streaked with grey, the lady suddenly disappeared, and in her place, the knight found only a wild rose-tree, that waved in the morning breeze, as if mocking him. He turned to seek his horse, muttering the while, that the father abbot's wine must have been over potent; but the steed had disappeared; so he resolved to proceed homeward on foot. As he walked on, to his astonishment, he found the face of the country changed. The ridges of Braid, and the bluff, flinty brow of Blackford, were the same as of old; but in some places where whilom the purple heather grew with many a tuft of dark green whin, since last night the yellow corn had sprung up, and was waving in the wind. Cottages, which he knew to be his own property, had sunk into ruin, and become mere piles of stones, or had totally disappeared; and elsewhere others had sprung up as if by magic, and now large trees were tossing their foliage where not a twig had grown the night before!

"At the Burn of Braid, where he had been wont to cross by a dangerous ford, and where a subtle kelpie had deluded and drowned many a belated man, my ancestor found a goodly bridge of stone, and he passed along it, as one in a dream. The Inch House, which whilom had been moated round by the river, stood now alone high and dry upon a grassy eminence; and the river itself, had shrunk between its banks to a mere mountain burn.

"Full of terror, the lord of Morton Hall turned to seek Kilmartin, the little cell we have just, left, and he saw it standing, as we see it now, all unchanged, on the brow of the hill, just where the saint was buried of old. He now discovered, that though yestereve he had been close-shaven in the old Scottish fashion, his beard had grown to a vast length, that it had become white as thistledown, and waved to and fro as he walked. His hands were changed too, as if with age, and his limbs, once so straight and strong, bent under the weight of his body, and seemed every moment to become more feeble.

"'Can this palsied wretch be myself—I who, at Dumbarton, struck down by a single blow of my axe the Red Stuart of Dundonald?' he thought, as he tottered on.

"A horror came over him, with the conviction that he had spent a long lifetime in a night, and he hastened towards the lonely chapel, the priest of which, Father Michael, was his chief friend and confessor. At the little arched door of the holy cell he met a churchman, whose face he knew not; but to whom he said, trembling,—

"'Is not Father Michael here?'

"The priest gazed upon him with surprise, and then replied, after a pause,—

"'Father Michael Ochiltree, if it be he you mean, old man, is with the saints, I trust.'

"'Dead!'

"'He became dean of Dunblane, and thereafter bishop of that see,' continued the priest, with increasing surprise; ''tis an old story, my son—Bishop Michael died in 1430, and is interred in the choir of his cathedral.'

"'Holy father,' said the lord of Morton Hall, with greater agitation and bewilderment; 'what year of God is this?'

"'It is 1520.'

"'Swear it.'

"'I swear it to thee, strange old man—it is the seventh year of our king's reign.'

"'And he is named——'

"'James.'

"'But James what?'

"'The *Fifth*.'

"'Mother of God!' exclaimed the knight; 'I knew but James the *First*. I have been ninety years among the elves—my wife, my children—yea, it may be my grandchildren, have all gone before me to the grave!'

"Rushing past the startled priest, he threw himself in a paroxysm of prayer at the foot of the altar.

"In terror, the father followed and entered; but only in time to see the tall and reverend figure of the knight crumble away to a few pieces of bone and impalpable dust. The skull alone remained, and you saw it lying upon the altar."

The anecdote or legend of the countess (one of a kind common to many countries) produced others, for the age was one of fable and fairy mythology; so the time passed swiftly as the shades of evening deepened, and the lovers rode lingeringly on.

"So, war is at hand," said the countess, after a pause; "O Florence, my soul trembles for you!"

"Fear not, dearest—for your sake I shall be wary."

"You can afford to be so, Florence; one of courage so approved, and in a close helmet——"

"Ah," said he smiling, "you fear that my face may have a ghastly scar, like my Lord Kilmaurs'! But I can guard my head better than he. As the doughty Douglas said to the King of France, 'I can aye gar my hands keep my face.'"

"What would you feel, Florence, were I laid before you, mutilated—mangled—dead?"

"Ah, why a thought so horrible!" he exclaimed, impressed by her strange manner.

"That you may imagine what I shall feel, if such should be your fate."

"For Heaven's love, Madeline, let us talk of other things."

The moon was rising from the glittering sea, when Florence, with a sigh, drew the bridle of his horse, a mile eastward of Carberry; for now they were close to the barony of Claude Hamilton, and to have proceeded further with the young countess would have been alike unwary and unwise.

"So here we part, dear Madeline!" said he sadly.

"And part, we know not when to meet again."

"Nay, I cannot leave you without knowing when that joy again awaits me. I must have promises, for they are better than hope."

"And I, Florence, have had a frightful dream, and dreams are said to be warnings."

"Nay, Madeline; they are but the reflection of the past, and not the foreshadowings of the future; so, no dream could scare me—but what was yours?"

"That your mother—that Lady Alison was slaying me."

Florence felt a pang even at this improbable idea; though he smiled, and to change the subject said,—

"May I hope that, at dusk to morrow, you will meet me—you pause—ah, promise me— —"

"Where!"

"In some secluded place—the church porch of Tranent—'tis always open for vespers."

"I have a horror of that gloomy place, where so many dead are lying, and at such an hour!"

"But what fear you, when I will be there?"

"I shall come—but Father John— —"

"Will not betray us, dearest Madeline! be assured of that; the good priest loves me well."

With some reluctance, she consented to meet him in the gloaming, at the place appointed, on the morrow's eve. He kissed her hand, and they separated; but so long as her light figure and her waving riding-skirt were visible, he continued to gaze after her, as slowly and thoughtfully he rode up the winding way that led to the gate of his home. He gave a glance towards Soltra and Dumprender Law; still their summits were dark, and no spark of light thereon as yet gave token of the coming foe.

The evening was dark, and the tints of the landscape were sombre and sad. It was the autumn of the year, and in his heart the ripe autumn of a love, that might have no spring or summer.

On this night the grim and indignant Lady Alison did not appear; and Florence, who, by his recent unexpected interview, and the hope of another with Madeline Home, felt as if he was in the midst of some tremendous treason against the peace and honour of his own family, experienced some relief in the absence of his mother; for such is the power that may be attained by a strong temper and resolute will over a gentle and affectionate, but better nature. And now such was the tender influence of Madeline, that Florence had returned with every angry passion and bitterness soothed, and he became happy again, for he seemed yet to hear her sweet voice lingering in his ear, and the last Mss they had exchanged in the old chapel of St. Martin seemed yet to be hovering on his lip and thrilling through his heart.

CHAPTER XXXIX
THE LURE

I will have such revenges on you both,
That all the world shall—I will do such things,—
What they are, yet I know not; but they shall be
The terrors of the earth. You think I'll weep;
No, I'll not weep.

King Lear.

Next day Lady Alison was moody, reserved, and sullen; she spoke little, or muttered as she sat in the bay of the hall window whirling her spindle, or secluded herself in her bower-chamber. Maud, the old nurse, who had lost a husband and two brothers in the feud with the Hamiltons, alone shared her angry communings; and even Roger, the bailie, who deemed himself one of the dame's chief counsellors and prime minister, on this day found her morose and unapproachable. Florence dreaded a renewal of the conversation of yesterday; thus, avoiding the presence of his mother, he busied himself among the horses of his retainers, seeing that all were carefully shod and proved to be sound in wind and limb, while an armourer from Edinburgh was at work on the iron trappings of steed and man. The grindstone was whirling in the court-yard; and songs were sung and tales told of the wars of James IV; while blades were burnished and pike-heads pointed and tempered anew: for now, like a thousand other castles in Scotland, the little fortalice of Fawside resounded with the bustle of military preparation.

So passed the noon of day. Florence watched the western verging of the sun as evening drew near, and the rays revolved round the dial. Then his heart beat quicker with anticipated happiness; for the hour of his meeting with Madeline drew nearer and more near. Yet time never seemed to pass so slowly.

As the hours of this long day succeeded each other, Lady Alison strove to smother the angry scorn her son's too peaceful spirit roused within her; but being loath to nurse this growing bitterness against him, she sought him in the garden, which then lay on the sloping bank to the southward of the tower wall.

On the face of a grassy terrace Florence reclined, with his head supported on his elbow, and so lost in thought that he did not hear her approach. In the hollow of his left hand lay the opal ring of Madeline; and it caught the keen eye of Lady Alison as she propped herself on her long cane and stooped over him. Startled by finding his deep and fond reverie so suddenly interrupted, Florence hastily placed the ring on one of his fingers, and resuming his volume of "Gologras and Gawaine," which lay near, arose with a flush of annoyance on his cheek. Rapid though the action, it was not done quickly enough to escape the keen eye of Dame Alison, and her sharp, angry, and anxious glance was at once riveted on the trinket. She saw that it was an opal; and the mysterious and malignant power which that stone was believed to possess and to exert over mortals at once occurred to her, and gave her maternal heart a twinge of alarm.

"Here is some new and fatal mystery!" she muttered; "dool and plague be on the hour I sent my only son to France! What bauble is this, Florence, that finds such favour in your sight?" she asked. And, as he expected the question, he replied calmly,—

"A trinket—only a trinket, mother; few gentlemen about the court are without such."

"My bairn," said she, seating herself by his side on the grassy slope of the terrace, and taking his hand in hers, while a fond smile spread over her face to conceal the anxious and searching glance of her grave grey eyes, "there was a time when a good sheaf of feathered arrows, a gay baldrick with pasements of gold, a crossbow with a stock inlaid with mother-o'-pearl, or a sword with a handsome guard, were toys that pleased you better, but that was before——"

"What, mother?"

"Before ye went to France, and to that devilish place Vendome? Ye have been sairly changed, my bairn, sinsyne, nor like the name ye inherit!"

"Dear mother," said he, kissing her hand with that combination of gallantry and affection which went out with the age of periwigs, "may I hope that I find more favour in your eyes to-day?"

"Favour, my winsome bairn!" she reiterated, while playing with his curly locks and the tassels of his ruff, and smiling fondly in spite of herself.

"Or am I still a lurdane and a maudlin fool?"

The old woman's brow darkened with an expression of care and trouble.

"I never thought ye either, Florence; but why has the just and natural bitterness of your heart for him who slew the nearest and dearest of your kinsmen turned all to peace and sweetness? Was it for this I brought ye hame frae France?—woe worth the day I ever sent thee there! There is magic in it; I tell thee, Florence, 'tis sorcery, and thou art under spell!"

"Perchance I am, mother," said he sadly, but with a fond smile, for he thought of Madeline.

"Perchance ye are?" she reiterated scornfully. "Art puling again like a yammering bairn, instead of acting like a bearded man—like the son of that brave father whom Preston and his people foully murdered in his harness, under tryst."

"Are you come again to taunt and to torment me?" said Florence, attempting to rise; but she clutched his right hand with fiery energy.

"Sit ye there and listen!" she exclaimed. "Ye are foully bewitched—I know it. Whence got ye that devilish bauble whilk ye were worshipping even just now as if it were a saint's bone or the true cross? 'Tis an opal; and know ye not the opal is a stone from the pillars of hell, and ever worketh the destruction of the wearer? Speak, ye witless one—speak!" she continued, raising her voice, while her grey eyes flashed with fire, and her wrinkled hand struck her cane again and again into the earth. "Some cursed witch of France hath wrought this mischief, and stolen alike thy manhood and thy heart. Give it me, that I may place it in the flames from whence it came, and so destroy the spell by which Preston is spared and thou art befooled. The ring, Florence—the ring, I say!"

"Nay, mother; in this you must hold me excused. But believe me, on the honour of a gentleman, no woman or witch of France gave this trinket to me."

His mother drew back a pace, and surveyed him with a singular combination of expressions in her dark-grey eyes: maternal love, rage, pity, and shame were there displayed by turns in all their strength.

"In our house, degenerate boy, have been ten knights created, where you will never kneel, under the king's banner, when its staff was planted in a foughten field where dead men lay thick as harvest sheaves; and of these ten, every man fell in battle with his belt and spurs on; but I trow, my silken page, thou wilt die comfortably in bed and with a whole skin."

Poor Florence felt the scorn of his mother deeply, and his anger at her determined injustice now began to kindle.

"I am under no spell, mother," said he calmly; "but I love a lady who is second to none in Scotland, save the queen herself."

"Indeed!" replied his mother, a new anxiety animating her breast. "And who may this peerless one be who has captivated the timid and peaceful heart of my renegade son?"

"Still so unkind and scornful! Dearest mother——"

"Who is she?" she repeated angrily.

"One whom you have never seen, mother,"

"Her name!" she demanded imperiously.

Florence paused; to tell his mother *all* would be perhaps to kill her on the spot, or to draw her bitterest malediction on his head.

"Her name, I say!" she reiterated fiercely, while a flush came over her wrinkled face; "say no ignoble name to me, Florence; but remember, degenerate as ye are, that your blood is the reddest in Scotland. Still pausing—still quailing before me, eh! 'Tis a woman you are ashamed of, and as a proof thereof, you dare not utter her name to your own mother."

Florence felt that a crisis in his fate was coming fast; and that an end should be put to a conversation so unseemly, so bitter and humiliating; so he replied,—

"Her name is Madeline Home."

His mother glared at him with a startled expression, as if she deemed him an enemy.

"Did I hear you aright?" she gasped in a low voice, while trembling like an aspen bough; "what mean you?"

"Mean?" murmured Florence, dreading the effect of his communication.

"Yes," she replied, still surveying him as if she deemed him a lunatic about to become troublesome.

"Mother, to end all this, I love Madeline Home, the Countess of Yarrow."

"Love—love *her*?" she gasped, for she was too old and too excited to raise her voice when suffering under deep emotion; but snatching her bodkin from her busk, she would have stabbed him, had not the nurse, Maud, arrested her hand and clung in terror upon her arm. There was a long pause broken only by her sighs. Florence attempted to take her hand, but she fiercely thrust him aside; for had Claude Hamilton appeared and made *her* a proposal of marriage, her intense disgust, bewilderment, and rage, could not have been greater. "My husband is in his grave," she said in a low and moaning voice; "the sea of life ebbs and flows as it rolls round the place of his sleep; but he hears its billows no more. Blessed be Heaven that spared him what I now feel; BUT, if the dead know aught that passes upon earth, beware boy, lest his bones may clatter in their bloody shroud—for it *was* a bloody shroud in which I wound him,—and his soul, at the foot of the throne of Him who died on Calvary, may curse thee, Florence, curse thee for loving a daughter of the race of Preston!"

Her calmness was more oppressive to Florence than her usually impotent anger.

"To love *her*—oh, to love *her*!" she continued,—"a wretch whose father, Quentin Home of Yarrow, drew his sword by Preston's side, in mere wickedness against your father, and may for aught I know, be one of his slayers. Boy, on thy peril, in thy raving, forget not our righteous feud!"

"Unhappy feud; what good has it ever done us?"

"Who thinks of good, when speaking of an hereditary foe? Shame on me that I bore thee! Shame on thy father that he begot thee! for by the holy Lamp of Lothian—yea, by the cross of the true Church, thou art fitted for naught in this world but to snuff candles, swing a censer and mumble latin, like old Mass John of Tranent. Oh, ungrateful, undutiful, and false! If ever thou hast a child, may it sting thy heart to the quick, even as at this hour thou stingest me! Thy father is in his grave——"

"By its side, Claude Hamilton is ready to make every honourable and religious amend; as Christians let us forgive——"

"'Tis the cant of shorn monks,—but is it the creed of a Scottish gentleman? Give me thy sword, and take my spindle and distaff; for by the God who hears us, they will become thee better than any warlike weapon. Thanks be to Heaven that I am the mother of another son who is there; but while on earth he knew his duty to his race and name. Hear me,—hear me!" she continued deeply, and wildly grasping his right arm, as much to support her feeble form as to give energy to her words: "With this right hand on the pale corpse of my husband, and with the other raised to heaven, I swore to have a dreadful vengeance on the house of Preston! With the same hand on the corpse of my Willie—that comely corpse,—sore gashed by Preston's curtal axe, I swore again that deadly vow; by the tombs in which they moulder side by side—that brave old father and most faithful son,—and on bended knees, by God's holy altar, a thousand times have I registered the same terrible vow,—registered it in *thy name*, Florence! I am a weak, very weak, and sorrow-stricken old woman; my trust is in thee, Florence; and woe to thee, woe, if that trust be unworthily placed!"

Exhausted by her emotions and this outburst, she sank upon a stone bench that was near, her fingers convulsively clutching her long cane, her pale lips quivering, and her bright but hollow eyes rolling on vacancy. After another long and painful pause, she spoke again through her grinding teeth.

"She is said to be beautiful—this earl's daughter,—this border churl's brat?"

"So beautiful and so winning, mother, that you could not fail to love her— —"

"What, I?"

"Yes; and so good and pious! Ask Father John if she ever misses a prayer, a mass, or other ordinance of the Church, and whether she is the mother of the poor whereever she goes."

"Marry come up!" exclaimed the fierce old dame, pressing her hands upon her throbbing heart; for this praise bestowed so ardently by her son upon one of that hated race stung her to the soul. "Oh that I had her in the vault of the tower," thought she, "or in yonder turret, or in my bower-chamber, gagged, and bound hand and foot! Verily, a hot iron would soon efface all trace of the fatal beauty by which this sorceress hath bewitched and spread a glamour ower thee!"

As *this terrible idea* occurred to her, she deemed it a wiser mode to dissemble with her son, than to quarrel with him, in attempting to exert an authority which at his years was absurd, and could not be enforced. So, with the cunning, rather than the wisdom of age, she gradually seemed to recover her composure; and for the purpose of luring information from her son, began to speak with pretended calmness, though her chest heaved with suppressed emotion, and when *his* face was averted, her eyes glared like those of a basilisk.

"These tidings of attachment are indeed something to startle and amaze," said she through her clenched teeth.

"Nothing is new under heaven, mother," said Florence, with a sigh; "the years and events that have passed are but the mirror of those to come."

"This love of thine, where hatred was wont to be, belies such musty morality. Love Madeline Home, indeed? It will be with the chance of having a score of rivals."

"Well," replied Florence smiling, "a score are better than one."

"One thou couldst kill."

"A score shall not kill me, at all events. And now, dear mother, if Madeline loves me, may not an earl's coronet, if one day blazoned in the old hall there, glint bravely in your old eyes?"

"The coronet of the Homes of Yarrow!" she said through her still grinding teeth; "and this earl's mother—who was she? An Achesson, of Gosford, or the Guseford, for they made their money in the days of the Regent Albany, by supplying the gluttons of Edinburgh with geese. Oho! of a verity, a brave alliance for one whose fathers have borne their crests on their helmets in battle five hundred years ago! But you see her frequently—this Countess of Yarrow?" she asked, on remembering her new tactics.

"Alas, no."

"Indeed! how cometh this about?" she asked, taking her son's hand in hers, with seeming fondness.

"Fate—yourself, mother, are alike adverse to us."

"When are ye to see her who hath so begowked thee—this bonnie bird, again?"

"Mother, you do not mean her evil?" asked Florence suddenly, for the expression of her eye bewildered him.

"Wherefore such a thought!" said she, as her withered cheek reddened; "but when do you meet?"

"To-night," said he, after some hesitation.

"So soon—hah! and where?"

"In the old porch of Tranent Church."

"Where they are lying—a fitting place for such a tryst!" she thought. "At what time?" she asked in a husky voice and while lowering her now stealthy eyes on the grass.

"The gloaming."

"'Tis two hours hence, by the dial. We may sit and converse yet awhile; but you look pale and weary, my bairn, and must take a cup of my medicated cordial."

"I thank you, dear lady and mother," said the unsuspecting youth, happy to perceive a change in the manner of the old lady, who summoned the nurse Maud, and, while giving her a key, whispered in her ear certain directions. In a minute after the old woman came out of the tower with a silver cup in her hand.

"Drink, my bairn—drink," said the nurse, patting the cheek of Florence; and he, heedless of what the contents might be if he pleased Lady Alison, drank them to the dregs, and turned with a smile to resume the conversation on the subject that was nearest his heart. He began to talk; but he knew not what, for his tongue seemed to speak without his control;

and within five minutes his utterance became heavy and inarticulate; he made a strong effort to recover himself, but his voice was gone; his eyes wandered—the tower, the garden, the terraces, and trees, seemed to be multiplied by a hundredfold, and to be chasing each other in a circle; then a deep drowsiness, against which he strove in vain to contend, fell upon him, and he lay motionless and still, but breathing heavily.

These two stern old women—the lady and the nurse—exchanged a glance of triumph and satisfaction; but the latter kindly covered him up with a mantle, and kissed his brow; while the former, in her fiery energy, almost tore the opal ring from his finger, and in doing so pressed the spring of the secret inclosure, which Madeline had referred to, when she first gave it to Florence. The stone arose, and under it was a little coil of hair, with the ominous words—

> "What ye resolve
> Death shall dissolve."

"So may it fare with the resolve of the donor!" said Lady Alison. "Maud, look ye to this moonstruck fool while I look to the false witch who hath begowked him. Now, ho! to keep this gay love-tryst at the kirk of Tranent!"

In ten minutes after this, accompanied by Roger of Westmains and three other armed men, who knew no will but hers, and had no scruple in obeying it; for they regarded her with as much veneration and fear as the dingy Hindoo does Brahma, or the miserable Persian does the bearded shah, she had left the tower of Fawside, and taken the eastern path direct to the church of the vicarage.

CHAPTER XL
THE WAKENING

He kneel'd in prayer in a lonely room,
　　Raised hand and streaming eye,
With a swimming brain, and a burning heart,
　　And a wild and bitter cry;
And a light came down on his stormy fears,
　　For a time; but the light grew dim:
And now, through the gloom of the pitiless years,
　　What hope, what hope for him?

Lyrics of Life.

The sun had set—the evening was grey and cloudy—when consciousness slowly returned to Florence. A swimming of the sight, a throbbing in the head, with an intense cold over all his limbs, were his first sensations on awakening from the long trance into which the potent drug given him by his mother had cast him two hours before.

"My appointment—the meeting—Madeline!" were his first thoughts; and he staggered up but to sink again upon his hands, with drooping head and bewildered brain; for the garden with its walks, trees, terraces, and shrubbery—the castle, with its grated windows and round tourelles (of which the corbelling now alone remains), and its large square chimneys—seemed to be all in pursuit of each other, as when he saw them last; and, in short, some minutes elapsed before he became fully conscious of existence, or able to stand erect and think with coherence, if not with calmness.

"Madeline's ring?" It was gone.

A sudden light seemed to break upon him. He recalled his mother's hatred and denunciations against her, and upon their love; her sudden change to assumed placidity; her remarks upon the ring; and then the cup of cordial—her own "medicated cordial"—given after a sudden whisper to Maud, who for years had been in all her secrets, the partner of her loves and hates, her sorrows and her joys. He saw it all; he had been duped—most foully duped—and his ring abstracted. He rushed into the castle and sprang up-stairs in search of Lady Alison; her bower chamber was vacant;

she was not in the hall; spindle, spinning-wheel, and distaff stood unused in the embayed window; and he was informed by Maud that she and Roger of Westmains, with three other armed men, had set out on horseback two hours ago.

"Strange and unusual this!" said he; "for, save to mass, my mother never leaves her own gate. Where has she gone?"

Maud replied, with eyes averted, she did not know.

"You do know!" exclaimed Florence impetuously,—"speak!"

The old woman fumbled with the lappets of her curchie, and endeavoured to withdraw.

"Speak!" continued Florence, confronting her. "I am the victim of some vile plot. Ye have half-poisoned me, beldame, by some damnable philter; for at this moment there is a bitter sickness in my heart and in my soul! Speak, old nursie, speak, or, though your foster-son, by Him who hears us on high, I will hang you over the tower wall as I would a hag of Egypt!"

"Weel," replied the woman, trembling, "she gaed by the loan end to the kirk."

"Hah—to Tranant! I see it all. Fool! fool!—dupe that I have been, not to read the cruelty that glittered in her eye, while her lips seemed to smile! My horse—quick—my horse!" he exclaimed; but, without waiting for the groom, he rushed bareheaded to the stable-yard, saddled the first nag that stood at hand, leaped on its back, and galloped madly over hedge and ditch, through field and meadow, straight for the kirk-town of Tranant.

The whole affair seemed to unravel itself now. Aware of the appointment in the gloaming, his mother had gone in his place to meet Madeline; and his heart trembled at the prospect of the terror, the insult, if not the actual danger, to which the young countess might be subjected by Lady Alison; his swollen heart beat painfully, and wildly he rode, spurring his panting horse, and pricking it with his poniard as it lingered at every desperate leap.

Much of the fine old wood which once covered the district has now been cut down, rendering the landscape somewhat dreary and bare; but though flat and (for Scottish scenery) unpicturesque, it was then, and is still, fertile and well cultivated.

On this evening it seemed particularly gloomy. The sun, long before he set beyond the dark hills of Dunblane, had been thickly enveloped in masses of dun and grey cloud, thus imparting a sombre aspect to the waves that tumbled in the estuary of the Forth, and flecked its breast with foam, while the breakers that roared and hissed upon the rugged shore were spotless as winter snow. The white sea-birds were skimming over the harvest-fields, betokening a storm at hand; and the red glare of the salt-pans, which belonged to the monks of St. Mary, and were perched upon the bleak and rifted reefs of freestone that jutted into the dashing sea, streaked the dull-grey background with sudden gleams of vertical fire, imparting a weird aspect to the scenery.

The gloom of the evening and the sombre aspect of nature inspired Florence with vague alarm, and with a strange foreboding that amounted to an emotion of horror, as he rode heedlessly and headlong towards the old church of the vicarage.

It stands upon the southern verge or slope of a long narrow vale, which was then covered by giant whins and wild gorse, and at the bottom of which a brawling brook forced its way past all obstruction to the sea. Of old it was named Travernent, which, say some, meant the hamlet in the valley; but, according to the writings of Father John, was the battle-shout of certain stout Scots who routed a party of Danish invaders and drove them into the sea. The church, a plain edifice of gloomy and forbidding aspect, built no one knows when or by whom, has a square tower and vaulted roof, and belonged of old to the monks of Holyrood. Its windows were few, and, by the immense number of dead interred for ages within and without its massive walls, this sombre temple seemed to have sunk far below the original level of the ground. On the steeple was a weather-cock, which, as the Hamiltons of Preston were wont to aver, tauntingly flapped its wings whenever a Fawside died.

The door, as in the churches of all Catholic countries, stood open, and when Florence dismounted and entered, the interior was so dark, that the only light came from the little tapers that twinkled before the altar which stood under the cross-arches of the rood-tower, and from the altar-tomb of Thorwald Lord of Travernent, whose effigy, cross-legged, for he had been a crusader, lay in the chancel, while on the wall near it there hung his rusty sword and mouldering hood of mail.

Florence passed the tombs of his father and brother with a hasty glance and with a shudder; for the memory of their faces, their fate, and the heritage of hatred they had bequeathed, came too vividly before him—too vividly at this terrible hour.

"Madeline!" he exclaimed; but there was no reply. The gloomy church was open, vacant, bare, and silent, and its solemn aspect was oppressive to his mind.

"Madeline!" he repeated, in a louder tone.

He was turning away to pursue his inquiries elsewhere. when he perceived, immediately under a monument on the wall, which still bears the shield and name of his father,

LORD Fawside of that Ilk

and within the shadow caused by the tomb, on which his armed effigy lay, the figure of a woman stretched without motion on the floor, over which a dark stream of blood was flowing even to his feet; and with a moan of agony, rather than a cry of alarm, he sprang towards her.

CHAPTER XLI
A BLOODY TRYST

O bide at hame, my lord, she said;
  O bide at hame my marrow,
For my three brethren will thee slay,
  On the dowie dens o' Yarrow.

Old Ballad.

On this gloomy evening, the 2nd of September, the tower of Preston, like every other tower and fortalice in Scotland, presented a scene of bustle and warlike preparation. Clumps of tall Scottish lances, newly shafted and freshly pointed, stood in rows against the barbican wall: the clink of the smith's hammer, as he welded horse-shoes or riveted armour that had been cut or broken in recent frays, was heard in various quarters; the hands of Symon Brodie, of Mungo-Tennant, and other sturdy vassals, were all busy, scouring breastplates, burganets, and gauntlets; and here, as in Fawside, the red sparks flew from the whirling grindstone, as the hard edge of the Jethart axe or the long fluted blade of the broadsword were applied thereto by those bronzed and bearded ploughmen whom the coming week was to see transformed into helmeted men-at-arms following the laird to the field for Scotland and her queen.

Amid this somewhat unwonted bustle the young Countess of Yarrow easily and unseen reached the castle garden, and from thence, by a private door, proceeded on foot to the place of rendezvous, attended only by a little footboy, who bore her missal in a velvet bag, on which her coat-of-arms was embroidered in the Scottish fashion for ladies, *i.e.*, without supporters, but surrounded by a cord of her colours, all fairly emblazoned by Sir David Lindesay of the Mount, and named in the courtly language of heraldry a cordeliere, or lace of love.

On reaching the church, which was little more than one Scottish mile from the gate of Preston, she sent her attendant on a message to the thatched village, with some bodily comforts for certain of her poor pensioners; and, without perceiving that Roger of Westmains, with three armed men in helmets, jacks, and plate sleeves, with four saddled horses, were half concealed in a thicket of thorns close by, she entered the gloomy fane just as the sun set enveloped in clouds, as already described, thus making more sombre the shadows of an edifice, the aspect and memories of which made her shudder, and blanched the beautiful smile which the hope of meeting her lover spread over her face.

"Florence!" she exclaimed timidly, pausing at the entrance of the church, which seemed so empty and desolate; and as she gazed anxiously up the nave, the figures of none met her eyes but those of armed men carved in stone, and stretched in death-like rigidity on their Gothic biers, surrounded by little figures called weepers, in niches—effigies all swept away by the mad fury of the Reformers, twelve years after.

"Florence!" she repeated, in a lower and more agitated voice; still there was no response; and she was about to withdraw with a mingled emotion of pique and alarm, when suddenly, from between the tombs of William Fawside and his father Sir John, there started up the tall and weird-like figure of a woman clad in a long black dooleweed, on the left shoulder of which was the usual mark of mourning, a white velvet cross. Her face was pale as that of a corpse, but her features were convulsed with all the energy of fierce and concentrated passion and venom. Her mouth was open, but her close rows of firm white teeth were clenched, and her hollow eyes shone with a baleful light. Towering above the shrinking Madeline, she put forth a long arm, and, with a wild exclamation of triumph, grasped her hand, and retained it with all the unyielding tenacity of an iron vice, and shook her wrathfully the while.

"Madam, madam!" exclaimed the poor countess, who believed herself in the power of an insane person, "what mean you by this?"

"That ye shall soon learn," hissed Lady Alison, shaking her more violently than ever.

"Help—help!" cried Madeline! "I will not be so abused! Woman, who are you, that dare to use me thus!"

"Dare?" she said; "dare?—ha! ha!"

"Yes, I repeat, dare! I am a lady of honour—Madeline Countess of Yarrow."

"And I am Alison of Fawside; and now, between these cold tombs, in each of which there lieth a murdered man—the corpse of the husband in whose kind bosom I slept for thirty years, and the corpse of the son I bore unto him and suckled at these breasts—murdered by Claude Hamilton of Preston, your nearest and only kinsman! Need I tell more to thee, Madeline Home?"

On this announcement Madeline remembered her recent dream; then a deadly terror possessed all her faculties and for a time froze her very utterance; while, as if feasting upon the fear her presence excited, the fierce old woman like an enraged Pythoness, surveyed her with gleaming eyes.

"Lady—Lady Alison, hear me; of all these horrors, I at least am innocent," faltered Madeline. "Release me, and on my knees I will unite with you in prayer for the dead."

"Prayer! thou sorceress, thou hell-doomed witch, who would rob me of my only living son!"

"Madam——"

"Nay, speak not, and crave no pity, for only such pity shall ye have as my winsome Willie had when bleeding he lay under Preston's curtal axe at the barriers of Edinburgh! And so my bonnie Florence loves thee? Aha! aha!"

"Oh God! is there no succour near?" sighed the shrinking girl; for there shone in the old woman's colourless face a pale and almost infernal light.

"He loves thee—ha! and yet thy beauty is no such wondrous matter, after all. A poor and pale-faced moppet like thee would never bear men to succeed the two stately knights who lie beside us! So, so! it is thou, witch, who wouldst rob me of the only son thy murderous race have left me—rob me of him by necromancy? Hah! Wretch! whence got ye that magic ring, that accursed opal, which I have thrown into the flames, but which hath cast a glamour in his eyes and made him love his enemies? Or got ye a love-philter from that quack apothegar, above whose door there swingeth a stuffed devil in the light of open day, Master Posset? Speak! 'Tis like the courtly ways of that woman of the house of Guise and those who serve her. Speak! thou pale-faced Jezebel—speak! lest I strangle thee!"

"Oh!" murmured Madeline, sinking lower on her knees, overcome by the horror of being an actor in such a scene as this. And now, endued by supernatural strength, this terrible dame dragged her between the tombs of the Fawsides. Then Madeline's spirit revolted against these insults, and she strove to rise and free herself, but Dame Alison by main strength held her down and retained her, kneeling at her feet. "Lady," exclaimed the countess, "you are alike unjust and cruel, insolent and wicked. I am a lady, an earl's daughter——"

"And what am I? A daughter of the house of Colean, whose sires were knights and barons in Carrick since the days of Malcolm IV. and William the Lion. Listen, thou trembling minx! My son came over the salt sea from France, hating, with a hatred deep as its waters, all who bore the name of

Hamilton, and intent on slaying the man who slew his father and brother under trust and tryst, foully, as Judas betrayed his holy Master. How is it now? He is James of Arran's soothfast man and tool, and thy plaything and toy—a puling moonstruck fool! And how came this to pass? By the agency of Satan and of such as thee; for, by St. Paul, I believe the holy water in yonder font would hiss upon thy pallid face if I cast it there, as it would do upon iron in a white heat? Love thee, indeed! Perchance he would have wedded thee, too! Ha! ha!"

"Madam," said Madeline, who was too patient and gentle not to be brave and resolute in a good cause, and who blushed amid her terror, "in that case he might, by the queen's grace, have shared the fair coronet my father bequeathed to me from the field of Solway."

"Foul shame and fell dishonour blight the new-fangled toy!" exclaimed Lady Alison with growing rage; "there were no earls in Yarrow when a laird of Fawside saved King David's life amid the Saxon host at Northallerton! But 'tis thy face that hath bewitched my son; and if a hot iron can mar and destroy the beauty he sees in it, by God's wrath it shall soon perish and shrivel up like parchment in the fire! Ho! Roger—Westmains, come hither!"

At these terrible words the fear of Madeline could no longer be controlled, and the recesses of the solitary church echoed with her cries for succour—cries which there were none to hear; and now, in the excitement of this struggle, a new idea seized the mind of Dame Alison. Wreathing her hands in the dishevelled hair of Madeline, she madly dashed her repeatedly against the tombs on each side. To save herself, the poor girl caught the carved projections, and, clinging, held them more than once; but such was the strength of Dame Alison, that her victim's grasp was repeatedly torn away.

"Here," exclaimed the stern widow—"here, between the bones of my dead husband and son, as on a shrine of vengeance, do I offer up your blood, even as the pagans of old offered up their sacrifices to the spirits of hatred and revenge! Die—die! and by the hand of her whose son ye sought by your damnable arts to ensnare and to destroy!"

With these words she drew the long steel bodkin from her busk, and thrusting it twice into the bosom of Madeline, rushed from the church, and left her stretched on the pavement gasping for breath, and choking in warm and weltering blood.

Some accounts say this terrible deed was perpetrated with a poniard; but the vicar of Tranent distinctly records that she used her "buske bodkyne."

CHAPTER XLII
THE PASSING BELL

Night-jars and ravens, with wide-stretch'd throats,
From yews and hollies send their baleful notes;
The ominous raven, with a dismal cheer,
   Through his hoarse beak, of following horror tells,
Begetting strange imaginary fear,
   With heavy echoes like to Passing Bells.

With his heart filled by emotions of horror which the pen cannot describe, Florence raised Madeline, whom, though stretched upon her face, he knew instantly. Ah, there was no mistaking the beautiful contour of her head, from which the little triangular hood had been torn so roughly; or those tresses of rich and silky hair, in which Lady Alison had so ruthlessly twisted her fingers, that trembled alike with wrath and rage. Madeline was deathly pale; her eyes were almost closed, and a crimson current flowed in a slender streak from, her mouth; while her bosom, like the pavement on which she had lain for some minutes, was covered with blood. Her dress, which was of pale yellow silk slashed with black, at the breast and shoulders was covered with gouts of the same sanguine tint as the tiled floor of the church.

Mechanically, as one in a dream, Florence raised her, and as he did so, he recalled her strange and boding words of yesterday. Then something rolled under his foot. He looked down; it was a long, slender, and sharp-pointed bodkin—his mother's busk-bodkin! Tinged with blood, it told the whole terrible tale. He uttered a moan of mental agony, and, reeling against his father's tomb, remained for some moments stupefied, and incapable of action or coherent thought.

Madeline was insensible, yet he pressed her to his heart; and while his tears fell on her cheek, he kissed away the blood that flowed from her lips. Steps were now heard, and the old vicar, Father John, with eyes dilated in horror of the inhuman deed, and at the sacrilege committed in his secluded church, approached hastily; for the little page had heard the cries of his mistress, and for succour had rushed to the vicarage, which adjoined the burial-ground—but the succour came too late.

"'Tis all over with us now, Father John?" exclaimed Florence in broken accents; "by this cruel act my mother has broken my heart, and cast eternal infamy upon our name; and in destroying Madeline she has slain her son more surely and more wickedly than even the sword of Preston could have done."

The priest knelt down and chafed the hands of Madeline; but they were cold and passive.

"The blow—a double blow, good father—has been struck! She is dying! Madeline!—Madeline! The stab that slays you slays me too! Oh, madness!—oh, agony! Oh, fiendish mother, to work a sorrow so deep as this! Madeline, do you hear me? For God's pity, grace, and love, good vicar, say something—do something—for I cannot lose her thus! Speak, or I shall go mad, and dash my head against my father's tomb!"

For a moment Madeline, roused by his voice and energy, opened her eyes; and, on recognizing Florence, a sweet, sad smile passed over her soft features.

"My mother did this, Madeline; say it was or it was not she; am I mistaken—speak—speak!"

Loath to give pain where she loved so well and tenderly, and believing herself to be dying, she did not answer, save with sad smiles, to his earnest inquiries respecting her wounds, and his unavailing protestations of love and sorrow.

At last, when he implored her to speak, she attempted to say something; but her lips and tongue had lost their power; her eye grew dull, and she became insensible; her hands and her head drooped, and her long hair swept over the floor of the church as she was borne away.

The alarm had now spread to the village; so, while this scene was passing in the dusky and half-lighted church, and Florence in his grief was uttering a succession of incoherences, a crowd, principally of women, who viewed him with louring and hostile eyes, had gathered round; and by them Madeline, amid many expressions of woe (for the influence of her family was great in the neighbourhood), was borne carefully and tenderly into the vicar's house; and while she was undressed, and her wounds—two small but deep orifices—were stanched, horsemen were sent at full speed to Preston-tower, to that quaint compatriot of Rabelais, Master Posset, at Edinburgh, and to a certain nun of Haddington, Christina Hepburn, prioress of the Cistercians, a kinswoman of the Earl of Bothwell—a lady who had great skill as a leech, and enjoyed a high reputation as a woman of holiness.

Pressing his lips to the brow of Madeline, whose features were cold and passive as her clammy hands, Florence left her in charge of the vicar and her new attendants, and mounting his horse, which he knew to be swift and strong, he prepared to follow, and if possible to outride, the messenger for Edinburgh, as he had the greatest faith in Master Posset's skill; and with something like a prayer to Heaven, mingling on his lips with an imprecation on his mother, he leaped into the saddle, urged his horse across the rugged ravine which the old church and vicarage overlooked, and then galloped westward, blind with grief and confusion of thought, for his brain was yet giddy with the potent drug by which he had been so wickedly deluded, and a half-stupor hung over his senses.

Darkness, dense and gloomy, had now set in. The sky was without stars, and the country was enveloped in obscurity. As he rode on, urging his horse from time to time, to get it well up in hand, a light at the horizon caught his eye. He turned, and felt a shock like that of electricity: but they knew nought of electricity in those days.

On the brow of Soltra the red beacon was in flame; and now another, that rose on the summit of Dunprender, expanded from a star to a sheet of fire; another and another, on many a tower and hill, were lit up in rapid succession; and soon a chain of fires garlanded with flame the far horizon of the night, from the southern borders, sending to the distant Highland glens the tidings that the foe was advancing and the day of battle was at hand.

A fierce sensation, almost of joy, glowed through the throbbing and agonized heart of Florence. He considered those certain signals of the coming war—the war that in another week was to lay all Lothian desolate, like the shores of the Dead Sea—as so many flaming lights that would guide him to Madeline in the other world; for by her changed aspect and dreadful pallor, he dared not hope that she would survive the night. As he paused a moment, to watch the beacons kindling and blazing in succession on the murky sky, there came over the open plain from Tranent, a sound which made him shudder, and caused the pulses of his heart to stand still.

It was, indeed, a dreadful sound—the solemn tolling of the passing bell, which informed him that Madeline Home was dying, or was already no more!

By this old custom, which of course was abolished in Scotland at the Reformation, all the faithful were invited to pray for the departing soul; and its sound was also supposed to scare away the fiends who were in waiting to wrest it from its guardian angels, as they winged their way towards the stars.

He stood upon the bleak, open heath as if transformed to stone, every knell of the solemn soul-bell seeming to echo in his heart and in his brain; yet his thoughts were without coherence and his lips without prayer. His mother—his dreadful, blood-imbrued mother, with her tall sombre figure, seemed to tower before his vision, like a shadowed angel of destruction! He dared not think of her.

The reins fell from his hands, and covering his hot, tearless eyes, he groaned aloud in his agony, and felt as if under a horrible spell.

Still the solemn bell continued its monotonous tolling, and it came to his ear by fits upon the hollow wind. Had Florence not been too certain that he was awake, he would have deemed that he was involved in some hideous dream or vision of the night.

"Oh, to shut out that dreadful sound, and to forget it for ever!" thought he. "A thousand times I have heard it ring before, but never with a cadence so dreadful as to-night."

At that moment he heard the galloping of a horse; its steps faltered as it came along, for it seemed worn and faint by the speed to which it was urged by whip and spur, and by the toil of the long journey it had undergone. On arriving near Florence, the rider reined suddenly up, and then, as if the endurance of life could be no longer taxed, the panting and foam-covered horse, sank lifeless, or nearly so, upon the roadway.

"Who are you that sit idly on your horse, in an hour like this, when every beacon in the land is in a flame?" asked the dismounted man breathlessly, as he disengaged himself from his stirrups, and rushed to the side of Florence; "speak, sir—who are you?"

"I am Florence of Fawside," replied the other; "and what then?"

"I am Livingstone of Champfleurie," said the other, stepping back with his hand on his sword.

"Hah!—go, go; in an hour like this, I am at peace even with you," said Florence mournfully.

"This is no time to speak of peace," replied Livingstone, still panting with his recent exertion; "I have ridden from Berwick on the spur—more than fifty miles to-day, after seeing the English vanguard close upon the Tweed, and when I last saw Home Castle, *four* lights were all ablaze upon its summit, as a token that they were in great strength, and bound this way. Through all the Merse and Lauderdale I have borne this—the cross of fire! Thou seest my horse, man—it can no further go, nor well can I. Take this, and ride to the Lord Regent—rouse the country as you go, and say the foe are bound direct for Lothian—you hear me, direct for Lothian! On, on—I say, and ride with this for Edinburgh. Luckily thou art mounted—ride, ride, for Scotland and the queen!"

With these words, which he poured forth all in a breath, Champfleurie thrust into the hand of Florence the *fiery* cross—the old Scottish symbol of war, the summons to arms, and then incapable of further action, he sank beside his dying horse, panting and breathless on the heath. Florence, as a loyal subject, knew at once what his duty required him to do; and anxious to find relief from the agony of his soul in any species of excitement, he turned his horse and rode off madly towards the west; but the solemn sound of the passing bell seemed to follow him, even when he drew up within the gates of Edinburgh, amid the wild clamour and hurrahs of the mustering craftsmen, the clanging of the alarm-bells, and the rattle of drums, as, in the glare of torch and cresset, the provost, the deacons, and magistrates, arrayed the bands of burgesses, under their various banners, in that long and magnificent street which still forms the main artery of life in the ancient city of the Stuarts; and there the murmur of the gathering thousands rose into the midnight air like the solemn chafing of a distant sea, or the wind passing through the leaves of a mighty forest.

Ten minutes after his entrance into the city by the Kirk-o'-field Porte, saw him in the presence of Arran, in the old Tower of Holyrood, along the shadowy corridors and past the tall windows of which lights were seen to flicker, and the glitter of armed figures, with helmets and partisans, flitting to and fro, like spectres, half seen and half lost in gloom, as gentlemen and men-at-arms betook them to their harness with soldier-like alacrity. Florence was introduced to the regent in that old tapestried room where, in the nights of after times, poor Mary Stuart wet many a pillow with her bitter tears, and from where Rizzio was dragged forth to die. He found the regent just roused from bed by the clamour in the city. He was clad in a loose robe of scarlet trimmed with miniver; his sheathed sword was in his hand, and around him were his brother, the lord chancellor, and the Abbot of Paisley, with many nobles and officers of state, who, on their first alarm, had hurried to the palace in arms.

Pale as ashes, and feeling as if death was in his heart, Florence entered the room, with his hands begrimed by the fire-scathed cross, which he had long since consigned to another messenger to bear elsewhere. He approached the regent, but, overcome by his emotions, tottered to a chair, and found himself incapable of speech or action.

"Wine—wine! 'tis Fawside, ever faithful and true; but faint and worn now," exclaimed Arran.

Dalserfe, the page, promptly brought a flask of wine; but Florence waved his hand, and again sank back; then fortunately there entered at that moment another messenger, the loyal old Earl of Mar.

"The English are in motion, my Lord of Arran," he exclaimed.

"A thousand beacons are telling all Scotland quite as much, lord earl," said Arran, with a quiet smile; "so they are advancing?"

"Their avant-garde, three thousand strong, under their lieutenant-general, the brave Earl of Warwick, is already on the march to Greenlaw; and their rear-guard, also three thousand strong, under the Lord Dacres, hath reached Berwick. I have ridden from the Merse, old as I am, to bear these sure tidings, for I saw them cross the Tweed to-day at noon!"

"Who hath them, under baton?"

"The duke—Edward of Somerset."

"Sit ye down, lord earl," said the Archbishop of St. Andrews; "for in sooth you seem weary."

"Nay, my lord, pardon me," replied this peer, like all his race a faithful adherent of the crown; "but in this room where last I knelt to James V.——"

"James V. was too good a Scotsman to have kept an old soldier, a true and valiant peer like thee, standing in thy seventieth year, like a very foot-page."

"And after a fifty miles ride from the Merse."

"But we have no time for idle compliments," said Arran impatiently; "summon the lords of council, and despatch couriers to every sheriffdom, stewartry, and constabulary; *the muster-place is Edmondstone Edge*. Dalserfe, my pages and armour!"

With these words Arran abruptly closed the interview.

CHAPTER XLIII
THE CROSS OF FIRE

Fast as the fatal symbol flies,
In arms the huts and hamlets rise;
From winding glen, from upland brown,
They pour'd, each hardy tenant, down.
Nor slack'd the messenger his pace;
He show'd the sign, he named the place,
And pressing forward like the wind,
Left clamour and surprise behind.

Lady of the Lake.

On this night the beacons blazed on continent and isle, athwart the whole kingdom,—from the shores of the Atlantic to those of the German Sea. In every city, burgh, hamlet, and castle, cottage, convent, and monastery, the tidings were known within an hour, that the invasion had begun; and by day-dawn THE CROSS OF FIRE had spread from hand to hand, with the summons to the muster-place, and it went from glen to glen with incredible speed, each bearer naming the gathering or rendezvous of his clan, burgh, or sheriffdom, with the place where the array of the kingdom was to meet the Regent Arran.

The Crian Tarigh—the cross of fire, or of shame, for it bore both names; first, from the circumstance of its arms being scathed with fire, and then dipped in the blood of an animal; and second, from the everlasting infamy attending all who disobeyed the bearer—was a terrible Celtic symbol never before used in the lowlands of Scotland; but on this occasion it proved most effectual.

It was usually borne by a messenger on foot. On reaching a hamlet he gave it to the first person he met, and the latter, on hazard of his life, was bound to leave his occupation, be it at home or afield,—a bridal or a burial,—a birth or a deathbed,—a scene of sorrow or a scene of joy,— and to convey it till he met another, to whom he simply mentioned the muster-place. On beholding this terrible cross, every man between the ages of sixteen and sixty, capable of bearing arms, was compelled to appear at the rendezvous in his best harness; and woe to the wretch who failed. The utmost vengeance of fire and sword, as indicated by the three burned and bloody arms of this ancient symbol of our Celtic fathers, fell upon the false and disobedient, the timid and untrue.

Thus by dawn next day the whole of Scotland was in arms! The barons and chiefs were all on the march, from every point, for Edmondstone Edge, the royal muster-place; while in every walled city and town throughout the realm the armed burghers kept watch and ward, or filled the great castles in the neighbourhood with men, cannon, and all the munitions of war. The military measures of the Regent Arran, at this important crisis, reflected the greatest credit upon his personal activity, and upon his government, which had hitherto been as weak and vacillating as his religious opinions, which wavered alternately between the new and stern, bare creed of Calvin, and the pictorial splendours of the Church of Rome.

On learning the tragic event which occurred in the church of Tranent, Claude Hamilton of Preston became reanimated by what he had striven to forget, or commit to oblivion, his feud with the Fawsides; and a longing for the direst vengeance on Dame Alison and on her son inspired him and all his followers. He would have attacked, sacked, and rased her little fortalice to its foundations, had not the Albany herald arrived, bearing a special message from his lord and chief, the Regent Arran, commanding him to forget his feud for the time, and to bring his vassals to the muster-place to aid the general cause; after the triumph of which, he should have all the satisfaction the power of the Justician of Scotland could award.

His summons to attend the array of the kingdom ran thus, as we render it in English.

"REGINA. Well-beloved friend, we greet you well. For so much as our dearest cousin the regent, and the lords of our council, are surely informed that our old enemies of England tend to invade our realm; he resolves, with the support of all true barons and faithful lieges, to resist them in our just defence. It is our will, and we pray you, to address you incontinent with your honourable household, all *bodin* in array of war, to attend our royal standard, in all haste, at Edmondstone Edge, as ye love the defence and common weal of our realm, and under the pain and *tynsale* of life, lands, and goods; and as regards your outstanding feud with the Fawsides of that ilk, and the cruel and bloody deed of the widow of the umquhile Sir John Fawside, we promise you all manner of vengeance at the hands of the Earl of Argyle, our lord justice general, and gage the honour of our crown therein. Written under our signet at Edinburgh, the 3rd day of September, 1547.[*]

JAMES REGENT."

"To our well-beloved friend, the Laird of Preston—*These*."

[*] Father John's MSS.

Sternly Claude Hamilton read this missive, and gulping down his anger and grief—for he dearly loved his beautiful kinswoman,—he stifled his furious passion for a time; and, meanwhile, the grim Dame Alison, with Roger of Westmains acting as her lieutenant-governor, watched well in her moated tower, with gates barred, and every falcon and arquebuse loaded; and though she secluded herself in her bower-chamber, it is to be doubted whether, even in her quietest hours of reflection, amid the still calm sleepless hours of the long night-watch, she felt any remorse for the terrible deed she had done. If she did feel it, she carefully veiled it under an exterior that to ordinary eyes was unreadable and impenetrable.

Animated by a horror of his mother—an emotion too strange and terrible for analysis or description,—sick at heart, and crushed in spirit, poor Florence returned to Fawside tower no more; but resided with Dick Hackerston, the hospitable and sturdy burgher, who occupied a mansion in a broad-wynd on the north side of the city, nearly opposite the hospital and chapel of La Maison Dieu, and the Black Turnpike, so famous in the annals of 1567, all of which have now been removed. There he was provided with suitable arms and armour for man and horse, and, until the army took the field, there he remained, tended as a brother would have been, by the worthy merchant's wife, who saw there was something noble and poignant in his sad and silent sorrow, which held communion with none; and being young, handsome, and gallant in bearing, it impressed her all the more.

But to return to the Regent Arran: by the grey dawn of that day, on which the alarm of the coming foe first crossed the land with giant strides of fire from mountain-top to mountain-top, the lords of the royal privy council assembled in the tower of James V. at Holyrood. There came the earls of Huntly, Mar, Argyle, Cassilis, and Glencairn; the lords of Lyle, Fleming, and Kilmaurs (with his sinister visage, his glistening eyes and teeth), and many other peers—those who were loyal and true, and those who were base and venial—to reconsider and debate upon the measures to be taken at the present emergency. Despite their bonds and promises, when the hour of danger came, and all the land was armed or arming, Glencairn, Cassilis, and others of their infamous and corrupt faction, found themselves swept away by the loyalty of the commons, as by a sea, the waves of which there was no resisting; and they were compelled to lead their vassals to the field, and to unsheath their swords, against those with whom they were in secret league, and whose gold they had hoped to pocket; but to that foul political leprosy—that inborn spirit of treason and anti-nationality, which was characteristic of too many of the Scottish nobles, and which they inherited with their titles and their blood—were the future disasters of Pinkey, like too many other national woes and degradations, distinctly traceable.

Even Claude Hamilton, for the time, forgot his proffered titles of Lord Preston and Earl of Gladsmuir, and found himself marching at the head of a goodly band of mounted spearmen, including Symon Brodie in his suit of beaked armour, for the muster-place, the green sloping braes of Edmondstone Edge; and now Ned Shelly's chance of obtaining a young Scottish countess seemed as distant as the realization of his leader's political hopes, or the chance of an English bride for Bothwell, who heard the din of preparation in the castle of Edinburgh, where he chafed like a caged lion at the external commotion, in which he could bear no part, for good, for evil, or for aggrandisement.

At the council board on this eventful morning, the peer whose advice had the most weight was George Gordon, Earl of Huntly, a loyal and noble lord, whose manners and education had been improved by study and by foreign travel. He had been made lieutenant of the north by James V., and captain-general of those forces which defeated the English at the battle of Haidonrig and baffled their next army under the Duke of Norfolk. When speaking of the matrimonial alliance with England, a marriage which Somerset seemed determined to form by the edge of the sword, he recommended that some accommodation might be made by a temporary truce or treaty.

On this, Mary of Lorraine, who had come to the council, gave him a glance of sorrowful reproach.

"My lords," said she, with a flush on her usually pale cheek, "when my dear husband was dying in Falkland Palace, as Monseigneur le Cardinal Beaton (who is now in heaven) told me, the setting sun shed a stream of light into the room where he lay, and with brilliance lit up the royal arms above the mantelpiece, the arms of Scotland, or, the lion *gules* within a double tressure, all were brightened as with a transient glory; but as the life of my beloved lord and king ebbed, and he sank lower on his pillow, dying—dying of a broken heart,—and breathed his last, the sun went down beyond the hills of Fife, and the arms of the kingdom became dark, so dark, in that chamber of death and gloom, as to be invisible; and this the cardinal, and all who were present, declared to be ominous of evil to come; and the evil *has* come upon the realm of my fatherless child when my lord of Huntly hath eyes of favour to the alliance of those who, for centuries, have striven, by the soldier's sword and the scrivener's guile, to dishonour the name and subvert the liberties of Scotland!"

As the beautiful Frenchwoman spoke, her fine hazel eyes became filled with a sparkling light; her bosom heaved, and her cheek was crimsoned by the excitement, that made her Valois blood course like lightning through her veins.

"You wrong me, royal lady," said the Highland earl; "be assured, madam, that the loyal spirit of my forefathers yet lives within me; and I trust that all who hear me will remember the words of the faithful and brave who, from the Abbey of Arbroath, addressed that ignoble Pope, John XXII., who leagued himself with England against them; and in the same spirit by which those Scottish barons adhered to Robert Bruce will we adhere to his descendant, your royal daughter. 'To *him*,' said they, 'we will adhere as our rightful king, the preserver of our people and the guardian of our liberties; but should he ever dream of subjecting us to England, then we will do our utmost to expel him from the throne as a traitor and an enemy; we will choose another king to rule over us, *for never, so long as one hundred Scotsmen are alive, will we be subject to the yoke of England*! We fight not for glory, we strive not for riches or honour, but for that liberty which no good man will consent to lose but with his life. We are willing to do anything for peace which may not compromise our freedom. If your Holiness disbelieve us, and continue to favour England, giving undue credit to her false assertions, then be sure that Heaven will impute to you all the calamities which our resistance must inevitably produce; and we commit the defence of our cause to God.' So spoke the faithful men of other days," continued the earl, "and, with the hand of that blessed God above their banner, may such to the latest posterity ever be the spirit of freedom which shall animate the Scottish people!"

These words filled the council with enthusiasm, and all separated to prepare for the mortal strife.

CHAPTER XLIV
THE INVASION

Our Scottish warriors on the heath,
   In close battalia stood;
To free their country and their queen,
   Or shed their reddest blood.
The Anglo-Saxons' restless band
   Has cross'd the river Tweed;
And ower the hills o' Lammermuir
   They've march'd wi' mickle speed.
                    Twinlaw—Old Ballad.

Edward Duke of Somerset, formerly and better known in Scotland as that Earl of Hertford who led the invasion in the year 1544, had arrived at Newcastle on the 27th of August at the head of fourteen thousand two hundred Englishmen and many foreign auxiliaries, with fifteen pieces of cannon drawn by horses, and nine hundred waggons laden with stores. Sir Francis Fleming was master of the ordnance, and had fourteen hundred pioneers, under Captain John Brem, to clear the way before the guns, to build fascines, and so forth. Master William Patten, who accompanied this army in the quality of judge marshal, a post to which, he had been advanced by the interest of Edward Shelly, in his history[*] of the "Expedition," has given us a minute account of the campaign, and an accurate list of all the commanders in the Protector's army, to aid which thirty-four ships of war and thirty-two transports, under the pennon of Edward Lord Clinton and Say (afterwards high admiral of England) and Sir William Woodhouse, anchored at the mouth of the Tyne.

> [*] "The Expedition into Scotland, of the most worthely fortunate Prince Edward, Duke of Somerset, &c., made in the first yere of his Maiestes most prosperous reign, and set out by way of diarie by W. Patten, Londoner. Vivat Victor! Out of the Parsonage of St. Mary Hill in London, this xxviii of January, 1548."

Lord Grey of Wilton, lieutenant of Boulogne, was high marshal and captain-general of the horse, who were all cap-a-pie in full armour, but of a light fashion. Sir Ralf Vane commanded four thousand men-at-arms and demi-lances; and Sir Francis Bryan (in the following year chief governor of Ireland) was captain of two thousand light horse. Sir Thomas Darcy led King Edward VI.'s band of pensioners.

Sir Peiter Mewtas was commander of the Almayners, or German infantry, who were all clad in buff coats and armed with arquebuses.

Don Pedro de Gamboa led the mounted Spanish arquebusiers; and these foreigners, being trained soldiers of fortune, who had served in many wars, were the flower of Somerset's forces. Many of them were veterans who had fought at the siege of Rhey, in 1521, when muskets were first used by the Spaniards, whose infantry were then deemed the finest in Europe.

Edward Shelly led the men-at-arms of Boulogne, who, like the mercenaries, were all trained and veteran soldiers, but dressed in blue doublets, slashed and faced with red. The celebrated Sir Ralf Sadler (whose papers were edited by Sir Walter Scott) was treasurer of this well-ordered army, and Sir James Wilford was provost-marshal.

On the 2nd September the Duke of Somerset entered Scotland, and marched along the eastern coast, keeping carefully in view of his fleet of sixty-four sail, which accompanied him towards the Firth of Forth. Unopposed, he reached that tremendous ravine, the Peaths, which is now spanned by a bridge that is perhaps the greatest in Europe, as it is two hundred and forty feet high by three hundred feet in length. Abrupt, precipitous, and narrow, this ravine formed one of the great passes into Scotland; and, being of easy defence, was deemed "a kind of sluice, by which the tide of war could be loosened or confined at pleasure."

For, an entire day Sir Francis Fleming and his gunners, and Captain Brem with his pioneers, toiled in that narrow and savage gorge to drag through the English artillery and waggons, while the Protector was busy storming several fortresses in the neighbourhood. Among these were the castles of Thornton and Dunglass, belonging to the Lord Home; and Inverwick, a house of the Hamiltons. These strongholds were blown up by gunpowder; but, "before we did so," saith Master Patten, "it would have rued any good housewife's heart to have beholden the great and unmerciful slaughter our men made of the brood geese and good laying hennes, which the wives had penned up in the holes and cellars of the castle [of Dunglass]. The spoil was not rich, to be sure; but of white bread, oaten cakes, and Scottish ale, was indifferent good store, and soon bestowed among my lord's soldiers accordingly."

The English marched in three great columns; each was flanked by horse and artillery; and each piece of cannon had a band of pioneers to guard it and clear the way before it. Somerset led the main body; Warwick still had the vanguard; and Thomas Lord Dacres of Gillesland, Knight of the Garter, led the rear.

Leaving Dunbar on his right, the duke pushed forward through East Lothian to the Tyne, which he crossed by the same old narrow bridge that spans it still; but there not unopposed, for the vassals of the house of Hepburn opened a cannonade of falcons and culverins from the ramparts of Bothwell's castle of Hailes, while a brisk assault was made upon the defiling columns by a famous border marauder named Dandy Kerr, of the house of Fernyherst, whose moss-troopers, after a rough encounter, were routed by the heavily-mounted men-at-arms of Warwick; then, laying the whole country in flames as they advanced, the English marched on until the 7th of September, when they halted at Long Niddry, in Haddingtonshire. There the coast is flat and low; and thus Somerset was enabled to communicate with his fleet, which came to anchor in the roads of Leith.

Somerset now became aware that a Scottish army was concentrated in the neighbourhood, as bands of their prickers, or light-armed horse, were seen galloping along all the eminences, hallooing and brandishing their long and slender spears in defiance. Despite these hostile appearances, the Lord Clinton was brave enough to come on shore and attend a council of war, at which it was arranged that he should anchor the fleet near the mouth of the Esk, to co-operate with the land forces, which Somerset proposed to halt finally eastward of Musselburgh, on the green links of that town, and in the parks of Wallyford and Drumore, where, on the evening of Friday, the 8th, he came in view of the camp of the Scots, thirty-six thousand strong, covering all the long green hill named Edmondstone Edge, at the base of which flowed the Esk.

Around the camp of Somerset, who pitched his own tent near the village of Saltpreston, the whole country was laid desolate by fire; and all who failed to escape perished by the sword. The tall square tower of Preston was soon stormed from a few old men and boys, who were headed by Mungo Tennant, and made a desperate resistance; but they were all slain; then the house was sacked by the English band of pensioners, and committed to the flames. The village of Tranent was burned, and its pretty little vicarage was gutted and destroyed; while in the church the altars and the tombs of the Fawsides were defaced and overthrown. Father John had fled no one knew whither; and for three days the whole landscape was shrouded in the smoke of burning hamlets, granges, mills, and stackyards. Amid this wicked devastation the old tower of Fawside, perched on the summit of its hill, escaped unscathed; but its time was coming.

All this destruction was visible from the Scottish camp, which consisted of four long rows or streets of white tents, that lay from east to west along the green slope of Edmondstone, surmounted by the many-coloured banners of chiefs, nobles, and burghs; and from amid these tents the weapons and armour of so many thousands of men caused a glittering that seemed incessant to the eyes of the English, as they surveyed the vast extent of ground occupied by the army of Arran. As at the battle of Falkirk in 1296, at that of Dunbar in 1650, and other fields, which the Scots have lost by the treason of their nobles or the imbecility of their preachers, the *first* position of the regent was strong and skilfully chosen.

In front flowed the beautiful Esk, between its steep rocky and wooded banks, from which the feathery ash, the green alder, and the wild rose-tree drooped to kiss the gurgling waters, which were deeper, broader, and more rapid than now. The old Roman bridge, so worn by war and time, which still spans the stream, and which formed the only avenue to their position, Arran had manned by archers and mounted with cannon. The left flank, towards the sea, was defended by an intrenchment of turf, also mounted with cannon and lined by arquebusiers; while a deep and pathless morass, through which nor horse nor man might march, covered the right.

Such was the position of the Scots before the disastrous field of Pinkey, or Inveresk — a battle, the issue of which was awaited breathlessly by Mary of Lorraine, at Edinburgh. By its strength, Somerset found himself completely baffled. To have assailed it would have been a hopeless task, which he saw would only end in a retreat that would cover his army with disgrace, if not with ruin and slaughter.

Arran surveyed the approach of the foe with a confidence in which our hero did not share; for he knew that the Scottish camp was filled by titled traitors, and that the auxiliaries under D'Essé had not yet left the coast of France. He had but one thought — to join Madeline, whom he believed to be in heaven, and to perish in the coming defeat — for what hope was there of victory for an army led by peers who in secret were the tools of Somerset!

From the slope of Edmondstone the Scots could see the high-pooped, low-waisted, and gaily-painted caravels of England coming in succession to anchor, by stem, and stern, off the mouth of the Esk, with their red ports open, and their brass cannon pointed to the shore. All bore the red cross of St. George, together with the banner of Thomas Lord Seymour of Sudley, K.G., high-admiral of England, Ireland, Calais, Boulogne, and the marches thereof; Normandy, Gascony, and Acquitaine; captain-general of the navy and seas — all of which high-sounding titles, did not save him from having his head ignominiously chopped off on the 20th January, 1549.

Amid the clamour, hurry, and bustle of the camp, Florence found but little relief from the agony that preyed upon his spirit. In the prospect of the coming battle, lay all his hope of relief—by plunging into the strife as into a raging sea, to drown his care, his sorrows past and present.

On the evening before the English halted in sight of the Scottish camp, he had left the hospitable mansion of bluff Dick Hackerston, for the last time; and the earnest and tender farewell which that good citizen took of his buxom wife, who laced on his mail with her own trembling hands and placed as an amulet round his neck a holy medal which an old grey friar had brought from Bethlehem; and the kisses which he bestowed again and again on his laughing and chubby-cheeked little ones, with the blessing which he knelt down to receive from his blind father—a frail old man, who for the last few years had vegetated in a huge leathern chair in the ingle-nook of the dining-chamber,—all formed a strong contrast in the mind of Florence to his desolate and friendless condition.

On this evening the old blind man was telling his beads,—for though he had heard Knox preach, and seen Friar Forest burned, he was still a devout Catholic; and by turns his withered fingers would quit the cedar-wood rosary, to play with the iron hilt of a large sword, which hung upon a knob of his chair. When his son knelt before him, he placed a hand upon his head, and a stern smile passed over the old man's face, when he felt the cold steel of Dick's helmet.

"Take this sword, my bairn," said he, "and go forth, believing that thine auld mother, who is now with the saints in heaven, is praying for thee and for thine. She lies in her grave in the kirkyard of St. Giles; but she bore me sax braw sons, Dick, beside thee; three fell by my side at Flodden, two at Ancrumford, and one at Haldonrig—all sword in hand for Scotland and her king. 'Tis but the tale that owre mony hae to tell. Ye were our last, Dick— born unto me in auld age, even as Isaac was born unto Abraham; but go forth—take this sword, and use it as I would use it again had my years been few as thine. Go—God and St. Mary bless you! Die if it be your weird; but turn not in battle, Dick Hackerston, lest the curse of thine auld blind father fall upon thee!"

And in this spirit did our people go forth to battle, like the Spartans of old!

CHAPTER XLV
THE MEN-AT-ARMS

Up, comrades, and saddle! to horse and away
  To the field where freedom's the prize, sirs!
There hearts of true mettle still carry the day,
  And men are the kings and the kaisers.
No shelter is there where a skulker may creep;
But each man's sword his own head must keep.

Schiller.

On the morning of the next day, when a bright sun was shining on the wide blue basin of the Forth, and a light silvery mist was creeping up from the low woods of Drumore and rolling along the green hill-sides, a body of fifteen hundred Scottish Light Horse, with all their helmets, their uplifted spears and bright appointments flashing, as they galloped forth with George Lord Home at their head, spread along the slope of Fawside Hill, in view of Somerset's camp. Being principally Border-prickers, they were fleetly mounted on strong and hardy horses, and were clad in open helmets with jacks of splinted steel, iron gorgets, and gloves. All had swords, Jethart axes, and long spears, which they brandished as they galloped or caracoled backwards and forwards in open squadrons, but irregularly and far apart, whooping, huzzaing, and taunting the English to attack them, by many injurious epithets.

Intent on meeting the earliest danger face to face, Florence joined this band of Border cavalry, and repeatedly rode near the gate of his own mansion. He felt a shudder as he surveyed it, and on perceiving, among many others on the bartizan of the tower, a dark figure which he thought was his mother, he sighed bitterly, and turning his head away, looked no more, save towards the masses of snow-white tents and hastily-constructed huts of the English camp, on the right and rear of which opened the beautiful Bay of Musselburgh, sweeping far away until its eastern promontory was lost in haze and distance; and on the left of which lay the wild ravine and smoke-blackened ruins of Tranent.

With the green banner of his family, charged with a lion rampant *argent*, armed and langued *gules*, borne by Home of Aytoune, the Border lord rode so close to the English camp that the Lord Grey of Wilton obtained the Duke of Somerset's permission to try the effect of a charge of the heavily-armed English horse upon these bravadoers. A long and glittering mass was then seen to defile from amid the white tents and the green chesnut-trees which shaded them. This mass formed in long squadrons as it advanced, with helmets and lances shining in the morning sun, and with pennons of every colour streaming on the wind behind. There were a thousand men-at-arms on barbed horses, with the demi-lances of Sir Ralf Vane. Among the latter rode Edward Shelly and many other gentlemen as volunteers. As they came on with a cheer, which was distinctly heard in both camps, the Border horse closed round Lord Home's green banner, and then, rushing on each other at full speed, and with all their lances levelled in the rest, the adverse columns met with a tremendous shock, which strewed the open meadows with hundreds of killed and wounded men and horses. Among those who fell first were the laird of Champfleurie and Allan Duthie of the Millheugh, who were slain side by side. The first was cloven down by a sword; the second had three feet of a lance thrust through his body.

It was impossible for the lightly-armed Scottish troopers to withstand the weight and fury of a charge from so many completely-mailed and heavily-mounted cavalry; they were soon broken, and after losing all order, continued a hand-to-hand conflict along the whole slope of Fawside Hill.

In fighting desperately to save his banner from Edward Shelly, whose gauntleted hand was placed thrice upon the pole, Lord Home was severely wounded, and his son the Master of Home, whom M. Beaugue styles a loyal Scottish chevalier, "inferior to none in the world, either in conduct or courage," was struck from his horse, disarmed, and with the laird of Garscadden and Captain Crawford of Jordanhill (afterwards so famous in the wars of Queen Mary's reign), was taken prisoner by Sir Ralf Vane and the Earl of Warwick.

In this conflict Florence ran his lance through the trunk hose of Master Patten; and as these were extravagantly bombasted with several pecks of bran, according to the English fashion, it continued to pour through the orifice as from a sack in which a hole had been torn, and to sow all the scene of the conflict, to the great amusement of friends and foes.

Still the strife went on. Surrounded by a mass of English men-at-arms, who by their very number impeded each other's actions and prevented his destruction, Florence Fawside, within a bowshot of his own gate, and within a green hollow, found himself fighting with all the resolution of a brave heart animated by despair, and coveting death rather than escape,— for he cared not to fly. His pressing danger was observed by his old enemy

Lord Kilmaurs, who leaped on horseback, and, attended by three gentlemen in complete armour, was leaving the Scottish vanguard, when his father, the Earl of Glencairn, sternly exclaimed,—

"Whither go you, my lord?"

"To the front."

"But why almost alone?—and wherefore?"

"To the front, where the laird of Fawside is fighting those devilish men-at-arms; see you not how sorely he is beset?"

"Beware of the odds."

"What care I for odds?" replied Kilmaurs, shortening his reins and waving his lance, the pennon of which bore the hayfork sable, the badge of his family.

"The danger——"

"It never deterred a Cunninghame."

"But remember the letters of the Guises and the Valois,—he is our enemy."

"No Scotsman is my enemy to-day," exclaimed the reckless young lord; "follow me, sirs! I would rather share the death of yonder gallant lad, than stand idly by and see it."

Kilmaurs and his three companions came along the hillside at full speed, and, with levelled lances, burst into the fray just as Florence had been struck from his saddle, and had placed his horse between himself and the swords of the men-at-arms. Thrice a demi-lancer of Sir Ralf Vane's band had made a deadly thrust at him; but thrice the weapon had been parried by the friendly sword of Edward Shelly, who had just joined the *mêlée*, for the same kind purpose that had brought hither Lord Kilmaurs.

"Mount, Fawside," exclaimed the Englishman, keeping between Florence and the Boulogners; "mount while there is time, and leave me to deal with my Lord of Kilmaurs,—another day will serve your turn and mine."

"Thanks," said Florence breathlessly, as he leaped on his horse; "for this good deed I strike not at you to-day."

"But to-morrow——"

"And why to-morrow, Shelly?—alas, I have no one left to live or fight for now; but to-morrow be it, for I warned you to avoid Scottish ground."

"And in good sooth a few of us find its air unwholesome for our English lungs to-day."

While Florence drew off for a few minutes to recover his breath, and from the exhaustion of the late encounter, a rough and desperate conflict took place between Shelly and Kilmaurs, whose former quarrel gave acrimony to their hate and energy to their hands.

"Thou traitor and bondsman of Somerset!" exclaimed Shelly.

"Spy!" taunted the other, and their ringing swords struck fire at every ward and cut. Kilmaurs received a severe wound on the bridle hand, and Shelly's helmet was nearly cloven in two, the vizor being struck completely off; but now other hands and weapons mingled in the combat, and here as in other portions of this extensive skirmish, the Scots were beaten, and had to fly at full speed to reach their own camp; but not until after the contest had been maintained for three hours, with the greatest valour and desperation; and until they had lost no less than thirteen hundred men and horses, did they entirely give way; and then the remnant were pursued round Fawside Hill for three miles to the right flank of the Scottish camp.

Fawside had his armour cut or riven in more than twenty places, by the long swords of the men-at-arms of Boulogne; and his fine grey charger, the gift of Mary of Lorraine, bore him through the Howemire and back to the camp, but so covered was it with wounds as to be disembowelled and dying.

Such was the result of this severe cavalry encounter, a prelude to the greater strife of the morrow; it filled the Scots with greater rancour, and the English (who knew that they must either win a battle or be driven into the sea) with a glow of triumph, which they were at no pains to conceal, for the livelong night their camp rang with rejoicing, and shouts of acclamation.

CHAPTER XLVI
THE PARLEY

Lo, I have ripen'd discord into war!
So let them now agree and form the league;
Since Trojan swords have spilt Ausonian blood;
The war stands sure; and hand to hand they've fought:
Such nuptial rites, — such Hymeneal feasts!

Æneid, viii.

After this conflict had been waged throughout the lower parts of the ground between the hostile camps, the Duke of Somerset, attended by Don Pedro de Gamboa, the Earl of Warwick, and others had ascended the steep green eminence of Inveresk, where, within the trenches of a Roman camp, stood the ancient church of St. Michael. From this lofty point, Somerset fully reconnoitred the position of the Scots; and he became more than ever convinced that any attempt to dislodge them would be attended with great loss, and perhaps by a total defeat. As he and his group of attendants were somewhat moodily descending the hill towards their own camp, they heard the sound of a trumpet issuing from a copsewood, and in a green lane which leads directly from St. Michael's Church towards the hill of Fawside, they were met, as we are told in history, by four Scotsmen. The first of these was a gentleman on horseback—Florence Fawside—in full armour except his head, on which he wore a blue velvet bonnet adorned by a tall white ostrich feather. He bore a steel gauntlet on his lance, and was attended by the Albany Herald in his tabard, the Ormond Pursuivant with his silver collar of SS around his neck, and by a trumpeter in the royal livery (red and yellow) who sharply blew the peculiar notes which invite a parley.

Florence had scarcely reached the Scottish camp, after the recent discomfiture of the Lord Home's mosstroopers, ere he was despatched to the English Protector, on a delicate mission by the Regent Arran and the Earl of Huntly.

"Well, Scots, what seek you?" asked Somerset, who was a stately man of a noble presence, with a fine open countenance, and a short-clipped beard, of the late King Henry's fashion. Over his armour, which was richly studded and inlaid with gold *damasquinée*, he wore an open cassock-coat of crimson velvet, lined with white ermine, and on his breast were the collar and order of the garter. Dudley Earl of Warwick was nearly dressed in the same fashion, and wore the same illustrious order. "Come you hither to offer me terms?" asked the duke.

"Such terms as your excellency may accept without dishonour," replied Fawside, bowing low, for in manner and bearing the noble Somerset looked every inch a prince, and indeed closely resembled his late monarch Henry VIII. in face, figure, and dress.

"'Tis well," said he; "but in whose name come you?"

"In the name of James Earl of Arran, Lord Hamilton of Cadzow, knight of the most Ancient Order of the Thistle, Chevalier of St. Michael in France, regent of Scotland and the Isles, for our Sovereign Lady the Queen, whom God long preserve!" replied the Albany Herald with due formality.

"And his purpose is— —"

"To receive back by cartel all the prisoners who may have been captured by your men-at-arms, in the conflict which is just ended; and on doing so, you will be permitted to retreat without molestation into England."

"This we decline," said Somerset bluntly; "and now for *your* purpose, fair sir?" he added, turning to Florence, whose pale and saddened countenance could not fail to interest him.

"I came in the name of George Earl of Huntly, Lord of Badenoch, Lochaber, and Auchindoune, also Chevalier of St. Michael, in France," replied Florence.

"And what would he with us?"

"This noble earl bids me say to you, Edward Duke of Somerset, that, being solicitous to avoid the unnecessary effusion of Christian blood, he is ready to decide this quarrel by single combat with you alone, or to encounter you with ten or twenty gentlemen on each side, on foot or on horseback, as may be arranged. Here lies his glove. Of these chosen combatants, I claim the honour of being one."

"And I, on the other side," exclaimed Don Pedro de Gamboa and several gentlemen, pressing forward.

"Nay," said Somerset loftily; "this cannot be. Knight, herald, pursuivant, and trumpeter, return to those fool-hardy lords who so unwisely sent you hither, and say that our quarrel, being a national and not a personal one, can only be decided by a general appeal to arms. And *thou*, sir," he added, with increasing hauteur, to Florence, "say to the Earl of Huntly, who sent thee, that in making such a challenge to me, being of such estate, he seemeth to lack wit, for, by the sufferance of God, I have committed to me the care of a mighty and precious jewel, even such a charge as the Lord Arran hath—the government of a youthful sovereign and the protection of a realm, while there be in my army many noble gentlemen, the Lord Huntly's equals, to whom he might have sent his cartel freely and without chance of refusal."

"Your excellency speaketh wisely and well. Here will I take up the glove, and in return send mine," exclaimed the fiery Earl of Warwick, drawing off his steel gauntlet, while his swarthy face glowed with excitement; "and I tell thee, trumpeter, thou shalt have one hundred silver crowns if thou bringest back a favourable answer from this Lord of Huntly and Badenoch."

"Dudley, this may not be," said Somerset; "Huntly, an earl, I believe, of a hundred years ago, is not peer to thee who representest our Norman earls of the twelfth century."

"Then give *me* the glove," exclaimed Don Pedro de Gamboa: "what care I for earl or for emperor?"

"Nor may this be," replied Florence. "The Earl of Huntly, a true and valiant Catholic lord, will not meet in single combat a renegade soldier of fortune, who, like Don Pedro, is beyond the pale of country and religion, since he sells his sword to those who are the avowed enemies of the faith of our fathers, the church of God and Rome."

The Spaniard, who was a dark, sallow-visaged, and black-bearded free companion, gave Florence a terrible frown, and his glowing eyes seemed to flash within the four bars of his casquetel. He had served under the Admiral Don Diego de Velasquez when, with three hundred Spaniards, that adventurous cavalier first landed in Cuba; and there Gamboa first won a name as a ferocious and daring soldier in the war with the natives, many of whom were roasted alive; others were torn to pieces by wild dogs, and the rest were awed into submission. Gamboa struck with his mailed hand the orders of our Lady of Montesa and San Julian de Alcantara, which sparkled on his cuirass; then he uttered a hoarse Spanish oath, and laid a hand on his sword. On this Florence lowered the point of his lance and reined back his steed to defend himself; but Somerset and Warwick adroitly urged their horses between them, and preserved the peace.

To end this interview, of which Master Patten and Father John of Tranent have left us such a minute account, Somerset said,—

"Sirs, what command hath the Lord Bothwell in yonder host upon the hill?"

"None," replied Florence; "he is now a prisoner in a royal castle, and deservedly so."

"A prisoner?"

"Accused of crimes against the state and queen."

"Hah—discovered!" said Somerset to Warwick; but the deep glance they exchanged was not unnoticed by Florence, who quite understood its import, and how deeply Bothwell (like too many others) was implicated with these invaders of his country.

"Tell the Regent Arran and the Earl of Huntly," resumed Somerset, "that we have now spent some eight days in your country; and that though your force far exceedeth ours, if they will march down into the plain they will have fighting enough; and I will give you, herald, and you, trumpeter, each one a thousand crowns for your pains. What say you, sir herald, to so fair a sum?"

"As Solon said to Croesus, king of Lydia."

"And what said he?"

"If another comes who hath more mettle, then he may be master of all this gold; and before to-morrow night we must win or lose a battle," replied the herald.

"A man of wit, by St. George! And to you, sir," added Somerset to Florence, "will I give a chain of gold worth thrice the sum, and knighthood from my sword, if you will take it from an Englishman."

"Knighthood could I have from no sword nobler than that of your highness, if I survive the battle, which, in my present mood, I deem most unlikely," replied Florence, with a stern and sombre air that seemed strange on his youthful face, as he bowed, reined back his horse, and, as if weary of the interview, withdrew to the Scottish camp to report that his mission had proved unavailing.

The result of this interview was a letter sent by Somerset to Arran about nightfall. It was borne by Edward Shelly, and contained an offer of retiring into England if the Scots would promise to keep their young queen at home until she attained such an age as might enable her to judge whether or not she would fulfil the original engagement with Edward VI., who would then have attained manhood; but so exasperated were the Scots by the unwarrantable aggressions of the English, that they rejected with scorn proposals which they knew arose rather from the pressing dictates of prudence, present danger, and political selfishness, and from the doubts and difficulties of Somerset's position, than from any sincere desire for peace, or for the welfare of Mary and her kingdom; so, from one end of their camp to the other, there rose a universal shout,—

"To battle! to battle!—no truce—no treaty!—to battle!"

And so the night closed in.

CHAPTER XLVII
THE BLACK SATURDAY

Yet turn ye to the eastern hand,
  And wae and wonder ye shall see;
How thirty thousand Scotsmen stand,
  Where yon rank river meets the sea.
There shall the lyon lose the gylte,
  And the leopards hear it clean away;
At Pinkycleuch there shall be spylte
  Much gentil blood that day.

Thomas the Rhymer.

The dawn of the next day, the 10th of September, 1547—by the Scots called, the Feast of St. Finian, by the English and others the Festival of St. Nicholas of Tolentino—was singularly beautiful. When the sun arose from his bed beyond the eastern sea, the waves rolled and glittered in amber light; the spray seemed to rise and fall in showers of snow and diamonds upon the rocky bluffs; while the dew of the past night lay heavy on every leaf and shrub. Between its green and far-stretching shores of yellow sand and opening bays, of mountain slopes and brown basaltic rocks, its grassy isles and covered headlands, the Forth lay almost waveless like a sea of gold, and receding far away as the eye could reach, until it melted into the eastern horizon, where cloud and wave were blent together.

The fertile hills and upheaved bluffs of Fife were tinted by the glory of the morning with saffron and purple, though mellowed by haze and distance; while the capital, with its castle, its steep ridge of towering mansions, St. Giles's tower, and Arthur's rocky cone, stood clearly forth from the deep unbroken blue of the west. As the sun rose higher, seeming to mount into heaven, through successive bars or horizontal lines of vapour, which turned to glowing gold and purple, the beauty of the morning increased, for it exhibited one of those glorious arrangements of massive cloud and blazing sunshine, brilliant light and sudden shadow, peculiar to the lowlands of Scotland.

Cleared of the grain, which was now stowed away in the vaults of baronial towers or of fortified granges, or else consumed by the flame and the troop-horses of the foe, the fields were bare now, and yellow stubble covered all the upland slopes, from the margin of the sea to the lonely Lammermuirs. In some places, the plough that lay now rusting and disused, had already been at work, and had turned up the long, brown furrows, above which the ravening gled and the black corbie, as if scenting the battle from afar, were wheeling in lazy circles. Westward, beyond the Esk, the stackyards were full of yellow grain, and along the river's bank, and among the old coppice that shrouded Pinkey House, Wallyford, and the Templar Hospital of St. Germains, the leaves were assuming those varied tints of orange, russet, green, and brown—the beautiful, but fading hues of the Scottish forests in autumn.

Such was the aspect of the morning and the scenery, when, on this Saturday in September, 1547, Florence Fawside reined up his horse on the slope of Inveresk Hill, and saw before him the whole arena of a battle-field; whereon manoeuvred the far-extended and glittering lines of more than *fifty thousand* Scots and Englishmen, prepared for mortal strife! And this was to gratify the mad ambition, of Henry VIII., who, from his deathbed bequeathed, like the first Edward, to his successors, the hopeless task of attempting to humble a free and warlike people.

The English had first begun to move about dawn, by sending some of their artillery to the summit of Inveresk and to Crookstone Loan, from whence they could play upon the camp of the Scots, towards whom their whole force moved in three great columns, Warwick still leading the van; Somerset led the second column, and Lord Dacres the third, or rear-guard; but on coming into the fertile plain, amid which the little stream named Pinkey Burn, flows through a cleuch or hollow, the English were astonished to find that the Scots, with singular imprudence, had accepted the duke's challenge, and left their strong position, to meet his better-trained and well-appointed army in the open field.

The regent of Scotland had unwisely mistaken the first movements of the English for an intention to seek safety in flight, by a precipitate retreat from the sands of Musselburgh on board their fleet. Alarmed lest they should thus escape, after their unwarrantable hostilities, and the devastations committed on their northern march, he resolved at once to cross the Esk, and get between them and their shipping, so as to cut off all chance of their retiring towards the sea. This movement he resolved to execute in defiance of the advice of the most wary and skilful soldiers in his army, which was armed almost entirely in the fashion of the middle ages, with lances, bows, swords, and battle-axes; while the English had many of the more modern appliances of warfare in the hands of their well-trained and veteran bands of Spaniards, Germans, and the garrisons of Calais and Boulogne, all of whom carried arquebuses or hand-guns.

The Earls of Arran, Huntly, Angus, and Argyle, on this day appeared each at the head of his division, sheathed in full armour, wearing above their cuirasses the Order of the Thistle, together with the Collar of St. Michael, which they had received from Francis I., two years before. Each wore around his helmet an earl's coronet, from the centre of which, beneath a plume of feathers, rose his gilded crest; thus, the first carried an oak-tree; the second, a stag's-head; the third, a salamander *vert* amid flames of fire; and the fourth, the wild boar's head of the Campbells, showing its ghastly tusks above his polished vizor.

"Reflect, lord regent," said the Earl of Huntly; "I pray you to reflect on this measure."

"Reflect on what?" asked Arran sharply, through his golden helmet.

"The sequel of a movement so rash as this."

"A brave soldier never reflects," replied Arran proudly.

"But a skilful captain doth," was the pointed response.

"True, my Lord Huntly," said the Earl of Angus; "you are in the right, and our friend Arran is most unwise to reject such prudent counsel."

"Enough, sirs—enough!" said Arran, who was burning with impatience, as he saw the long lines of the English glittering in the sunshine, and a longing for vengeance on Somerset, whose invasion had convulsed the realm, and whose plots, spies, assassins, and bribes, had so long disturbed the Scottish government, gathered in his heart; "let us attack them ere they escape by sea. You smile, my Lord Kilmaurs!" he added, turning wrathfully to that young lord.

"Nay, my lord regent—this is no time to smile; nor did I," replied the other bluntly.

"Methought a strange expression crossed your face."

Kilmaurs grew pale with rage, for being in the English interest, he *had* felt some satisfaction on foreseeing the ruin of Arran's army.

"Your grace is scarcely well bred in reproaching me with a wound received in the service of my country," said he, pointing to the scar which traversed his cheek, and the spasmodic twitching of which was a constant source of annoyance to him. He then put spurs to his horse and galloped to the head of his father's vassals, all stout yeomen of Cunninghame and Kyle, who were arrayed in a dense and steely mass under the banner with the hayfork sable, and were preparing to cross the fatal river at a ford.

The rash movement of Arran was urged by the Earl of Glencairn and many others, who are now known to have been the pensioners of England, and in secret league with Somerset; but dearly did it cost the earl and his Cunninghames.

"The lord regent is right," said he; "let us down at one fell swoop upon them; for what is yonder host but a banded horde of English clowns and Irish kerne—of Spanish robbers and German boors, come hither in steel bonnets to seek for blood and beer? Down at once, I say, and bear me this horde of invaders at spear-point to the sea!"

"But the German infantry," said Huntly, "and those arquebuses of Spain——"

"A rabble of tawny loons clad in armour so heavy, and mounted on horses so gorgeously trapped, that they can never escape your Highlandmen or the Lord Home's light Border-prickers."

The Earl of Angus now refused to advance, swearing "by St. Bryde of Douglas it was rank madness to cast advantage at their horses' heels."

"On pain of treason to our lady the queen, I charge you, lord earl, to pass forward with the van, or beware our speedy vengeance!" said Arran.

"My fear is less of thee than for my queen and country," replied the Douglas calmly, as he led his squadron girdle-deep through the stream, which swept some of them through the arches of the bridge, and away into the sea beyond.

"What says your leal and right-hand man, the young Laird of Fawside?" asked the Earl of Cassilis with a scarcely perceptible sneer; "doubtless that he is ready, on either side of the Esk, to die for your grace and the queen."

"To say so, my lord, were an empty boast," replied Florence quietly (his heart was too heavy for anger). "In yonder plain are six-and-thirty thousand Scots, who far excel me, I hope, in their readiness to die."

"To battle, then!" exclaimed Arran, waving his truncheon. "God and St. Andrew are with us!"

By this time the whole Scottish army had defiled across the high Roman bridge of Esk, and formed in dense columns of horse, foot, and archers, as they advanced towards the foe, presenting a splendid array, with all their polished helmets and cuirasses shining in the sun—their many square, triangular, and swallow-tailed banners waving, and their tall, uplifted lances, eighteen feet in length, and not less than fifteen thousand in number, swaying heavily to and fro, like a field of giant corn, as the close ranks marched on shoulder to shoulder, until the whole thirty-six thousand men stood in firm order of battle on the plain beyond the hill of Inveresk, which overlooked their left flank, while the green upland slope of Fawside rose upon their right.

With the shrill fife, the rattling drum (or *Almainie swesche*, as the Scots named it), the droning bagpipe, the twanging bugle-horn, the kettle, the clashing cymbal, and the sharp brass trumpet, filling the air with harsh but martial music, the Scottish lines drew near the English; and then the shouts, the cheers, the war-cries (the *slogan* of the Lowlanders, the *cathghairm* of the Celts), by which the soldiers of hastily-collected levies usually encourage each other, or taunt the foe, began to load the air with a confusion of sounds, after the deep boom of the first English cannon from the green brow of Inveresk had pealed through the clear welkin, and made a ghastly lane amid the nearest close column of Scottish infantry, causing the silken banners to rustle, the ranks to swerve, and the tall ash spears to sway like a corn-field bending beneath a blast of wind; and then to heaven went up a louder and a deeper shout, as the ranks closed over the mangled dead, and the forward march went on.

The centre was led by the Regent Arran in person. It consisted of the hardy clans from Stathearn, with the flower of the Scottish infantry, the men of Lothian, of Kinross, and of Stirlingshire. With many barons, he had also at least eight hundred chosen citizens of Edinburgh, led by William Craik, their provost. In their centre, Dick Hackerston bore the "Blue Blanket," or ancient banner of the city—a great swallow-tailed pennon of azure silk, worked for the burgesses by Margaret of Oldenburg. Among the men of Strathearn were the MacNabs, in their red, glaring tartans; and amid them were twelve stately warriors, conspicuous in their long lurichs of steel. These were Ian Mion and his eleven brothers, the heroes of the savage story of Lochearn, and on their banner was painted a human head *affrontée*.

The right wing consisted of six thousand western Highlanders, and brave and hardy islesmen, inured to battle and to storm, under MacLeod, MacGregor, and Archibald Earl of Argyle, the regent's son-in-law. On both its flanks and rear this column was covered by artillery. The other divisions presented the aspect either of dull or uniform masses covered with shining steel or brown leather; but this displayed the varied tartans of many Celtic tribes; and from its marching masses, with the incessant brandishing of swords and round targets, rose the wildest and most tumultuary shouts and outcries.

The left division of the Scots consisted of ten thousand infantry of Fife, Mearn, and the eastern counties, led by Archibald Earl of Angus, flanked by culverins and light horse. In their centre there marched a singular force, consisting of more than a thousand Scottish monks, who had been drawn from their cloisters by a terror of the Reformation (which Henry had so roughly established in England) being spread into Scotland, if Somerset's expedition proved successful. They were clad in plain black armour, and wore white or grey surcoats with crosses on the breast and back, to distinguish them as Dominicans, Cistercians, or Franciscans; and in their centre waved a white silk banner, which had been consecrated with many solemn ceremonies by the abbot of Dunfermline, after it had been made by Mary of Lorraine and the Countesses of Yarrow and Arran. Thereon was depicted a female kneeling with dishevelled hair before a cross, and around her was the motto—

"Afflictæ Ecclesiæ ne Obliviscaris"

The great squares or close columns of Scottish infantry were formed in admirable order, but in the ancient and somewhat unwieldy fashion of their country. Drawn up shoulder to shoulder, each soldier carried his spear, which was six Scots ells (*i.e.* eighteen feet) in length, pointing to the front; the first rank knelt, the next stooped, the third stood erect; but *all* had their weapons levelled at three angles towards the foe; thus the Scots were "so completely defended by the close order in which they were formed, and by the length of their lances, that to charge them seemed to be as rash as to oppose your bare hands to a hedgehog's bristles."

Lances, two-handed swords, and daggers, with mauls and Jethart staves, were the arms of the cavalry, who were all in complete mail, except the Borderers, who were always lightly armed, and seldom wore more than a skull-cap and breastplate or splinted jack, with plate sleeves and gloves of steel. A few were armed with wheel-lock pistols, which were brought from Italy or Flanders; but in the art of war, in order, and, above all, in perfect obedience, as well as in the discipline of the Boulogners and the new fashion of weapons, arquebuse and culiver, by which their auxiliaries the foreign horse and foot were armed, the English on this day were every way superior to the Scots.

CHAPTER XLVIII
THE BATTLE

Near Ilus' tomb, in order ranged around,
The Trojan lines possess'd the rising ground;
The sea with ships, the fields with armies spread,
The victors rage, the dying and the dead.

Iliad, book xi.

The joy of Somerset was great on perceiving that the Scots had quitted their formidable position, and, between his fleet on one flank and his artillery on the other, were deliberately marching into a mouth of fire. He and the Earl of Warwick warmly congratulated each other, and then repaired to their posts. The earl formed his division on the slope of Inveresk hill; the duke formed his line from thence till its other flank reached the plain. The mounted arquebusiers of Don de Gamboa and the men-at-arms of Lord Grey, flushed by their victory of yesterday, formed the extreme left, while Lord Dacres commanded the seaward line.

Being armed with shorter pikes than the Scots, the long and serried array of the English looked compact and low; the sun was in their rear, and above their long lines of glittering helmets poured aslant his morning rays, in which every polished sword and point of steel flashed and sparkled brightly.

On this day the royal standard of England was borne by Sir Andrew Flammock, a gentleman of approved valour, who rode near Somerset, on a magnificently caparisoned horse, and in the centre of the whole army. This scarlet banner, with its three yellow leopards, was the mark of many an eye, the aim of many a Highland archer, and Lowland cannonier; thus the unfortunate bearer had no sinecure of his office; and on Arran saying to those about him,—

"Sirs, I would give a fair barony to have yonder standard in my hand!"

"I care not for baronies," said Florence, who rode by his side; "I care not for life itself, lord earl,—and thou shalt have the banner, if human strength can win it."

"Then," adds the vicar of Tranent, who records this episode, "ere the Lord Arran could reply, the battaile began with a mighty furie."

As the chief intention of Arran was to throw the division of the Earl of Angus—if not the whole Scottish army—between the English and their fleet, the flank which marched near the sea, became (as Somerset had foreseen) exposed to an immediate cannonade from the whole line of the English ships, sixty-four in number. The booming of their artillery echoed along the indented shore with a thousand reverberations, while the pale smoke enveloped all the line of anchored ships, from their low-waisted and high-pooped hulls, to the gaudy banners and long wavy streamers which decorated their masts; and their shot of stone or iron, bowled with fatal precision among the dense masses of the men of Fife and Mearn, making long and terrible lanes of death and mutilation—of shattered limbs and dismembered bodies. This caused a flank movement by which the whole Scottish line swerved south and westward towards the slope of Fawside Hill. On perceiving this, Somerset ordered the Lord Grey at the head of his mailed men-at-arms, and Edward Shelly with his Boulogners to charge the right wing of the Scots, to the end, that both their flanks might be driven upon the centre. With this body went the bearer of the royal standard; and true to his pledge, Florence galloped to join the right wing of the Scots, that he might be nearer his intended prize.

"St. George! St. George for England! Come on, my valiant Boulogners, my true-bred English fighting-cocks!" cried Shelly, standing in his stirrups, and waving his lance as he spurred in front of the line.

In solid squadrons, with their barbed horses making the ground shake beneath their mighty rush, the men-at-arms all clad in shining steel, with swords uplifted and their faces glowing through their barred helmets with ardour and excitement, came furiously on, their trumpets sounding, and the red cross of England waving above them. On came Edward Shelly at the head of his mounted Boulogners, the last of those "five hundred light horsemen, cloathed in blue jackets with red guards," whom King Henry had taken to Boulogne;[*] and with them came Sir Ralf Vane, Sir Thomas Darcy, and the Lord Fitzwalter, all wearing magnificent armour, streaming plumes, and gay colours, leading the column of demi-lancers, a thousand heavy horse, and sixteen hundred chosen infantry, to break that portion of the Scottish line.

[*] *Vide* "Relations of the Most Famous Kingdoms." 1630.

The brilliant horsemen first gained the slope of Fawside Hill, and then making a sweeping wheel to their right, like a rolling sea of shining men and foaming chargers, they rushed with tremendous fury down upon the

Scottish flank. There was a sudden and a fearful shock; and again, like a rolling sea from the face of a flinty bluff, this human tide of valour was hurled back upon itself in confusion and disorder.

Foremost in the *mêlée* fought Florence, with his eyes fixed on the standard, and many a mounted man went down before him, till at last, with a shout of triumph, he laid his hand upon the pole, as it swayed to and fro, above the fighting and the falling.

"The standard!" cried Lord Grey; "by Heaven and King Harry's bones, let us save the standard!"

He made a blow at the left hand of Florence, who gave him a severe cut across the mouth just as his helmet flew open, and then by a wound in the neck completed his discomfiture. Sir Andrew Flammock was roughly unhorsed by Sir George Douglas; but he retained the standard, by tearing it (as he fell) from the pole, which remained in the hand of Florence as a trophy of victory.

It was at the present farm-house of Barbauchly that this encounter took place; and into its muddy ditch, back from the triple line of gleaming Scottish pikes, there rolled two hundred of Somerset's best cavaliers. Ratcliff, Clarence, and many others were slain, many more were wounded; while hundreds of riderless horses, wild with affright, fled over the field in every direction, some with their entrails hanging out, having been stabbed in the belly by the spears, the long double-edged daggers, or Tynedale knives of the Scots. "Rendered furious by their wounds, many of these chargers carried disorder into the English companies, which were thrown into such confusion (says an historian) that the Lord Grey had the greatest difficulty in extricating them and retreating."

While he drew off his discomfited cavalry to re-form them, there lingered near the Scottish line a single horseman, whose blue surcoat, trimmed with gold and slashed with scarlet, worn loosely and open above his armour, and whose lofty plume, as well as his trappings and bearing, marked him as an approved soldier and man of distinction. This was Edward Shelly, in the livery of a Boulogner. Rising in his stirrups, he thrice waved his lance aloft; and Florence, remembering their quarrel and appointed duel, rode forth at once to meet him. He had long since broken his lance; but he now couched in the fashion of one the pole of the English standard, which he still retained, and with it he rushed at full speed upon his challenger.

They met with a furious concussion; but as Shelly's horse swerved, his lance was broken in two athwart the breast-plate of Florence, whose impromptu weapon was splintered into twenty fragments on the right shoulder of the sturdy Englishman, who kept his saddle, but with difficulty.

Each in a moment tossed aside the truncheon or fragment which remained in his hand, reined up his horse, and drew his sword; then, in full view of the Scottish right and of the English left wing, began a sharp hand-to-hand conflict, in which the utmost skill in the use of the bridle and sword was displayed by both combatants.

Florence, being reckless alike of life and danger, had evidently the best of it, as he drove his adversary, at every thrust and stroke, further up the hill towards the right, until they were within a bowshot of the tower of Fawside, the barbican of which was crowded by women and by the old men of the barony, who were all armed, in case of the place being attacked. It soon became evident that they recognized their young master, for shouts of

"Forth—forth, and feir nocht!" faintly reached his ear, mingled with shrill cries of alarm.

Suddenly his horse stumbled and came heavily down on its knees, throwing him prone to the earth. Ere he could rise, while a shriek burst from the women in the tower, Shelly had sprung from his horse, and throwing the bridle over his arm, placed his sword at the throat of the fallen.

"Here might I slay or capture you, Scot," said he; "but I have not forgotten your generosity on the night we met in that lonely castle of the Torwood. Here ends our quarrel; and in this field let us meet no more, unless it be that the fair one, whose name I jestingly mentioned on that night——"

"Nay, speak not of her," said Florence mournfully. "I seek not life, Master Shelly, but rather death; and from so honoured a sword as thine it were indeed more welcome!"

"Wherefore so sad?" said the Englishman. "Up, man, and be doing; for, by St. George! you Scots will have your hands full to-day. Here come our demi-lances again; away to your own band—you have not a moment to lose!"

Shelly remounted; Florence saluted him, and leaped lightly on his own horse.

"Farewell, Edward Shelly," exclaimed Florence with an emotion of enthusiasm; "thou art a soldier as generous as brave. I would rather be thy friend than thine enemy."

"To-day you have been both, fair sir," replied Shelly, as he wheeled his horse round. At that moment there came a loud whiz through the air, and struck by the ball of an arquebuse, which had been fired from the tower of Fawside, the brave Shelly fell dead from his terrified horse, which dragged him by the stirrup into the ditch where so many English were already lying killed and wounded.

Florence cast his eyes upward to the tower-head, from whence the pale light smoke was still curling. He saw the tall dark figure of a woman brandishing an arquebuse, and he knew in a moment that the hand of his stern mother had fired the fatal shot.

"She again!—oh, ruthless hand!" he muttered with a half-smothered groan; and turning his horse, galloped again to the Regent Arran.

On beholding Shelly's fall a shout of rage arose from his comrades the Boulogners, and from the long array of demi-lances, whom the Duke of Somerset once more ordered to attack the Scottish right.

"By my faith, duke, you might as well bid me charge a castle wall?" was the angry reply of the Lord Grey, from whose face and neck the blood was still streaming; but now, by the advice of the skilful Earl of Warwick, the Spanish and German arquebusiers, with a body of English archers, were ordered to assail the Scottish columns in front, while several pieces of cannon played upon one flank from Fawside Hill, and the shipping still swept the other with terrible results. The foreign auxiliaries, in ranks eight deep, poured in their heavy shot, firing over forks or rests, full into the faces of the Scottish infantry, who, by the destruction of their light cavalry on the preceding day, were without means of attacking either the cannoniers or the continental troops. Thus the battle soon became general along the whole plain, and the cry of the Scots,—

"Come on, ye dogs! ye heretics!" rose incessantly above the din of the strife; for now there was the rancorous rivalry of creed to inflame the rivalry of race, and the transmitted hatred of a thousand years. Moreover, in this engagement the English were burning to avenge the defeat of their troops at Ancrumford and Paniershaugh, where Sir Ralf Evers and many men had been cut to pieces by the Earl of Angus; and now, filled with fury on beholding the destruction of his castle and the pitiless devastation of his lands, no man in all the army of Arran on this day of blood hewed a passage further into the English host than old Claude Hamilton of Preston, who forgot all about his proffered titles, and with his two-handed sword sent many a younger man to his long home.

The combined movement of the Spaniards, under Gamboa, with the Germans, under Sir Pietre Mewtas, seconded by a body of English archers showering flight and sheaf arrows point-blank into the teeth of the Scottish line, on which (as already related) the cannon were playing from both flanks, drove it into confusion; and, after suffering dreadful losses, the great column of Angus first began insensibly to retire.

At this crisis the whole air seemed laden with sound; The booming of cannon; the rattling explosion of arquebuses, hand-guns, and calivers; the smoke of which rolled like carded wool before the wind; the twang of bows; the whiz of passing arrows, which planted all the turf as they stuck with feathers upward; the clang of swords on swords or helmets; the galloping of horses; the voices of many thousands of men uttering triumphant hurrahs, fierce and bitter imprecations or cries of agony, as they were struck down wounded and bleeding to the earth;—all were there to make a mighty medley of uproar. The air of the sunny morning became dusky with the dust raised by the feet of men rushing in tens of thousands to the mortal shock; and sulphureous with the smoke of gunpowder, which was then almost a new element in Scottish war; and to this new ally in the hands of their foreign auxiliaries on one side, and to the treason and incapacity of the Scottish leaders on the other, England eventually owed the victory.

The recoil of Lord Angus's division caused a panic to run along the whole Scottish line.

It began to waver, to pause, and fall back!

"Treason! treason! to your ranks—to your standards! forward and follow me!" cried Arran, whose magnificent armour, covered with gold embossings made him the aim of many an archer, as he galloped along the line to restore order. He had already had three horses killed under him; the golden oak and pearl-studded coronet had been hewn from his helmet; the diamond cross of St. Andrew and the golden shells of St. Michael had been torn from his breast; he had broken his sword and lance, and now wielded a steel truncheon; his eyes were wild and bloodshot, and his voice had become hoarse by the reiterated orders he had issued. His efforts were vain; and vain also were those of Florence, and a few who attempted to second them; for the rapid advance of the Earl of Warwick's column, and another well-directed volley from the foreign auxiliaries, completed the discomfiture of the ill-led, ill-posted, and ill-disciplined Scots. A total and most disastrous rout ensued! The great army, which one historian likens to "a steely sea agitated by the wind," after a few moments was seen breaking into a thousand fragments, and dispersed in all directions.

"They fly! they fly!" burst from the victors.

All became flight, chaos, confusion; and the fugitives, in their haste to escape the English cavalry, threw aside all that might encumber their movements. More than twenty thousand spears and partisans strewed the ground, with helmets, cuirasses, back-plates, bucklers, gauntlets, swords, daggers, mauls, Jedwood axes, bows, belts, sheafs of arrows, drums, banners, trumpets, cannon, pistols, hand-guns, and all the *débris* of a mighty host; and the pursuit of the unarmed fugitives continued from one in the day until six in the evening—nor even *then* were the English sated with slaughter.

Exasperated by their first defeat, the demi-lances and the men-at-arms of Boulogne, were especially severe in their actions.

"Remember Paniershaugh!" was their cry; and others shouted,—

"Shelly, Shelly! remember Ned Shelly!" for, says Master Patten, "On the field we found that worthy gentleman and gallant officer, pitifully disfigured, mangled, and discernible only by his beard."

In their haste to escape, many of the Scots cast aside their shoes and doublets, and fled in their shirts and breeches. Many concealed themselves in the furrows of the fields, and were passed unseen by the English cavalry, who swept on after others. In short, it was one of those routs or panics to which undisciplined troops are at all times liable.

To Edinburgh the din of the distant battle had come by fits upon the autumnal breeze; and when the English infantry reached Edmondstone Edge, and found themselves among the plunder of the Scottish tents and camp-equipage, the shout they raised was distinctly heard in the streets of the capital, where that day's slaughter made three hundred and sixty widows. Among those who fell was the merchant John Hamilton, mentioned in the thirty-first chapter of our story.

Thousands of the Scots threw themselves into the Esk, and perished miserably under the cannon from the ships, the shot of the Spaniards, or the swords of the English horsemen, when they scrambled ashore. On the narrow Roman bridge, the press of fugitives was frightful, as the Lord Clinton's great ship was pouring her broadsides upon it, and on the defiling masses. Here were slain the good Lord Fleming of Cumbernauld; the Masters of Livingstone, Buchan, Ogilvy, and Erskine, all sons of earls; the Lairds of Lochinvar, Merchiston, Craigcrook, Priestfield, Lee, and many others, with their friends and followers, till the barricade of mail-clad dead impeded the passage of the living; and so little did their consecrated banner avail the band of armed monks, that they nearly perished to a man, and the symbol of "the afflicted Church" was found on the field, soaked in their blood, torn and trampled under foot. The Esk was literally crimsoned with blood, for nearly half the Scottish army perished along its banks, the English having made a vow before the battle, "that if victorious, they would kill *many* and spare *few*."

The aspect of the field, says Master Patten, was frightful; the bodies lay so thick and close.

"Some without legs, some houghed and half-dead, others the arms cut off, divers their necks half asunder, many their heads cloven, the brains of sundry dashed out, others their heads quite off, with a thousand kinds of killing. In the chase," continues this minute reporter, who writes of the affair with great gusto, "all, for the most part, were killed either in the head or in the neck; for our horsemen could not well reach them lower with their swords. And thus, with blood and slaughter, the chase continued five miles westward from the place of their standing, which was in the fallow-fields of Inveresk, unto Edinburgh Park (about the base of Arthur's Seat), and well-nigh to the gates of the town itself, and unto Leith; and in breadth, from the shore of the Firth up to Dalkeith southward; in all of which space *the dead bodies lay as thick as cattle grazing in a full-replenished pasture.* The river Esk was red with blood, so that in the same chase were counted, as well by some of our men who diligently observed it, as by several of the prisoners, who greatly lamented the result, upwards of fourteen thousand slain. It was a wonder to see how soon the dead bodies of the slain were stripped quite naked, whereby the persons of the enemy might be easily viewed. For tallness of stature, cleanness of skin, largeness of bone, and due proportion, I could not have believed there were so many in all their country."

The Lord Chancellor, the Earl of Huntly, with fifteen hundred men, were captured, and, with thirty thousand suits of mail found in the camp and on the field, sent on board the fleet.

Previous to all this, Florence collected a few horsemen by the force of example, and made three desperate charges, which kept Gamboa's fiery Spaniards and the Lord Fitzwalter's demi-lances in check until the regent and his train had passed the Esk. On achieving this, Arran, whose helmet was now completely cloven, and the housings of whose horse were covered with blood, exclaimed,—

"Fawside, the day is totally lost, and I am living: and without a single wound!"

"And I too, though seeking death everywhere."

"So much the better; I have for you a task of honour and peril to perform."

"Name it—quick, my lord; we have not a moment to lose," cried Florence breathlessly.

"Ride for Edinburgh—get forth the queen and queen-mother, and, with whatever men you can collect, take the road for the north—there await my orders—away!"

"Farewell; but I must have one other dash at these English demi-lances," he exclaimed, wheeling round his horse.

Cold in the cause of Scotland, and heedless whether the field was lost or won, too many of the peers showed but an indifferent example to their soldiers; others, with an eye to the promised pensions, gold, titles, and rewards, wished well to Somerset, and openly fled, like traitors, as Arran called them. Hence the rhyme, with which the poor Scots consoled themselves,—

> 'Twas English gold and Scots traitors wan
> The field of Pinkey, but no Englishman.

According to Buchanan, the Highlanders escaped without loss, as they formed themselves into a dense circle, and in this strange order retreated over the most difficult and rocky ground, where no men-at-arms could follow them. Their retreat was covered by the MacNabs, among whom the twelve tall sons of Aileen were conspicuous by their vigour and bravery.

Arran retired with a body of fugitives to Stirling, and on the day after the battle fresh scenes of disaster and devastation occurred in Edinburgh. In every street rapine and outrage were triumphant. Holyrood was sacked, the churches were despoiled, and Leith was set in flames.

There was one citizen of Edinburgh, who, after bearing himself gallantly throughout that bloody day, on finding that he was unable to bear away, like the pious Eneis, his blind and aged father, while having a young wife and her babes to protect, stood for nearly an hour amid the flames of rapine and a hundred weapons that gleamed around him, defending with his two-handed sword the archway that led to his house. A horde of assailants, flushed with ale, wine, triumph, and ferocity, opposed him; but valiantly he faced them all, until a ball from the arquebuse of a Spaniard pierced his heart and he fell dead. This citizen was Dick Hackerston; but to this hour his name is borne by the street or wynd which he so valiantly defended.

While the English were stripping the dead and slaying the wounded on the field, the little garrison in Fawside tower fired on them briskly, from bartizan and loophole, until they were environed by a body of men-at-arms under Sir Ralf Vane, who on finding the defender was a lady, tied a handkerchief to his sword and riding forward called upon her to yield.

"Yield thou!—false kite, what make ye here?" was the scoffing reply of the fierce Dame Alison, in whom the events of the day had kindled the keenest excitement. "I hold my house of the queen of Scotland, and will yield it to no Englishman,—least of all to a popinjay squire like thee."

"I am Sir Ralf Vane, madam, a captain of demi-lances, and ere now have had a château yielded to me by a marshal of France."

"The more fool he," she replied; while Roger of Westmains, sent a bullet close to Vane's right ear.

"Surrender to thee, indeed!" he exclaimed; "thou loon and heretic tyke, I would as soon think of ploughing up the devil's croft."

A cannon was now brought up; a single shot blew the gate open; then the tower was given to the flames; and as none were allowed to come forth by the doors, and the windows were (as we may still see them) grated with iron, all within perished miserably.

"The house was set on fire," saith Master Patten complaisantly in his seventy-fourth page; "and for their good-will all were burnt or smothered within." So Lady Alison died by the same dreadful death, which, but a few days before, she had devised for the Hamiltons of Preston.

Roger of Westmains, many other old men, and the wives of all her tenants perished with her: but, as already mentioned, the spirit of this stern woman is still said to haunt the ruined tower on each anniversary of that day of cattle and disaster, the Black Saturday of 1547.

CHAPTER XLIX
THE FLIGHT

The deeds of our sires if our bards should rehearse,
Let a blush or a blow be the meed of their verse;
Be mute every string, and be hush'd every tone,
That shall bid us remember the fame that has flown.

Scott.

Such was this disastrous defeat on the 10th September; a defeat which though less fatal than Flodden to a class whom Scotland well could spare — her noble families — was severely felt by the commons; for among the fourteen thousand dead, who lay on the field of Pinkey, were no less than two thousand lesser barons and landed gentlemen.

The aspect of the plain next day, as the sun arose, was terrible, when Master Posset and a few other good Samaritans, undeterred by the dread of English plunderers and camp-followers, attempted the herculean task of attending to the wants of the wounded and dying.

Great numbers of the English wounded had been borne to Pinkey House, a fine old mansion of the Abbots of Dunfermline, which stands near the field, embosomed among aged chestnuts and sycamores, above which its round turrets and steep roofs still attract the eye of the passer; and in one of its chambers, a place well suited to gloom and spectral horrors, the blood of the wounded English could be traced until effaced by some recent repairs.

Flowing from amid its coppiced banks towards the sea, the Esk lay gleaming in the golden sunrise, but crimsoned still with the gashed corpse of many an armed man, lying in its current, among the rocks, the weeds, and sedges — the bread-winner of many a little brood, — the pride and care of many a tender mother: for in its flood the fugitive Scots perished by whole companies. The shock and din of the battle, with the confused murmur of the flight that whilom sounded like a sea chafing, or a multitude cheering at a vast distance, had now died away, and under the rising sun the dewy landscape, from which the morning mists were rising, lay placid, still, and calm. The green clench of Pinkey in which the carnage had deepened most, the far extent of stubble fields upon the upland slope over which the iron squadrons of Gamboa's Spaniards and the demi-lancers of Vane and Fitzwalter had swept yesterday, were silent and voiceless as the roofless, windowless, black, and gaping ruins of the old tower of Fawside on the hill; and where yesterday more than fifty thousand gallant Britons had closed in the shock of battle, all was mournfully still and deserted now.

On the pale upturned faces and glazed eyes of the dead, and the distorted features of the dying, shone the level glory of the autumn sun as he came up in his morning splendour from the German Sea. On that field, planted thick with arrows, furrowed by iron shot, and trodden by charging squadrons, strewed by so many dead bodies, and covered still with broken arms, crushed helmets, pikes, and torn banners, so thickly that it seemed as if the clouds had rained them down, the merry mavis and the laverock were twittering and singing, as before they had sung and twittered among the yellow summer corn; but now the black gled and obscene raven were wheeling in low circles, or alighting where so many troopers and their steeds were lying dead in the muddy ditch, or in the scroggy cleuch, where more than one abandoned Scottish cannon lay with wheels broken, and the corpses of the gunners piled around it.

From under the dewy grass myriads of insects came forth to batten in those horrid purple pools, that lay where human hands and human bravery had formed the greatest heaps of slain; and all this carnage, which shed a horror over that lovely autumn landscape, was to gratify, as we have said elsewhere, the mad ambition, and to fulfil the dying bequest, of one who had already gone to his terrible account—Henry VIII. of England.

In the distance rose the smoke and flames of Leith and its shipping; and at various parts of the horizon there towered into the blue sky tall columns of dusky vapour, that indicated where the work of rapine was still proceeding; while a cloud of the same sombre nature, like a funeral pall, shrouded all the ancient capital—a pall, however, streaked with sudden and incessant fire, as the castle of Edinburgh was vigorously defended by Sir James Hamilton of Stainhouse, whose cannon completely repulsed the enemy.

When the latter retreated, a week after the battle, they found most of the dead lying still unburied. A few had been hastily covered up by sods in the churchyards of Tranent and St. Michael at Inveresk; and beside these uncouth graves the poor people "had set up," says Master Patten, "a stick with a clout, a rag, an old shoe, or some other mark thereon," by which the body within might be known, when more leisure came for the rites of sepulture on the retirement of the English from Scotland.

But to return to our hero.

On beholding the total rout of the army, he became heedless of all that might ensue; and having now nothing that he cared to live for, his first thought had been to seek death amid the masses of the pursuing host; and hence the vigour and fury of the three desperate charges, by which he was enabled for a time to repel the soldiers of Don Pedro, of the Lord Fitzwalter, and of Sir Ralf Vane, and to cover the retreat of Arran; nor was it until this was fully accomplished that he perceived that, in this fortunate movement, he had put himself at the head of the vassals of his enemy, Hamilton of Preston. As the latter was nowhere visible, he was supposed to have perished on the field or in the river. The order of Arran to attend to the safety of Mary of Lorraine and her daughter, gave a new turn to the desperate thoughts of Florence, and made him remember that, in the fulfilment of his duty to the queen and country, he still had something which made existence valuable; though the loss of Madeline, of whom for days before the battle he could discover no trace,—the miserable fate of his mother, who, with all her stern peculiarities and bitter prejudices, had loved him well,—the destruction of his ancestral home and all his household, together with the shame and slaughter of that disastrous day, filled him with mingled horror, rage, and despair.

Swept away by a tide of fugitives, horse and foot, pikemen, archers, and men-at-arms, he crossed the Esk near the Red Craigs, leaping his horse in at a place where the stream was deepest, and then forcing it up the opposite bank, he escaped, though the Earl of Glencairn, Findlay Mhor Farquharson of Invercauld, who bore the royal standard, and several others who accompanied him, perished under the shot of a few German arquebusiers and Kendal archers who lined the river's eastern bank, and nestled in security among the thick furze, beech, and hazel trees, that covered it. After this he found himself almost alone, and rode slowly to breathe his horse, which, like himself, had fortunately escaped without a wound. Occasionally there crossed his path or fled before him a fugitive foot-soldier, making off by the nearest way towards his own home or locality, but denuded of helmet, corslet, arms, and all that might impede his flight; for in their mad panic the Scots cast aside everything, and fell the readier victims in the pursuit.

To conduct the queen-mother and little queen from Edinburgh, he required an escort; and among these fugitives an efficient one could scarcely be formed. The royal guard were all with the army; their captain had been slain; and, like the army itself, his force had doubtless been dissipated and disorganized.

Florence conceived he might obtain a few good men-at-arms from the castles of Craigmillar, Dalkeith, or any other baronial fortress, for the queen's service, and ride with them at once to Edinburgh, as there was no time to lose now, and the sun was verging towards the western horizon. Keeping in the wooded hollow through which the Esk winds to the Forth, he was riding towards the Douglas's castle of Dalkeith, when a loud outcry and the report of firearms warned him that some of Gamboa's mounted arquebusiers were on his track, and forced him to spur on at the fullest speed. Their ironical cheers, taunting cries, and occasionally a shot, followed him; but still, while rage filled his heart and made it beat with lightning speed, Florence rode furiously on, intent on obeying the orders of Arran. Closely the pursuers followed him; for after perceiving that his armour and trappings were rich, they became intent on plunder, and, being fleetly mounted on good Spanish horses, they easily kept pace with the utmost speed of the animal he rode. Down through the deep wooded dell, where the south and north Esks unite below the old castle of Dalkeith, and insulate the quaint old town of the same name—through swamp and bog—through copse and den, and up the river's bank by the Thorny-cruick—they followed him close; while others joined in the pursuit from various points—through the leafy oak woods and beautiful haugh of Newbattle Abbey they swept on the spur; still with a boiling heart the Scot rode on, and still the pursuing Spaniards followed; till in a dark, woody, and secluded hollow, through which the Esk flows, after he had totally failed to gain a shelter in the castle of Dalhousie, they shot his horse, and it sank beneath him in the middle of the stream. Fortunately it was shallow there; he scrambled ashore, and sought a refuge in the copsewood; but the Spaniards and the Kendal archers followed him closely; and as the weight and joints of his armour impeded every action, they gained upon him rapidly. He dreaded the clothyard shafts of the Kendal men more than the large leaden bullets of the Spaniards, who levelled their ponderous arquebuses over their horses' heads, and almost invariably shot wide of the mark they aimed at. Still the balls which whistled past him every minute, stripping the bark from the trees, and flattening out like stars as they crashed upon the rocks, added spurs to his speed; while ever and anon, with a whizzing or a humming sound, a feathered English arrow would quiver in the trunk of a tree close by.

Thus his flight and their pursuit was continued through the oak woods of Dryden till he entered the deeper and more sequestered glen, where, between walls of rock, and shrouded in the densest foliage of every kind, the Esk chafes and gurgles over its stony bed beneath that abrupt and precipitous cliff which is crowned by the ancient castle of Hawthornden, then in ruins, as it had been left by the English during Somerset's previous invasion in 1544, but in after years the poetical home of the loyal and gentle Drummond, one of Scotland's sweetest bards.

Perched on the brow of a grey, detached, and stormbeaten mass of limestone, nothing remained then of the old castle but two square towers and the high arched windows of the hall which faced the south. The cliff starts to a vast height above the bed of the stream, and in every cleft of it and of the adjacent rocks where rooting could be found were those hawthorns from which the *den* receives its name growing in wild luxuriance; and there, too, were the pink foxglove and the blue harebells tossing their cups upon the wind. The silver hazel, the feathery ash, and the branching oak fringed all the cliffs around the gorge—a gorge of rock that is undermined, or literally honey-combed, by deep and tortuous caverns, which formed hiding-places for the Scots of Lothian in the wars of other times; and of their shelter, at this desperate crisis, Florence did not hesitate to avail himself, as he knew the locality well. Having eluded his pursuers, whose shouts had now died away, he sought the entrance of one of these subterranean retreats, and having found it immediately under one of the square towers of the old ruin, he dashed through the natural screen of wild briars, hazel, and hawthorn which concealed it, and entering the cavern, threw himself upon its stony floor, breathless, weary, and prostrated in energy and strength.

The time was evening now; and without a horse, without men, money, or adherents, with the whole surrounding country in possession of an army flushed by a sudden and bloody victory, what hope had he of obeying Arran's order, and achieving the safety of the two queens, who might fall into the hands of the conqueror?

He took off his hot helmet, and pressing his hands upon his throbbing temples, closed his eyes and strove to shut out thought, memory, and even the dim twilight that struggled into the damp cavern where he lay, prostrate and weary in body and in spirit.

CHAPTER L
HAWTHORNDEN

The hazel throws his silvery branches down.
There, starting into view, a castled cliff,
Whose roof is lichen'd o'er, purple and green,
O'erhangs thy wandering stream, romantic Esk,
And rears its head among the ancient trees.

These caverns are spacious and circuitous, and occupy the entire rock under the ancient castle; and Scottish antiquaries (a hard and dry, yet credulous race at all times) have been lost in a maze of conjectures concerning their origin and use, as they are in a great part artificial. Tradition avers them to have been a stronghold and place of retreat for the Pictish princes who once held the Lowlands; and they still bear the names of "the gallery," "the guard-room," and "the king's bedchamber;" for in these vaults, according to the Vicar of Tranent, Lothus, who gave his name to Lothian, resided with his queen, Anna, daughter of Aurelius Ambrosius, King of the Britons when Hengist and his Saxons sorely troubled all the isle by their invasion. In one of the caverns is a deep draw-well, beautifully hewn like a vast cylinder through the living rock, where, in the pure cold depth of its water, the reflected stars are sometimes seen at noonday.

The sun was setting now beyond the purple Pentland Hills, and Florence, with the roar of the recent battle yet buzzing in his ears, with sorrow, gloom, and bitterness in his aching heart, crushed in soul and vague in purpose, lay watching the sinking beams through a fissure in the rocks, around which the dark-green ivy, the fragrant wild briar, and the dog-rose grew together.

Far westward spread the lovely landscape, tinted with the ruddy light of eve and with autumnal brown; murmuring over its rocky bed, which occupies the entire space between the wood-crowned cliffs or walls of rock that border in the narrow vale, the Esk flowed ceaselessly on. The dense foliage that covered its banks exhibited all the varying tints of the season; while on the rent and fissured fronts of the opposing bluffs, that start abruptly up like ruined towers or fantastic feudal castles, the western sun poured a warm glow, that faded slowly as his wavering rays shot upward and sank beyond the summits of the Pentlands. Grey lichens, green velvet moss, the purple foxglove, the pink rose of Gueldres, and every species of wild flower peculiar to the lowlands, covered the rugged banks and freestone rocks, through the fissures of which many a tiny rill poured down into the deep and lonely dell to join the Esk upon its passage through a thousand windings, till it joined the sea near Pinkey's corpse-strewn field.

Rock, wood, and water, silence and solitude, broken only by the voices of the birds above and the brawl of the stream below, with the deepening tints of the autumn evening—all that can make a sylvan landscape charm, were there; but these accessories rendered the thoughts of the wanderer more sad and bitter as he surveyed them, for Florence loved his country well, and he had that day seen her banner trodden in the dust. Then he remembered how, two hundred and fifty years before, it was in these same caverns that the valiant Sir Alexander Ramsay of Dalhousie and the Black Knight of Liddesdale, during the memorable and disastrous wars of the earlier Edwards, lurked with a band of young and desperate patriots, and thus were enabled to elude the pursuit of the temporary victors; that from thence they had sallied forth to destroy the Flemings under Guy of Namur, Count of Gueldres, in battle on the Burghmuir; that from thence they issued to storm the castles of Edinburgh and Dunbar, and to perform a hundred other brilliant feats of chivalry.

As these old memories occurred to him, he arose, and thought that, as the darkness was at hand, he might make his way to the capital unseen and on foot; but now, hearing a sound near the cavern mouth, he drew his sword, to be prepared for any emergency.

Steps were heard; the screen of ivy and hawthorn was hastily torn aside; the gleam of the western sky glittered on the polished helmet and cuirass of an armed man, who with difficulty, as if wounded or weary, made several ineffectual efforts to reach the cavern. None but a native of the locality—one at least belonging to Lothian—could know of this place, thought Florence, as he put forth a hand to assist the stranger to clamber in, and found himself confronted by the pale face and snow-white beard of Claude Hamilton of Preston!

They surveyed each other in painful silence for nearly a minute.

The old baron was weary, wan, and by the blood-spots and dints which his armour exhibited, his torn plume, and red sword-handle, had evidently borne his full share in the dangers of that terrible field. He, too, had been pursued by the stragglers of the foe, who were now all mustering among the Scottish tents on Edmondstone Edge, previous to an advance upon the capital, and its seaport. His horse, which had borne him from the conflict, pierced by many arrows, and half disembowelled by a sword-thrust, had sunk under him at the ford near Lasswade; and now he was fain to seek the sheltering caves of Hawthornden, for age and toll had rendered him almost incapable of further exertion. But on recognizing Florence, his cheek crimsoned, and his eyes sparkled with a sudden fury.

"We meet at last," said he, in a voice querulous with age, anger, and weariness;—"meet after I have sought you everywhere, for these ten days past; and now fortunately meet where there are none to see, and none to separate us."

"Alas, sir!" replied Florence, "too well I know what you would say to me."

"Thou whining loon, is it so with thee?" exclaimed the other scornfully; "yes, I would speak of my kinswoman—of Madeline Home, the Countess of Yarrow. What hast thou done with her? Where secluded her if alive—where buried her if dead? How hast thou spirited her away from me? Speak, lest I have thee riven at a horse's tail!"

"What shall I say—what *can* I say?" was the bewildered response of Florence.

"Some say thy mother slew her, Florence Fawside," continued the old man hoarsely, as he grasped the young man's arm, and shook him vehemently in his grief and rage; "others say 'twas *thou——*"

"I—oh horror!"

"I care not which; but vengeance I will have, for the sake of my sister who bore her, and of her father, that true and valiant earl, who, on many a day since Flodden Field, has fought by my side, and who loved me so well. Vengeance, I say, thou accursed son of a wicked beldame—dost hear me?"

"Slay me, Claude Hamilton, if you will—I resist not," replied Florence mournfully. "Weary of life, I sought death in every part of yonder bloody field; but like that fated Jew who mocked his blessed Lord upon the slope of Calvary in the days of old, he fled me everywhere. The arrows rained upon me, harmless as snowflakes; and swords, and spears, and cannon-shot have alike failed to maim me; and I live yet—live without a wounds; but without joy—without desire or hope!"

"What is all this to me—I would speak of my dear kinswoman—my dead sister's only child——"

"Alas! I know nothing, and can say nothing of her."

"Nothing?" continued Hamilton, furiously drawing his dagger; "know ye that stabbed—foully stabbed by the hand of the sacrilegious hag who bore thee, her pure blood has stained the floor of the church of God!"

"The cause of your injurious words procures their pardon. Stabbed! oh, too well know I that, for her blood dyed my hands as I knelt by her side; a dagger was there—a bodkin—my mother—Madeline...." muttered Florence incoherently. "God knows I am every way innocent, sakeless, and free of Madeline's blood—my Madeline, whom I loved with a love akin to worship! You have your dagger, Claude Hamilton—you and I are each the last of our races—strike! add one more item to the gory catalogue of this day's slaughter. Strike!" he added, sinking on one knee; "I care not to leave the last and final blow, with the triumph, if a triumph it is—and the fatal inheritance of our houses—the hatred and the feud, to thee!"

Mad with a fury which rendered him pitiless as a hungry tiger, Hamilton raised the dagger, and it flashed in the twilight which straggled through the ivy screen that closed the cavern-mouth, when his uplifted arm was arrested by the hand of some one behind, and the *Countess of Yarrow*, with the vicar of Tranent, appeared before them, as suddenly as if they had sprung from the floor of rock below.

"Guide me God, and every saint in heaven!" cried the old man, as he dashed his poniard down; "am I going mad? or do I see before me things that are not in existence!"

CHAPTER LI
JOY

Full on this casement shone the wintry moon,
 And threw gules on Madeline's fair breast,
As down she knelt for Heaven's grace and boon;
 Rose-blossoms on her hands together prest.—*Keats.*

It was, indeed, Madeline, and no illusion or shadowy mockery, that stood before them, smiling, and smiling sweetly; looking her own fair self again, but paler, and, it might be, somewhat sickly in aspect; for the skilful nun of Haddington, by her simples and leechcraft, had really cured her; and barely was she able to be moved in a litter, when the sudden advance of the English, and the destruction of the village, the church, and vicarage of Tranent, compelled the vicar with his charge to seek safety in flight. Failing to reach the capital, which was already crowded by thousands of fugitives from all the southern and eastern towns and villages, on that very evening, after wandering from place to place, by a strange coincidence they had taken shelter in the same cavern to which Florence and her uncle had been driven by the force of events, or by the tide of war. Thus rage on one hand, and grief on the other, gave place to mutual explanations, and the details of dangers escaped and toils endured.

"But tell me, Father John," said Florence, "whence came the sound of that passing bell, which on the fatal evening struck such a horror on my heart?"

"It was a mistake of my sacristan."

"Blessed be Heaven that spared her——"

"To life and *you*," interrupted the good old priest, pressing his hand.

Claude Hamilton was about to speak, when the vicar resumed hurriedly, while lifting up his withered hands,—

"Alas, sirs! of a verity this hath been a black Saturday for Scotland!"

"And our monks, with their grey frocks and white banner," added Claude Hamilton bitterly; "what availed its solemn consecration, amid incense and Latin, in the abbey of Dunfermline? By the Black Rood of

Scotland! I saw them lying round it as thick as leaves in autumn, in their shaven crowns and black armour; and small mercy those heretics of England gave them!"

"Our church, which my friend in youth, Dunbar the poet likens to a ship—the holy bark of St. Peter—tossing on a tempestuous sea of Lollardy, will yet ride out the storm; and on the next field where we meet these heretical English, foot to foot and hand to hand, God will make Himself manifest, and defend the right."

"I hope so. Heaven taking all the monks to itself, however, seems a sorry commencement. But I begin to put more faith in stout men-at-arms than in miracles, and more faith in a hackbut than a homily."

"Yet thy kinswoman hath been restored to thee hale and sound," said the vicar reproachfully.

"True, Father John; and for that good deed will I hang in your church a lamp of silver, that shall light its altar till the day of doom, in memory of my gratitude and devotion."

"But tell me of the field—this fatal, gory field,—and how it went," said the politic priest; "and meanwhile let us leave the young laird to make some reparation to the young countess for the sore evil his mother wrought her; so come this way with me, and I will show you how the fires of these destroyers redden all the sky to the westward."

At first Claude Hamilton was unwilling to leave his niece, even for a moment, as she hung affectionately on his breast; but the priest gently separated them, and led him within the caverns to a point from whence, through an orifice or fissure in the limestone rocks, they could see all the valley to the westward lighted by a broad and lurid blaze of light, that wavered, reddened, waned, and sank to rise and glare again, upon the impending cliffs which overhung the river; on its waters, which bore a hundred varying hues; and on all the copsewood and thickets that fringed the sylvan glen. This unwonted blaze came from the princely castle of the Sinclairs of Roslin, which some of Somerset's devastators had sacked and set in flames; and now the conflagration shone far over all the valley of the Esk, like the fated light of the legend, that bodes when death or evil menace the "lordly line of high St. Clair." Many wild animals fled before this startling light. The wolf sent up its wild baying cry from the caverns in the glen; the red-deer and the timid hart fled down the stream, as if the hunter's arrow and the shaggy, brown-eyed dogs were on their trail; and the gled and the mountain-eagle were screaming as they whirled and wheeled in mid air, as if in fury at being scared from their eyry.

Claude Hamilton remembered that but lately he had seen the fire rending and the smoke blackening the walls of his own baronial home: he muttered a fierce malediction; and grasping the dagger which had so recently menaced the life of Florence, he continued to gaze upon the flames, and to listen to the shouts of armed stragglers, who, by the frequent sound of horns, cries, and explosion of arquebuses, seemed to be wandering in the valley of the Esk, exchanging signals or slaying those who fell into their hands. These alarming noises became more frequent, and ultimately seemed to approach the place of his concealment.

Meantime, though left thus together, though their tongues and hearts were laden with inquiries, Florence and the young countess were silent, and full of thoughts which could find but little utterance or coherence; for the course of recent events had been so startling and rapid that both were bewildered.

"You are well—restored—recovered, Madeline!" said the lover in a low and earnest whisper, as he pressed her to his breast, closely and convulsively.

"Restored and recovered by God's grace and the skill of sister Christina of Haddington."

"Heaven bless her, Madeline! My mother—what shall I say of my mother!"

"Speak not of her now," said the countess in a low and agitated voice; "I would not pain your heart for worlds."

"She wronged you deeply—cruelly, dearest! But this day—God rest her soul!—she died a horrible death."

"Died—did you say she died?"

"Amid the flames of our tower, which the English attacked and burned, while I was disputing the passage of the Esk at the head of a few horsemen; but she defended her house, by bow, pike, and arquebuse, to the last, and died as she had lived, unflinching, resolute, and unyielding,—died, as roof and rafter, cope and turret, went surging down into the sea of fire below. Oh, it was an awful end! All her animosities, her hate, her mistakes, and her faults, have passed away; so let us think of them no more. But the slaughter of to day, the treason of our peers, and dispersion of the army, have plunged the land in danger and dishonour, the end of which I cannot foresee! A thousand times to-night I have said—would that I were dead!"

"Florence," said the countess softly, taking his hand in hers, "at this miserable time, do not let us exaggerate our sorrows. Let us rather bear up together against our misfortunes. All hope is not dead for us. Something yet remains, for Mary of Lorraine is my friend, and hope whispers to me that we shall both be happy yet."

"Together, Madeline?"

"Together."

"And you my wife?"

She did not reply, but returned gently the pressure of his hand, and then tenderly passed hers over his tearful and bloodshot eyes.

"Bless you, Madeline, for that assurance and the hope it gives me: but your kinsman, Claude— —"

"Remember only that I love you, Florence—for I do love you, dearly."

"These words should lighten everything. When you are near me I no longer seem to suffer aught from recollection of the past, or dread of the future. Even this dark, dank cavern becomes bright and beautiful!"

Madeline smiled, for he could see her eyes sparkle, and her teeth glitter like two rows of pearl in the twilight.

"You smile now, dear and merry one, even in this place, and after such a day of woe."

"The joy of being restored to you counterbalances every evil," she whispered in his ear.

"Mine own sweetheart! Then think of the time when I shall be always with you, and when we shall never be parted again."

There was a tender and mute embrace, which was suddenly interrupted by a sound of alarm.

"Hark—what is that?" exclaimed Madeline starting back.

"The explosion of an arquebuse— —"

"And voices— —"

"Quite near us, too—be still—we are beset!"

"To your sword, Fawside," cried Claude Hamilton, coming hastily forward; "some of these pestilent English stragglers are close by. Remove the countess—Father John, lead her within, and leave the young laird and me to make what service we may, and to keep the mouth of this dark hole while life and blood and steel remain to us."

Madeline was led away, while Florence and the old knight of Preston, with their swords drawn, crept close to the mouth of the cavern, from whence, as the moon was now up, a clear, broad, and yellow one, for the season was harvest, they could distinctly sec the coming danger. Several of the enemy's pillagers had been passing near, and had too evidently heard the sound of voices in these caverns, the echoes of which repeat each other with many reverberations.

CHAPTER LII
PEDRO DE GAMBOA

The rascal who would not give cut and thrust for his country, as long as he had a breath to draw or a leg to stand on, should be tied neck and heels, without benefit of clergy, and thrown over Leith pier, to swim for his life like a mangy dog.—*Mansie Wauch.*

On looking through the screen of leaves which partially shrouded the mouth or entrance of their remarkable hiding-place, they saw the moonlight reflected from, the conical helmets, the globular cuirasses, and long polished gun-barrels of some ten or twelve arquebusiers, whom, by their black beards, swarthy countenances, and strange language, they knew to belong to Gamboa's Spanish band; and, indeed, that formidable Don himself, in a suit of black armour, profusely engraved with gold, spurred his horse rapidly after them from the river-side, and ascended the steep path that led to the ruined castle on the limestone cliff. With this party were a few green-doubleted English archers and billmen, who had with them several horses, linked together by halters; and these were laden with all kinds of trappings and household goods, too evidently the plunder of the village and castle of Roslin, the flames of which were now beginning to waver and sink. In short, this was evidently a party of foragers or devastators, who were returning to Edmondstone Edge, where the main body of Somerset's army were now encamped, and where his soldiers were making merry among the Scottish tents; but having, as I have said, heard voices in the echoing cave, or having discovered by means of a hound which accompanied them, that some unfortunate fugitives were concealed thereabout, the yet unsated lust of blood, or hope of plunder, made the Spaniards resolve to have them discovered, and killed or taken.

As they warily drew near, with the matches of their arquebuses burning, and in every half-drawn bow an arrow-pointed, Florence remembered the future safety of Madeline, the unobeyed orders of Arran; and the hopelessness of achieving either filled his heart again with sickness.

Perceiving nothing but the ivied face of the rock, and hearing no sound, the Spaniards uttered a shout, and came more hastily up the narrow path;

then, most unhappily, Madeline, being unable to repress her alarm, uttered an exclamation, which, however low, reached the ears of Gamboa.

"*Voto á tal!*" he exclaimed; "there are women here—one, at least, and I shall watch her as Argus did Io, that is, if she proves as handsome."

"It may be a spirit guarding buried treasure," suggested one of his soldiers, shrinking back.

"And which dost thou shrink from, Gil Alvarez, the spirit or the treasure?" asked his leader. "I have heard of such things in Germany, and, by my beard and beads! this old place looketh like many a castle we have seen upon the Rhine and in the Schwarzwald. Push on, *hombres!* Diavolo! here are men-at-arms afraid of a few ivy-leaves!"

There was another shout from the Spaniards, and he who was named Gil Alvarez made a rush into the gloom that lay beyond the screen of ivy and wild roses; but he found himself encountered by unseen enemies, for at the same moment that Claude Hamilton wrenched away his arquebuse, Florence tore off his collar of bandoleers, and bestowed a sword-thrust into his open mouth, hurling him back, bleeding and senseless, upon his comrades below.

This was an immediate signal for a general assault.

Whiz came the long arrows, to shiver and splinter on the walls of rock; and with the flash of the arquebuses came their leaden bullets, to crash and flatten on the same place; and then both the English and Spaniards withdrew behind some masses of the fallen walls and the trunks of trees, to consider the best means of assailing those hidden defenders, of whose number and power they were ignorant.

"There are twenty charges of powder in the bandoleer," said Claude Hamilton, counting them in the dark, "and there are not above twenty of those cut-throats opposed to us. Your eye is keener, Fawside, and your hand more sure, than mine; take the arquebuse, and pick me off these fellows as fast as they show themselves. Two men to man this cavern-mouth are as good as a hundred; let us fight bravely, lad, for we know not but aid may come anon."

By the glitter of its beams on the polished armour of Gamboa's men, the bright moon showed with fatal distinctness where they nestled among the green hawthorns or behind the heaps of stones which had fallen from the old castle above; thus Florence, when he loaded and levelled by the silvery light without, felt that Madeline's safety, honour, her life perhaps, depended upon the precision of his aim.

He almost trembled as he selected an object; and Claude Hamilton could perceive that his face was pale, even in the usually ruddy light of the match, in which his polished mail seemed to glitter with a lambent glow, as his eye glared along the barrel. He fired; and the explosion, which made the cavern echo with seeming thunder, was followed by a cry of agony, and then an armed man was seen rolling down the slope towards the Esk.

"To thine arquebuse again, lad!" said Hamilton, sternly but cheerily, and with grim satisfaction; "thou hast given one of these tawny loons a shot in his stomach, and a weighty one, too; I warrant they go four, at least, to the Lanark pound. Couldst notch the helmet of that pernicious heretic Pedro Gamboa, think you? By St. Andrew! were he within reach of *my* hand I could spelder him by one stroke of my axe, yea, spelder him as I would a haddock!" he added, as another volley of shot and arrows whizzed and rattled on the rocks around them.

A second bullet from the arquebuse of Florence, followed by the cry of—

"Holy Virgin, I am a dead man!" announced that this time an English billman had fallen; and with a yell of rage his comrades rushed forward to storm the retreat of these hidden enemies. While Florence reloaded and blew the match of his arquebuse, Claude Hamilton with his two-handed sword manned the cavern mouth, and being on firm vantage ground (while the assailants required all their hands. feet, and energy, to clamber upward), he cut down three of them in succession with ease, and by a single thrust tossed a fourth nearly ten yards into the woody hollow below. In a minute more two others hac fallen, killed or wounded, under the deadly aim of Florence.

"How stands your bandoleer?" asked the laird of Preston, resting on his long sword.

"I have shots enough for them all at this rate."

"Good—by the black rood of Scotland, good! We'll beat them yet; level low and true—we fight for our lives!"

"Oh, laird of Preston," exclaimed Florence, in a voice to which emotion lent a chord that was soft and musical; "even in this hour of terror hear me. I fight only for Madeline, and for the love I bear her—a love beyond the grave—see that she is in safety."

"Thanks, my ancient enemy—may Heaven nerve your eye and hand!"

Florence fired again, and while the deep vaults and the rocky glen rang with a thousand echoes, a Spaniard fell, and was seen tossing his arms in the moonlight, as he shrieked on "the Holy of Holies" (el Santo de los Santos) to have pity upon him. On beholding the slaughter of his men, Gamboa uttered a dreadful oath in Spanish.

"Let us smoke forth these Scots!" he exclaimed.

"How, *smoke* them say you?" asked an Englishman, who proved to be no other than Master Patten, the future historian of the expedition, who rode up at that moment.

"Exactly," rejoined the Spaniard, who spoke the English language with great fluency: "many a brood of yellow Indians I have smoked out of their holes in Hispaniola and Tortuga. You know nothing of life in Cuba—but I do. There I have often roasted thirteen Indian devils alive on a Good Friday, in honour of our blessed Lord and the twelve Apostles. God smite ye, fellows! cut brushwood—bring fire—fill the cavern-mouth, and burn them as we would castanos in their shells."

This proposition, which made the blood of Florence run cold, was received with a loud hurrah, and relinquishing their arquebuses, the Spaniards drew their short swords, and together with the English billmen, proceeded to form piles and bundles of wood, by uprooting shrubs and bushes—cutting down small trees, and tearing branches from firs and beeches; and now, from the ruins of the old castle above (a place where they were secure from the arquebuse of Florence), they began to throw down vast heaps of this hastily-gathered fuel, together with an entire stack of straw, which they found near; and as these combustibles accumulated about the cavern-mouth, and gradually covered it up, excluding the moonlight and the external air, the imminence of their danger could no longer be concealed from the countess and the vicar; and to save them at least from so horrible a death, Florence proposed that a capitulation should be asked for.

"To capitulate is to be destroyed!" exclaimed Hamilton fiercely; "what hope of quarter have we from mercenaries like these?"

"To remain here is also to be destroyed, and by a death too dreadful for contemplation—suffocation in a dark pit," replied Florence, pressing Madeline to his breast closely and tenderly.

"Bring hither a lighted match; but, by the Holy of Holies," they heard the superstitious Don Pedro exclaiming; "I am loath to smother a woman at the close of a day of victory—a woman whose name may be *Mary*, too!"

"What matters it, whether her name be Mary or Maud—Giles or Joan?" asked Master Patten, staring in wonder through the bars of his helmet, and laughing the while.

"It matters much to me, Señor Inglese, for I was reared in Old Castile, and on the banks of the Ebro, where my mother taught me it was a sin to make love on a Friday, or to kiss a woman whose name was Mary on a day of fasting; for though I serve King Edward's banner, and fight against the Scots, I am nevertheless, thank Heaven! a good Catholic and a true Castilian, without the taint of Jew, infidel, or Morisco in my blood."

On hearing this, just as fire from a gunmatch was about to be put into the vast pile of fuel, over which the arquebusiers had sprinkled powder from their priming-flasks, the Vicar of Tranent rushed to the entrance of the grotto, and tearing aside the screen of ivy with one hand, waved a white handkerchief with the other, exclaiming, —

"*Gloria tibi, Domine!* we shall be saved! I am a priest, sir Spaniard, and in the name of our holy Church and of Him I serve, command you to spare me, and those who are with me!" A shout of derision from Patten's men was the sole reply to this.

"Command, quotha—what manner of ware have we here?" said one mockingly.

"A priest and a woman in that dark hole! holy father how farest thou?" said a second.

"By St. George, 'tis a rare one to eschew the world, the flesh, and the devil!" added a third.

"Shoot, shoot! Cogsbones—'twas no priest's hand that slew the best lad in Kendal," exclaimed Patten, "or handled his arquebuse like one of our men at Finsbury!" Two archers drew each an arrow to their heads; but Pedro de Gamboa interposed his drawn sword before them, exclaiming:

"Hold—hold, sirs. I will have naught to do with priests. I have seen enough in my time to prove that Heaven always avenges a sacrilege."

"What!" asked Patten; "hast any qualms about killing a scurvy shaveling—a Scot, too? Don Spaniard, you should have smelled the fires o' Smithfield in old King Harry's time. Go to! we are not now either in Old Castile or on the banks of the Ebro."

"Silence, Englishman!" replied the Spaniard gravely; "for though your land hath become as a land of heathens, and, to my sorrow, I serve it, I am a good Catholic, yet one, it may be, who is in the habit of swearing more by the saints than of praying to them. I am a soldier of fortune, yet I war not on priests or women, but simply on such as come armed against me; and 'tis the memory of *what I was* in Old Castile and on the banks of the Ebro that in an hour like this prevents me from slaying a priest of that Church in the faith of which my mother reared me. For one act of sacrilege and blasphemy I have seen nearly the whole population of a city perish in an hour."

"Fore George, this *must* have been in Old Castile!" said Patten, in a jibing tone.

"It was *not*," replied the Spaniard angrily, while his dark eyes flashed under the peak of his helmet. "But darest thou gibe me, Englishman—I, who have fought by the side of Cortes in Mexico, and by the order of Pizzaro slew Diego Almagro—I, who served with Velasquez in distant climes that are far away, in the lands of gold and silver, snow and fire, where the boasted red cross of your country has never yet been seen by sea or shore; but there I have seen that which this night forbids me to commit a sacrilege!"

In Spanish, he now commanded his soldiers to remove the pile of brushwood and straw that lay before the cavern-mouth; and while they obeyed with alacrity, he again turned sternly to Master Patten, and said,—

"Listen! In 1534 I was at San Iago de Guatemala, in old Mexico, and resided with a noble Spanish gentlewoman of the city, named Doña Maria de Castilia, or of Castile, for she came, like myself, from the sunny banks of the Ebro. In one week her husband was slain in battle and her children were destroyed by the Mexican savages from Petapa. Driven to frenzy by the loss of all she loved, she smote a priest who attempted to console her, and in his presence blasphemed Heaven, exclaiming, while she rent her garments,—

"'El Espiritu Santo, what more can it do to me now than has been done, save take away a miserable life which I regard not!'

"As she spoke, there was heard a dreadful rushing sound. For a time we knew not whether it came from heaven above or the earth beneath us; but anon there came also shouts of terror from a thousand tongues, and lo! from the old volcano, a mountain nine miles in height, which overhangs the city, there burst a mighty flood of water, which drowned this impious woman and many hundreds of the people, while streets and churches were alike overturned and swept away. A few persons escaped: among them I, by the speed of my horse: but the ruins of La Cividad Vieja still remain to attest how sacrilege may be punished. And now, as I vowed to perform at least one deed of charity to-day, if I escaped the battle scathless, I release this priest and those who are with him. Come forth, good father, and fear not; I pledge my word for your safety—I, Don Pedro de Gamboa."

The lofty air and determined manner of the Spaniard, together with the knowledge that his veterans were the more numerous and better-armed party, awed Master Patten and his petulant archers into silent acquiescence; and the old vicar, leading the countess by the hand, stepped forth into the moonlight, followed by Florence and Claude Hamilton.

"Is this your whole party, señor padre?" asked the Spanish captain, with a courteous salute.

"All; and in the name of Him I serve and the Church you still venerate, I crave their liberty with me."

"It is granted."

"*Deo gratias*, sir Spaniard."

"I am too good a Castilian, *padre mio*, to refuse aught to a priest or to a lady; and as neither you nor she can travel hence afoot, I give you here two of our captured nags. Go, reverend sir, and God speed you! If, between the night and morning, you can find time to say an Ave or Credo for one who has long since forgotten how to pray for himself, insert in your prayer the name of Pedro de Gamboa, the poor soldier of fortune. Adieu!"

In five minutes after this fortunate and sudden release our friends found themselves alone, and pursuing, by the most sequestered paths, as rapidly as possible, and lighted by the clear and brilliant moon, the way to Edinburgh; while the cavalier, with his party of arquebusiers and bowmen, with their train of horses and plunder, proceeded to Somerset's new halting-place on Edmondstone Edge.

The vicar and the countess were mounted; and on each side of the horse ridden by the latter, Florence and Claude Hamilton walked on foot as hastily as their iron trappings would permit them.

CHAPTER LIII
THE GUISE PALACE

Oh, these bright days are past,
  And their joys are buried deep;
Sweet flowers that couldna last,
  They've gane with those we weep.
The world is now grown cold,
  And the mirth and love and glee,
That wont to cheer of old,
  We never mair can see.—*Anon.*

In the pure splendour of that brilliant moon, when every herb and leaf were gemmed with glittering dew—when the heaven above was all one azure vault of stars, and the distant landscape mellowed far away in silence and placidity—when a silver haze rose from every hollow—and when, save their own voices, no sound came to the ears of the countess and her three companions, it was difficult for them to realize—the actual amount of danger through which they had passed—that they were now free; and none who surveyed that quiet moonlight scene, or the blue and star-studded sky over head, could have imagined that more than fourteen thousand men, who when the sun rose had been in all the prime of life and vigour, were now lying, within a few miles' compass, as cold and pale as death could make them.

Seeking the most secluded paths, the little party proceeded with all speed towards Edinburgh, passing the ancient grange of Gilmerton, through the deep and sylvan dell of the Staine-house, over the hills of Braid, and past the cell of St. Martin, which had been sacked, ruined, and stained by the blood of its poor hermit, who was slain by the English. From thence, after traversing the Burghmuir undisturbed and unquestioned, they entered the city by the porte at the Kirk-of-field Wynd. There the gate was open; no guard or warder was there now. The town-house of the Regent Arran, which stood in this steep, ancient, and narrow street (now known as the College Wynd), was deserted and dark; but as they proceeded further into the city, the effects of that day's defeat became everywhere painfully apparent. The bells in the numerous churches, oratories, and monasteries, were being tolled mournfully; and at every altar were people praying for the dead. The streets were thronged by crowds, principally of women, who wept and wailed as they bore forth their children and most valuable goods and chattels by the light of cressets, links, and torches, that sputtered in the night-wind and flared on the reddened eyes and pale affrighted faces of the multitude, as from the archways of the quaint narrow alleys and wynds of that old "romantic town" they took their way towards the west, to the Pentland hills, to the sea-shore, or anywhere to escape the victorious foe, as all despaired of defending a city the flower of whose men had fallen in that day's disastrous battle.

In answer to the anxious inquiries of Florence, as to whether the queen-mother had quitted the city, and if so for where, none could inform them; but on reaching the Guise Palace, as the citizens named the little mansion and oratory of Mary of Lorraine on the north side of the Castle Hill, they found a number of well-armed horsemen arrayed in the street, with swords drawn, and bearing lighted torches; while a train of horses, some of which were saddled, others laden with trunks, mails, and bales of such valuables as the queen-mother and the ladies of her suite wished to preserve, were held by grooms and lackeys in the royal livery. Among them was a powerful Clydesdale nag, which was led by a groom, and had securely strapped to its back a curtained horse-litter, which, as it was surmounted by a royal crown, was evidently destined for the little queen of Scotland.

The present was no time for ceremony, and as Mary of Lorraine stood under the royal canopy in her presence-chamber, hooded, cloaked, and ready for her journey to the north or west, according to the recommendation of those about her, the Countess of Yarrow and those who accompanied her were at once introduced. Mary of Lorraine folded Madeline in her arms and kissed her on both cheeks with great emotion, receiving her as one restored from the dead; for she had heard of the terrible episode in the church of Tranent—of her mysterious disappearance; and she loved the young countess as a sister.

The beautiful widow of James V. was pale, but calm, firm, and collected. In the chamber were many of her ladies—Helen Countess of Argyle, Elizabeth Countess of Athole, and others, all prepared for the road in their riding-dresses; and there, also, were several of the noblesse, whose dinted and blood-stained harness or bandaged visages afforded an index how they had maintained themselves in the lost battle of the past day. Some had lost their scabbards, and still had their notched and discoloured swords in their hands; the blade of one, that of the Lord Aboyne, was so bent that the sheath would not receive it.

"Florence Fawside!" exclaimed the queen with emotion presenting her hand, "M. Fawside and M. Hamilton of Preston! I do rejoice to see you together, and safe, at this most dreadful crisis?"

"You see us together, madam, because the present pressure of evil makes all Scotsmen brothers, or at least comrades," replied Preston coldly and sternly, while he coloured with shame and vexation on being seen thus on quiet terms with one who was well known to be his hereditary foe.

"Have you any tidings of your chief, the lord regent?" she asked.

"Tidings?" reiterated Hamilton with surprise.

"Yes, of this Earl of Arran, of whose utter incapacity to govern a realm or lead an army we have had such fatal proofs to day; through whom, by leaving his strong position, we have lost a battle by defeat which else had been a glorious victory," said the Earl of Mar, with stern vehemence.

"Yea—a fool—a very fool!" added the Lord Aboyne, whose son and heir had perished on the field, and whose sentiments were consequently the more bitter.

"Naught know I of him, but that he was to retreat with the main body of the army towards Stirling," said Hamilton.

"Retreat for thirty miles through a country full of strong military positions!" exclaimed the Earl of Mar with growing indignation.

"And leaving alike the queen and queen-mother behind. Truly well and wisely planned, most sapient regent!" said Mary of Lorraine bitterly.

"On seeing the field was lost," said Florence, "his last orders to *me*, madam, were to get you forth the city and conduct you and your royal daughter to a place of greater safety."

"I know not in whom to believe, M. Fawside," said the queen mournfully; "or to whom to turn."

"Ah, turn to me, madam," said the young man, with a glance of honest confidence and enthusiasm, as some of the ever-watchful courtiers withdrew a little space to confer among themselves; "my counsel may be feeble, it may even be unwise; but my sword is ever ready, my heart steadfast and true."

"But a queen—especially a young queen (I am only thirty-two)," she added with a charming French smile, "is always surrounded by so many flatterers!"

Poor Florence now coloured absolutely crimson, for with all his love for Madeline he felt how seductive and dangerous was this intimacy and familiarity with Mary of Lorraine. The latter saw the triumph of her beauty, felt its power and smiled again; for amid all her domestic and political troubles, she was too much of a Frenchwoman and a Guise not to find a pleasure and consolation in this.

"Ah, monsieur," she added, "do you love your little queen?"

"I love her, madam, as becomes a Scottish gentleman and faithful subject,—as the daughter of that good King James for whom my father drew his sword at Falamuir, at Ancrumford, and Solway Moss!"

"She is yet a child—alas!——"

"A child in whose person are embodied all the destinies of Scotland, past, present, and future; yea, and it may be the future destiny of Britain itself!" said the Earl of Mar without knowing how truly he spoke.

"Be it so," replied the queen, "fair sirs—look here!"

She drew back the arras, and there within a carved oak cradle, which stood within a recess, and the canopy of which was surmounted by a royal crown, lay the little queen of Scots asleep, with a white kitten in her arms, and Janet Sinclair, her nurse, seated on a tabourette close by. The white-haired Earl of Mar raised higher the visor of his helmet, and knelt down to kiss her tiny dimpled hands.

Then the tears sparkled in the eyes of Mary of Lorraine, as she saw so many brave lords and gentlemen in their blood-spotted armour, fresh from the terrors of that lost battle, follow the example of the noble chief of the Erskines. She placed her beautiful hand caressingly on the old earl's shoulder, and said,—

"Thou good and faithful Mar! to thee her father turned his eyes, ere he died at Falkland, when around him were Scotland's bravest and most true, men whose advice had been faithful to him in council, and whose swords had never failed him in peril, for in good sooth, Mar, he loved thine old face well."

"Madam," said Claude Hamilton impatiently, "if indeed your grace is to ride for Stirling, the sooner we set forth the better; for the morning wears apace and dawn draws nigh. The English will ere long break up from their camp at Edmondstone Edge, and advance on the city. Methinks I hear the sound of their artillery already."

"The laird of Preston speaketh wisely, madam; let us to horse, for ladies, litters, and sumpter-nags are a sore hindrance when men have to cut a passage through a stand of pikes," said the laird of Balmuto, a Fifeshire baron, whose suit of black armour was encrusted with blood, and whose eyes were wandering, wild in expression, tearless and bloodshot.

"You are wounded?" said the queen, with deep commiseration.

"Nay, madam, my hands could ever keep my head."

"But this blood?——"

"Is the blood of my enemies, and of—my ain bairns!" he added bitterly.

"Your bairns!"

"Two of my sons gave up their lives on yonder field, the English cannon slew them by my side, upon the bridge of Esk; but blessed be God and their leal mother, I have three mair at hame, to handle their swords when the time comes."

"Heaven may requite this devotion, my brave Balmuto, but Mary of Lorraine never can!" replied the queen, with growing emotion.

"Madam, forth, I say, ere the day break, and we hear the English trumpets in the Nether Bow—forth, and fear not," resumed Claude Hamilton; "fear not, though we have lost the battle. I have this sword, which I drew at Flodden, and my father drew at Sark, and which his sire drew at Vernuiel— 'tis at your service still, and thus can thirty thousand other Scotsmen say, who like me, are ready to peril all for the child and crown of King James the Fifth!"

"To horse, then," said the queen; and giving her hand to the Earl of Mar, she prepared to leave her favourite little palace, and surveyed the apartment sadly as she withdrew.

Florence turned towards the Countess of Yarrow; but with a cold and stern expression in his eye, Claude Hamilton, quick as thought, anticipated him; and presenting his gauntleted hand to his niece and ward, led her from the apartment to the street; and with a sinking heart the young laird of the ruined tower followed them.

Deeming some explanation necessary, while the queen and her train were mounting, Hamilton turned to him, and said in a low but determined tone,—

"Here ends our temporary peace and truce. You scorned my alliance and every reparation to the dead as well as to the living, at a time when, with a full heart and a purpose leal and true, I proffered it; so think not to win my kinswoman's love, for that can never be the prize of one whose kindred shed her pure and sinless blood so wickedly as Dame Alison did, on that terrible night in the church of Tranent. Enough, sir—we now know each other—adieu!"

Florence, chilled by these stern and unexpected words, turned to Father John, who stood near, regarding them both wistfully; but the old priest shook his head with an air of sadness, and drew back, while Madeline held her veil close to conceal the tears that filled her eyes.

CHAPTER LIV
THE DEPARTURE

Woe, woe to ye! ye haughty towers;
　No sound of sweetest strain,
No music, song, nor roundelay
　Shall haunt your halls again;
Naught—naught but sighs and groans,
　And tread of slaves in grim affright,
Till, crush'd in dust and ashes,
　Ye feel the avenger's might!—*Uhland.*

In the pale grey of the morning, when the moon was waning and the stars fading out of the sky, when the cold, heavy shadows lay deep in the high and narrow wynds and alleys of the city, from whose towering mansions so many generations have looked down on scenes of wonder, awe and terror, broil, bloodshed, and disaster, the child-queen of Scotland (still tenaciously grasping her favourite kitten) was placed in her warm litter, and its curtains were carefully drawn. The queen-mother, with the few nobles and ladies of her train, mounted; the lackeys led all the spare and sumpter horses; and with a band of some forty spearmen on horseback, an escort provided by the care of the Earl of Mar, she set forth from Edinburgh.

The streets were still encumbered by crowds of fugitives and terrified people, pale with weeping for the slain and watching in the night. Many surrounded the train of the queen, and strove to keep pace with it, crying for aid, advice, or protection from the coming English.

"Alms—largess—largess!" cried many, while poor women held aloft the babes, whom the strife of yesterday had made fatherless.

"For alms and largess ye shall have the first rents I receive from my lordship of Monteith and my castle of Doune," replied the queen, who was moved to tears by the scenes she saw; but among the dense masses at the city gate were many Reformers, who on seeing her began to shout,—

"Down with the league with France—no French alliance!"

"Woe to the day that Mary of Lorraine brought forth a female bairn!" cried one.

"And that our gude auld Scottish crown fell from the sword to the distaff!" added another.

"Down with the bloody house of Guise! A Hamilton—a Hamilton!"

The poor queen-mother grew deadly pale on hearing these hostile and unexpected shouts from the populace, whose favour has ever been in all ages variable as the wind; but Florence felt his blood boil! He had been reared in a land where gallantry was a science; he had heard Francis I.—the most splendid of European monarchs—declare that a court without ladies was like a spring without flowers; he had stood by his side, bearing the train of Anne of Albany, when Laura's tomb at Avignon was opened, and when flowers and verses were cast upon her bones, as a tribute to her past beauty and to Petrarch's love and muse. The fourth and fifth Jameses were in their graves, and Scotland no longer understood the sentiment of chivalry; but, filled with indignation by the reiterated insults of a lank-haired fellow who followed the queen's train, in a suit of sad-coloured clothes, Florence drew his sword and would have smote him down, when she quickly arrested his hand, and said, with one of her most alluring smiles,—

"I pray you to spare the poor man, and I shall tell you a story. One day some drunken archers of Paris, in my hearing, insulted Catherine de Médicis, and said a hundred bitter and abusive things to her, as she was proceeding on foot under her canopy through the Rue de l'Arbre Sec towards the Louvre. Perceiving my kinsman, the Cardinal de Lorraine, start angrily from her side, she grasped his scarlet cope, saying,—

"'Whither goes your eminence?'

"'To see those poltroons hanged without delay!'

"'Nay, nay,' said she, 'not so; let them alone. I will this day show to after-ages that, in the same person, a woman, a queen, and an Italian, controlled both pride and passion.' If the terrible Catherine could do this, why not may I, who have ever been deemed so tender and gentle?"

"Most true, madam," replied Florence, bowing low as he sheathed his sword; "your wish is law to me."

Her train left Edinburgh by the Lower Bow Porte, on the parapet of which was a bare white skull, that seemed to grin mockingly at the turmoil and terror of those who crowded the steep and winding street below. Mary shuddered as she saw it, for this poor relic of mortality was the head of the terrible "Bastard of Arran," Sir James Hamilton of Finnard, whilom captain of Linlithgow, royal cup-bearer, and grand inquisitor of Scotland, executed for treason against James V.; and all who passed the old arch beneath were wont to sign the cross, for it was alleged that this head, after it was cut off, had thrice cried *"Jesus Christus"* as it rolled about the scaffold, and that no blood came from it; moreover, on the day it was first spiked, a certain honest farmer, the gudeman of St. Giles's Grange, when passing under the gate with a cartload of turnips to market, beheld them all turn into human heads, which winked and grinned at him for the full space of three minutes.

As the royal train issued forth upon the western road that led to Stirling, the sun arose in his ruddy splendour and shed a blaze of yellow light across the eastern quarter of the sky; and against this glow Edinburgh uprose, with its castles, towers, and spires, its hills and mass of roofs, its strange piles of gables and chimneys, in outline, strongly and darkly defined. Then the blue flag, with the white cross of St. Andrew, was seen to wave upon the summit of King David's keep; and the flash and boom of a culverin from the rampart below it, as the light smoke floated away on the soft breeze of the early morning, announced that the governor of the castle, Hamilton of Stainhouse, had fired the first gun at the approaching foe.

A wail arose from the city beneath; for that hostile sound also announced that the English, with sword and torch, flushed by victory and fired by the spirits of rancour and devastation, were at hand; but the queen and her train, warned by it of coming danger, added spurs to their speed, as they galloped past the long shallow loch, the ancient church, the rocky hills, and reedy marshes of Corstorphine.

CHAPTER LV
SEQUEL TO THE INVASION

Ayliffe. —'Tis bold—'tis very bold!
Restalrig. —　　　I tell you, sir,
　　　There be more Arrans and more Lennoxes
　　　On Scottish ground than you in England wot of.
　　　　　　Earl Gowrie—A Tragedy.

Four days after the battle, *i.e.*, the 14th of September, Holyrood Day, or the Festival of the Exaltation of the Cross, a time when children were wont of old to commence nutting in the woods, the town of Stirling, the great abbey of Cambus Kenneth, and all the strongholds in their vicinity, were crowded with fugitives; and masses of retreating soldiers occupied all the passages, fords, and roads towards the north. Mary of Lorraine, with her suite, and the Regent Arran, attended by many officers of state and barons of his house held a solemn and somewhat bitter council, to deliberate on the future, in that vaulted chamber of the castle of Stirling wherein, a hundred and eighteen years before, Queen Jane had brought James II. into the world, and in which the traitor Walter, son of Murdoch Duke of Albany, passed his last night on earth, the 18th of May, 1426. On this day many met who deemed each other had perished on the field.

Hither came the Lord Kilmaurs, now fifth Earl of Glencairn, wearing a black scarf over his armour as mourning for his father's fall; hither came also the regent's brother, John Abbot of Paisley, lord high treasurer; William Commendator of Culross, the comptroller of Scotland; and David Panater, the classic bishop of Ross, who was still secretary of state; Lord Errol, the high constable; the Earls of Cassilis, Mar, and many others, including the lairds of Fawside and Preston.

Arran was pale, and his eye was red and feverish. He still wore the suit of hacked and dinted mail, which he had never put off since the day on which he fought the fatal battle. It had lost all its brilliance; and he was now without his splendid orders of St. Andrew, St. Michael, and the Golden Fleece, all of which he had lost in that dreadful *mêlée* when his main body closed with the English under the Earl of Warwick.

"Taunt me not, my lords," said he bitterly, in reply to the angry remarks of some who were present; "I feel too keenly my own position and this crisis of the national affairs. Alas!" he added, striking his gauntleted hand on the oak table, "I can never more hold up my crest in Scotland; and it is a crest, sirs, that has never yet stooped, even to those kings with whom we have been allied."

"Say not so, my lord," said the gentle Mary of Lorraine, on whom the countesses of Yarrow, Huntly, Mar, and Athole were in attendance, and who felt a sympathy for the somewhat unmerited shame that stung the proud heart of Arran; "do not blame yourself for having fought this field of Pinkey."

"I do not blame myself for having fought, but for having lost it, madam."

"After this admission, my lord, even your enemies can have nothing more to urge."

"Nay," said the fierce young Earl of Glencairn, while his eyes shot a baleful gleam, "lay the blame on those hireling Germans of Pieter Mewtas and those heretical Spaniards, whose graves I hope to dig in some deep glen between the Torwood and the Tweed. What availed our old-fashioned battle-axes, our mauls and maces, spears and bows, against gunpowder and the close-volleyed shot of culverins and arquebuses?"

"The English are loitering in Lothian still," observed the Earl of Cassilis, "and the dead are yet unburied on the field."

"Woe is me!" added the abbot of Paisley, who fought there among the band of monks, "how close and thick the slain were lying!"

"Yea, my lord abbot; Duke Somerset's plunderers may win a bushel of golden spurs for the Lombard Jews in London, if they choose to glean among the dead men's heels—my brave father's among the rest," said Glencairn; "for, shot dead by a Spanish arquebuse, he fell by my side, when together we attempted to ford the water of the Esk."

"But *you* escaped, my Lord Kilmaurs," said Arran significantly; for he knew well the secret treason of the father and son, and cordially hated them both.

"Escaped by favour of the patron saint of Scotland," added the abbot of Paisley, to soften the taunt of which he dreaded the result.

"Escaped by favour of a sharp sword and fleet horse," rejoined Glencairn sourly; "for I may assure ye, sirs, that the patron saint of Scotland seemed to have other business on hand than attending to any of us on that day—my unworthy self in particular."

"Or it might be that the smoke of the gunpowder bewildered him, as it did his grace the regent," was the taunting surmise of Cassilis.

"And now, my brave Fawside," said Arran, turning to Florence, as he felt the earl's insolence, and wished to change the conversation, "what recompense can I give you for your services—for your valour on that fatal tenth of September."

"I have performed no services superior to those of other men, my lord," said Florence modestly.

"Do you consider bearing to me the letters of Henry of Valois; that covering our retreat at Inveresk, and routing by three desperate charges the demi-lances of Vane and the Spaniards of Gamboa; that saving the life of the Countess of Yarrow, and assisting to escort the queen to Stirling, are no services?"

"Lord regent, they were but duties which every loyal gentleman owed to the crown, and nothing more."

"I dispute while I admire your modest spirit. You shall be a knight, as your father was; though that is but a meagre recompense as knighthoods go in these days of ours. Have you no boon to ask?"

Florence glanced timidly towards the Countess of Yarrow, and was silent, though his poor heart was beating with love and anxiety. Claude Hamilton detected the glance, rapid and covert though it was, and frowned so deeply, that Arran, though unable to understand what new turn matters had taken between these troublesome and hereditary enemies, was too politic to notice it, but held out his right hand to the old baron, saying,—

"And thou, stout kinsman, I rejoice to see thee safe, for I heard somewhat of a dangerous wound."

"Nay, Arran, I am free even of a scratch."

"'Twas not your fault, laird, if you escaped so well."

Preston felt the compliment these words conveyed, and bowed low in reply. These conversational remarks over, the regent and others were about to resume the consideration of the present warlike and political crisis, when the constable of the castle entered hurriedly to announce "a messenger from Edinburgh, with tidings for my lord regent."

"Admit him instantly," exclaimed Arran, starting from his seat; and all eyes were turned towards the door.

The messenger appeared, clad still in his riding-cloak, armour, and muddy boots, the spurs of which bore traces of blood, for he had ridden hard and fast.

"The Master of Lyle!" exclaimed Arran. "Speak, sir, are the English advancing hither!"

"Nay, my lord regent—the reverse," replied the master smiling.

"Retreating?"

"Yes, as I myself have seen," replied Lyle gaily enough, though he was one of the traitor faction, or had been so until the merciless slaughter of Pinkey soured his heart against England. "This day at noon the Duke of Somerset broke up from his camp and commenced his homeward march, drawing together all his ravagers and foraging parties, while his fleet, under the Lord Clinton, has already left the Firth of Forth, and sailed towards their own seas."

This intelligence, which other messengers soon confirmed, caused the utmost rejoicing in the minds of all save Arran, who, covered with shame and mortification by his late defeat, was longing for another trial of strength with the foe, while Mary of Lorraine was desirous of peace at any price, as she felt sure that *now* the Scots would never break their ancient league with France; and that the fatal events of the 10th September, would soon place the regency of the realm in her own hands, and thus enable her to advance the interest of the House of Guise and the Church of Rome.

To keep Florence near her own person, as she found him useful, faithful, and liked his society, she made him captain of her guard, in place of Livingstone of Champfleurie; but the Countess of Yarrow was no longer at court, as Claude Hamilton, in his capacity of tutor or guardian, appointed by the will of her father the earl, had removed her to Edinburgh. Thus Florence felt an irrepressible gloom over him, a moodiness of spirit, which not even the dazzling favour, or seductive society of Mary of Lorraine could relieve.

The English Protector had fortunately neither the enterprise nor firmness of mind to improve the victory he had won, by making a rapid march to Stirling,—a movement by which he might perhaps have secured the great object of his wanton and daring campaign, the person of the young queen, before she could be sent to France. Instead of this decisive advance, which, at all events would have complicated and protracted the war, he wasted his time in petty ravages throughout the Lothians; and on hearing tidings of a conspiracy formed against him in England, he made all preparations for a sudden retreat, and finally did so, on the 18th September, thus remaining exactly one week after the battle was won.

The events of this campaign, together with an inroad made on the 8th September, by the Lord Wharton, and Mathew Stuart, the outlawed Earl of Lennox, who with five thousand men, ravaged all the Western Borders and stormed the stronghold of Castle-milk, destroyed the town of Annan, and blew up its church, increased the general indignation of the people at the rash attempts to force them into a matrimonial alliance with England; and now, by the affectionate energy of Mary of Lorraine, prompt measures were at once adopted for the transmission of the little queen to France.

This proposal was warmly received by Monsieur d'Oysell the ambassador of Henry II., who assured the Scottish peers that the House of Valois would never fail in maintaining the ancient alliance which had subsisted between the two countries since the days of Charlemagne.

"And be assured, my lords," added Mary of Lorraine, who had all the boldness which characterized the House of Guise, "that the dauphin of France, heir of the first kingdom in Europe, is a more suitable consort for Mary of Scotland than this English king, whose pretensions to her hand have been supported by every violence and barbarity of which the worst of men are capable."

Soon after these proceedings, the Sieur Nicholas de Villegaignon, in the same ship which brought Florence from France, anchored in the Firth of Forth, to receive the queen, who, with her train, had been removed to the sequestered priory of Inchmahoma, or "the Isle of Rest" in the Loch of Menteith.

"Thus," according to one of our historians, "England discovered that the idea that a free country was to be compelled into a pacific matrimonial alliance amid the groans of its dying citizens, and the flames of its cities and seaports, was revolting and absurd!"

Such was the *sequel* to the campaign of 1547.

CHAPTER LVI
THE ISLE OF REST

This dowry now our Scottish virgin brings,
A nation famous for a race of kings,
By firmest leagues to France for ages join'd,
With splendid feats and friendly ties combined,
A happy presage of connubial joy,
Which neither time nor tempests shall destroy,
A people yet in battle unsubdued,
Though all the land has been in blood imbued.

Buchanan.

So wrote the most classic of Scottish scholars in his *Epithalamium*, or "Ode on the marriage of Francis of Valois and Mary, sovereigns of France and Scotland," the ungrateful Buchanan; but we are somewhat anticipating history and our own narrative in the heading of our chapter.

Inchmahoma, the secure and temporary abode of the two queens and their court, is a singularly beautiful islet, so small and so green, in the midst of the lake of Menteith, that when viewed from the mountains it resembles a large emerald in the centre of a shield of silver.

Of the Augustinian priory — which was founded in the twelfth century by Edgar, King of Scotland (the son of Cean-mhor), a prince who reigned only nine years, but lived "reverenced and beloved by the good, and so formidable to the bad, that in all his reign there was no sedition or fear of a foreign enemy," — there remains *now* but one beautiful gothic arch, the dormitory, and the vaults embosomed in a grove of aged and mossgrown timber. These trees are all chestnuts, and were planted by the canons before the Reformation. A few decaying fruit trees, and traces of a terrace, show where the garden of these sequestered churchmen lay; and where, in her sportive glee, the little queen of Scots with her auburn hair streaming behind her, played for many an hour with the ladies of her mother's train; and heard the white-bearded fathers of St. Augustine tell old tales of their holy isle, and show the oak chair wherein the stout King Robert sat when, in 1310, four years before Bannockburn, he came there to visit them; and legends of the stalwart Earls of Menteith, whose ruined castle stands on the

Isle of Tulla, and whose graves are in Mahoma; of Arnchly, or "the bloody field of the sword," where, at the western end of the loch, stood a little chapel, wherein a monk said mass daily for the souls of the slain. And, in that terraced garden, to lighten care and chase sad thoughts away, Florence spent many an hour with this beautiful child, whose "pure and sinless brow" was encircled by the Scottish crown of thorns, and with her four Maries, who were the daughters of four loyal lords,—all women celebrated in after life—by song, by tradition, and by Scotland's brave but mournful history.

These young ladies—to wit, Mary Fleming, daughter of that Lord Fleming who fell at Pinkey; Mary Livingstone, Mary Seaton, and Mary Beaton (a kinswoman of the murdered cardinal), all received precisely the same education as their beautiful mistress, and were taught every language and accomplishment by the same instructors, and they all loved each other with deep affection.

Their favourite amusement was *palm play*, which Florence taught them as he had learned it at the Louvre and Vendome. It is an old French game, which simply consisted in receiving a ball in the palm of the hand, and propelling it back again; but it became so fashionable in the kingdom of the Louis, that the nobles, when they lost large sums, and found their purses empty, to continue the play would stake their mantles, armour, poniards, jewels, or anything, in the ardour with which they pursued it.

On a little eminence close to the verge of the loch, there still remains a box-wood summer-house, with a fine old hawthorn in its centre; and in this the little queen and her mother, with the four Maries, are said to have sat in the autumn evenings, and heard Florence read the ancient chronicles of Scotland, the *Bruce* of Barbour, and tell old tales of wizards and fairies, giants and dwarfs, till the light of day faded from the romantic summit of Ghoille-dun; till the vesper lights began to twinkle through the Gothic windows of the old priory upon the tremulous waters of the lake, and the ancient tower of Tulla, on the Earl's Isle (where dwelt Earl John, who in that year, 1547, was slain by the tutor of Appin) cast its lengthening shadow to the shore.

Amid the romantic mountain scenery which surrounded this lake and isle, Florence, while attending to the somewhat trivial and monotonous duties which the queen-mother assigned him as captain of her guard— duties which he varied occasionally by hawking on the long, narrow, promontory that runs out from the southern shore, or by fishing for pike by baited lines tied to the leg of a goose—a strange custom then common in Monteith—longed to be once again in the Scottish capital, for now he never saw, nor by rumour, letter, or report, heard from the Countess of Yarrow. His love affair seemed literally to be an end! The angry spirit of the old feud, thought he, may have gathered again in the heart of her kinsman; and there were times when he bitterly upbraided himself for having so sternly declined that kinsman's proffered friendship and alliance; "but, alas! what could I do?" he would exclaim—"the blood of my father, the blood of my brother, were alike upon his hands." Then he would strive to recal some of the anger, bitterness, and antipathy that filled his heart when he first left France on board of the galley of Villegaignon, with no other thought but to fulfil the terrible injunction of his mother's homeward summons—to slay the Laird of Preston as he would have slain a snake or tiger—but the soft image of Madeline arose before him, and he strove in vain!

If the sentiments of Claude Hamilton had really grown more hostile, and Madeline Home had learned to share them, she might also gradually learn to love *another*, or to wed in mere indifference, for she had many suitors—but he thrust these ideas aside, and vainly strove to think of other things.

So time passed slowly, heavily on, and brown October spread her russet hues upon the foliage; the swallows disappeared, and the woodcocks came through dark and misty skies from the shores of the Baltic to replace them.

By the old chesnuts that cast at eve their shadows on the grey walls of the ancient priory, and by the waves of the lake, poor Florence sat and pondered, till the sweet voice of Madeline seemed to come to his ear, amid the ripples that chafed on the little beach, and amid the rustle of the dry leaves, as the autumn gusts shook them down from the tossing branches.

Michaelmas came; but even in that remote Highland region, where, *yet*, so many old customs linger, few traces remained of the feast of St. Michael, as it was held of old; though Mary of Lorraine and the prior of the isle, or Earl John of Monteith, in Tulla Hall, partook of roasted goose, duly and solemnly, on the eleventh of the month, as an indispensable ceremony— all unaware that it was the last remnant of a creed that flourished long anterior to Christianity; for on this day the Pagans of old sacrificed a goose to Proserpine, the infernal goddess of Death.

'Twas November now; and the piercing wind that swept over the mountains seemed as if anxious to tear the last brown leaves of autumn from the naked trees; and then came snow to whiten the hills and valleys— to bury deep the rocky passes; and with it came the frost, to seal up the waters of the lake; for, unlike those of the present age, the winters of the olden time were somewhat Arctic in their aspect, with the strong and bitter

Scottish frost, of which Annsæus Julius Floras, the satirical Roman poet and historian, wrote, when, armed with his pen, he entered the lists against the Emperor Adrian:—

"Ego nolo Cæsar esse,
Ambulare per Brittanos,
Scoticas pati pruinas."

And so the Highland winter came on with all its dreariness; and amid the cloistral seclusion of the Isle of Rest, and of Mary of Lorraine's little court, Florence thought ever of Madeline Home, and longed again to hear her voice—to see her smile—to touch her pretty hand. Mary of Lorraine saw that he was sad, pre-occupied, and thoughtful; and, with the natural gaiety of a Frenchwoman, she rallied him on the subject of his pensiveness, and bade him be of good cheer; for though man proposed, God disposed, and all would yet be well.

With early summer final preparations were made for the young queen's departure to France; and after sailing from Leith, round the stormy Pentland Firth, a gallant fleet of caravels dropped their anchors in the waters of the Clyde.

On a bright July morning, when the wooded hills that rise around the blue lake, the ancient priory, and the green Isle of Rest were clothed in their heaviest summer foliage, Florence was seated in the boxwood bower beside the old hawthorn-tree, reading to the little queen. With her dove-like eyes turned up to his face in wonder, she heard how the valiant paladin, Sir Palomides, sorrowed for la Belle Isonde—of the siege perilous, and the marvellous adventure of the sword in a stone; but now Mary of Lorraine approached them with a grave and mournful expression in her face; kissing her daughter, she desired her to withdraw, and the young sovereign at once obeyed. She now desired Florence, who had instantly arisen and closed his book, which was Sir Thomas Malori's romance of "King Arthur," to listen, as she had a serious matter whereon to confer with him.

"In a week," said she, "my daughter sails for France."

"France, within a week—so soon!" he exclaimed, with regret and surprise; "and in charge of whom, madam?"

"The lords Livingstone, Erskine, and a chosen and gallant train; but more immediately would I confide her to the care of one whose character I have studied carefully and closely, and in whom I can repose implicit faith."

"Your grace is right; but who is this honoured person?"

"Yourself, fair sir," replied Mary with one of her most beautiful smiles.

"I!" he exclaimed with astonishment.

"You, Florence Fawside."

"Oh, madam, you overwhelm me!" he replied, casting down his eyes: for his first thought was the total separation from Madeline Home, that was consequent to this important trust, which he durst not decline.

"You express more surprise than satisfaction," said the queen, who was an acute reader of the human face, and could read all its varying expressions. "You dislike the high trust I would repose in you?" she added, with a proud but peculiar smile.

"Oh, madam, do not say so—I but——"

"Or the journey by sea, or a residence in Paris, or I know not what. *Mon Dieu!* would that I could go with her to merry France again; but that may never, never be. I have her turbulent kingdom to watch over as a sacred trust; and as its regent—for regent of Scotland I *shall* be!—I must bide any time in Holyrood."

"Your majesty must pardon me; I dislike neither the journey nor the splendid trust you would repose in me; but—but——"

"But what?" Florence coloured deeply, played with the plume in his bonnet, and hesitated.

"Queens are unused to doubts; but since you seem so averse to my offer, I must e'en repose the greater trust in the Countess of Yarrow, who has already consented to go."

"Consented to go!—to leave me; has Madeline really consented?" exclaimed poor Florence, in his desperation forgetting all his prudence.

"She has," replied the smiling queen.

"Oh, madam, can she go thus and leave me behind—who love her so tenderly—so well!"

"What would you have her to do!" said Mary of Lorraine; "it is arranged that, in charge of the Lords Livingstone and Erskine, together with the Earl and Countess of Yarrow, my daughter proceeds to France in the ship of M. de Villegaignon."

"And this—this Earl of Yarrow?" muttered Florence in a breathless voice, as he grew pale with sudden grief, fury, and confusion.

"Is——" the queen hesitated provokingly.

"Who—who?—pardon my vehemence!"

"Cannot you guess?"

"Madam, my heart is sick; I have neither wit nor skill for riddles!" replied Florence, who trembled and became painfully agitated.

"Oh, thou man of little faith," said the queen merrily, as she patted his cheek with her white hand; and then drawing two documents from the velvet pouch which hung at her girdle—"Look here!" she added, "and read."

Florence read them over hurriedly, and could scarcely believe his eyes. The first was a contract of marriage between himself and Madeline, Countess of Yarrow, signed by Madeline's own hand, by her uncle, and the Regent Arran; *his own* signature alone being wanting. The second document was a patent of nobility under the great seal of Scotland, granting the title of Earl of Yarrow and Baron Fawside to Florence Fawside, for the leal and true service rendered by his father, umquhile Sir John of that ilk, at Flodden, and by the said Florence at Pinkeycleuch; and for the good and leal services ever rendered by his forbears to the throne and ancestors of our dearest sovereign lady the queen. With these documents was a letter from Claude Hamilton, at least a letter written by a notary's hand and signed by the signet ring of the old baron, who had but small skill in clerking, and in it there occurred the following passage:—

"We have in sooth been owre near neighbours to be gude friends, as our auld Scots proverb hath it; but all the reparation I promised in the Torwood—reparation to the living and to the dead—am I still willing to make Florence Fawside; and to end this old hereditary feud, which hath been the curse of our forefathers, and all quarrels anent our marches, rights of fuel and pasture, fishing and forestry, let them henceforth become *one*; and let your wedding with my kinswoman be the bond of amity between us, and Father John be the notary who frames it. 'Tis well! And my fair lands of Preston shall be hers, after me, for pin-money for holding and her abulyements. With the broad seas of Scotland and France between us, laird, we shall be better friends than our forefathers when they could scowl from their barred gates at ilk other owre the waste of Gladsmuir; and so I commit you to God. "PRESTON."

"Now, sir," said Mary of Lorraine; "will you sail to France with my daughter, or will you stay at home?"

"Ah, madam, pardon me," exclaimed Florence, sinking on one knee; "I am without thought or speech—I have no words, no voice to thank you."

"I want not thanks; but your signature to the contract, and the benediction of the old vicar of Tranent on the marriage."

"Madam, who has done me all this kindness—all this most undeserved honour?"

"Say not so—but your good angel has been your dearest friend—Mary of Lorraine—from the first, my poor boy, I loved and valued your worth."

"I knew it—I knew it!" he exclaimed, kissing her hands with ardour; "but your grace must show me some mode by which I may requite this."

"In France be faithful to my daughter, be tender and be true," said the queen in an imploring voice, that seemed full of soul.

"True to death,—true as I would be to Madeline Home!"

"Come, then, for the countess has arrived; she is now with the Abbot of Inchmahoma, and awaits you in the priory," said the queen with a winning smile, as she presented her hand to the bewildered young man.

And thus our story, like a good old-fashioned comedy, ends by one marriage, and opens the way to another. After this, we have but little more to add.

On a bright morning in July, 1548, when the hot sun exhaled a silver mist from the broad blue bosom of the Clyde; when its fertile and beautiful shores lay steeped in golden haze that mellowed each grey rock, green wood, and purple hill, bay, beach, and headland that stretched in distance, far, far away; and when the sunbeams played gaily upon the long, swelling ripples that seemed to vibrate in the heat, and churned the waves into little lines of foam as they rolled on the pebbled shore, the thunder of brass cannon from "Balclutha's walls of towers," the double peak of Dunbarton, boomed in the still air, while the bells rang their farewell peal in the spire of many a village church, as the fleet of the Sieur Nicholas de Villegaignon, Knight of Malta, and Grand-admiral of France, got under weigh.

Above the lesser ships that spread their white sails to the eastern breeze, his great caravel towered conspicuously.

High-pooped, with turrets of pepper-box aspect, she had three enormous lanterns at her stern, which, like her bow, rose nearly thirty feet above the water-line, and had a gilded iron gallery before each row of painted windows. This poop was covered with every variety of cunning work in wood, painting, and gilding, with niches containing saints with swords, wheels, and scourges, the emblems of their martyrdom; while long carved mouldings ran along the bends between the brass muzzles of the polished culverins that rose above each other in tiers and glittered in the sun as its rays played upon the rippling water. Many a gay pennon and streamer floated gracefully out like long and silken ribands on the breeze;

but high over all were the lion *gules* of Scotland, the silver fleur-de-lis of old France, and the family banner of the Grand-admiral de Villegaignon, which floated from the mizzen-mast head, bearing two anchors crossed behind his paternal shield.

On board of this gay caravel were Florence and his bride the countess, with the little queen and her two noble preceptors, the abbot of the Isle of Rest, and her three kinsmen, the Lord James Stuart (afterwards Regent Moray), the commendator of Holyrood, and the Lord Robert, Prior of Orkney, with a train of two hundred lords, ladies, and gentlemen, all of the best families in Scotland. The young bride of France was weeping bitterly, and the arm of the Countess of Yarrow was around her.

"The young queen," says the Captain Beaugue, a gallant French officer, who witnessed the embarkation, "was at that time one of the most perfect creatures the God of Nature ever formed, for her equal was nowhere to be found, nor had the world another child of her fortune and hopes."

As the ships got under weigh, and began to drop down the lovely river in the sunshine, and enveloped in the smoke of their cannon, which fired salutes, a cheer, which sounded somewhat like a wail of sorrow, as it floated over the Clyde, arose from a group that stood upon its shore, where Mary of Lorraine was lingering, to witness the departure of the daughter she was never to behold again; and there she watched the lessening sails until they melted into the haze and distance.

Escaping all the efforts of Somerset, who daringly sent out a fleet to intercept her, the young queen and her train landed in safety at Roscoff, three miles north of St. Pol de Leon, in the vicinity of Cape Finisterre, and on the 20th of August arrived at Morlaix; from there she proceeded to the palace of St. Germains, where Henry of Valois received her with every demonstration of respect and affection; and where he bestowed on the Earl of Yarrow, and the three great lords who accompanied her, the collar of St. Michael.

Soon after this, the Earl of Arran, on being created Duke of Chatelherault, in Poitou, and receiving the long-promised succours from France under General d'Essé d' Epainvilliers, solemnly abdicated the regency of Scotland in favour of Mary of Lorraine, who, by her perseverance, her wisdom, and skill, attained that power and dignity which had been so long the darling object of her wishes, and the ambition of the House of Guise.

NOTES

I.—FAWSIDE OF THAT ILK

In the text I have not exaggerated the antiquity of this old family, the ruins of whose fortalice are still existing in Haddingtonshire.

In the reign of David I., during a portion of the twelfth century, the name of William de Ffauside occurs in Parliament, and Edmundo de Ffauside witnesses the charter by which that monarch grants certain lands to Thor, the son of Swan of Tranent; and in the time of William the Lion, Gilbert de Fawside witnessed a charter of the monastery of St. Marie of Newbattle.

In 1246, Donatus Sybald witnessed a charter by De Quincy, Earl of Winton and Winchester, to Adam of Seaton, *de Maritagio hoeredis Alani de Faside* (Nisbet), and seven years afterwards Allan obliged himself "to pay yearly to the monks of Dunfermline, *quinque solidas argenti*," out of his lands.

In 1292 Robert de Fawside signed the Ragman Roll, and four years after we find a Roger and William of the same name swearing fealty to Edward I. Roger obtained a grant of the lands from Robert Bruce.

In 1306 Sir Christopher Seaton (who married Bruce's sister) was executed by Edward I. He was succeeded by his son, Sir Alexander Seaton, who obtained from his uncle, King Robert, the lands of Tranent, including *Fawside* and Lougniddry, which formerly belonged to Alan de la Zouch. He and his second son were slain in battle by the English, near Kinghorn, in 1332, leaving a son, Sir Alexander, eighth baron of Seaton, the gallant defender of Berwick, whose sons, though given as hostages to Edward I., are alleged to have been basely hanged by that ferocious prince, in their father's view, before the walls of the town.

In 1350 a Sir Thomas of Fawside witnessed a charter of Duncan Earl of Fife to the monastery of Lindores; and in 1366 a charter of Malcolm of Fawside was witnessed by Symon Preston of Craigmillar, sheriff of Edinburgh. In 1371 William de Seaton granted to John of Fawside, for true and faithful service, the whole lands of Wester-Fawside, in the barony of Travernent,—a gift confirmed by Robert II. on the 20th of June.

In 1425 William of Fawside and Marjorie Fleming his spouse obtained the lands and will of Tolygart, and the lands of Wester-Fawside are confirmed to John of that ilk (Great Seal Office) in June.

In 1472 John Fawside married Margaret, daughter of Sir John Swinton of that ilk; and on his death, in 1503, she became prioress of the Cistercian nunnery at Elcho.

In 1528 there is a remission under the great seal to their son George Fawside of that ilk, for certain crimes committed by him; and in 1547, after the battle of Pinkey, as related in the story, his castle was burned by the English, after a stout resistance, and all within it were, as Patten relates, "brent and smoothered."

Twenty years after this, Thomas Fawside of that ilk signed the Bond of Association, for defending the coronation and government of the young king, James VI., against the supporters of his unfortunate mother; and in 1570, he was one of the assyse who tried Carkettle of Moreles for treason. In 1579, he became surety for Alexander Dalmahoy of that ilk, who, according to the fashion of the age, had employed his leisure time in besieging the house of Somerville (*Pitcairn*).

In 1600, on the occasion of the escape of James VI. from the plot of the Earl of Gourie, "this night (6th August) bonfires were sett upone Arthure Seate, *Fawside Hill*, and all places farre and neere" (Calderwood's Historie).

Sixteen years after, we find James Fawside of that ilk becoming pledge and surety for Sir Patrick Chirnsyde, of East Nisbet, who was accused before the Justiciary Court of abducting a girl of thirteen from Haddington; and in the same year (1616), his servitor, Robert Robertson, was "delatit for the crewel slaughter of umquhile John Fawside, in the barne of Fawside, with a knife or dagger, on the 10th of November," for which he was beheaded on the Castle Hill of Edinburgh (*Pitcairn*). On a dormer window of the ruins at Fawside are carved

I F—I E. 1618.

In 1631, Robert Fawside of that ilk is one of a commission for augmenting the stipend of Inveresk; and about this time the family sold their estate to Hamilton, a merchant in Edinburgh.

In 1666, James, eldest son of the *deceased* Fawside of that ilk, witnessed a charter of George Earl of Haddington. He would seem to have been the last of the line. Their lands belong to Dundas of Arniston, and now nothing remains of this old Scottish family, but their ruined tower upon the hill, and in the church of Tranent, a half-defaced tablet inscribed

II.—THE BATTLE OF PINKEY

Of this great defeat no trace remains in Scotland but the memory of its slaughter. Upwards of two thousand nobles and landed gentlemen fell, and the following list of a few of these, compiled from authorities too numerous to mention, may interest our Scottish readers, some of whom may find their ancestors therein:—William Cunninghame, Earl of Glencairn; Malcolm Lord Fleming, Lord High Chancellor; Allan Lord Cathcart; Alexander Lord Elphinstone; Henry Lord Methven; Robert Lord Grahame; John Master of Buchan; Robert Master of Erskine; John Master of Livingstone; Robert Master of Rosse; Adam Gordon, son of the Lord Aboyne; Sir James Gordon, Knight, of Lochinvar; Sir George Douglas, Knight, of the House of Angus; Sir Robert Douglas, Knight, of Lochlevin; Sir George Home, Knight, of Wedderburn; William Adamson of Craigcrook, near Edinburgh; Alexander Napier of Merchiston, near Edinburgh; John Brisbane of Bishoptoun, in Cunninghame; Alexander Frazer of Durris, Kincardine; Alexander Halyburton of Pitcur, in Angus; John Buchanan of Auchmar and Arnprior; John Norrie of Finarsie, Aberdeenshire; Gilbert MacIlvayne of Grummet, Argyle; Thomas Corrie of Kelwood, James Montfoyd of Montfoyd, Bernard Mure of Park, John Crawford of Giffertland, Quentin Hunter of Hunterstoun, Ayrshire; Robert Bothwick of Gordonshall, John Ramsay of Arbekie, John Strang of Balcaskie, William Barclay of Rhyud, David Reid of Aikenhead, James Wemyss of Myrecairnie, Andrew Anstruther (younger) of that ilk, Alexander Inglis of Tarvet, John Airth of Strathour-Wester, David Wemyss of Caskieberry, Stephen Duddingston of Kildinington, Fife; Ludovic Thornton of that ilk, Forfarshire; Cuthbert Aschennan of Park, John Gordon of Blaiket, John Ramsay of Sypland, Kirkcudbright; Thomas Hamilton of Priestfield, near Edinburgh; David Anderson of Inchcannon, in the barony of Errol; John Kincaid of Wester Lawes, in the barony of Kinnaird; John Leckie of that ilk, Stirlingshire; John Macdoull of Garthland, Wigton; Patrick Bissett of Lessindrum; Walter Macfarlane of Tarbet; Richard Melville of Baldovie, parson of Marytown; David Arbuthnot (younger) of that ilk, parson of Menmure; William Johnston of that ilk; Robert Munro of Foulis; John Murray of Abercairnie; David Murray of Auchtertyre; John Halket of Pitfirran; David and Robert Boswal, sons of the laird of Balmuto; Allan Lockhart of the Lee; Duncan Macfarlane of that ilk; Finlay Mhor, Farquharson of Invercauld, royal standard-bearer; George Henderson of Fordelhenderson; Alexander Skene of that ilk; James Innes of Rathmackenzie; Robert Leslie of Wardes; John Kinnaird of that ilk; William Cunninghame of Glengarnock; John and Arthur Forbes, sons of the Red Laird of Pitsligo; Cuthbert Hamilton of Candor, David Hamilton of Broomhill;[*] Gabriel Cunninghame of Craigends; John and Robert, sons of Sir Walter Lindsay of Edzell, who fell at Flodden; John Ogilvie of Durn; John Hamilton, merchant in the West Bow, Edinburgh; Walter Cullen, bailie of Aberdeen, and twenty-eight burghers of that city.

> [*] Two brothers, slain when attempting to rescue the Lord
> Semple, who was taken prisoner.

The *seven* sons of Sir Thomas Urquhart of Cromarty are also said to have fallen, in this disastrous field; but their names do not appear in the "Scottish Baronage."

It was frequently named the Field of Inveresk and of Musselburgh.

In Bunbury Church, Cheshire, is a monument to Sir George Beeston, who was knighted by Queen Elizabeth for his bravery against the Armada in 1588. He died in 1601, at the age of 102, and would seem to have fought against the Scots at Pinkey. "Contra Scotos apud *Musselborrow*," is on his tomb.

In the following "Acquittaunce," rendered into English, the battle is styled Inveresk:—

"I, Walter Scot of Branxholm, Knight, grant me to have received from an honourable man, Sir Patrick Cheyne of Essilmont, Knight, the sum of eight score English nobles, for which I was bound and obliged to content and pay to Thomas Dacre of Lanercost, Knight, Englishman, taker of the said Sir Patrick at the field of *Inveresk*, for his ransom, of the which sum I hold me well-content and payed. In witness whereof, I have subscribed this my letter of acquittaunce with my hand, at Edinburgh, the 2nd March, 1548." — *Aberdeen Collections*, vol. ii.